THE HAUNTING
⌐○ OF ○⌐
MOSCOW
HOUSE

Olesya Salnikova Gilmore is the author of *The Witch and the Tsar* and *The Haunting of Moscow House*. Originally from Moscow, she was raised in the US and graduated from Pepperdine University with a BA in English/political science, and from Northwestern School of Law with a JD. She practiced litigation at a large law firm for several years before pursuing her dream of becoming an author. Now she is happiest writing novels in a variety of genres, including fantasy, paranormal, gothic horror, and historical fiction. She also loves exploring Eastern European history and folklore. Her work has appeared in *LitHub*, *Tor.com*, *CrimeReads*, *Writer's Digest*, *Historical Novels Review*, *Bookish*, and *Washington Independent Review of Books*, among others. She lives in a wooded, lakeside suburb of Chicago with her husband and two daughters.

Also by Olesya Salnikova Gilmore

The Witch and the Tsar

THE HAUNTING OF MOSCOW HOUSE

OLESYA SALNIKOVA GILMORE

HARPER
Voyager

Harper*Voyager*
An imprint of HarperCollins*Publishers* Ltd
1 London Bridge Street
London SE1 9GF

www.harpercollins.co.uk

HarperCollins*Publishers*
Macken House,
39/40 Mayor Street Upper,
Dublin 1
D01 C9W8
Ireland

First published by HarperCollins*Publishers* Ltd 2024
This paperback edition 2025
1

Copyright © Olesya Salnikova Gilmore 2024

Book design by Alison Cnockaert

Olesya Salnikova Gilmore asserts the moral right to
be identified as the author of this work.

A catalogue record for this book is available from the British Library.

ISBN: 978-0-00-855567-2

This novel is entirely a work of fiction.
The names, characters and incidents portrayed in it are
the work of the author's imagination. Any resemblance to
actual persons, living or dead, events or localities is
entirely coincidental.

Printed and bound in the UK using 100% Renewable Electricity
by CPI Group (UK) Ltd

All rights reserved. No part of this publication may be reproduced,
stored in a retrieval system, or transmitted, in any form or by any means,
electronic, mechanical, photocopying, recording or otherwise,
without the prior written permission of the publishers.

Without limiting the exclusive rights of any author, contributor or the publisher
of this publication, any unauthorised use of this publication to train generative
artificial intelligence (AI) technologies is expressly prohibited. HarperCollins also
exercise their rights under Article 4(3) of the Digital Single Market Directive 2019/790
and expressly reserve this publication from the text and data mining exception.

This book contains FSC™ certified paper and other controlled sources
to ensure responsible forest management.

For more information visit: www.harpercollins.co.uk/green

*For my sister, Katerina, for the love, support, and magic
And for sisters everywhere*

Do you know that I love now to recall and visit at certain dates the places where I was once happy in my own way? I love to build up my present in harmony with the irrevocable past . . .
   FYODOR DOSTOEVSKY, "WHITE NIGHTS",
    AS TRANSLATED BY CONSTANCE GARNETT

They will not hear, they will not look, they will not listen to me!
   NIKOLAI GOGOL, "DIARY OF A MADMAN"

1

The Sisters of the House of Golitev

LATE AUGUST 1921
Moscow

I F SOMEONE FROM their past should catch a glimpse of the formerly aristocratic Goliteva sisters, they would find two wraiths instead of countesses.

That is what Irina thinks as she trudges down the empty Moscow street with her sister Lili to barter their priceless family heirlooms for food at the bazaar. Their stomachs are empty, their pockets even more so, their coats shabby and stripped of most finery since the Revolution. Between them, they clutch a large oil painting of Grand-père Sergei Sherbatsky in its gilt frame. They should call him Dedushka. French might have been denounced as a bourgeois language, but their family still speaks it in secret. Their lives are sustained by secrets. That and memories, though those, too, are best kept hidden.

The awkward frame digs into the flesh of Irina's palm, her other hand gripping the handle of a battered old leather valise. From time to time, she stumbles on the uneven pavement with its potholes and cracked stones, shooting her sister an apologetic half smile, even as Lili swears under her breath about the Bolsheviks' fine efforts at city repair and reconstruction.

The street is wide and broad but dirty and deserted, no longer busy with finely dressed people or magnificent carriages. Aside from a few ragged children with empty eyes, pausing their half-hearted play to watch them, or the distant rumble of a tram or horse-drawn droshky cab, it is unnaturally still. So Irina talks to Lili as nowhere else. Lili is eighteen to her twenty-eight years, and Irina doesn't always understand her younger sister. But on the streets, the long years between them blur, and all they have is each other.

The clouds hang low and stubby in a bone-white sky, the cold against Irina's skin biting, entirely unreasonable for August. There is no sun. She thinks it may have burnt itself out during the heat and drought of that summer, when the crops failed and famine came for Russia, like the Revolution four years before, like the Great War three years before that. But Russia is synonymous with tragedy. So Irina isn't surprised.

When they stop for a rest, she props the painting against the valise and burrows into her coat, feeling for the cameo brooch with the silhouette of their mother that she has sewn into the lining. While Lili cannot abide such trinkets, as they remind her of a past she'd rather ignore, Irina finds comfort in them. She supposes it's because she's had more of it. She runs her fingers over Maman's worn hair and face—recalling her rare, perfumed embraces; her slight nod of approval at a particularly fine ball gown, significant due to Maman's position as a maid of honor at court. Irina hastily pushes the trinket back into hiding. The thought of a ball triggers one of her dead fiancé. The brooch resides out of sight for a reason. So do the memories.

Being *former people*, they have lost the privilege of fine things—that is, except for their names. To the new Soviet republic, the Bolsheviks, and the Cheka secret police, they are still countesses Irina and Liliya Goliteva, the people's class enemy as descendants of one of the greatest and most ancient aristocratic clans of an imperial Russia dead and buried. Like most of their family. But unlike many former people, Irina's family didn't flee Russia. They stayed in hope of a return to normalcy. Now it is too late. Even if they could obtain papers, how could a household of women and children brave the danger of travel and exile?

So here they are, surviving as best they can, living as quietly as is possible for Golitevs. In fairy tales, paupers became princesses, not the other way around. But Soviet Russia is a warped Wonderland, where all is topsy-turvy and not what it should be.

Irina tries not to look at the neglected buildings as they continue on. Also topsy-turvy, with holes from artillery and machine-gun fire, some gutted and burned, others mere craters, black and cavernous like missing teeth. Shops are boarded up and wreathed thickly in cobwebs, most missing windowpanes. Fragments of glass crunch under their booted feet. Irina feels as if they shouldn't be here. And what will Aunt Marie say when she discovers the painting missing?

"Oh, no, I know what that face means, Irishka. Your conscience is rearing its ugly head," Lili needles, her specialty from the days when she would sneak into Irina's rooms and play pranks on her, down to the same elfish smile and naughty glimmer. "Don't look so glum! If we trade enough, we'll fill our stomachs for once, fueling us to wage our battles with Auntie."

"She will not like it," Irina says, though it is safer to disregard their promise to Auntie not to sell their family's possessions. But Irina cannot ignore her guilt; their aunt may be a force to be reckoned with, at times controlling and manipulative, but she is their matriarch and adoptive mother. Despite losing her son and husband three years earlier on top of her precious position also as a maid of honor, Auntie took on their dead mother's role without complaint. For this reason, whenever Lili starts to complain about her, Irina is the first to defend their aunt.

"Let her notice." Lili doesn't smile fully—no one does—but there is Papa's mischievous glint in her hazel eyes. "Besides, will the damn thing feed you? Grand-mère? Natasha and Seryozha? No. Besides, the Bolsheviks will take it from us sooner or later."

Irina's mind is instantly on Seryozha, her cousin for all intents and purposes. Only Auntie knows the truth—that he is Irina's son with the dead fiancé. Since he was born out of wedlock during the Revolution, when such a predicament still spelled social downfall, Auntie had saved Irina by arranging for her brother, Pavel—nicknamed

Pasha—to adopt the boy. Irina feels the usual pang at this. Even in a topsy-turvy world, with their uncle and his wife dead, Irina remains the boy's mother in all but name. Only tradition cloaked in secrets dies hard.

Now, at nearly five years old, Seryozha is small and scrawny. His adoptive sister, fourteen-year-old Natasha, is so thin she has taken to rewearing her old dresses. And Lili has had to cut her wonderfully long honey-brown hair to her shoulders because of how lank it has become, her diminutive frame more boyish than ever. How absurdly sentimental she has been, Irina berates herself. She, who takes such pride in her sensible and practical nature.

"You're right. I only wish your art could sustain us." She nods at Lili's coat pocket, the edges of her sketch pad pressing faintly through the threadbare wool. Lili sketches portraits, scenes of Moscow, even former people. Alas, it brings in a pittance.

"I wish it, too. Do you think I like selling off what's left of our inheritance?" Lili's fingers tighten on the gilt frame, knuckles whitening, as if loath to part with it. "I learned everything I know about art from paintings like this one at Moscow House, thanks to Uncle Pasha. But I won't allow Auntie's backwardness to let us starve. I do *not* fear her." Lili swaggers a little at that.

Irina doesn't believe her bravado. Though impulsive and outspoken, Lili is just as hesitant to incur Auntie's displeasure. Irina tries not to think about the house.

Moscow House, built during the reign of Catherine the Great, was one of their family's many homes. Yet it was the house Irina and her family escaped to following the February Revolution in St. Petersburg, renamed Petrograd during the Great War. And they've managed to keep it all these years, their one remaining White oasis in the sea of Bolshevik Red. Dread blooms in Irina's chest at the thought of the house. Once a place of light, of talk and laughter, it now stands dark and sullen, empty except for the memories and what is left of her family.

"Be thankful for the roof over your head," she reminds Lili, slipping all too easily into her elder sister role, thinking about the homeless, all those crammed into communal housing. "Most are not so fortunate."

Lili slips into her own role of needling, impish sister. "Oh, Irishka, so serious. I forgive you. As long as you don't frighten away the entire bazaar. I wish to trade for some tea, maybe a tin of coffee. I swear Grand-mère's boiled water is laced with metal."

Irina draws in an exasperated breath. With it, the filthy smell of the streets. Piss and several years' worth of waste. The ground floors of the abandoned buildings were turned into public toilets long ago. She remembers they used to laugh and pinch their noses. Now they breathe deeply of the air, and they don't laugh. That is the smell of their new Russia. One must get used to it—or die.

2

The Americans

NOT FAR FROM the bazaar, Irina suddenly hears the violent screeching of tires. Her body tenses—a pair of black motorcars is barreling toward them, their white headlamps stabbing through the gray day.

Lili's face pales, all lightness gone. "Is it . . . ?"

Them, the Cheka. Or the head of the Soviet government, Vladimir Ilyich Lenin, motoring in the automobiles he stole from families like theirs. But at second glance, the motorcars are bulky, freshly painted, foreign looking. Irina sharply veers toward the sidewalk, pushing herself and Lili out of the way of the speeding automobiles.

Just in time—the cars brake to a halt in a cloud of noxious black exhaust.

Irina takes one inhale of the engine fumes and dissolves into coughing. Her chest heats with outrage. Children live and play in the streets, their reflexes slow from lack of food.

Through the smoke, she sees three or four men slide out of each car and crowd the street with their tall, elegantly suited figures, their trunks and luggage. Irina steps toward them, about to air her thoughts, and not at all politely. She stops short upon hearing their words. Not

Russian, but those of the dead last tsar and his wife, Nicholas and Alexandra; of the imperial family and the court—English, with hard American *r*s.

What are Americans doing in Moscow?

No more questions, Irina tells herself sternly, suppressing her curiosity for anything foreign. She glances about the street furtively, expecting a hidden Chekist to slither out of the shadows. Merely exchanging a few words with a foreigner is enough for a Muscovite to end up behind bars, or worse.

"Are you sure this is it, Carroll?" One man speaks, low, with foreboding. "It looks like a prison."

"Took us days to secure, but this is it" comes the grim reply.

The men are uneasy, shifting their feet, stealing glances at the gray stone building.

"You almost ran us over," Lili calls out, in halting English. Then, to Irina's horror, she marches up to the men. "Did you even look where you were motoring in your monstrosities?"

A few of the men turn to glance at her, then at Irina, who feels like melting into the building behind her. Reluctantly leaving the valise and painting, Irina hurries to her sister. "There are many homeless children here," she adds, in her own rusty English. Her eyes glide across the men, rumpled though well-fed, their garments and luggage dusty though nice. She would scoff if it weren't for the manners buried inside her.

A man with plump, clean-shaven cheeks and slicked-back hair ambles over. "The street looked empty to us," he says, long faced yet exuding arrogance.

"Ignore the brute—I do." Another man steps forward with a bright smile. He is so tall, he practically towers over them. "I apologize for any offense we may have caused."

All Irina can see is his smile. It is so different from the one the dead fiancé would give her, which was haughty, self-assured, with green eyes flicking to her possessively. . . .

"Will Hardwick," the man with the smile introduces himself. "And this brute here is Harold Rollins. We've officially gone into Bololand with the American Relief Administration."

"Relief? As in, help?" Irina translates the word. "How is it possible?" And what is *Bololand*?

Soviet Russia has been cut off, unrecognized, from the West for over three years. She casts another furtive glance about. They have done it—spoken to foreigners, Americans.

"Haven't you heard? We are here to feed the children of Russia." Harold looks down at them curiously. "Say, your English is quite good for Russian girls. We'll need Russian interpreters, bookkeepers, secretaries, clerks. You should apply for jobs—if you can rein in that temper."

"Why, you—" Lili starts to say before Irina pinches her arm.

The men are now walking toward the building.

"I apologize on Harold's behalf," Will says, hanging back. Irina notices stubble on his cheeks and chin, at least a week old. He is rough around the edges, shirt unbuttoned under his coat, blond hair long and shaggy, but with eyes that remind her of the sea. "On the whole, we are a nice, well-mannered lot and really will need the help. Most of us don't know a word of Russian, which will complicate our relief mission."

"Your mission being—?"

"Why, helping Russia with the famine."

Lili gives a snort. "Russians working for Americans . . . you really don't know Soviet Russia at all. We would end up in Butyrka prison."

Will smiles. "Ours is a relief organization, nothing more. We've been instructed to distance ourselves from politics, fully aware Comrade Lenin is watching us. And the Bolos—er, that's what we call your Bolsheviks—have agreed to let Russians assist us. We may hire anybody we want—with no danger from your government or that dreaded secret police." Seeing their hesitation, Will shrugs. "Why don't you think it over? If interested, come back in a few days, mention my name to the porter, and we'll get you a pair of job applications." Again that bright, carefree smile. "Oh, and we will pay very well. Not only in rubles. In food also."

The doors slam after him, leaving Irina alone in the street with her sister. Her mind is awhirl, her mouth watering at the thought of American food.

She looks up at the street sign, faded and scratched yet still there: Spiridonovka Street. She shivers, as if a cold breeze has swept through. The mansions on this street belonged to families like theirs—until they were taken by the Soviet government and nationalized. How can they now house Americans—an aid organization, no less? Irina bites at the inside of her cheek. Tastes blood and memories. She can almost see the British Colony Hospital for Wounded Russian Soldiers within the maze of the red-bricked Pokrovskaya Hospital on Vasilyevsky Island. The Petrograd hospital where she had volunteered as a nurse during the Great War. Suddenly, the sharp smell of alcohol hits her hard, then blood. The clang of scalpels, the moans and screams. The stretchers, operating tables, more stretchers, more operating tables. The chloroform masks pulled over faces twisted in agony from wounds only dreamed up in nightmares, the rotten, septic smells dispelling only with the hastily opened windows.

"Irina? Where did you go?" Lili is leaning over her with rare concern, the kind they only reserve for each other, on these streets, when the past intrudes.

Irina swallows. "Back there." The English, the Americans—it all reminded her . . .

"It won't do." Lili gives a shake of her head. "Come back, Irinushka, come back."

Tears prick Irina's eyes, but the memories—the sounds, the smells, the blood—recede. Her sister might be young and immature, but in these moments, she is there for Irina. Irina blinks rapidly and, with one last glance at the street, takes up the valise and painting. "We should hurry, or we will miss the bazaar."

Lili lifts her side of the painting. "Yes, I want that tea, even if it tastes like shit."

Irina clucks her tongue. "Your language is worse than a muzhik's." Though she allows a half smile. "I'll take the tea over the boiling water."

"Do you think," Lili falters, "we can take the long way home after the bazaar?"

A shadow skims over Irina. At Moscow House's dark insides, their dour aunt and mournful grand-mère, thrown into gloomy contrast to the lighthearted Americans. And at Auntie's recriminations when she notices the missing heirlooms. "Very well," Irina says softly, and they resume their trudge to the bazaar—with a fresh stream of talk between them to keep the chilling silence, if not their hunger, at bay.

3

The Mansion on Vozdvizhenka Street

As they turn onto Vozdvizhenka Street, the glass dome of Moscow House takes shape like a ghostly apparition materializing out of mist limb by limb. Lili's hands start to shake, damn them. She nearly drops the tin of coffee traded for that hideous painting at the bazaar, and the bag of flour, for the diamond diadem worn by Maman to the Winter Palace. She must be rolling over in her grave, wherever that is, at their selling it. But with people starving, food is worth more than hated bourgeois jewels. Lili cannot believe they used to sew them into their corsets.

The house is a ghastly sight from this vantage point, in this murky light. The paint is peeling in flecks of faded, crusted teal, like very dry skin. The formerly white columns and window frames are stained moth gray. Lili thinks, *Monster*. As if it can hear, the darkened, smudged windows glare back. Her chest tightens in dread.

Irina calls her fanciful whenever she mentions ghosts. Still, something isn't right about the house, hasn't been right since Uncle Pasha was shot dead there three years before, and Grand-père Sergei succumbed to his illness mere days after.

Though she's never seen one, Lili has believed in ghosts for quite a long time.

Do you think the dead can rise? Her voice, from a long-forgotten memory.

Of course, Nicky had answered, as if it were the most natural thing in the world.

They were reading fairy tales, their mothers caught in the usual stream of gossip and tea over the steaming brass and silver samovar. Lili had known Prince Nikolai Naroshin ever since she could remember, his family as old and aristocratic as hers. But to Lili, he was just Nicky, thin and gangly, dark-haired and with eyes the color of the rich, nearly black coffee Maman refused to let her have. The only person except Uncle Pasha she could be herself with.

Nicky never treated her like a mere girl but as his equal, his partner in adventure, indulging any of her whims or fancies—whether it was exploring Petersburg, a museum or their houses, an old cemetery. Reading stories and poems. Wondering if ghosts were real.

Lili flopped onto her stomach, jabbing her finger at the fairy tale they were reading about a lazy maiden who steals into a graveyard at night, then steals the shroud off a corpse. *Do you think this can happen?* she asked. Nicky lay down beside her, their arms touching, his strangely fuzzy with hair. And there was a bold, spicy, French scent to him that was unfamiliar. Lili felt very warm. She didn't know why.

Yes, I've seen a corpse before—my grandmother's, and I could imagine it reanimating. If only to haunt us out of spite.

Remembering the mean old lady convinced Lili that yes, the dead *could* rise.

Come. Nicky's smile was narrow. *Let's read another.*

Her heart skipped a beat at his whisper, the intimacy in it. The way Irina's fiancé spoke to her when he thought no one was listening. Lili's hands worried at a ribbon. She wanted to tear the damn thing from her hair, undo her braids. For the first time in her life, she had wanted to be anything but a little girl.

Lili presses down the memory, like the rest of the past, like Nicky, whom she has not heard from since her family fled Petrograd for

Moscow. Likely dead. She wonders why he hasn't haunted her—if only to tell her ghosts are real because he is one.

Now she'd rather go back to that cold, sad bazaar with the white-haired aristocratic ladies selling baubles for bread than remember the past, that smile, him.

At first, Lili doesn't notice the activity in front of the house. Or the men, in their dark leather jackets with their Nagant revolvers and irritatingly small mustaches.

Then she hears the loud, boastful speech, inhales the cigarette smoke. Ash fills her mouth as Irina's cold hand grabs her free one, the other weighed down with the coffee and flour. For all her bravado, her intention to live without fear, Lili grips Irina's hand right back. Is it the Cheka? Some of the men don't wear leather, carry books instead of revolvers. Still, they are Bolsheviks, every last one of them. Could they have seen Lili and Irina with the Americans? Or heard their offer to apply for jobs? No, that is paranoid. Not even the Cheka works this fast. Does it?

As they near the house's gate, a dark-haired, severe-looking man in his thirties waves them on. "Move along, Comrades," he says, the slash across his lip quivering.

Lili is usually quick to offer a retort. But her throat closes up and her hands start to shake—in fear now. She cannot speak, flashing back to that night three years before when the dining room doors had burst open with a firecracker-like bang, and the Chekists flooded in—murdering Uncle Pasha, then taking Papa and Uncle Aleksei.

Lili can barely hear Irina say, "We live here, sir."

Irina, usually the dark-haired, violet-eyed beauty in any place, even on Moscow's bleak streets, even as angular as she's become, is reduced to a simple girl in this moment.

"Irina Alexandrovna Goliteva and Lili Alexandrovna Goliteva?" The man doesn't wait for their answer. "Come with me," he says, his voice as cold and callous as his icy-blue eyes. "And don't even think about trying anything." The holstered revolver at his waist glints in warning.

Lili's body is now shaking. She meets Irina's steely gaze and hot embarrassment rushes in at her damnably ill-timed timidity. Lili wishes for her boldness to return, the pluck she'd felt with the Americans. Maman would be seething with disapproval at her decidedly un-countess-like behavior. But her mother is dead, so it doesn't matter. And the Bolshevik is hurrying them past the chaotically parked motorcars at the curb, the men milling by the house's gates, the courtyard with its sooty bricks and dried-up, rusted old fountain.

"How dare you?" Auntie's voice shrills from inside the house. "This is *priceless*."

Lili picks up her pace, nearly stumbling over the discarded furniture piled up at the entrance doors. Tables and cabinets, screens and commodes—all of it theirs, all of it painstakingly collected by Uncle Pasha from their other estates during the Revolution. All of it bourgeois and destroyed whenever the Bolsheviks set their sights on a house like theirs. Men stream in and out with more trunks and chests. A black mantilla struggles out of an ancient-looking suitcase, flapping in the breeze like a pirate flag flaring into view.

"Keep walking," says the man behind them, following too closely with that revolver of his.

"Felix!" somebody calls out.

Lili turns to see their escort, Felix, melt into the throng of other men. But his ice-blue eyes stay with her.

The shaking has lessened, and Lili is almost herself, maybe because Felix is gone. She and Irina pass through the drafty vestibule with the flickering glass lantern and broken telephone into an entrance hall echoing with laughter and jeers. Auntie is surrounded by twenty or so men. Her normally prim, swept-up salt-and-pepper hair streams wild and free, her increasingly pointy chin and blazing black eyes accentuated by evident indignation. She clutches at a large portrait of her husband, Uncle Aleksei, in his cavalry officer uniform.

Also, a black marble statue of Eurydice, the Greek poet Orpheus's bride, said to have been bitten by a viper and sent to the underworld on her wedding night.

Lili notices the rest of her family, hovering in the elaborately carved doorway to the East Wing. Beyond it are a series of drab rooms buried in gloom. They used to be the glittering site of soirées, of intimate conversations punctuated by peals of elegant laughter, of piping hot samovars and platters of mouthwatering pastilla desserts their butler Dmitri would set out proudly. Can she see Uncle Pasha's tall figure? Papa's shorter frame, his charming face? No, they are dead. And the rooms are cold and silent. There are only empty spaces where the furniture has been removed, like craters in place of Moscow's destroyed buildings, the remaining furniture shrouded in white sheets rising up like the ghosts from her and Nicky's fairy tales. The smell of old things, of a past long dead, rising with them.

Lili forces the memories away, deep inside her where they live.

She turns back to her family. Sees Natasha shiver in her threadbare blue dress. Her vivaciousness is drained, her dark blonde hair ratty, and her blue eyes alarmingly empty of their spirited luster. A white-faced Seryozha clings to her skirts. He is oddly subdued, none of his mischief in sight. Grand-mère stands beside them, stiff and regal with her cane, a sentry to her young charges at a ball. Though she isn't the formidable countess of Lili's childhood. She seems years older than even hours earlier and very frail, hair nearly as white as fresh snow, face as small as Seryozha's.

Irina bolts to them. She has time to grasp Seryozha's tiny hand before a man nearby shakes his head and escorts her back to Lili's side.

"Listen up!" says an older man with silver hair and a wispy silver mustache, just as another man hurries over to the wall with a red bundle and a hammer.

The strike of each nail reverberates through Lili. The hated flag unfurls its bloody Bolshevik red, the yellow hammer and sickle in the corner.

The Soviet government has requisitioned most of the former people's property, sometimes allowing the owners-turned-owned to live with their class enemies. Irina worried they would be next. She was right.

"Several members of the Soviet government are moving into 6 Vozdvizhenka Street," announces the silver-haired man. "You may continue to live here. We will occupy the West Wing, and you are to move to the top floor by the end of the day."

"The attic?" bursts from Auntie before it can burst from Lili despite the fear. "But no one has lived there in years! Suzhensky, be reasonable—"

He opens his mouth to respond when a parakeet swoops down in a whirl of emerald-green wings and lands on his head with a screech. Comrade Suzhensky startles, his hands flying up. But before he can get a hold of the bird, she is off again. "What was that?" he blusters, reminding Lili of a big-bellied teapot about to burst. "Was that a bird?"

It was indeed. Lili's bird, Cleo. A gift from Uncle Pasha. Normally, she would laugh at the joke. But fear stifles any humor.

"Whose bird is that?" demands Comrade Suzhensky.

Lili steps forward shakily. "Mine, Comrade."

"I don't want to see it again. Such bourgeois eccentricities have no place in my household, am I clear?" He turns away before she can reply.

"Comrade Suzhensky." Auntie speaks up, having regained those wits of hers. "There are dozens of rooms, including the entire East Wing—" But even Lili knows it isn't about the lack of rooms; rather, it is to deliver a blow to pride, to humiliate and demean. After all, no self-respecting Soviet citizen is allowed to occupy this much space. Quite simply, it is obscene.

And she is right. Lili watches Comrade Suzhensky's mustache quiver. "If you are unsatisfied with the terms," he says to Auntie, "you may leave. Meanwhile, Tolya"—he snaps his fingers at the man who hung the flag—"will kindly relieve you of your painting and statue. This excessively large house is nevertheless too cluttered."

Tolya wrenches the items from Auntie and roughly sweeps past her, pushing her to the floor. Her black skirts pool like spilled ink, or dark blood.

It takes every ounce of Lili's self-control not to rush over to Auntie. She is not as close to their aunt as Irina is, has next to nothing in common with her, and does a damn good job of avoiding her. Still, Lili doesn't like seeing Auntie so defeated. Only the memory of Uncle Pasha's dead body forces her to stay in place.

Irina tilts her chin up, as taught by the matrons before the Revolution. "We will stay, Comrade Suzhensky."

Why must she always be so restrained, so like Maman?

But Lili is picturing blood expanding on parquet, mingling with the dregs of tea and crushed caviar. She remains as docile as a lamb as the hated Bolsheviks start a bonfire in the courtyard to burn their possessions. And then again as they force her and her family to carry what necessaries and furniture they'll need up four flights of stairs to their new living quarters.

4

Only in Fairy Tales

THEIR QUARTERS ARE two unheated rooms that Lili and her sister must first clear of years of accumulated filth and dust, even mummified remains of dead rodents and insects. The closest lavatory is on the landing below. The only saving grace is the attic happens to be above the East Wing, providing much-needed distance from the Bolsheviks.

"What disrespect, what humiliation," Auntie muses. She is pacing restlessly before the doorway to Lili and Irina's room with a prattling Seryozha in her arms.

"Do not be vulgar, Marie," Grand-mère says from her cot, not deigning to glance up from her embroidery. "Ça ne te va pas." *It does not suit you.*

Lili nearly laughs, though nothing about their circumstances is diverting.

The attic is claustrophobic, its half-moon windows woefully small and dimmed with grime. The wooden rafters where Cleo flutters are hung with spiderwebs that glow spectral in the greasy, dirty lamplight. Lili's skin prickles with cold. Her coat retains the dead smell of the streets, but she doesn't remove it. Instead, she jumps onto Irina's cot and presses tightly against her sister and dozing cousin, coat and all.

"Are you hungry, Seryozhinka?" Grand-mère glances up. "Ladies?"

"We are always hungry," Lili grumbles, stomach empty of its usual modest supper. Seryozha seconds this with an indignant yowl of hunger.

There isn't much Grand-mère can say. It's not as if they can easily walk to the kitchen with the Bolsheviks crawling all over the house. They might just starve up here.

"Then I shall tell you about a ball." Grand-mère pushes aside her embroidery. "The last ball of imperial Russia . . ."

—was in 1903, held at the Winter Palace . . . Lili can recite the entire story. She's heard Grand-mère's reminiscences about imperial Russia's glory days countless times. They used to hold her rapt, until she realized no good comes from looking back at a past dead and gone. She is relieved when Auntie continues her tirade.

"The circumstances we have been reduced to, living in the attic of our own house like servants." Auntie's face pales, as if she's seen a ghost from that ball. "No, we did not even force servants to live this way. They should not be here. They promised."

Lili is entirely at sea. "Who promised?"

"Shouldn't you be keeping yourself busy, Liliya?"

"I *am* busy, Auntie—busy thinking about food." And she is.

Lili has been distracting herself by sketching their old cook's elaborate French meals, which she used to hate yet even then swallowed happily in one sitting. Besides, putting her thoughts onto paper eases and grounds Lili. It reminds her of Uncle Pasha, who first gave her a sketch pad. But back to the food. She remembers the rich flavors, the sheer variety. Sardines and anchovies, entire hams and chickens, bœuf bourguignon, pâté de foie gras, even stinky blue cheeses and multicolored sauces. She envisions Maman's face, puckered in disapproval.

You shouldn't eat so much, Liliya, or you will grow fat and lazy.

Lili shakes her head, forcing Maman's voice out. She looks for Cleo in the rafters.

"There must be something we can do," Auntie is saying.

"Assez, Marie, *enough*." Grand-mère shakes her head.

Auntie pauses in their doorway. "Natasha, did you finish your homework?"

The mound of blankets that is Natasha gives a twitch before a giggle slips out. Knowing Natasha, *finish* is a relative term. She'd rather sleep or dream or wander Moscow.

"Irina and Liliya, who did you see today?"

Lili meets Irina's gaze, thinking of the Americans, their aid organization, the jobs they spoke of. "No one," replies Irina, to Lili's relief. The less Auntie knows, the better.

The shattering of glass comes from downstairs suddenly. Lili stills, dead from fear.

Overhead, Cleo gives a squawk.

"Now they are breaking our priceless objets d'art. Dear Lord, protect us from the uneducated riffraff, the proletarian swine." Auntie takes in a rattling breath, catching a glimpse of Seryozha's pale, frightened face. "Oh, mon cher, forgive me." She strokes his dark hair and presses him tightly to her breast before walking over and handing him to Irina. "Distract our boy. Read him a fairy tale or two."

Lili meets her sister's gaze again; this time, she has to bite the inside of her cheek to keep from smiling. With her free hand, she reaches for her and Nicky's old book of fairy tales from a chest-turned-table. The gold lettering on the brown leather cover is faded, a few letters missing entirely. Lili thumbs to a tale called "The Oracle," about a prankster pagan spirit that would certainly be handy with the beastly men downstairs.

She reads the story aloud. It follows a peasant family whose izba hut seems to turn against them. They cannot sleep for the clanging of pots and pans in the pech oven, the smashing of dishes and the crashing of furniture. Their candles are snuffed out, too, as if by a ghostly hand. One morning, the youngest daughter wakes to complain of a cold, prickly touch as the moon was high and bright. Her family laughs. But that night, they find the girl dead in her bed.

Lili inadvertently thinks of her and Irina's younger sister, Xenia, who died two years before from scarlet fever. She wonders morbidly if Xenia had felt the same touch. Shaking her head to banish her sister's specter, Lili reads on. "Varya had told the truth. The spirit had visited her, his cold touch portending misfortune or death—"

"Enough!"

Lili glances up. It takes a lot to rattle Auntie. But her face is corpse white, as Lili had imagined Nicky's grandmother in her coffin. "What is it, Auntie?"

"Stop reading! It is nonsense. It is worse than nonsense. It is—it is . . ." Auntie swoons. Just as she is about to collapse, she grabs for the doorway and rights herself with one thin, shaking arm. Her eyes stare into nothing. They freeze the blood in Lili's veins, bulging terribly, entangled in some private nightmare.

Lili's voice dries up. She shuts the book with hands that are trembling again. Irina passes Seryozha to her, warm yet also trembling, and dashes to Auntie.

"Are you well?" Irina takes Auntie's face between her hands, trying to get through to her. "Marie? Shall we call for a doctor?"

Auntie stills, more than ever resembling a corpse. Then, to Lili's horror, she smiles. And all Lili wants to do is run into her sister's arms and be a little girl again, ignorant of these horrors. She settles for Cleo flying down and snuggling up to her. That, and clutching her sketch pad to her chest as if it were Uncle Pasha himself.

5

Hunger and Shadows

THAT NIGHT, IRINA doesn't sleep. Wild laughter and bursts of carousing song reach them, the men's revelry spinning fiercely and without regard for decorum into the night. Irina keeps picturing her aunt's face drained of blood, that horrific smile. She and Lili had put her to bed, thinking the requisition had been too much for her.

Irina aches something terrible for their previously quiet, hard-working household—Auntie cooking and cleaning, Grand-mère mending and baking, she and Lili out searching for food, Natasha learning (and eating) at school, Seryozha keeping up their spirits with his grins and winks, his childish prattle and quests.

A moody morning filters into the attic, ashen gray and lifeless, not improving Irina's mood. Especially when Seryozha wriggles in her arms to face her with large, pleading eyes. "I'm hungry," he whispers.

Perversely, she wonders what his father would say if he saw his son in such dire straits and her unable to provide for him. In a flash, the American and his offer to apply for the relief jobs returns. Supposedly *with no danger from your government or that dreaded secret police* . . . Irina's stomach rumbles, as if eager for the American food.

"The flour we got yesterday," Lili mumbles sleepily, lifting her head from Irina's shoulder as Cleo emits a drowsy tweet from the crook of her arm. "Oladushki?"

"Oh, yes!" Seryozha's dull brown eyes lighten to chestnut. "Irina, can we?"

"Without milk and eggs?" They would make sad pancakes indeed.

"Oh, but we have coffee now." Lili's eyes are closed, but her mouth quirks up.

No, there's always a danger when it comes to Americans, and Irina isn't that desperate. "Let's see what we can do, hm?" she says to her boy, who hops off her lap with a fresh burst of energy. She yawns, stretching her stiff limbs before rising more slowly.

Cleo flaps her wings, blinking wide awake and shooting up to the rafters. Lili flops onto Irina's place. She cuddles up to a still-sleeping Natasha. Irina shakes her head at their childish ignorance. But her lips twitch into a smile. Let them be children for a while longer. She catches Seryozha's little hand in hers as they tiptoe through the adjoining room, resounding with Auntie's snores and creaking cot, before descending the cramped stairs.

Halfway down, Irina grinds to a stop. Her heart has leaped into her throat.

A shadow has appeared on the wall—one of the men?—moving toward them with startling speed. But it is small, too small for a hearty Soviet.

Irina feels sick. She imagines her dead sister, Xenia, sprinting through the twisting corridors. But as the shadow draws nearer, it shrinks, becoming bent and deformed. Grand-père, in the last months of his life, walking this very hall with his cane striking the parquet.

A large black rat hops around the corner, and Irina draws back in disgust. Relief, too. Is she Lili, to be imagining ghosts? The rat is as startled as they are; it gives an indignant squeak before scrambling away. Seryozha, ever the curious little boy, makes to run after it. But Irina pulls him forward—to the next landing, then down the marble steps of the grand staircase, toward the dark-wood and tile-checkered kitchen.

"Make borscht for us, old woman." A man's voice comes from behind the door, and Irina hastens inside the room, keeping a tight, steady hold on her son.

"What will *we* eat?" Grand-mère is flushed from the stove, her reddened hands planted on her thin, aproned waist. "It is our food. If you bring me yours, I will gladly make anything you like."

Men are everywhere, brushing past Irina, slamming cupboards and pantry doors. On the counters, she glimpses rows of dusty vodka and wine bottles from their stores, as well as their remaining food—a loaf of stale black bread; a sack of turnips; a few radishes, carrots, beets; the sack of flour and tin of coffee.

"Nah, I think we'll use your food." A large, thuggish man smirks at Grand-mère. "You can starve for all I care." His eyes are flinty, hooded, revealing a total lack of decency, maybe humanity. Certainly, no brains.

Grand-mère glances at Irina with such a lost expression that her heart contracts. What did the American call the Bolsheviks? *Bolos?* She marches up to the man angrily. "You have no right to take our food." Though they do, and she knows it.

"You"—the man's gaze slips, eel-like, down her body—"will do as you are told."

Irina's empty stomach gives a sick lurch. She pushes Seryozha toward Grand-mère, just as the man thrusts his face into hers in a rush of stale alcohol.

"You see, little countess, I can do much worse than take your food." He runs one paw-like, sweaty hand down her arm. His wetness seeps through her blouse. Then a *slap!* on her behind. Her eyes water from its force.

Irina clenches her jaw and raises her chin in defiance, as if her legs aren't wobbling, her behind smarting. As if the kitchen hasn't just gone silent. "Don't you dare do that again. Or I will take the matter up with your superior. Then you won't be so cavalier. You won't be here at all."

"You hear that, Boriska?" one man says, laughing. "What will you do?"

But Boriska is, quite simply, a dolt; his eyes shift from the men to Irina, befuddled, clearly not having thought this far ahead. "Why, you little—" But no words come, and he turns confusedly back to his laughing comrades.

Irina kneels before Seryozha, who is rubbing his belly—hunger pains, again. She wants to press him close, to tell him to hold on. She will make things better. She will try.

That day, Irina convinces Lili to leave Moscow House earlier than usual to barter their wares and look for jobs, even the lowliest and most humiliating. Irina cannot help but think of the American jobs, likely in some warm soup kitchen. But they aren't possible. No, she will clean streets, gutters, toilets, anything for a little money or food to sneak into their attic. Night falls, and with it descends a bitter, soaking, deadening kind of cold.

They return dejected and disheartened. Worse, empty-handed.

6

A Party Irina Cannot See

ON THE THIRD night, the attic starts to remind Irina of a prison cell that smells suspiciously of their house, of dusty tapestries, carpets, mothballs. Wisely, Cleo is keeping away.

Irina goes to open a window, her head inadvertently brushing against a low-hanging cobweb. A spider falls into her dress. She can feel its legs against the skin of her back as it crawls up the length of her vertebrae. Irina covers her mouth to muffle a scream before finally flicking the spider away. She rushes to the window, throwing it open and gulping in the cool air, saddened, not comforted. It is damp with leaves already on the cusp of dying.

Thankfully, the men's drunken revelry downstairs has quieted. Irina hears only the scratch of Lili's pencil against her sketch pad from behind the lacquer screen dividing their room. She walks back to the table, thinking of checking on Seryozha and Natasha again. But no noise comes from the other room where the children have gone to bed with Grand-mère. Auntie never really rose that morning, mostly sleeping since her fit.

Irina picks up a yellowing map from the table, Papa's eighteenth birthday present to her. She can see him even now, the mischievous curl of his lip, the jovial glint in his chartreuse-green eyes. *I wish to give you the world, Irinushka. If you have a map, you will have an idea of where you'd like to go.*

How she had wanted to travel, to see the world Papa had wished for her to see! Irina runs a hand across the map, the foreign lands and vast seas tumbling in blue-green streaks, the mountain ranges carved deep into the earth like memories upon the mind. And America, that unexplored frontier, an ocean, a life, away.

Irina wonders which state the Americans are from. . . .

The candle beside her shivers, bringing her back. She lifts a stack of photographs from the crate at her feet. They are stuck and fused together. Like the map, she hasn't looked at them in a long time. It is not safe to look at them. But tonight, she cannot resist.

The first photograph is of her parents—Papa in an elegant suit, Maman with a feathered hat and a luxurious fur-lined cape, both with slight smiles on their young, handsome faces. Irina can almost see the violet in her mother's eyes through the black color. The next photograph is of a young woman with wonderfully coiffed hair, the impeccable Meriel, daughter of the former British ambassador to Russia. Irina can still picture her friend's small yet animated features as she imparted the latest gossip from the English court. Or spoke of her imposing mother, Lady Georgina, and her campaigns to save the Russian people.

The hospital where Irina worked flashes into her mind again, the alcohol and blood, the screams of agony . . . *No, Irina. Come back.*

She skips the next photograph—of her and Meriel in their white nursing uniforms—and takes up another.

"Julia," Irina whispers with pained affection. The American Princess Cantacuzène-Speransky stares back, her stately Russian husband, Prince Mikhail, hovering behind her. Irina recalls Julia's knowing smile, whether at the Mariinsky Theatre or at her splendid suite at the Hotel d'Europe. Her rooms had brimmed with priceless art and ambassadors, including the American David Francis.

You simply must come to Washington, Julia would say. *I was born there, you know, in the White House where Granddaddy was president.*

Irina would drink up Julia's descriptions of that grand columned portico; of Pennsylvania Avenue, dotted with carriages and fashionable people, the great dome of the Capitol shining in the distance. How new it all seemed to Irina, how filled with promise. A future to breathe in without the constraints of hundreds of years of history, of Petersburg, of her mother and the matrons telling her how to live.

The image fades to the last one of Julia, harried and in her travel clothes. The squeeze of her hand before the hastily whispered, *Farewell, darling.*

Is she in Washington, safe and happy and free? Likely. Without a thought for her *dear, violet-eyed Irina*. And, no doubt, Meriel is back in England.

Irina shuffles the photographs so she doesn't have to look at her friends. No matter how much they insisted they *will miss Russia! And you!* they left both Russia and her without a thought. She is surprised it no longer hurts as much. Her mind flicks back to the Americans, the possible jobs, what it would be like to work for them.

Irina's fingers stiffen on the last photograph, her eyes sweeping over the man pictured there. His closely cropped black hair, his eyes—black in the photograph yet green in her memory—his polished dark green and red Preobrazhensky Regiment officers' uniform. The smile, all at once charming and off-putting with its arrogance.

Prince Georgy Dolgonog, her fiancé and Seryozha's father.

Georgy stares back at her from his photograph. From a past long dead, like her parents. Parts of her, too. She remembers the ballroom where they met, the officer with the mane of red hair who had approached her, though she doesn't remember his name, some friend of Georgy's.

Do you see that man over there?

Irina nodded, thinking the officer's conspiratorial whisper flirtation. Yet he pointed to Prince Georgy Dolgonog, of the oldest and princeliest aristocratic family, dating back to the founding of the Russian lands.

He is in love with you, said the officer.

Then why not talk to me himself? asked Irina. Was the prince a coward, a weak man?

He will—if you agree to dance the next waltz with him.

When Irina met Georgy's gaze, it sparkled like Grand-mère's emerald brooch. Not only unafraid but filled with a daring, a loftiness that seemed to say, *See how powerful I am? I send others to do my bidding, even in matters of love.*

Irina glided toward the dance floor and Georgy. Not because she found him handsome, though he was. Not because she knew him; she didn't, as he had been away serving in the army. But because Maman's face glowed with pride. And the other guests whispered and stared. They parted before Irina in a sea of bold color, rippling silk, and sparkle. Of pure envy. At his name, at what that represented. Status, family, marriage, motherhood—everything she had been taught to desire and strive for, putting an end to Papa's dreams of travel for her, her own curiosity about the world beyond Russia.

Now Irina flashes back to the last time she saw Georgy, thin and pale, his face without its assurance, scattered, lost. And those once sparkling green eyes, dulled and haunted from years of war.

No. Irina leaps from her chair and strides to the door. She will not think of him, of his face, brought into such razor-sharp focus. As if she had really looked into his eyes.

"Where are you going?" she hears Lili ask.

But it is as if Georgy is before her with his haunted face. "I need air."

"Then open the window wider! Don't go looking for trouble. Irina?"

But Irina cannot *think*, she cannot *breathe*, she *needs air*. She tugs her coat off the door hanger and pushes into the next room, past the cots with her sleeping family reduced to formless shadows, then through the attic door into the stairwell—and the likewise slumbering house.

On the threshold, Irina inhales the brisk night air greedily. Her gaze falls on the dried-up fountain, and the oak tree behind it. Though it's still August, it riots red orange like a flame, drawing the eye. Must all ghosts be raised this night?

Irina whirls, shutting her eyes against the oak, the grave beneath, the usual dark feeling at the sight.

An owl hoots, a disturbing, otherworldly sound given her thoughts.

She hastily steps back inside, stinging wind to dense stillness. But she isn't ready to return to the attic, either. She needs to distract herself from the memories.

Irina veers right off the entrance hall, into the abandoned East Wing—a series of reception and drawing rooms leading to the ballroom. Now they are nothing but white sheets and hulking shapes and gaping empty spaces. Her heavy felt boots kick up puffs of dust from the parquet like powdery snow. She sneezes, suddenly and violently, the sound reverberating against the cavernous silence hanging over the rooms.

As Irina is crossing into the next room, she feels a prickle of cold on her arm. A draft of air. But the damask curtains are sealed tight. No, it is as if someone has moved past her. She turns sharply, as fearful as the other morning. Odd. She has never been afraid in the house. She doesn't have Lili's active imagination. Nor is she given over to delusions. It is only the howl and tear of the wind, the rattle of the windows in their casements, the faint give of a latch. With all this noise, she almost doesn't hear it.

The creak of parquet, somewhere near. And again, unmistakable now. *Creak. Creeeaak.*

Footsteps. Small, like a child's.

Irina backs away with wide eyes—when there is a deep growl. Then an earsplitting screech, and a dark shape hurtles across her path. A glint of red, as though red eyes have snapped to hers. The next second, the thumping of bare feet, then nothing.

What was that? Some animal, trapped in the house?

That's when the air implodes all around her. As if the windows have been flung open to let in the wind. It rushes at Irina, sweeping up her hair and skirt in a perfect tempest. The heavy patterned carpets billow under her feet. She barely manages to keep her balance. Throws her hands over her head as she hears furniture crashing, things smashing, the old Gobelin tapestries pounding against the walls so hard she thinks they will be torn down.

The noise dissipates as suddenly as it had started, a small child's tantrum blustering to nothing. Irina lowers her arms, breathing hard. She can tell by the dark outlines of overturned furniture and objects that everything in the room has been upset. Before Irina can move, she hears a sharp *click-clack*. This time, heavier footfalls, bouncing dully against the walls. As if heels are striking the parquet, becoming muffled as they hit the carpet.

"Who's there?" She peers around. Can it be one of the men, intent on making her the subject of ridicule? She throws her shoulders back and tries again, in a steadier voice: "Quit tormenting me with ill-timed jokes."

A whispering fills her ears. Everywhere and nowhere. Irina spins on her heel, still peering into thick, very still darkness. But the words are like the rustle of dried-up leaves, a conversation achingly close yet too distant to distinguish. An echo of a laugh bursts out, a gown rustles.

She draws in a shaking breath, catching a whiff of perfume that is heady, floral. Maman's orange blossom. The scents of jasmine and sandalwood, too, followed oddly by strong black tea and something sharp and salty, caviar or perhaps pickled fish. As though their dead butler, Dmitri, has drawn too near with a platter of zakuski balanced in his ghostly hands. Irina is trying to hold herself straight, but it is as if her limbs are waterlogged.

She is brought back ten years before, when Moscow House sparkled with balls and soirées, guests milling in these rooms filled with the lively hum of conversation and the flicker of intimate candlelight.

In the distance, something flickers, then vanishes. Flickers, vanishes.

Despite her thundering heart, the irrational fear, Irina walks on. Perversely, wanting to see more, like the eye snagging on a dead body in the street.

The other sounds recede, the scents shifting to fragrant, spicy smoke. Cigars, she realizes, with a musky note underneath, vanilla intertwined with cedar. Her breath dies in her throat—Papa's eau de cologne. But Papa cannot be here. He is gone. The man playing this sick joke on her must wear the same scent.

The flicker wavers, reminding her of a shoulder turning, or a hand motioning. It is still far, still unreachable. And yet. Irina picks up her pace, walking very fast, then starting to jog.

Memories of Papa rush in, the images as jagged as broken glass. Papa handing her the map. Papa listening to her, head tilted, face intent. Papa excitedly tugging a new gown out of his trunk for her after his latest visit to Paris. His love of travel and adventure surpassed only by his joy of giving them presents upon his return.

Papa's father had been a diplomat to Tsar Nicholas's father, and Papa followed him into civil service, first into the Chevalier Guard Regiment, then as Moscow's deputy governor, then as Petrograd's civil governor, and finally as master of ceremonies at the imperial court. Papa's charm won everyone over. That smile, warm, inviting, filled with love. Now reduced to ashes. Papa is dead. Irina saw the letter, from some minor government official, the word *typhus* scrawled there with a careless hand.

The flicker wavers on the air, closer now. She sees it is a shadow wrought from pale colors. A form, a figure—of a man? Irina is running after the shadow, room into room, corridor after corridor, trying to see, to reach it.

Finally, panting, she stops—just outside the ballroom's shut gilded doors.

The flicker has evaporated into darkness like a drop of moisture.

Irina takes breath after breath of the air, back to its dusty scent, smothering against her throat. Tears sting her eyes. She imagines herself holding that letter all over again, seeing the fatal word that with such heavy permanence kills all hope—*Dead*. Pure, cold horror clutches at her. Could the shadow have been her dead papa?

Enough. Irina straightens. Her eyes land on a darkened shape, and her heart gives a panicked lurch.

A man lies motionless before a high fireplace, surrounded by broken glass lamps and shattered marble statues.

Perhaps he stumbled in the dark, walking the house like her, and they crashed down on him from the mantel. She is still shaky, panicky, but instinct takes over. Irina strides over to the man and kneels beside him. She sees it is Tolya, the man who put up the Soviet flag. *Please be responsive*, she pleads with him silently.

But his chest doesn't rise and fall with his breath. He is rigid, white-faced, with blood crusted over and blackened on the side of his head. Irina reaches for his hand—deathly cold, maybe days cold. With her hands steadier than she feels, she listens for his pulse. Hears nothing. Swallows past a throat now tight with gathering fear. Despite her years as a nurse, she feels the distinctly human horror at the proximity to death.

"Help!" Irina forces out. Then she draws in a sharp, jagged breath and screams, "Somebody, help me!"

After an interval and more screaming, she hears heavy boots on parquet and men's voices growing closer, louder, ringing with alertness. Then they are crowding her in a blur of feet and legs, arms and chests.

It is only later that Irina wonders why she didn't leave the dead man where he was. But she was remembering that hospital, the rush and purpose of it. Everything she has missed while living entombed in Moscow House. Maybe it was also adrenaline—from hearing, smelling, seeing those rooms come back to life. And her dead papa with them.

7

Decisions

ONCE THE POLICE, several Soviet officials, and a pair of Cheka agents descend upon Moscow House, filing their reports, conducting their inquiries, and sending for their doctor to examine the dead man, a young Soviet boy with pale, unevenly parted hair escorts Irina to Comrade Suzhensky for her statement. She keeps her back straight, rigid with tension. The entrance hall is a hive of men with cold, businesslike voices. They fall silent, looking up and staring as she and her escort veer into the West Wing.

While its second floor is used for the men's bedrooms, the ground floor consists of the library—two stories of books and Pasha's salvaged artworks—and Grand-père's rooms, including his study, as dark and austere as Irina remembers it.

An old oil lamp burns forlornly on the large mahogany desk, where Comrade Suzhensky sits bent over a sheaf of papers. With alarm, Irina also glimpses the severe-looking, blue-eyed man Felix, whom she and Lili met in the street the day of the requisition. Behind the two men, pictures of Lenin and Politburo member Lev Kamenev have been hammered into Grand-père's wall. They stare at Irina, watchful, as she lowers into a chair and tilts her chin up. She has nothing to hide.

Felix dismisses the Soviet boy with a flick of his wrist before lighting a cigarette and offering it to Irina. She shakes her head, not taking anything from the man on principle. Then the questions come: *Why were you in the East Wing, at night? Do you know it is a restricted part of the house?* Irina hasn't smoked since the war, when she and the other nurses would sneak a cigarette or two at the hospital. But the more questions that come, the more she wants that cigarette. *Did you know Tolya? That he has been dead for at least forty-eight hours?*

Irina imagines that unnaturally pale, still face. The crusted-over blood. The men likely already know everything about her. So she gets ahead of the questioning. "I followed the protocols I was taught at the British Colony Hospital for Wounded Russian Soldiers."

"You did," allows Comrade Suzhensky. "You saw nothing else?"

Irina's heart skitters. That red-eyed shape, the shadow . . . "No," she replies. "Except for the shattered lamps and statues." *The man was likely blind drunk.* Yes, that would make sense.

Comrade Suzhensky smiles, very wide and wolfish. "What do you think should happen to whoever did this? If it wasn't an accident, that is."

Irina blinks, senses a trap, thinks fast. "Of course they should be prosecuted and punished accordingly."

The Old Bolshevik leans toward her. She has no doubt that is what he is, given the practiced wolfishness, his air of authority and experience. "Would your answer be any different if you knew Tolya was a drunk?" he asks.

"Of course not," she says mechanically, swallowing her thoughts from before.

Suddenly, the lamp's yellow wick gives a tremble, throwing the room into ripples of shadow and a chill over Irina's skin. Though there is no breeze, and the glass would protect the flame if there were. She notices the men's uneasy glances at each other as the light continues to tremble. It is almost as though someone is fooling around with the lamp. . . . She answers the next question distractedly. "I've been out looking for work—and food."

Comrade Suzhensky ignores her pointed look. "And in the evenings?"

"In the attic." Irina holds herself very still, trying to suppress her uneasiness. Do they believe she or her family killed this man? Ridiculous. She found him and raised the alarm. "Ask my sister. She was with me."

"Crimes *have* been committed in pairs, you know," Felix interjects, voice and eyes suspicious. "Boriska tells me you two had an altercation."

The light dims, gives an oily wink. Starts to flicker madly. The chill is back. The lamp, that thuggish man . . .

"Fix that," Comrade Suzhensky snaps at Felix.

"Boris was stealing our food and making inappropriate advances toward me," Irina says, trying to ignore the flickering, the intense cold, the unease. Desperate to leave the cursed study. "I can provide names of the people who saw us about town. Your men have seen us leaving and returning. My grandmother, Katerina Sherbatskaya, will corroborate. You don't doubt her word, do you? She can appeal to Lev Kamenev if so." Irina was waiting to use this trump card. The Politburo man has known Grand-mère since before the Revolution and was a useful inside source following Papa's and Aleksei's arrests.

"We don't care—" Felix pitches forward, his head thrown dangerously close to the table's edge. He thrusts his hands out just in time. Almost knocks over the lamp.

"Chyort vozmi, you idiot!" Comrade Suzhensky leaps up and gives Felix a shove. Then he swings toward Irina with hastily honeyed words. "My sincere apologies, Irina Alexandrovna. For Boris Borisovich's improper behavior as much as for Felix Ivanovich's. I'll speak to them both. No appeal will be necessary, I assure you."

Felix huffs as Irina takes in a relieved breath. But not of cigarettes— of pipe smoke. She coughs, bewildered. It is Grand-père's distinctive scent.

Comrade Suzhensky sniffs at the air, as if he, too, can smell Grand-père. "I . . . will interview my men and verify your witnesses. All perfectly discreet, of course. Not even a notice will appear in the paper.

But my investigation will be thorough. To that end, I will need to interview your family." He spreads his hands apologetically. "Procedures, you understand."

Irina pictures the Soviet officials and Cheka agents downstairs, thinks Comrade Suzhensky is likely a Chekist himself. He has power over this investigation, after all. But why not just arrest them? Former people have been taken to Butyrka for less. "Why help us?" she cannot help but ask. "You can . . ." She stops short of saying *arrest*.

Comrade Suzhensky ignores Felix's ugly laugh. "We respect your venerable babushka. Comrade Kamenev does as well. It is why you have been allowed to stay here. That, and . . . other circumstances. But I should tell you"—he leans forward in his chair—"no weapon has been found. The head wound is such that it may have been an accident, or not. Either way, we will need to conduct a proper search of the attic."

No. Irina puts up a hand, thinking how frightened Seryozha and Natasha would be. "Comrade Suzhensky, we have nothing to hide, but please, the children—"

"I think we have chatted long enough, don't you?" Comrade Suzhensky turns back to the papers on the desk. Yet his face is pale, and he glances around uneasily.

Irina wants to plead with him, but she sees any attempt will be in vain. She summons all her dignity. "Thank you," she says, and sweeps out of the study.

Felix is on her heels. As soon as the door shuts, he grabs her shoulder, hard. "Your pretty face and manners might have fooled old man Suzhensky, but not me," he whispers fiercely. "You are a wolf in sheep's clothing. Your family, nothing but upyrs, draining the country with your bourgeois excesses. You are up to something, and I will find out what it is."

Vampires, blood. The living dead. A nightmare. "Kindly remove your hand, Felix Ivanovich," Irina forces out through her teeth. She will not let this small man make her feel small. To her surprise, he withdraws his hand. Irina walks away even as her heart turns to ice.

Not only at the loathing in that hard gaze but at the pipe smoke—as if Grand-père had really been in his study.

"You should have refused," Auntie fumes, her rage a quiet simmer. Her painted face watches Irina in the mottled mirror of her old wooden vanity. "A search, as though we are criminals. Why, it is undignified. Disrespectful. Insolent."

Despite Irina's head aching something fierce, she wonders when Auntie managed to bring up that vanity from her rooms. Or the photographs in their tarnished silver frames—of Auntie's husband and son; of her, Maman, and Pasha with their tall hats and bright smiles, dappled in sunlight and exuding their contented, relaxed luxury.

Auntie raises one heavily penciled brow at Irina, waiting for an explanation.

Irina bristles. What does her aunt expect? "It would have looked suspicious."

"What about Seryozha, hm? Have you thought how it will affect him?" *Your son*, unspoken, hangs there suspended. *Like a threat*, Irina thinks.

The boy, sitting in Grand-mère's lap, stares back at Irina solemnly. An ache blooms in her heart, radiating up and down her left arm painfully, horribly. Auntie knows exactly what to say to wound her, to make her doubt herself. She had the same thought, after all.

Lili marches over to Irina, slipping an arm around her waist. "Irina is perfectly right. Let the damn Bolsheviks search to their hearts' content. Shall I give them my statement next?"

Irina grips Lili's arm right back, grateful. The guilt and doubts ease.

"Such eagerness for an interrogation. Have I taught you nothing, Liliya?" Auntie shakes her head before applying a sweep of rouge to her high-boned cheeks. She says something to Grand-mère in French.

But Irina cannot tear her gaze from her aunt. Her skeleton presses against her pallid skin as if to leap out. Shadows of fatigue swarm her face, bat-like, eyes frightfully large and luminescent. Irina hasn't seen her aunt with makeup or in such a dour, old-fashioned black gown in years. Not since Uncle Pasha's death.

"Why did you paint your face, Auntie?" Natasha peeks over Irina's shoulder.

Lili leans forward, frowning. "Your eyes are so big, Auntie. Did you use belladonna?"

"Well, I need to put on my face if I am to be humiliated in my own home."

The girls cackle—and despite the gravity of the situation, the Soviet men on their way, Irina smiles.

"Can *I* put on my face?" Natasha quips, using any excuse to play with makeup.

Grand-mère blanches. "Oh, mon Dieu!"

"Absolutely not," says their aunt.

Irina laughs then, really laughs. A dour Auntie with a twinkle of her old humor cuts a comical figure. Grand-mère, even Auntie, also smile.

The attic is searched, no weapon or other evidence found. The family, even little Seryozha, are questioned. It is only as a dreary blue dawn seeps in between their old muslin curtains that they are finally allowed to rest.

Their family is asleep by the time Irina and Lili have tidied up and changed into their nightgowns. "What happened tonight, Irishka?" Lili finally asks, stealing a glance at her.

Irina settles into her cot thoughtfully. The mattress and covers are soft and downy after all the hard chairs. She wants to tell Lili about what she saw and heard, the scuttling shape, that shadow, the scent of Papa and Maman and Grand-père. But it was her imagination, had to be, doubtless overactive due to the strain of the requisition. That, or she is in a fit of delirium. The supernatural does not exist. Ghosts do not exist. The dead do not walk.

"I needed air," she finally confesses. "I... looked at some photographs."

"I knew it." Lili throws up her hands. "Nothing good can come of that, Irishka. We will all end up in Butyrka for your little peeks. To say nothing about finding dead bodies."

When she tries to close her eyes and sleep, all Irina can see is the dead man.

Tree branches scratch at the house. It shifts with the wind in a haunting chorus of groans and creaks, bangs and moans. The air smells rotten, as if more insects and rodents, even pigeons, are trapped in the walls. Her stomach clenches, knotted tight with emptiness without its supper. As she lays there, Irina assesses the situation. Soviet men, their class enemies, are sharing their ancestral house. They face hunger, deprivation, no work. And there is an investigation into a man's death.

But there is the possibility *of work*, whispers a little voice inside Irina—with the American and his relief organization. What did he call it? *The American Relief Administration*.

She stills, the sheets hot and scratchy against her overheated skin. How strange—it is so cold.

Maybe the notion of working for the Americans is not so ridiculous, or impossible. Maybe she *can* apply for the job. At the very least, learn more. If she doesn't, they will freeze or starve, sicken, possibly die. How long will the Soviet men let them stay? Weeks, months? They've already occupied most of the house, restricted the rest. And here is the job Irina has been desperate for, the promise of money and food and safety should they be turned out. A future she has not allowed herself to envision. And work. Purpose. Something outside of the house.

The American said the Soviet government, even the Cheka, knows of the organization. That Russians will work for it, that it is sanctioned by Lenin himself. Her fears of speaking to, maybe working for, the Americans may be unfounded. They can hire anyone, Will said. That must include former people. And there might be protection in working for the Americans—from the Soviet men in the house as much as from the Cheka.

Irina pictures Seryozha's small, hungry face, Natasha's and Lili's gaunt frames.

They need food—preferably packaged food, to better hide from the men.

They *are* desperate. Irina is desperate.

Her stomach growls—again—sealing her decision. She will apply. She will ask questions. And if there is too much danger to the family, she will not take the risk.

SEPTEMBER 1921

Irina bides her time—until, some days later, as September whirls in with its bone-chilling gales, Comrade Suzhensky notifies her the investigation has been closed, the man's death ruled an accident. She blinks at him with a mixture of surprise and relief, one more impediment to the American job removed.

"An unfortunate accident." Comrade Suzhensky is mournful, his moustache turned down. "Though Tolya *was* a drunk, so perhaps it is not *that* shocking." He tips his cap to Irina and withdraws, his boots striking the parquet like Grand-père's cane.

A few days after that, Irina walks over to 30 Spiridonovka, a distance just shy of two kilometers from Moscow House. It feels longer than the half hour that it is.

Rain falls on Irina in cold droplets that leave her skin wet and numb. The wind thrashes, vicious, out for the kill. With it, the tinge of soaked leaves, a bitter autumn. Irina glances around for watchful eyes. But the street is empty, bare, except for the fallen, still-green leaves. Flapping bright and papery like bird wings, yet dead.

Irina hesitates before the building, slate gray in the rain. Maybe she should turn back. Then she thinks, What kind of mother is she if she doesn't do all in her power to feed her child, her sister and family? To protect them and give them a future? Even if it ultimately costs her her freedom, maybe even her life, Irina has to do this. Then she is walking up to the old mansion, giving her name and Will's to the porter, and filling out two applications for work with the American Relief Administration—for her and, if she wishes it, her sister—come what will.

8

The Horror of Both Past and Present

NIGHT IS FALLING fast and hard, and Lili's stomach is aching from hunger. More so at the thought of Grand-mère cooking for the Bolsheviks instead of her. Auntie's simmering rebuke to Natasha and Seryozha wafts over to Lili through the closed door. Auntie must also be hungry. It is time for supper, and yet Irina and Cleo are nowhere to be seen.

A *bang*, and the closest window bursts open in a billow of curtains. The rain-drenched wind gusts inside, shaking the house so violently that Lili thinks it might be constructed of hay instead of stone, that the roof will collapse on them like in "The Three Little Pigs." Then a *flash!* and Lili is remembering the house shaking from a different kind of violence on an autumn night so damnably like this one. Only, three years before—the last time the Bolsheviks forced their way into Moscow House.

Despite her promises to ignore and forget, Lili is reliving it all over again—she, fifteen, sketching absently as the dining room doors burst open and the leather-jacketed men stream in. The crush of sight and sound. The pounding of heavy boots, the click of bullets in the revolvers, at the ready, aimed directly at Lili and her family.

She remembers dimly thinking, *This is it. This is when I get a bullet to the head.* It could only be the dreaded Cheka, feared by most everyone in Russia. While nightly visitations to former people had not been unusual, her grandparents and Uncle Pasha had friendly relations with Soviet officials, even converting the family's former estates into state-owned museums. But of course, no one was safe from the Cheka.

A man walked into the dining room then, with a comical shock of dark hair, a hideously large and long forehead, and a villainous absence of expression. "Hands up!" he barked.

Even Lili recognized him—one of the Cheka's founders, Comrade Yakov Peters.

She was faintly aware of a gasp—Irina's, as her sister reached out a trembling hand to Seryozha.

Their family raised their hands but remained seated. Dmitri lowered the tray with the gleaming samovar and pot of zavarka brew to the floor. The smell of that strong, black tea burned into Lili's nose along with her panic. Her hands started to shake, nearly dropping her pencil.

"Where is Count Sergei Sherbatsky?" Comrade Peters asked, using Grand-père's title with a startling mixture of disdain and begrudging respect.

Pasha, the eldest, stood. "My father is on his deathbed. He is not to be disturbed."

"I will decide who is to be disturbed."

"Oh, for the love of God!" Uncle Pasha brought his fist down on the table, setting the service and silverware rattling. "Do you respect nothing? The man is dying—"

"No. You are."

A single shot rang out.

Lili shut her eyes. Shock, pure and numbing, jolted through her. She felt lightheaded, about to fall, about to be sick. Her ears couldn't stop ringing. It couldn't be. They couldn't have. It wasn't possible!

She opened her eyes, looking for her uncle. Her favorite, her beloved Uncle Pasha. But he had dropped onto the table and was sliding down to the floor. An alarmingly red stain expanded on the bright white tablecloth. Fat red drops trickled onto the parquet, swelled there to become a puddle beneath Uncle Pasha's body. The crystal glassware, the porcelain plate of caviar, his teacup with the untouched tea, it all went crashing down.

Lili couldn't see or hear anything—except for the dripping blood.

She barely registered Comrade Peters's instructions to Nurse Masha to take her, Seryozha, Xenia, and Natasha to the nursery, while the adults were to be locked in the dining room with a dead Uncle Pasha for the night. Lili's knees were shaking, her dress so heavy it weighed her down. And in place of the shock, a very real, very raw awareness. In that moment, she had lost not only her beloved uncle but her youth.

She didn't think; she dropped into a curtsy before Comrade Peters.

A fleeting look of surprise skittered across that still, emotionless face, then the lips curved up into a barely suppressed smile.

Lili had been proud of her little act of rebellion. But Uncle Pasha remained dead. And Papa and Uncle Aleksei were still arrested and taken to Butyrka. Uncle Aleksei was lucky enough to die in prison; Papa was tried and sentenced to hard labor, then sent into exile. He died in middle-of-nowhere Russia, along with Maman, who had followed him there.

Now the gunshot echoes in Lili's ears. *Bam!* Earsplitting, intensely violent.

But it is only the banging of the open window.

She curses, rushing to it. The rain is pouring in, heavy, relentless, so cold. Her blouse and trousers become soaked in seconds as she fumbles with the latch, wet and slippery.

Outside, the oak is swaying, flinging leaves out in all directions. Below the tree, something shifts. A movement, a step, toward the house and her. A shadow, a figure? Tall, familiar, back straight and proud from years of noble and military training. But the next minute, it evaporates like smoke until there is only the tree and the grave underneath.

Lili slams the window closed, the glass rattling in its frame.

Rain streams down her arms in cold rivulets, raising the hair on her skin. The figure is making her flash back, remember. *No.* She dashes a hand across her wet face before rushing to her cot and grabbing for her sketch pad. It is the only way to stop the tumble of jagged images, those bloody flashbacks, leaving her reeling and sick.

Raindrops seep into the paper, turning it damp and stained as she sketches.

The oak, three years ago. Black-clad men, with shovels raised. Uncle Pasha, lying at their feet. Her pencil tears through paper. Yet she still sees the scene, on paper and in memory—as the men buried her poor uncle under the oak. Lili had watched from the nursery as dawn painted the sky a scarlet, bloody red.

"Enough," she growls, angry at herself for letting it all in. For remembering.

She tosses the sketch aside, seizes a candlestick in her shaking hands, and strides to the door. She needs to get out of this cramped room, to lose herself in motion, to forget.

"Liliya?" Auntie calls out as Lili hastens through the adjoining room with tears stinging her eyes. The stair's creaks blessedly replace her aunt's voice, asking where in God's name she is going, and she is alone.

A *bang*, like that gunshot, and Lili stills on the landing below.

But it is a *tap, tap, tapping*. She thinks of the dead man Irina had found. Lili didn't see him, but now she imagines the blood, the ghastly pale skin, the rigid, lifeless body.

A *creak*—down the hall.

Lili doesn't move.

Creaaak. A step, she is sure.

Her candle quivers, casting shadows that shift on the walls, monstrous shapes morphing into frightening creatures from her and Nicky's storybooks—of wild-haired Baba Yaga in her mortar, zmeys and serpents, half-bird sirens. The light glints off the cracked oil paint in the portraits of Maman's family, the aristocratic House of Sherbatsky. The hall's shabbiness twists their figures into sinister phantoms with jutting limbs, bulbous noses, all-seeing eyes. Lili imagines them reaching out their dead hands to grab at her from the dark.

She is about to leap down the grand staircase—to look for her sister, a meal, anything to take her mind off monsters and dead men—when the tapping starts up again. It is behind her now. And the creaking explodes into many steps. Footsteps. A burst of movement, a sprint. The feet are not heavy or large. But dainty, a little girl's feet.

Lili squints into the darkness and almost drops her candle.

A flash of gold flares and dims, dims and flares—like a yellow will-o'-the-wisp. Then a giggle rips through the silence. More creaks, more steps, the air imploding as something whooshes past. In its wake, another giggle, the flare of gold, a waft of rot along with cold air that chills Lili from the inside out.

Something brushes against her leg. . . .

She is completely frozen. Her little sister, Xenia, had worn a skirt that rippled gold.

The tapping grows louder, more insistent—near a canvas in an elaborate bronze frame. It is an oil painting of Catherine the Great in ceremonial dress. *Tap, tap, tap* thuds the frame against the wall, buoyed by an unseen wind. A shadow passes over the portrait, slipping onto the ceiling, where it contorts into a long and twisting shape. A snake, poised to strike. Then Lili hears a screech, high and keening. Her candlestick quivers, its flame nearly snuffed out, as a sigh of air races down the hall. The tapestries and carpets billow, flapping in her face, almost knocking her over. She manages to keep her footing while heaving out violent coughs from the clouds of dust.

The old Sherbatskys continue to stare, still dead, still inanimate and ghastly.

Lili's breath is stuck to her throat. She collides with a closed door.

Behind it, someone coughs. Hacking, sick, the kind that leaves a smear of blood on the handkerchief. Horror pierces her at the realization that it is the sickroom where Grand-père died. The doorknob rattles, stops. A small pause, and everything stills. Lili is about to move, to do *something*, when a faint singing drifts up to her.

It is a soft song, a lullaby. The nursery was on the landing below, she realizes. She remembers Uncle Pasha's wife, Aunt Luba, preparing the room for the latest baby, humming in the very same way. . . .

Lili backs away, tasting a scream in her throat, building, ready to tear out—

"Lili?" Irina steps into the circle of light. The darkness stills beyond as if by magic.

Like a princess waking from a curse, Lili draws in a sharp breath. There is an influx of blood, of warmth, to her skin. The tips of her fingers tingle and thaw.

"Are you all right, Lil?"

Lili doesn't care if she looks like a coward. She rushes to her sister, who first carefully places the candlestick on the floor, ever the responsible, thoughtful Irina. But then she pulls Lili into a fierce embrace, and Lili lets her. She buries her face in the wool of Irina's coat, squeezing her eyes shut as relief floods every cell of her body.

And all the while, Irina is asking, "What is it? What did you see?"

9

An Invitation on the Heels of the Horror

LILI CONSIDERS HOW much to tell her sister as they huddle together under a scratchy blanket on her cot. Was it real, or has her imagination finally got the best of her? She doesn't wish for Irina to think her any more fanciful, or *mad*, as Maman so generously liked to put it.

But Irina speaks first. "I know we don't talk much here, around the family . . . but I need to. Is that all right?"

Lili stares at her sister, momentarily thrown off. Irina doesn't usually have time for this, for her, being too busy taking care of the children or the house. Something warm kindles within Lili. She'd like to talk to Irina. She would like it very much. "Let's make an exception, Irishka. Everybody is asleep, after all." Lili winks, casting a glance at the door, behind which she hears Auntie's cot creaking, Grand-mère's snores.

Irina nods. "You were afraid tonight. And you are never afraid."

Lili pauses, gives a quick bob of her head, curious where Irina is going with this.

"You told me the house has felt off since . . . Pasha was killed. I dismissed it as your imagination. But what if there *is* something wrong with it?" She pales to the lips.

Her sister is rational above all. Which means . . . "What did you see, Irishka?"

"I wasn't entirely honest with you the night I found Tolya. The truth is, I . . . saw something as I was walking through the house. That is, I *felt*—as if I had traveled back in time, to one of Grand-mère's soirées. I thought I smelled perfume, guests, Maman. And I saw a shadow. It had Papa's scent. Lil, I think it led me to the dead man."

Lili has gone very still, as if her insides have frozen over. Cleo, too, in the crook of her arm. The candle casts a shadowy yellow flicker that waltzes on the rafters like dancers swaying to music—what decadence. An ache pierces Lili's heart at that, and at the memory of Papa, his easy smiles, their private jokes.

"And the house seemed to implode with a strange wind," adds Irina. "A shape, some animal, appeared to me, then vanished. I assumed I was seeing things, but—"

"I'm glad you told me, Irishka." Lili places a hand on hers. It is as if they are on their way to the bazaar, Lili forgetting how much older and more mature her sister is. "I don't know about an animal, but I saw a shadow, too—under the oak. It looked like . . ."

"Uncle Pasha . . ." Irina's whisper is a trembling, frightened thing, but Lili goes on.

"And downstairs, I felt the same strange wind and heard a cough from Grand-père's sickroom, faint singing, and giggles, even something brushing against me with a skirt spun in gold." Lili's stomach churns at the memory.

"Lil?" She hears Irina through her suddenly rasping breaths.

A moment later, a cup is thrust into her hands, and she mechanically takes a drink.

The cold, bitter tea revives her a little, her breathing steadying.

Lili takes another sip. Tries to steady her thoughts, too, to pick through them. With all the years Moscow House has seen, including Uncle Pasha's violent death, only now do they notice anything remotely ghostly. She doesn't shy from the word *ghost*. The stories she has read with Nicky, the terror they have lived through during the

Revolution and beyond, their friends and family dead, Lili is surprised they didn't see traces of ghosts sooner.

She says as much to Irina, who only raises her lovely violet eyes up to the rafters.

"You still don't believe," Lili says with her usual boldness, which comforts her a little.

"Now that I know you saw it, too, I'm realizing it isn't only . . . the strain from all the change, some delusion—you know I don't have much of an imagination."

"Or any." Lili bumps Irina's shoulder playfully.

"But it cannot be, Lil. They are *dead*. They died!"

"Hypothetically, if it can be, why now?"

"Maybe it has to do with the requisition. I saw . . . what I saw a few days after that."

Cleo ruffles her wings, the feathers skimming Lili's throat. "And a man did die in the house."

Irina gives a grim nod. "Whatever it is"—she casts a glance toward the door, their family blissfully ignorant on the other side—"we cannot leave the children alone."

"And you cannot afford to find another dead body." Lili suddenly recalls her sister's absence earlier. Her stomach rumbles indignantly. "You skipped supper. Where were you?"

Irina takes a creased envelope from her skirt pocket and places it in Lili's hands with a nervousness unlike her. As if bored by the turn of the conversation, Cleo fluffs her wings and shoots up to the rafters. Lili pulls a sheet of paper out of the envelope.

As soon as she reads *You are invited to* . . . , she stares open-mouthed at her sister.

Especially when careful, circumspect Irina proceeds to tell her she filled out two applications for jobs—with *the Americans*. And here are two invitations to interview at the American Relief Administration the very next day.

Lili's emotions oscillate between shock, embarrassing fear, maybe curiosity, and . . . excitement, if her thudding heart is any indication.

An interview means tomorrow she won't need to sit in this attic or be out in the increasingly cold and dark streets, scavenging for food and work. Her spirits lift. Milk, eggs, butter, edible bread, maybe meat, even something sweet, might be theirs for the taking. Her stomach clenches at the thought of real food and at being around people, handsome American men. But then she thinks of the Cheka, the Bolsheviks in the house, that ghostly gunshot . . .

"Say something," Irina says finally.

Lili presses down her fear, reaches for the excitement. "I am impressed."

"You aren't angry I filled out an application for you?" Irina's face is pinched in genuine worry. "You don't need to interview."

Lili shakes her head, marveling at her sister's surprising solution while she'd forgotten all about the Americans. "Of course I will interview. Our very names spell danger, Irishka. But if we can get these jobs, they will put food in our bellies and rubles in our pockets."

"You don't think it is *too* dangerous?" A dent forms between Irina's neatly trimmed dark brows. "It might draw the men's attention, given the prior investigation."

"The pigs aren't leaving us much of a choice. They eat all in sight except the dregs of Grand-mère's horridly watery cabbage soup." Lili can hardly sleep for the hunger. It gnaws on her insides like a vicious parasite, until she's forced to drink unboiled water from the lavatory sink just to fill her stomach. "I'm not sure how long we will survive otherwise. And I know you. The fact that you made this decision means we need it."

Irina nods. "So we interview and—"

"—if we get the jobs, we take them," Lili finishes.

"Only after we have all the information. And we don't tell the others—about the jobs or the other thing. Not until we know more. I don't wish to worry them."

"Agreed. I cannot handle any more questions from Auntie. She's behaving . . . oddly, even for her."

"She is," Irina agrees, to Lili's surprise. "The old-fashioned gowns, the makeup. She is in her dressing gown well into the afternoon, as before the Revolution. No cooking or cleaning, either, not since the men moved in."

"Mm, only her pugs are missing." Lili remembers the fat, rambling creatures, all of a sudden missing their wrinkled faces. She used to play the best (and most well-intentioned) pranks on them. "I told you she went mad long ago." Lili cracks a smile.

Again she is surprised when Irina, Auntie's fiercest advocate, smiles back.

That night, Lili is jittery and restless, thinking about the interview.

She listens to the scrape of branches against the windowpanes, the creaks of a darkened house moving along with the blusters of wind. The night, black and heavy, presses in. Or maybe it is Uncle Pasha, knocking against the glass with a ghostly hand. . . .

Lili squeezes her tired, swollen eyes shut. Thinks she hears a rustle—of a skirt of gold—and blinks her eyes open. Her entire body prickles with cold sweat. And, despite herself, a very sharp, real fear—at the shred of gold on the floor. But no, it isn't moving, spinning, *twirling*. Only a bit of ribbon absent-minded Natasha forgot earlier.

Lili relaxes into the bed. Yet she follows the shadows stirring on the walls, a coiling, seething mass of branches and leaves and murky moonlight. It reminds her of the monsters from her and Nicky's fairy tales. The dark is somehow alive, a true presence.

She recoils when a noise vibrates against her back.

A scrabbling, or a rooting. From deep within the wall. A trapped animal? Lili pushes away, too quickly and forcefully. She almost falls off the damn cot, cursing and swinging herself back onto it before she can hit the hard wood. She is about to tell herself to stop the silliness when she hears a dragging from the direction of the table beyond the screen. As if the table itself is being dragged. Lili wishes to bury herself under the covers.

Instead, she slips out into the cold. She needs to know if she is imagining things or if it is . . . like earlier.

Slowly, she tiptoes past the screen. Peers at the table, searching for the source of the noise, gone now.

Rhythmic breathing comes from Irina's darkened cot.

Lili is about to return to her own cot, angry at not sleeping as peacefully as her sister, when the window curtain gives a twitch. She glances past it to the oak. Beyond the undulating branches and scattering leaves, a shadow takes shape on the grave—a figure, clearly visible this time. Lili's breath tangles in her throat.

A face comes into view, with an aquiline nose, high cheekbones, and a beard, neat and trim. This is followed by the body, seemingly appearing out of nothingness. It is her uncle, in the clothing from that night. Only, the suit's trousers are torn and rife with holes and dirt, the jacket gone, the shirt stained. With blood, Lili realizes. There are bruises on his pale face, his eyes empty and ringed in a hair-raising blue. But it is the bullet hole in his forehead that makes her finally gasp out in horror.

In a burst of movement, Lili hurtles back to her cot and throws the covers over her head.

There is no denying it. She saw a ghost. Really saw it. Him. Uncle Pasha. Still shadow, but more than a flicker. More than just air. The darkness beneath the covers is stifling, yet she doesn't dare move a muscle. She has believed in ghosts, but seeing one is different. The horror becomes a living thing. It makes a home deep inside.

Suddenly, a noise shatters the silence—*Cock-a-doodle-doo!*

Her heartbeat explodes into a sprint. A rooster, in the city? Impossible.

Cock-a-doodle-doo!

Lili's heartbeat slows. Now she is remembering another ghost.

The horror comes alive at night, Nicky said, pointing to the green-backed book of Nikolai Gogol's tales of hauntings and ghosts, demons and dead girls blinking awake in coffins, witches flying through the night with the Devil in their hearts. *As though by magic, the crow of the rooster brings morning, and all the horror scurries into hiding, into shadowy corners, under darkened beds. Into our hearts, where it lives to wait.*

Feeling the hair rise on her arms, Lili scooted closer to Nicky on the bench.

Not because it was twilight, when darkness descended upon Petrograd, and the war with the Germans seemed closer than ever. She wasn't thinking about that true horror. But about the ghosts, these stories, him, a delicious kind of horror and one to be savored. It set her body tingling, her heart thudding, her imagination flying. It brought her nearer to Nicky.

What is it about night that brings out the ghosts, you think?

Don't you know? He had smiled, heavy lidded, teasing, his face incredibly close. *Night belongs to the unholy and the dead, morning to God and the living. The rooster gives good fortune, protects, erases the night. He chases away the horror.*

Maybe it is the ghostly crowing, or the memory of Nicky's voice. As if enchanted, Lili's eyes fall closed. And she dives into a dreamless sleep a little like a starless night.

10

The ARA and Someone from Lili's Past

WILL MEETS LILI and Irina in a foyer exactly like the one they have at Moscow House. Lili hates it immediately. It only brings on thoughts of Uncle Pasha, the night before. But Irina, as ever, is right, and Lili needs to focus.

"Welcome to the ARA." Will flashes them his wide American smile, shaking first Irina's hand, then Lili's. "Thank you for accepting our invitation to interview."

"Thank you for the opportunity," Irina says too eagerly, as Will leads them through a series of reception rooms converted into leather- and cigarette-scented offices.

The men milling there are mere boys, no more than a few years older than Lili, despite their grown-up airs and suits. Her nerves ease as they walk past the long wooden tables. Some rise, others crane their necks for a look, still others approach to shake their hands and chat, a veritable slew of Johns, Roberts, Walters—and Harold.

"Give the girls their breathing room, for Pete's sake," he says highhandedly, his condescension toward Lili and her sister apparently forgotten. "Welcome to our little abode, ladies."

But Lili doesn't like the man on principle and tunes him out.

She has never seen so much paper. It litters every surface. What look like typewriters and telephones, too. The glass lamps are already lit, the light sifting in through the thickly curtained windows misty and graveyard-like. For being American, this place retains its dark Russianness well. Except for the pictures of what she assumes are American men on the wood paneling. Lili approaches the wall and peers at the unfamiliar faces with interest.

"You should've seen this place when we first moved in," Harold is saying. "Thirty rooms, in an absolute state of filth. The central heating, kaput! Electricity, dead! Plumbing, nonexistent! We ordered fifty oil-burner heaters from London *straightaway*."

Will launches into a speech about the ARA then. Something about the American Congress paying for the relief, in thirty-two—or is it thirty-three?—countries, under their "fearless leader," the ARA chief Herbert Hoover. Probably one of the men in the pictures.

Lili wishes they would get on with the interviews, impatience replacing the jitters. But darling Irina keeps asking questions. Funny, as she must have nearly turned back at least a dozen times, worrying over Seryozha and Natasha. Lili had hurried to point out that Natasha would be at school while Seryozha would be more than well cared for—and spoiled—by Grand-mère and Auntie.

"So, the operation feeds children?" Irina is asking.

Will is only too excited to humor her. "With plans to expand to adults, too. And provide medicines and supplies to hospitals and children's homes, even help with rebuilding. Fixing telephone and telegraph systems and such. Acting as a liaison for the Allied Powers."

"In the interest of American humanitarianism?" Irina quips—cheekily, Lili thinks.

"What else?" Will's smile turns sharp. Are they *flirting*?

"But where is the aid, the relief?"

"Not here. This is our headquarters and living space. But there will be food kitchens all over Moscow and Russia. The SS *Phoenix* arrived in Petrograd from Hamburg on September first with seven hundred tons of rations. We've already opened a food kitchen on Moika

Street in Petrograd and one here in Moscow in that old restaurant—the Hermitage?"

"That stuffy dump?" Lili wrinkles her nose. Yet images from the past flood in—the horse-drawn carriage that would take them to the Tavern, as her family so fondly called it, and those elaborate meals, too rich and fancy for her simple stomach. At Irina's look of disapproval, Lili hastens to plaster on a smile and apologize.

"My sister and I are eager to help those less fortunate. Are the jobs for work in the kitchens?" Irina is positively tireless.

"You wish!" comes a ringing voice.

A woman in a starched white uniform walks through the doors, with deep brown skin and sparkling light brown eyes hinting delightfully at mischief. Lili has seen Black people before, especially in imperial Russia prior to everybody fleeing the Revolution. But the woman is still intriguing. Maybe it is her liveliness, her sparkle, shining through, different from other women Lili knows, including her sister—more like Lili herself.

"So you've finally come to see me," Harold says to the woman, opening his arms to her.

"I'd rather ship off to Siberia than be caught dead with you—in an office." She sidesteps him to a few laughs. "I'm only stopping in on my way to the kitchen."

Lili is now *really* intrigued, especially since noticing the woman's accent. It is different from the other Americans', more leisurely, with a drawl, a twang to it, the vowels charmingly elongated. Lili wonders where in America she is from but refrains from asking. There is a shadow that has crossed the woman's face, making her more reserved, watchful, as Lili introduces herself to her.

"And I'm Emma, from New Orleans, the *unofficial* head of the ARA kitchens," the woman replies, as if reading Lili's mind, visibly a little more at ease, letting a little of her cynicism bleed through her words.

Lili has heard much of New Orleans, a city said to be located in America's Deep South, haunted, eerie, filled with jazz music and crumbling cemeteries and ghosts. Uncle Pasha had been there, saw and told her about it. About the racism, too. Lili shivers at that. Maybe that was the shadow that crossed Emma's lovely features and dampened her light. Maybe she didn't know how Lili would react to her. Interestingly, Emma seems comfortable, at home, with Will and Harold. Maybe she has known them awhile, has worked among white American men like them before, is used to them. Whatever the reason, Lili gives Emma a bright smile, tells her it is good to meet her, and means it. Lili wants a friend, recognizes something like-minded in this woman that calls to her.

"So you are the sisters everybody is talking about," Emma says slowly, thoughtfully, not unkindly. "Princesses, are you? Welcome to the fraternity," she adds, straight-faced. Yet the latent humor is undeniably there. "I'm just sorry I'm not here to supervise. These boys are beasts. Try not to indulge them."

"Not all of us are beasts," Will protests. His eyes settle on Irina, then shift away.

So Lili didn't imagine the flirting. She almost laughs. The poor boy suffers from the same malady as all men: lovesickness over her beautiful sister.

Emma gives a dry laugh. "Enough of your nonsense. Where is my Russian prince?"

"Waiting for you in the wings."

A bolt of shock races through Lili at the voice. *His* voice.

The men crowding her and Irina part as a dark-haired man strides forward with a cigarette in his mouth. His elegant black suit is impeccable, worthy of the balls of old.

The high cheekbones, the dark eyes under heavy brows, the curve of his mouth—the same and not. It looks like Nicky. But Nicky is dead. Or so she thought. If it is him, he isn't the snub-nosed, gangly boy she chased around Petersburg and read ghost stories with.

Lili can still see the two of them that last time behind the sweep of velvet drapery, as their mamans sipped their tea. Not with their usual gusto, but with low, fearful murmurs. It complemented Petrograd's increasingly threatening mood, the protests, the Revolution gaining steam like one of their monsters. Nicky and Lili were debating whether they would see a witch riding her broom through the cold, starry sky that Christmas, as Gogol had in "The Night Before Christmas." It was a game, a joke, to lighten their spirits.

Lili suggested it could only be possible with a clear night and a crescent moon. Nicky didn't laugh as she had expected. He grew quiet, his eyes darkening to black. Suddenly, hastily, he leaned down, so they were face-to-face, and he brushed her lips with his. It was a bare catch of the mouth. Then it was over. He had gone back to being a fourteen-year-old boy, boasting how another boy had dared him to kiss a girl, and now he had done it.

Back at the ARA, Lili flushes with pure, hot embarrassment. For her past self, thinking it was a real kiss, and for remembering it now. In that moment, his eyes find her. They deepen, becoming fathomless— as before that stupid, nonreal kiss.

"Well, if it isn't Countess Lili Goliteva." He smirks, as if Lili still has freckles on her cheeks and ribbons in her hair.

Relief melts the embarrassment. She exhales a breath she didn't realize she was holding. It *is* Nicky, it really is. Alive. And he recognized her. "Nicky Naroshin." She smirks back as Irina rushes over to him with open arms, embracing Nicky and kissing his cheeks. How she used to proclaim her hatred of having to watch them!

"You are acquainted?" Will glances between them. "Niko's a driver for us, and—"

"He isn't just a driver." It takes Lili a moment to understand she's the one who spoke. But the words needed to be said. Nicky is many things, a driver being only one.

She doesn't hear Will's reply. Emma and Nikolai are now walking away, but not before Lili feels a warm hand at her elbow and hears his whisper, in Russian, always in Russian, as he knows her hatred of French. "Thank you for that. It is good to see you, Lil. I hope it isn't the last time."

She feels the staticky impression of his fingers, then nothing. Questions tumble into her mind, the ones she's kept at bay. *How is he here, in Moscow, at the ARA? Is his family alive? Why hasn't he looked me up?*

No, Lil, she tells herself sternly, packing away the questions. No dwelling, no past, only the here and now. Besides, she may have known the boy, but not the man.

The ARA men disperse, as does the illusion they are chatting with old friends. Lili follows Will and Irina with a straightening of her spine and a press of the lips like her sister.

The next and last room is quieter. Only a few men glance up from their typewriters. Lili's stomach rumbles at the rich smell of their coffee. Meanwhile, Will is talking about job positions she cannot distinguish between—clerk and secretary, interpreter and translator. He moves on to their education and experience—well educated thanks to the governesses Auntie had insisted upon, but no experience for Lili. Then their languages—Russian, English, French, and a little German, though Lili hates all except Russian and English. Too throaty.

Apparently, it is because of all their languages that they are interviewing for office positions, which Lili is suddenly not keen on. Especially when Will sets them up with two typewriters, to compose letters and translate dull-looking documents.

"You may need to communicate with Soviet officials, facilitating office, kitchen, and warehouse openings, as well as shipments of rations and supplies. Also handling arrangements with the officials for ARA trips to the heart of the famine, not to mention translation and interpretation at government meetings—"

For all her resolve to ignore the fear, Lili's hands give a tremble. She hears the ghost of that gunshot. But this is no time or place for fear. Irina has already slipped off her coat, hanging it carefully on her chair before sitting with a straight back and knowing air. With an encouraging nod at Lili, she lowers her fingers onto the skeletal keys and begins to type. Lili eyes her own typewriter. Well, how hard can it be?

She is about to find out when the scratch of a pencil reaches her ears. She follows the sound on instinct back to the front of the room, Irina's furious whisper receding behind her. A thin Black man with freckles on his cheeks and a line of concentration on his brow sketches at one of the desks there. Lili stops and peers over his shoulder.

"What is that?" She points at his sketch, crudely drawn, not very good.

"Moscow." He looks up. "Why, can't you tell?"

She shakes her head. "Not really." Too honest?

"All right." He stands and gestures to his chair—to her surprise, not offended, but with a spark of challenge in his warm brown eyes. "You try." He hands her his pencil.

Lili sits, suddenly self-conscious. Has her impulsivity cost her the job? But the feel of the pencil against the crisp paper steadies her. Focuses her mind as always. She draws the bazaar where they trade their family's heirlooms. Then Irina, the day they met the Americans. Her face, so like Maman's but sadder and veiled with a lovely melancholy.

"What a striking likeness, don't you think, Frank?" comes from behind. Lili is jolted back into the present. Will is standing beside her and studying the sketch.

"That *is* quite good," Frank agrees, not resentfully.

Irina looks up from her typewriter, her lips pressed into a thin, disapproving line.

The men step away, their heads bent close together, nodding and talking in low tones. Like Emma, Frank appears to be comfortable and at ease with Will, seemingly his equal, at least at the ARA, at least here in Moscow. Lili squeezes her hands into fists under the table, trying not to let the nerves get the best of her. Why didn't she think before acting for once? Now she has blown her one damn chance. At a glance from the men, she shrinks in her chair like a naughty child. They are probably discussing how to throw her out, maybe mention her to those same Soviet officials.... *Stop it, Lil*, she tells herself as the men walk back. *Here we go.*

Instead, they lead her behind one of the antique screens, into a private little office with photographs all over the walls. Lili drops into a chair across from the men uneasily.

"Where did you learn to draw like that?" Frank asks without preamble.

She is completely at sea but says, "From Ilya Repin and Marc Chagall."

Uncle Pasha had arranged for lessons with the great artists soon after learning of her interest in art. Lili flashes back to that room at his house where she had studied, the whole thing kept secret from Maman. She can still smell the paint, see the blank canvases, all the light. And the painting that sparked it all for her at just seven years old.

Lili had been passing the large canvas with Uncle Pasha while on a visit to the Winter Palace's Hermitage Museum, a favorite pastime of theirs. Tiepolo's *The Banquet of Cleopatra* showed the sumptuously attired queen of Egypt, alone in a crowd of men, going toe-to-toe with the arrogant Mark Antony. Her arm is raised, as if in challenge. Refusing to back down, to lose what Lili later discovered was a wager.

I cannot look away, she said. *Do you think women will ever again be this bold?*

Only if Russia moves on from the Romanovs and autocracy, Uncle Pasha replied, his usual refrain. He slid out a notepad and handed it to Lili along with a pencil.

What's this for? she remembers asking dumbly.

To draw her, Lilichka—so you remember. And so you are as bold as her in fighting for what you want and what you believe in, regardless of the cost. For that is to matter.

Lili recalls that first drawing, a mere childish scrawl. But with it, something real and powerful took hold of her. A way to express all those feelings bottled up inside, to put her restless hands to work, to give her purpose. Most importantly, to believe another life was possible, a different one from her sister's, from marriage and motherhood.

The drawing was lost during a revolution ironically started by women. But that day never left Lili. She even named her parakeet Cleo.

"You studied with Marc Chagall?" Frank's voice brings her back.

"So you have been formally taught, though not at school," Will sums up, skimming over the artists, not knowing them, or not caring. "Fair?"

"Fair. And yes, I studied with Marc." Lili can tell Frank is impressed.

The men exchange a look. Will says, "We are journalists turned ARA men, having been with the Administration since its inception. But we are journalists first, right?"

"That's right, my man." Frank grins.

"The Russian mission will be the ARA's largest and most challenging. It will be our legacy. So with our chiefs' permission, Frank and I are developing what will eventually be its own department—the liaison division. It will record the history of the Russian operation and include press, communications, publicity, and marketing."

"Our biggest need," Frank puts in, "is getting word out to the Russians about the ARA. We require posters, sketches, drawings, you name it."

"We were thinking of bringing over an American for this, but it would take weeks. Besides, we like your work. What do you think?" Will leans forward.

"Are you offering me a job? I cannot type," Lili blurts out stupidly.

"Yes, but you can draw," Frank says, with a sharp smile.

Will points to a camera lying on his desk. "Can you use one of these things, or learn to?"

"May I?" Lili is already reaching for the camera. Uncle Pasha showed her how to use this exact model. She turns it over, pressing a button on the side. The front panel pops out with the lens, and she aims the camera at the two men. The shutter clicks, and there is a bright flash as the photograph is taken. "I know how to use it."

Will slaps his hand against the desk. "The job is yours if you want it, Lil."

Lili puts the camera back down carefully. Her thoughts are racing. For most of her life, her art has been treated as nothing more than a silly girl's passing hobby. And here she is being offered a job for it. In fact, these men are watching her eagerly, waiting for her answer. Lili smiles, wide for once, with teeth. And she says *yes*.

She has been hired for *a job*, a real one, with *Americans*, doing what she loves and getting paid for it. Best of all, now she has someplace to be besides Moscow House.

11

Sandwiches and Dolls

IRINA AND WILL are in Chief Philip Carroll's large office, also located in the last room of the office wing. The chair is hard at her back, yet Irina summons the countess within her, the poise and dignified air, as she faces Mr. Carroll's inquiries. He is a clean, polished man with neatly parted hair and a tailored suit that enhances his Americanness.

"Welcome to the American Relief Administration, Ms. Goliteva," Mr. Carroll says, with a flash of his strong, white teeth.

Irina is stunned, though she can admit the interview went well. She spoke of her hospital work—her nursing patients, assisting in surgeries, helping administratively. How Lady Georgina Buchanan taught her staff to type, compose letters, translate between English and Russian. Still, it doesn't seem real. *Papa would be proud* is her first thought. He encouraged her to find her own way, to explore the world outside of marriage.

"—it is all hands on deck here," Mr. Carroll is saying, "and the administrative clerk would be setting up kitchens and warehouses, finding space for ARA offices and housing, organizing shipments, working on payroll, assisting with office tasks, and so on. If that suits you—" He leans over his desk and offers her his hand.

She recalls Auntie's and Maman's horror at her hospital work, though even the grand duchesses had done it. Doubt, *fear*, niggles at her—at the thought of the Soviet men, the investigation, Felix . . . "May I ask a question, sir?" He withdraws his hand, surprised, and Irina says, "My family is well-known. Does this . . . affect your offer?"

"Not at all. We are aware of your former standing."

Former standing. "But is it safe? I have a family, children in my care."

"I told you," Will cannot resist putting in, "we have 'complete freedom' in personnel matters, as per the Riga Agreement. You have nothing to fear."

Mr. Carroll gives Will a stern look before turning back to Irina. "I won't pretend the Soviet government will be happy with our hiring former people. But your class is educated, with the language and skills we need. There will be a risk, but one we will hopefully be able to mitigate."

So Irina can either take the job, the wages and food parcels with it, or return to the streets, scrubbing gutters and toilets, demeaning herself and barely scraping up a kopek or a few bruised potatoes. Auntie is blissfully unaware of this, believing Irina and Lili to be merely standing in breadlines and other queues. Their working in an office like a man would horrify her. But Seryozha and Natasha flash into Irina's mind, hollow cheeked and hungry. . . .

"I would very much like the job," she says in a rush. *Even if Auntie is horrified. Even if I end up in Butyrka.* For her son and cousin, for her family, Irina will take on the risk.

She shakes hands with the men, and Philip Carroll escorts her out, instructing Will to show her around the offices. "You start today," he says, a statement broaching no further conversation, and hurries on.

The industriousness of the ARA offices reminds Irina of Lady Georgina's hospital. Though there, Irina never had her own desk, this one close to Mr. Carroll's office, or a typewriter and telephone. As Will is explaining something to her, she glimpses Lili, bent over her own desk across the room. Irina still cannot believe her sister got a job after the stunt she pulled. But that is Lili, all impulse, all luck. Though for once Irina isn't irritated. They both need these jobs.

Later, Will offers her luncheon—cucumber sandwiches and tea, though weak and lightly scented. Not Russian. He has pulled up a chair to her desk, so close she can smell his soap—fresh, with a hint of mint, something else just him. What a contrast to Georgy's expensive French colognes, the arrogant catch of his eye, the wicked angles of his clean-shaven face, not one hair or thread out of place. From what she can see, Will is very different, with his messy blond hair and stubble, his grounded manner. Irina takes a sip of tea, chasing away thoughts of Georgy.

"What is it?" Will's eyes on her are a very clear, very pale blue. Straightforward, unlike Georgy's calculating glances, all courtier, all slippery and sly, like a magnificent snake.

She hesitates, wishing to ask Will about something he said during the interview. But first. "Are you . . . my superior?"

"Technically, Phil Carroll is. Why?"

Irina glances toward Mr. Carroll's office, hearing his clipped, commanding speech. *Just ask, Irina.* "Will I need to speak to Soviet officials?"

Will chuckles. "Don't worry, we will acquaint you with our American brand of dealing with the Bolos, then you won't be so afraid. And Carroll covers his bases more than most."

"He is right to. We live with a group of Soviet officials."

Will draws back. "No kidding. That must be your own personal hell, given—"

His face falls, and there is a concerned look in it, something she rarely receives. It makes her itchy, uncomfortable. "Will you hire more people like us?" Irina redirects.

Will takes a long gulp of tea. "Many more—for HQ and other offices."

Irina wonders if she will know any of them. Former people may visit some of the same bazaars and queues, but they keep their heads and eyes down. Conversing would only emphasize their fallen circumstances. At the ARA, though, they will have no choice. Irina suddenly realizes how she aches to speak to them. Absently, she reaches for another sandwich. She stills when she sees Will watching. Her face flames in humiliation. She must have taken too many.

"No, no." He grabs several sandwiches and hands them to her. "It's . . . refreshing for a woman to actually eat. Come, please. Take more, some for your, erm, children."

"Cousins," she corrects, with the familiar pang for Seryozha. Irina meets Will's gaze, kind yet not pitying. She appreciates that. And his help. "Thank you. I know this job—jobs—are because of you."

"No, it was you—and your sister. I just got your foot in the door is all." Will grows solemn. Turns his sandwich over; a slice of cucumber slips out. He catches it in time, pops it into his mouth. It leaves a sliver of butter on his lower lip that Irina wishes to wipe away.

She glances down. The thought is much too intimate. Entirely inappropriate.

"We heard stories about—that time. How families like yours lost all. I am sorry."

No one has ever told her they are sorry. And Auntie expects her to bear their burdens in silence. "Thank you," Irina forces out. "But we are fortunate. We have our house still, even eat here and there. Yes, extremely fortunate."

Will looks at her a little too long. Maybe he doesn't believe her. Maybe if Irina did speak about the past, their current troubles—unlike Georgy, this man would listen.

Leaving Lili at the ARA to work on her posters, Irina meets Natasha following her after-school programs. Darkness descends as they walk back to Moscow House. It is bitter cold, but Irina's mood doesn't sour. She feels the sandwiches in her bag, the tin of tea and can of milk for the children. She grows warm at the memory of Will's earnest look as he gave her the sandwiches, how he hastened to the ARA commissary for the tea and milk.

The men are thankfully at their supper, Grand-mère presumably waiting on them. Irina shudders at the thought of seeing Felix, or Boriska, though he's lately been more subdued.

In the attic, Seryozha leaps from Auntie's lap and sprints into her arms. "Irina!"

"Seryozhinka, my darling! How was your day?" She looks into his eager little face, too excited to first wash up or put her things away. "I have a surprise for you," she says, lowering him and pulling out the ARA goods.

Seryozha's eyes light up as Natasha gasps in delight. Without a word, the two fall upon the sandwiches.

Heady aromas of cucumber and herb waft over to Irina, and her heart lifts. She did something right. She provided for her son and family. Warmed by this, she leaves the children to eat while she goes into her and Lili's room to boil water for tea on their little kerosene stove.

"Where did you get the food, Irina?" Auntie comes up behind her. She is in another black gown, this one with black pearls on the bodice. Her face is still pale, her eyes distracted.

Irina busies herself with the teapot for the zavarka. If she imagined that keeping a secret *from* Auntie, as opposed to *with* her, would be simple, she was sorely mistaken. "At a bazaar."

"A Soviet bazaar?" Auntie says flatly. "Did you forget I found your maman your English governess? The canned milk has English on the label. Explain yourself."

"I didn't realize it, Auntie. How is Seryozha?"

"In the best of care, naturally. Where is Liliya?"

"Still out looking for food. You won't believe who we saw today," Irina hastens to distract her aunt. "Nicky Naroshin!" Auntie lives for sightings of former people, meticulously cataloging how much worse off they are.

"Hmph. And here I thought all the Naroshins were dead."

Irina turns from her aunt's searching gaze, thinking of Nicky. She is glad he is alive and safe. "And here I thought your gowns from the last century were also dead."

"Watch yourself," Auntie warns, but with a glimmer, a little of her wry humor. She lets out a resigned sigh. "I am a countess. I have had enough of those hideous proletarian skirts. Now go and read to Seryozha. I shall make tea—in a samovar, as it should be made. And, Irina?"

"Yes, Auntie?"

"I hope you know you can tell me anything." She tilts her face toward Irina.

"Of course, Auntie." A quick peck on her aunt's dry cheek before swiping Lili's book of fairy tales from the makeshift nightstand.

In the other room, a sheepish-looking Seryozha and Natasha have finished all the food. Already their cheeks are pink, their eyes bright. Irina settles onto Grand-mère's cot, sliding her arms around the children's thin shoulders, inhaling cucumber and milk. "What shall we read?" she asks, glancing down and for the first time noticing the sheets on the bed. Fresh, expensive, with Grand-mère's initials embroidered into the linen. The same linens are on the other cots, with Auntie's and the children's initials. They packed away such bourgeois items long ago, traces of a life long erased. Irina grits her teeth. She was willing to overlook the gowns, but this—by the look of it, towels, napkins, and tablecloths, too—Irina will need to confront Auntie about.

Given the men, there can be no return to such extravagances.

"Baba Yaga!" Seryozha clambers, unable to sit still. "I want Baba Yaga!" He squirms, twists, pulls at Natasha's hair until his cousin starts to complain loudly.

Irina wipes breadcrumbs from his cheeks; they scatter onto the linens. "Since when do you want Baba Yaga?" His stories are usually full of daring bogatyr heroes, princes and fools, wolves and bears, foxes and hens and goats.

"The girl likes Baba Yaga, so I like Baba Yaga."

The laughter stills in Irina's throat. *Girl? What girl?*

Natasha pinches her arm. "Oh, just read, Irina. He is being naughty, is all."

Still uneasy, Irina flips through the book for her favorite Baba Yaga tale—"Vasilisa the Beautiful," about a merchant's daughter whose mother dies, leaving her a little doll and her maternal blessing. When the maiden grows up and her stepmother forces her into the woods to visit Baba Yaga for a light, the doll saves her. She does Baba Yaga's bidding until the requisite three days are done, and the witch allows the maiden to return home—with a light, having pleased her.

Natasha sighs. "I wish I had a doll from my mother."

Irina fleetingly thinks of the unfortunate Luba, who died in childbirth when Irina was pregnant with Seryozha. "As do I." Irina cuddles her son's little, warm body, flushed with food and milk. Yet something niggles at her, an irritating, incessant thought.

"She led me to her doll." Seryozha's voice is singsong.

Irina's smile falls away. "Who did? The girl?"

He nods. "She is my friend. I think I knew her long ago."

Irina is brought back to Xenia begging her to read the likes of "Vasilisa the Beautiful," "The Sea King and Vasilisa the Wise," "The Frog Princess"—all with the hideous, iron-nosed witch of legend. *I shall be Baba Yaga when I grow up!* Xenia would trill. "Where is this doll?" Irina demands.

Seryozha hops from Grand-mère's bed and beelines for his cot, reaching underneath.

Irina lets out a scream when he straightens. Gripped in his little hand is a porcelain doll—in an old-fashioned, moth-gray gown and cape, the delicate lacework yellowed. Patches of hair are missing. The skin is chipped, reminding Irina of Xenia's scarlet-red rash. The doll's eyelids are melted, scratched, giving her a chillingly narrow gaze. It is Xenia's old doll.

"Give it back!" Seryozha screams when Irina wrestles the vile thing away from him.

She kneels eye level with her son. "Seryozha, you must not play with this. And you must tell me if the little girl returns. Do you understand?" She is cold, so cold.

"No!" He stomps his foot. "It is *mine*!"

"Where did he find this?" Irina rounds on Auntie, hovering in the doorway and watching them.

Her aunt lifts one bony, black-swathed shoulder. "He already told you. And it is a fine doll." She pulls it out of Irina's hand and props it up on her vanity.

The head droops. One piercing, deformed eye peeks out, loathsome, evil.

Could her dead sister really have led Seryozha to the doll? Does Auntie know? It all feels wrong and somehow dark. All Irina knows is she will not let her son anywhere near the vile thing. Now she can only wait for her sister, the doll's pernicious presence driving her to distraction.

12

The Past Belongs to the Old and the Dead

OVER THE NEXT few days, with Auntie avoiding Lili and her sister, Xenia's old doll following their every move with her malevolent stare, and nights that allow little sleep, Lili tries to lose herself in her ARA work.

It falls into a comforting rhythm. In the mornings, she and Irina walk over to 30 Spiridonovka before their family or the Bolos awaken, usually with a scrap or two of stale bread in hand. Once they fetch their coffee, they head to their respective desks, Lili to her sketches, Irina to her own work. Lili feels a twinge of guilt for not asking her sister what that work is. But the project with Frank and Will has been consuming.

She is supposed to be sketching a poster of a lady with an American flag wrapped around her shoulders, handing out bread to the hungry children of Russia. Once she is done, she was told to write "ARA" and "Gift of the American People" in large letters at the top. Lili finds herself sketching the bazaar instead, with roosters wandering the square. She can almost hear their ghostly crowing, almost see Nicky's face, telling her about them.

She hasn't seen him since her interview. *And good riddance.*

"Roosters?" Frank is peering over her shoulder.

"Sorry." Lili pushes the sketch away. "I'll start on that poster."

His tobacco and clover scent hangs on the air. "If you include a crate with the ARA name, or a can of food with English on the label, we can keep the sketch."

She turns to him, brightening. "Even the roosters?"

But Frank is still studying the picture. "Were these old women really princesses, hobnobbing in palaces with the tsar and his dukes?"

"Yes, Francis, and now they are paupers." Much like Lili and her family. She calls Frank by his full name, which he made the mistake of revealing, and which is a great deal more diverting. They've fallen into an easy camaraderie ever since.

"Haven't I asked you to call me Frank?" His lips are pursed, yet they twitch. "Must be your countess upbringing, resisting instruction, following the tsar's word only."

The joke falls flat. Lili imagines the tsar, his tsaritsa, their daughters, her former playmate Anastasia, all lying in a bloody heap in some forgotten wood with diamonds scattered around them. . . . Lili shakes her head, pushing the ugly image far away.

"It is swell to have royalty in the office. More will be starting soon."

"Really?" Lili perks up, curious, despite her resolve to leave them in the past.

"Oh, yes. Before we know it, the entire ARA will be held up by Russia's former ruling classes, feeding the children of the very state that killed off their families." Frank clears his throat. "Sorry."

But Lili is recalling how Will said their department will eventually record the Russian operation's history. If it *will* be held up by former people, it is only natural that such work should be recorded. Their voices, after all, have been silenced with the Revolution.

Lili has a saying: *Remembering is for the old and the dead.* It has been her mantra for survival. That she is young and will live in the damn present as she is meant to. But seeing Uncle Pasha, sketching that bazaar, being at the ARA, where her art can make a difference, brings back her uncle's advice. To be bold. To fight for what she wants and what she believes. *For that is to matter.*

Maybe this job isn't just about her art. Maybe it is to believe in something, to fight for something. For children who are starving as much as for people like her, many of whom have lost their homes and possessions to the Bolos, uncles like Pasha and other family murdered. Lili assumes no one has heard of their plight outside, even inside, Russia. And like her, these people are now getting a second chance at life working for the ARA, maybe even a future. What if she finds the voices of the former people here, at the ARA? She could document with sketches and photographs their work for the Americans and for Russia's future generations. . . .

To do that, though, Lili would need to face the hated past she's been ignoring and, when she can manage it, suppressing. Is she ready for this? She doesn't know. She only wishes for her art to matter, not just to her and the Americans but to people like her uncle.

"Say, Frank, when I finish these posters, may I help with your documentation project?" At his look of surprise, a flush creeps into Lili's cheeks. "If I have time, that is"—she fumbles for words—"I'd like to . . . capture the former people's role at the ARA."

"Russian princesses serving American food," Frank muses, scrunching his nose in thought. "It is true that not many are aware of those who stayed in Russia, people like you who are now bringing the ARA to the Bolos. It's brilliant, Lil. Tell you what, if you finish your other tasks, work on this. I'll help. We'll make an article out of it for some Western newspaper. What do you think?"

Lili's heart gives a hard thud. Has she found a purpose, something to fight for that will matter? "I love it," she says. At Frank's smile, she directs her attention back to her poster with fresh energy. It will take no time at all. Especially with Frank now absorbed in his own sketching.

In the past few days, Lili has gotten to know him and some of the other Americans. After graduating from Harvard with degrees in journalism and photography, Will worked for a Boston newspaper before joining the ARA to see the world, first in London, then in

Prague and other eastern European cities. He met up with his old college mate Harold in Prague, where they learned about a new ARA operation in the heart of Russia. Together with Frank, another college mate, they decided to sign up for the adventure of their lives—to see the socialist experiment at work behind the Red Curtain. But not before inviting Emma to join them. She had met Will years ago while working in the New York City soup kitchens, through an article he was writing as a reporter, and later he introduced her to the ARA and its work.

The men's chatter, their cigarette smoke, the peculiar smell of the sardine and cucumber sandwiches they constantly nibble on, all pushes Moscow House quite out of Lili's mind. Just as she is becoming immersed in her work, Irina approaches her desk.

"Irishka, you won't believe this," Lili tells her sister excitedly, "but I'll be working on a recording project with Frank, documenting former people's work for the ARA. What do you think?" Irina, more accepting of the past, should like it, should be proud of her. At least, she hopes.

Irina smiles sadly and gives Lili's arm a squeeze. "You are so like Pasha," she murmurs. Lili knows they are both thinking of their uncle's writing the Sherbatsky-Golitev histories, cataloging their artworks and historical and cultural objects. "I can ask Mr. Carroll for a look at the ARA payroll, which should show us the former people being hired."

"Oh, Irishka, that would be swell." Irina rolls her eyes at the American word, but Lili has also heard her use it and laughs. They are among Americans, after all.

Irina shoves a creamy card into Lili's hand then. "Auntie left this for me in the morning." They didn't walk to the ARA together, as Irina had to visit Natasha's school.

Lili's pretend steadiness falls away when she glimpses the words.

Formal Family Dinner, 12 a.m., Dining Room

"Do you think she would reopen it?" Lili tastes bile in her throat. That room, where Uncle Pasha was shot . . . They abandoned, shuttered, locked it. Though it had been their gathering place each night for dinner and family meetings.

"And why have a dinner at midnight? Try not to dally tonight. Come back as soon as you are done. Auntie was not surprised by the doll, or Xenia. She knows something."

"Very well. And I don't dally." A lie. Lili hates to return to Moscow House and the Bolos, finding any excuse to delay it. Maybe she has also stayed to see if a certain boy would return from his never-ending errands. On her way out, she may even have glanced for him among the fleet of ARA motorcars—apparently called Cadillacs.

Stop this nonsense, Lil. You don't wish to see him anyway. The question of why he hadn't looked her up is a sore point that, admittedly, still bruises her heart.

A swollen-skied day transitions into a bleak, windswept night. Lili gathers up her things, pulls on her coat, and trudges out into the frost. It is very late, despite her promises. She glances about for watchful eyes. There are few streetlights left in Moscow, and the dark gives the town a deserted look and feel.

"I hardly think your mother would approve of you being out so late, Countess."

Her heart gives a violent thud. Nikolai is leaning against a motorcar, smoking. "She is dead," Lili says flatly. His face falls, and she tries for softness. "My mother wouldn't approve of anything I do." She leaves it at that. First, he disappears from her life without a word, now he is bringing up the past.

Nikolai lifts the cigarette to his lips. Its orange tip flares to life and smoke blooms on his exhale, drifting to Lili. "What wouldn't she approve of?" He leans back, smoking and watching her with that dark, fathomless gaze.

Lili eyes the cigarette, irritated he is still talking. "Working here, for one, or at all. 'Young ladies must know their place.'" She mimics

Maman's voice, as she remembers it. "Being with a man"—she gestures to the empty street—"alone."

"I doubt your mother would mind me, given how often she left us to our own devices." He laughs, and Lili's cheeks heat up. "What was that look on your face just now?"

"What look?" comes out a little strangled. Does he also remember the non-kiss?

Nikolai considers. "As if you were walking the plank of a pirate ship, with the sea churning below." He laughs again, evoking their favorite stories, of one-eyed pirates and chilling sea voyages, of high-stakes adventure from the likes of *Treasure Island*, *Robinson Crusoe*, *The Count of Monte Cristo*. He offers her his cigarette.

"I don't smoke," she says automatically.

"Me neither," he says, smiling. "My mother wouldn't approve."

"Nor mine." Before she can think twice, Lili grabs the cigarette and inhales—too quickly. She dissolves into a fit of coughing.

Nikolai's fingers brush against hers as he takes the cigarette and brings it to his lips. A practiced inhale, and he passes it back to her.

The coughing isn't as bad the second time. Lili pauses with the cigarette burning between her fingers, pretending at worldliness. "How is your mother?" she asks, despite her initial reluctance to talk. *Is she alive?* she almost adds but doesn't.

"How is your aunt?" Nikolai asks, as if to say, *What do you expect?* "Though I heard about your mother's passing," he adds, taking the cigarette. "I am sorry, Lili. Heavenly Kingdom to her." He crosses himself with his free hand.

"Thank you." She mimics the gesture. Then, to her shame, it comes out, at least part of it. "A man died in our house, and I think I saw Uncle Pasha come back from the dead." Lili rubs her face, her burning eyes. "I cannot believe I just told you that." Had to be the cigarette. Or maybe it felt good to talk to Nicky. They had loved talking about specters, the dead reanimating, their delicious horror.

"I am sorry about Pavel Sergeyevich, too," Nikolai says, using

Uncle Pasha's patronymic as a sign of respect and with genuine sorrow in his voice.

He had joined Lili and her uncle on many excursions in and around Petersburg. And after all this time, how funny that Nicky still doesn't bat an eye at her mentioning the dead. Maybe he isn't as different as she thinks. She cracks a smile. "Here I thought you had become a serious man who would laugh at such childish nonsense."

But Nikolai doesn't laugh. "We live in a country that is more like a graveyard, Lilichka. I have since learned to believe we were right all along. Are you afraid of Pavel Sergeyevich's spirit? Or the dead man?"

How is it that Nicky still understands her? "You think Uncle Pasha can be back?"

"It is more than possible." Nikolai shrugs. "Knowing Pavel Sergeyevich, he is trying to tell you something. Or help you in some way. Maybe warn you."

Lili meditates on that. If the dead *can* reanimate, and the ghosts of her dead family *have* returned, Irina might really have seen Papa, and he might really have led her to the dead Bolo. Likewise, could Uncle Pasha have returned to help Lili, right when the Bolos have moved in? If so, there could be a connection between the men and the hauntings, and the ghosts may not be what they should fear.

Nikolai grinds his cigarette into the asphalt with the heel of his nice leather shoe. "Let me take you home."

As they motor over to Moscow House, they don't speak. Lili glances at Nikolai's profile, half in shadow, his eyes intent on the road. In that moment, she sees her friend Nicky from long ago, and she wishes to talk to him some more, to sit a little closer to him. But he doesn't smile or say anything. And Lili thinks perhaps he really has become just a stranger to her. Or else a spell has veiled them from each other. Then she only wishes to get home, the past sitting between them like a person they cannot see. A past Lili doesn't wish to remember, much less relive. It belongs to the old and the dead. At least, for now.

The Haunting of Moscow House

❖ ❖ ❖

It turns out *now* is a relative concept and might be sooner than Lili thought.

Irina and Natasha run up to her as soon as she pulls open the entrance doors to the house.

"Auntie is gone—with Seryozha and Grand-mère." Her sister grabs her arm. "I showed Natasha Auntie's note and told her about the . . . happenings in the house. The men are in the West Wing—we saw Comrade Suzhensky—but someone is in the dining room."

Lili becomes aware of music, soft and lilting. She hesitates, dreading seeing that room again. Then she hears a chirp, and Cleo flutters onto her shoulder. Lili gives her parakeet a grateful smile, suddenly feeling strong enough to see that room, to deal with Auntie. She follows her sister and Natasha through the entrance hall. Instead of turning right into the East Wing or left into the West Wing, they hasten deeper into the house.

Oddly, the dining room isn't by the kitchen; it's down a hallway parallel to the East Wing.

Here, the air presses in heavily, as if they are descending into the earth's depths.

Lili huddles closer to her sister and cousin, grabbing hold of their hands as they approach the dining room. She meets their gazes and gives them an encouraging nod. Yet Lili can tell Cleo is uneasy. The parakeet fluffs her wings, squawks, restlessly swivels her head. Lili has a feeling they should listen to her.

But Irina is already pulling open the doors.

Lili comes to an abrupt halt. It's not only the dreadful feeling of this room—dark, noxious, smelling of death. The mahogany table is impeccably set for a formal dinner of old with their finest Limoges service, as though by Dmitri's hand. The fashionable Sèvres porcelain is out. The Lalique glassware, too, along with the blazing ormolu French candelabra. It is all feverish, flickering candlelight in a room onto which the pall of tragedy has settled, suspending it in time like a photograph. Lili's breaths tumble out, spurt-like, in tune with her trembling hands.

As on that night three years ago, Auntie is sitting nearest the window, Grand-mère on the right side of the table, Seryozha on the left. The rest of the chairs are empty, waiting. Lili's eyes stray to Uncle Pasha's seat. She can almost see the shards of glass, the upset tea, the blood. The music is strangely faint, vanishing the moment she strains her ears.

"There you are," says Auntie. "I thought you may not have seen my note."

Before Irina can reply reasonably, Lili throws her hands up. "Are you mad?"

Cleo flies up to Auntie and beats furious wings in her face. Suddenly, it is all too much. Lili leans against the doorway, limbs weak, stomach feeling sick.

Irina slides a steadying arm around her waist. Natasha leans on her sister's other arm. Even Cleo has stopped squawking. She flutters from seat to empty seat. "Do you see what you are doing, Marie?" Irina's voice is one Lili hasn't heard her use with Auntie. "I was willing to overlook the gowns and linens, but . . . this? What if the men see?" Irina glances at Grand-mère, who looks down at her plate. "And you let her do this."

Lili steps away from her sister, stands on her own. Only then does she realize how bitterly cold it is. An icy breeze snakes through the open window behind Auntie, along with the black night. It lends an eerie chill to the still-swirling, vanishing music.

"Sit down, ladies." Auntie's refrain from their childhood.

"This is a dangerous kind of madness, Marie," Irina says, for once not leaping to do Auntie's bidding. "Come, Seryozhinka, let's go back upstairs."

"No!" howls the spoiled boy. "I want to see Xenia. Mama and Papa, too!"

Natasha drifts over to the dining table and lowers herself onto the chair beside Seryozha. "If it is indeed possible, I, too, wish to see

Mama and Papa." Her eyes are shining with tears. "I . . . never had a chance to say goodbye." She, too, is spoiled.

"You see? They wish to be here. Now, do sit down, ladies."

Lili meets Irina's gaze. Maybe, like Lili, her sister wishes to be anywhere but here, pretending to the past. They don't move. Cleo perches on Lili's shoulder. Another small comfort in this comfortless place of stalemate.

"We have lived in this humiliating state for far too long and must return to our old ways of life. Dinner together each evening. Clean linens and tablecloths. Proper gowns." Auntie gives Lili and Irina a once-over. "Not those hideous peasant skirts."

Grand-mère is now muttering in French. Lili catches *folle, elle a perdu la tête, état hystérique*. Apparently, Grand-mère doesn't wish to be here, either.

"Is all this you trying to return to the past?" Irina shakes her head. "Marie, that is impossible. We cannot go back. Nor can we start indulging in it. The men will notice. It is too dangerous." Then, softer, "Has Xenia been playing with Seryozha? Is she back? Are they all?"

Auntie drifts to the window, opening it farther. "I must return to that night," she mutters. "To change its course. To atone. But we need to wait until midnight."

By some perverse magic, the enamel peacock clock chimes loudly in that moment. The peal is like bells from great distances, or like the bone-chilling music. Even with these noises, somewhere behind her, Lili hears a hiss—so distinct she is sure it is a snake or some other kind of reptile. She whirls on her heel to face a pair of eyes glittering at her from the black hallway. She takes a step toward the eyes, but they vanish just as quickly.

"Did you see that?" Lili dips her chin to Cleo, who grinds her beak in assent and spreads her wings with a whistle, taking off down the hallway.

The back of Lili's neck starts to prickle painfully with a cold that has suddenly rushed at her. Beside her, Irina lets out a gasp. Slowly, hesitantly, Lili turns back.

Around the dining table, pale, nearly transparent figures are flickering to life.

Next to Auntie is Uncle Aleksei, with a dark red stain over his heart. Beside him, Papa, with his blue-tinged face and pockmarks where the rash had been. A blur of filmy white, a mist shaping into a woman's face, and lips cracked from cold appear, the same lips that had once pressed to Lili's temple in a kiss—Maman. An echo of a little girl, Xenia, giggles at Lili's feet and looks up at her with reddened cheeks. And by the door to the bufetnaya, a shadow of a man hovers with a suit streaked in the same dark brownish red. Blood. Old blood.

"Dmitri," Lili whispers, her lips numb and strange. Their old butler died during a raid on the house shortly after the Cheka visit. They *are* back. Reanimated. Alive. Like Uncle Pasha, the figures are more than see-through shadows, more than air. They have substance to them, even a little depth. Can Auntie's rituals be making them stronger? And where *is* Uncle Pasha?

Other figures are blinking to life in the room. A shadow of their cousin Andrei, his wink of a smile; a hint of Uncle Pasha's wife, Luba, one ghostly hand resting on her pregnant belly; the stooped figure of Grand-père with his cane at his side. These figures are hazier, flickering in and out like dying stars.

Lili's ears fill with whispers, too faint to hear. Then Natasha's indrawn breath, Seryozha's excited little trill, Grand-mère's anguished cry. And the smell of rot.

Maybe Lili should be happy her family is back. But she cannot ignore these traces of death, so unnatural and dark, and the man already dead in the house. . . . Lili presses her back against the closed doors. Alarm bells chime in her head. Who shut them, and when? If only a rooster would crow. But it is long until daybreak and the relief that comes with it. All she can think about is telling Nicky how she truly believes in ghosts now. How on their heels, death follows.

The floor under Lili shakes. She hears shouts from behind the doors, the pounding of men's booted feet. The spell is broken, and the figures vanish. Lili is still frozen.

Irina tugs her away from the doors—just as they burst open, and the Bolsheviks stream past them in their usual fashion. A flustered, wheezing Comrade Suzhensky barrels in, stops, points a fat finger at Auntie. "Princess Maria Sablorova"—he purposely addresses her with the Russian form of Marie—"you are under arrest."

Lili is rooted in horror, and not the delicious kind she shares with Nicky. The dinner, the men, the arrest are all so damnably like that night. The sickness is back, clutching at her, twisting her up until she tastes bile in her throat and feels air in her head. Her vision oscillates, then goes black.

13

All's Fair When One Is Dead

"Another one of my men lies dead, Irina Alexandrovna. My hands are tied."

Irina is back in Grand-père's study with Comrade Suzhensky and Felix, Moscow House once more crawling with police, Cheka agents, and Soviet officials.

Another head wound, another would-be accident. This time, Boriska—found in the hallway to the kitchen. Unease ripples through Irina. Given their altercation about the food, he is dead almost as if she had wished it. But she tells herself she is safe. Poor Auntie was arrested, and Irina was nowhere near the house when it happened.

She is the last to be questioned, the children and Grand-mère allowed to sleep. Irina is still shaky, still picturing the dead flickering back to life around the dining room table, horrific wounds and all. How is this possible? She still doesn't believe in the supernatural, but it is growing harder and harder to refute its existence.

Auntie's last words echo in her mind: *Take care of the children, your grandmother, the house. Do not preoccupy yourself with me. Do you hear, Irina?*

After Auntie was taken away—head held high, lips pressed into a thin, disapproving line—Irina and Natasha revived Lili. A few men offered to carry her up to the attic, but Lili categorically refused, weak as she was. In the end, Natasha and Irina half carried her, followed closely by a distraught, weeping Grand-mère and a white-faced Seryozha. Comrade Suzhensky questioned her family right there in the attic, a small comfort, then summoned Irina to the study, where he asked her much the same questions as before.

He towers over her now with a face that is drawn as much as it is darkened.

Irina must convince the Old Bolshevik that she and her family had nothing to do with the deaths, that Auntie is innocent and needs to be released. Irina will do all she can for her. She must protect her son and what is left of her family—from these men and from the dead. They have not yet been arrested, due to Grand-mère's connection to the Politburo's Lev Kamenev, maybe to Comrade Suzhensky's leniency. Irina must keep it that way. She channels Auntie's determination, her imperiousness. She takes in a slow breath, the air heavy with Grand-père's pipe smoke.

"My aunt was in the dining room with us. It could not have been her. So why was she arrested?" Irina fixes Comrade Suzhensky with Auntie's level look.

He peers down at her. "Did you see your aunt before your return to the house this evening, Irina Alexandrovna?"

"Well, no."

"The doctor said Boris Borisovich had been dead for at least several hours," Felix spits out. "If you cannot account for your aunt's activity before the dining room, she is a suspect. Part of me believes you are, too. Maybe you told your good aunt about Boriska's mistreatment. Or asked her to kill him for you. Maybe she did it on her own. Wasn't she the interfering type?"

"Too far, Felix," the Old Bolshevik warns. "There is no evidence of this. The men all say that since I spoke to Boris Borisovich, his behavior toward Irina Alexandrovna has been perfectly civil."

Irina ignores Felix. "Did you ask my cousin Sergei Pavlovich as to my aunt's whereabouts? She was supposed to have been with him all day."

"The boy said she left him for about an hour this evening," replies Felix, smug.

"Oh, but this is preposterous!" Irina cries out. "My aunt has been taking all this . . . change hard. She had the misguided notion to organize a dinner for us. She was likely preparing it when she left my cousin."

"Your cousin," Felix repeats thoughtfully. "Or your son?"

Irina's insides plummet. No one except her, Auntie, and Uncle Pasha knows. Or so she thought. She takes in a shaky breath, tries to steady herself, press down the *how?*

Felix leans over the desk. "He is Sergei Georgyevich Dolgonog, is he not?"

He is not. He is not. Irina forces herself to speak. "He was adopted by my uncle, Pavel Sergeyevich, so he is Sergei Pavlovich Sherbatsky."

Felix's smile doesn't dim. "Your family doesn't know, do they?"

"What does this have to do with the investigation?"

"I only hope you are telling us all you know. Secrets have a way of resurfacing."

Suddenly, a movement catches Irina's eye. In a corner of the room, a figure materializes in the shadows. It is nearly transparent, blending with the yellowish-gray lamplight. But she can see the figure is tall and gaunt. Hollowed out by illness. Grand-père? Yet the men give no indication they are aware of her grandfather.

"I am telling you all I know, Felix Ivanovich," Irina says, trying to ignore the specter. "There is no need for threats."

"No, there is not." Comrade Suzhensky speaks finally. "After all, why would an upstanding Soviet mother gamble with her son's life?"

"Then why work for the Americans?" Felix asks, delivering his death blow.

This time, Irina isn't surprised. She holds herself straight. She has rehearsed this speech many times. "I cannot find a job anywhere else. Do you suggest I let my son starve? Besides, Comrade Lenin invited the American Relief Administration into Russia, fully aware and acquiescent to the fact that we Russians will work for it. Am I not doing my duty to my country and to Comrade Lenin?" Irina keeps her gaze on Felix, who now looks a little like a lost boy. She drives the point home. "Are you blaming these deaths on the ARA? If so, this is a diplomatic matter and beyond your purview. Perhaps I should appeal to Lev Kamenev."

Is there a hint of a smile on the specter's shadowy face?

"We are saying nothing of the sort, Irina Alexandrovna." Comrade Suzhensky is again the benevolent official.

"You have questioned us and performed another search. If you discovered nothing, and my son and job have nothing to do with your investigation, why am I here?"

"We are simply chatting, Irina Alexandrovna." Comrade Suzhensky stares expectantly at the younger man, and Felix gives Irina a reluctant, begrudging nod.

"My aunt comes from a family respected by the Politburo. She is not a murderess." It is ridiculous to even say the words aloud. Irina cannot picture her prim, proper, conservative aunt, with her unwavering faith in God, hurting, much less killing, another human being. "I ask you again, on what grounds was she arrested?"

Felix opens his mouth, but Comrade Suzhensky swiftly silences him with another stare. "The hour that was unaccounted for, her bourgeois dinner, her hostility at the requisition," lists the Old Bolshevik. "And it is the second death in this house. I will question each of my men, of course. But we need a suspect. And your aunt, aside from the aforementioned circumstantial evidence, has been scaring my men. How well do you really know her, Irina Alexandrovna?"

"I know she did not kill those men," Irina says, voice and gaze hard.

"Do not push me, Irina Alexandrovna," Comrade Suzhensky says quietly. "Or you and the children will be next."

Irina feels like the air has been knocked out of her. She is failing her aunt. But she presses her mouth closed.

Comrade Suzhensky lets out a tired breath. "I have always believed women's constitutions to be too delicate for the ugliness of murder. I will continue my investigation but make inquiries after your aunt. In the meantime, you will agree not to ask any further questions."

"Suzhensky, you cannot make such promises." Felix's face twists in rage.

That's when the specter lunges at Felix. It happens so fast Irina sees only the moment when the shadowy figure passes through the man's body on the lunge. Then it has evaporated, and everything is as before.

She cannot smother her gasp. Can the specters touch the living? They can do something of the sort, for Felix is clutching at his chest. His eyes are dazed and wide in horror. He stumbles into the desk as if drunk.

Comrade Suzhensky blinks, whispering something about nechistaya sila—the *unclean force*—and turns back to a frozen Irina. "Thank you, Irina Alexandrovna, you may go."

Felix is still clutching at his chest, his eyes frantically searching the room for an explanation.

As Irina hastens out of the study, she thinks that Grand-père's specter may have protected her. But two men lie dead, and Auntie has been arrested. Irina needs to get her aunt released and find out why the dead are back—before another man dies, and the rest of her family pays the price.

Irina returns to the attic to find only Lili awake. Paper is strewn all over her bed, sketches of familiar yet forgotten faces of people from their past and scenes of Petersburg.

Irina perches on the edge of Lili's cot, Cleo chirping at her in greeting. "They know about the ARA," Irina says without preamble. "But I believe they will leave us alone. We should tell Grand-mère about the jobs." Irina pauses, studying Lili, not liking how pale and hollow eyed she is.

But her sister's shoulders lower in relief, and she nods. Irina, meanwhile, will never again be relieved. The men know about Seryozha. It is on her tongue, *He is my son—*

"What about Auntie?" Lili asks, and the moment passes.

"Auntie is a suspect." Irina skims over Felix's implications, not wishing to worry her sister. She flips through the sketches on the bed. Lifts one of a handsome man with dark hair and a sardonic smile—Nicky. She steals a glance at Lili, wondering if she has seen any more of him. Once upon a time, the family was convinced they would be married. Now he is back in their lives. What can it mean? Something to think about later. Irina puts a hand on Lili's arm, her skin ice-cold. "I will try my best to get Auntie released, Lil. But we need to find out what is happening . . . here." Irina listens to the house, the little creaks and groans of its existence. "I think I saw Grand-père's specter in the study. He lunged at Felix, who seems to have felt him. I am starting to believe . . ."

Lili voices Irina's thought from earlier. "Maybe Grand-père was protecting you. When I last saw Uncle Pasha, he was more himself, more substantive. It is as if the dead are reanimating from the time of their deaths. Can they become as alive as you and me, their human faculties and all?"

Irina tries to suppress the horror that has suddenly clutched at her. "And what does Auntie know?"

"Clearly, she arranged the dinner for the dead—to re-create the night Uncle Pasha was killed." *To change its course. To atone.* "I was also thinking Auntie's rituals from the past might strengthen the ghosts and make them more alive. At least, at midnight, and with us present."

"But what about the killings? And why haven't we seen the spirits of the dead Bolsheviks?"

Lili shrugs. "If all this relates to that night, it makes sense that we are seeing only the family. And maybe the ghosts of the family are doing the killing. But, Irishka, I saw that creature. So did Cleo." The parakeet gives a tiny chirp of assent.

Those red eyes, the scuttling shape. "It could be an animal."

"It could." But the unspoken words, *Likely not*, hang between them.

"Do you—" Irina hesitates. "Do you want them back? The family?" She misses them as they were, but these specters feel different, dark and somehow wrong.

Lili strokes Cleo's wings thoughtfully. "Nicky and I used to read stories about spirits and ghosts, the dead coming back to life—all of it leading to very bad things, to bloodshed and madness. Our ghosts seem just as unnatural. And the damn Bolsheviks keep dropping dead. No, Irishka, I don't want them back. And I don't think they would want to be back. Not like this. At least, not Uncle Pasha. But why are they here, and what do they want? Given the timing, what if . . . they are trying to warn us?"

This possibility *has* crossed Irina's mind. The specters of Grand-père and Papa *did* try to help or lead her to something. "But warn us about what?"

"Something about the night Uncle Pasha was killed. Papa's and Uncle Aleksei's arrests on that night led to their deaths, too. In the stories, ghosts are absolutely obsessed with their deaths. So maybe we start with this idea, that night, Uncle Pasha. His rooms. Maybe we can find something helpful there."

"We can take a look at Auntie's rooms, too. But only before midnight, just in case."

Lili pauses for a beat. "Do you think the attic is safe?"

What, exactly, is *safe*? "Well, so far, we've seen the specters in places in the house that they might have a tie to. Pasha on his grave, Grand-père in his study, Papa by the ballroom, Xenia in the corridors, everyone else in the dining room. No one ever visited the attic, so maybe we are safe for now." Irina can only hope she is right. Her glance flickers to the door. "We should also see what Grand-mère knows."

"But she's never talked about that night," Lili points out, and she is right.

Grand-mère belongs to the old world, where secrets were swept conveniently away. "Then who else would know? Servants, but in Moscow, we mostly only had Dmitri. And he is dead." Irina doesn't remember much from that time. Part she suppressed, the other she spent in bed, in shock over Georgy's death and her son's adoption.

"Several people helped us in Moscow, don't you remember?" Lili gives her a funny look. "True, they left by November 1918, when the Cheka killed Uncle Pasha, but some came and went throughout that year. This might be a stretch, but if they are still around, maybe they know something about the family, or Auntie, or that night. And what it all has to do with the now."

Irina now dimly recalls those people. "Sorry, you are right," she backtracks, reddening. "I . . . was sick then." Irina tries to focus. She doesn't quite remember what they looked like, but she might recognize their names if she were to see them somewhere—on a payroll, for instance. Why, that's it. "When I look up the former people for you on the ARA payroll," she says excitedly, "I can keep an eye out for people who have worked for the family, both here in Moscow and in Petersburg. I don't doubt they will apply for jobs with the ARA."

Lili smirks. "That would be a big coincidence, don't you think?"

"No. Who has more applicable skills than the people who worked for houses like ours?"

A smile spreads slowly on Lili's face. "You *are* wise, Irishka. And I can also include these former servants in my project. But I don't think we should discount former people. Maybe a former person or two had contact with Auntie or Grand-mère, even the rest of the family, after we moved to Moscow."

"Good thinking, Lil. We will get answers, one way or another." Irina takes Lili's hand in hers and gives it a reassuring squeeze. Despite the hauntings, the Soviet men, Auntie's arrest, Irina realizes that she and her sister are becoming closer than ever. And this edges away the horror.

14

A Plan with More Questions Than Answers

THAT NIGHT, THOUGH she needs rest or her eyes will be tired and puffy, Irina cannot sleep.

Slippery, gut-churning questions dart through her mind. How can Irina hope to get Auntie released, given Comrade Suzhensky's warnings?

Auntie had held them up—with her strength and wisdom, her indomitable presence. Now Irina is alone. Not only responsible for her younger sister, two children, and a fragile old lady, but faced with that which she doesn't understand. A slick, cold sweat envelops Irina, and she pulls the sheet with her initials—a leftover extravagance—over her body like a shroud. She feels dead inside, helpless. As if overnight, she has turned into a little girl again.

The night is still, magnifying the house's nocturnal sounds. The floorboards creak, even the walls.

Irina raises her head. But it is just the closed door, the sliver beneath darkened, her family asleep. She almost wakes her sister, but after Lili's fainting spell, Irina forces herself not to disturb her. Instead, she focuses on the comforting emerald-green spot in the rafters—Cleo, also asleep. The cobwebs sway in a draft that leaves a trace of cold on Irina's skin. Like the unsettling cold from those ghostly apparitions in the dining room. She thinks she hears a cough from the floor below and becomes intensely aware of the window, what lies beyond it.

A scratching starts up then. A scrabbling, rooting, jaw-clenching sound. At first, Irina wonders if an animal is trapped in the attic walls. But it is methodical, a creature—with red eyes?—digging through the house, eating into it. She can barely take a breath. It rattles, her throat parchment dry.

The sound dies down, and she finally sleeps. Fitfully, horribly. She pictures Pasha under the oak, red eyes peering from cobwebbed shadows, Grand-père puffing on his pipe.

When Irina awakens, only a little light sifts through the ragged curtains. It bathes the room in a blurred ocean blue, the color of the American's eyes. She folds the covers aside neatly and rises. Her skin stings from the cold. Candlelight shines below the door, which means Grand-mère is awake. Irina remembers her promise to speak to her grandmother. She slips on her coat, feeling for Maman's brooch in the lining, which fortifies her a little.

In the adjoining room, Grand-mère is hunched over a bit of embroidery on her cot. A stubby candle gutters at her side. Irina walks past a sleeping Natasha and Seryozha, pulling the covers over them, before sitting beside her grandmother.

"Comment ça va, Grand-mère?"

"Une autre fille, disparue." A shake of the head. *Another daughter, gone.*

Irina places a hand over her grandmother's mottled one. The skin there is paper-thin. "We will get Auntie released." Only the *how* eludes Irina.

Grand-mère's rheumy eyes are unfocused. Or it could be the morning light pouring in, now the color of very clear water. "One daughter is back," Grand-mère says, making the hair on Irina's arms rise. "I can smell orange blossom all over the house." She sniffs. "And last night, my grandchildren visited me in the kitchen. Can you believe it?"

"Natasha and Seryozha?"

"Andrei. Xenia, too. I must be close to death, for I am seeing the dead."

"We are all seeing the dead, Grand-mère," Irina soothes, despite the cold seeping in. "What happened the night the Cheka killed Pasha?" she asks softly. "I am trying to understand why Auntie wished to reopen the dining room, how the dead are here."

There is an oddly distant look in Grand-mère's eyes. But she shakes her head violently. "I do not know anything. Please do not ask me."

She knows something. Maybe if Irina pushes a little harder... "But—"

"Leave it, Irina. Your aunt is gone." Grand-mère licks her lips, nervous, not herself. "Why is Pasha standing out there in the cold?" Then, all at once, she snaps back. "No, he is gone. They are all gone. Do not ask me."

Irina gives her grandmother's hands one last pat and begins to ready for work. She will try again later—and search Auntie's rooms. In the meantime, she will bring Seryozha to Madame Trobelska, a fellow former person with a daughter in the same class as Natasha and a son Seryozha's age. With Natasha at school and Grand-mère in the kitchen, Irina refuses to leave her son alone in the house, unprotected as much from the living men as from the dead, even if the specters sleep during the day like vampires. A tremor goes through her at that.

Before leaving, Irina tells Grand-mère about the ARA jobs.

Her grandmother's gaze is glassy. "All right, Anna."

"It's Irina, Grand-mère." Cold settles into Irina's bones at Maman's name. She calls for Seryozha and the girls, turning back to her grandmother worriedly. "Perhaps you will stay and rest?" Grand-mère appears so frail that Irina can see the bones in her face, the flesh there stretched translucent and white. Deathlike.

"I shall rest when I die," says Grand-mère, "which is very soon. Anna told me. She said he will visit me in the night."

He? Irina's heart hammers out a warning. "Who?" Maybe she should stay and help her grandmother.... Before she can voice the thought, Grand-mère speaks again.

"Go, I can handle myself." Her voice is that of a countess, firm, final.

But Irina continues to worry even as she, Seryozha, and the girls descend the grand staircase. She hears shuffling footsteps and voices, though muffled and low.

"—not only Boriska's death. The damn singing is not giving me any peace."

Irina grabs Seryozha's hand and throws a warning glance over her shoulder at Lili and Natasha. They meet one another's gazes, stop as one. Irina holds her breath.

"What do you think it is?" another man says from around the stair's corner.

"The Devil knows. Some nechistaya sila."

"The house is cursed. Do you know, I got up to piss in the night, and I heard noises in the library. Two men, crying out, *Take cover! The Reds are coming!* Then rapid footsteps, as if they are really taking cover. Two White soldiers . . . ghosts."

When the men see Irina, they don't joke, tease, or playfully call her *Countess*. They go perfectly still. One clutches a cross at his chest. Reasonable Soviet men, wearing superstitious bourgeois trappings from the past. They *must* be spooked. But then, so is she. She suspects the singing is Luba's, to the child that would never be born. The two White soldiers, her cousin and fiancé, both having died in the Civil War.

Irina loses herself in her ARA work, trying not to think of the haunted Soviet men with their crosses, talking of phantom singing and ghostly White soldiers. Her grandmother is also still worrying her. Can the specter of Maman really have told Grand-mère of her death?

It is only later in the afternoon that Irina is clearheaded enough to take out the payroll.

She reads the list of Russian employees for familiar people carefully. The list includes first, patronymic, and family names in the Russian style. The names don't seem to be in alphabetical order, perhaps written down as people were hired.

Galina Antonovna Stryapko

A maid, at Peter or Moscow House? Or a kitchen assistant?

Ludmila Dmitriyevna Khozyayeva

One of the head housekeepers at Peter House. Was she called Luda?

Svetlana Vasilyevna Boleznova

A maid who worked for Auntie at some point. Irina clearly remembers Auntie's shrill *Sveta!* every time the young woman was late with tea or fulfilling some other whim. She wishes to tell Lili of these findings, but her sister left earlier with Frank, she doesn't know to where.

Irina returns to the list, and to the next name: Paulina Nikolayevna Gonchurova. She pictures dark eyes and rosy cheeks, fashionable mink furs about a slender neck, only the best for the daughter of one of imperial Russia's wealthiest merchants. Paulina was a fixture at Peter House, along with her mother and a sister whose name Irina has forgotten. Paulina's mother knew Irina's family well and might be worth speaking to.

Irina stops at the next name abruptly.

Kirill Ivanovich Serpukhov

Prince Kirill, alive, and in Moscow?
Irina heard his family was murdered on their country estate in the spring of 1917. She assumed it was his fate also. Kirill had been Andrei's closest friend and confidant. He spent weeks, sometimes months, at Auntie's Petersburg house. The two went to war together in 1914,

along with Georgy. Andrei and Georgy had then gone on to fight for the Whites in the Civil War. And Kirill, Irina doesn't know.

She wonders if Kirill and Paulina will be working at headquarters or elsewhere. The ARA is renting more buildings from the Soviet government. But in the spaces next to their names, and Svetlana's, there are blanks instead of office assignments. They must not have been placed yet. Though the other women have—at the ARA kitchen in the former Hermitage Restaurant. Irina notes down the relevant names on her own list and looks up.

The offices are quieter than usual, only a murmur here and there, the rustle of paper or the flicker of a lamp. The ARA chiefs are on an inspection of the famine zone along the Volga River, hundreds of kilometers from Moscow, the rest of the men lulled into a drowsy spell. Maybe she can convince Will to take her to the Hermitage Restaurant. Irina inhales a nervous breath, along with the scent of burnt coffee. And before she can talk herself out of it, she embraces her inner countess and marches to his office.

"Do you intend to show me the ARA kitchens or not?"

Will holds the telephone receiver from his ear, covering the mouthpiece with an incredulous look. "I'm speaking with somebody. . . ."

"Well, now you are speaking to me. I am tired of this office and keen on learning how the ARA operation works."

Will leans back in his chair, considering her. She tries not to fidget as he uncovers the telephone receiver. "I'm going to have to call you back, John." He hangs up before unfolding his lanky body from behind his desk and scooping up his camera with a flash of one of his American smiles. Bright and full of teeth. "Let's go, then."

She likes this about him, the unencumbered way he goes through life. The lack of restraints and the easy acquiescence. The freedom. Entirely the opposite of Georgy, herself, Russia. "Can we see the Hermitage kitchen first?" she asks.

His eyes are sky blue. "As you wish, Countess Irina."

"You still don't know how to pronounce my family name, do you?"

"I like *Irina* too much to say any other name."

The American is flirting with her.... Despite Georgy's memory and the long years since she has flirted, Irina gives Will a teasing smile. She likes her name on his tongue. It is softly accented yet thick, expansive, smoky like his voice. She imagines American cigarettes. Her name said elsewhere, in a faraway place that might as well be the Thrice-Tenth Kingdom from Seryozha's fairy tales.

The Hermitage Restaurant looks the same as ever—the yellowish-gray stones, the Parisian flair, the dome floating above it like a crown. Yet it has an air of abandonment to it, a pitiful kind of shabbiness. The paint is peeling, the windows broken. No horse-drawn carriages or Muscovites in evening wear, sparkling with jewels and laughter.

"After you." Will pulls open the heavy door, and Irina steps inside.

A sweetly wholesome smell envelops her. It has replaced the expensive perfumes, fine cigars, and savory foods. Yet Irina can still taste the poulet à la broche, caviar, fried langoustines; feel the warmth of the champagne and consommé. Her stomach rumbles hungrily.

As they enter the previously shining, columned space, Irina sees the white-clothed tables have been replaced by long wooden ones. And instead of the murmur of fancily dressed couples and gypsy music, there are children in dirty rags, quiet and sullen. As one, they turn, and Irina feels all the judgment of a classroom filled with pupils. Something within her breaks at the sight of the children, so familiar to her. They could be anyone, even Seryozha.

The chill from outside bleeds into the room. A little boy of no more than five years stands by a stove. He sticks out his tiny hands and wriggles his fingers.

Irina walks over and kneels beside him. "What is your name?"

The boy turns empty eyes on her. "Pasha."

"That was my uncle's name."

"He is dead, isn't he?" His seriousness, odd in one so young, shocks Irina into silence. "I miss Mama, though she isn't dead yet. But what

The Haunting of Moscow House

can we do, eh?" He gives a small shrug before waving over a little girl around his age. "This is my friend Dusya."

"Hello, Dusya." Irina touches the girl's cheek gently.

"Are you a princess?"

"No," Irina says, too quickly. Then, "Not anymore."

Soon she is surrounded by a group of girls and boys, tugging at her skirt, talking all at once, telling her their stories. By the time she leaves the gaggle of children, a Russian woman has joined Will and is gesturing animatedly.

"—nothing I can do," she is saying, in heavily accented English, as Irina approaches. "It is after four p.m. and growing dark. They need to go home, and so do I."

"But the children need their supper." Will rubs his face. "Where is Emma?"

"She in other kitchen today." The woman is in her early to mid-sixties, with a hawkish face, commanding speech, and a proper bearing, yet kind and intelligent eyes.

Irina recognizes Ludmila Dmitriyevna, or Luda for short, from her list. She did not interact with the former head housekeeper much, as Luda was not with the family long and tended to remain belowstairs, only ascending to scold a maid or two, or cast a critical eye over preparations for a ball or banquet. "Ludmila Dmitriyevna—is it you?" Irina ventures carefully.

The woman's eyes snap to her and widen. "Countess Goliteva?"

Irina nods eagerly, and Luda dissolves into humility. She throws her meaty arms around Irina in a puff of that sweet, wholesome air. A furtive glance, then in Russian, "We were so afraid! We heard from Count Sherbatsky, your dear uncle, when he had us send some of his possessions to Moscow. But then we were told he, maybe your whole family, was dead!" She crosses herself, shedding a fat tear. "I am so happy to see you!"

"Will you stay and feed the children?" Will puts in hopefully.

"Oy! These Americans, ready to work at all hours," Luda mutters, still in Russian.

"Can't we do it?" Irina switches to English, genuinely baffled. And she needs to convince Luda to stay long enough to ask her questions. "Ludmila Dmitriyevna, would you show us?"

Luda sighs. Pauses. Gives in. "Oh, all right."

Will flashes Irina a grateful smile. They throw on aprons and dive behind the counter. Each meal, Luda explains, consists of a hundred grams of bread and a bowl of what Irina learns are grits made of corn, a vegetable previously unknown to her and the source of the sweet, wholesome smell. As Will chats with Pasha and Dusya, Irina and Luda prepare the meals by the crates of food piled in a storeroom behind the counter.

"Thank you, Ludmila Dmitriyevna," Irina says at length, in Russian, as they are alone.

"It's only out of respect for *you*, Countess Goliteva," she responds blithely. "I have no love for the Americans. Now, tell me, how *is* your dear family?"

"Only my grandmother, sister, and cousins are left. Aunt Maria was arrested."

"Oh, I thought she had been arrested a long time ago." Luda reddens, wipes her brow. "Not to speak ill of her, Countess Goliteva."

"No, please . . ." Irina tempers her eagerness. "What do you mean?"

"Just that your aunt—well, she had fixed ideas about the Bolsheviks, the Revolution, Russia. Back then, people like her were taken out and shot." Luda gives another furtive glance about. "Forgive me, I am an old, thoughtless woman."

"I don't know as much about that time as I should." Irina hears Will call for the children to line up and takes her chance. "You wish to go home. Oh, how lucky I am to have found you again, my dear Ludmila Dmitriyevna! May I visit you again, with my sister? It would be so lovely and . . . help us to move on from what happened."

Luda's eyes cloud with pity. "Mornings after breakfast are quietest," she says, to Irina's relief. "Galina Antonovna helps with meal preparation. She assisted in the kitchen at Moscow House. Perhaps she will also be willing to speak to you. You may see us then." Without waiting for a response, Luda bustles away with a huff.

Will smiles at Irina as she takes her place next to him behind the counter. She bends toward each child with a kind word or two before placing a meal on the tray. A little head bobs above the counter and tiny hands snatch up the tray, exchanging their cards for food and hurrying to the benches. Then Irina is on to the next meal, the next child, forgetting herself in the hustle. But not that she has a lead. That stays.

Later, she and Will walk the two kilometers or so back to 30 Spiridonovka. It takes them a little over a half hour. Despite the cold wetness, Irina feels the warmth of satisfaction, of making someone's life more bearable. Not since her hospital days has she felt this way. And she has found two women from her family's employ who may know more. Irina chats with Will about their work and Moscow, the ARA kitchen and the children there, how much they reminded Irina of her "cousins," and Will's reporter job in Boston and Boston itself, that bustling port town of tea parties. Irina is curious about it all. Maman would be horrified at her lack of restraint or a chaperone.

The memory of Georgy's laugh rushes into Irina's mind, teasing, boastful. And her barely held-in excitement as she told him about the hospital where she worked on one of his visits from the front.

You are a woman, my own darling! he said with a condescending shake of the head. *Once we are married, you shall not do anything but be in bed with me.*

Irina, being a proper lady, blushed furiously at that. But men had dropped all pretense to old-fashioned courting after the horrors of the front. *What about the children?*

We will have nurses for that. Georgy smirked. *You shall be mine, all mine. Not even your patients or books will have you.*

Irina's chest tightened. She had wished to be married, but to not read, to not even take care of their children! What on earth would she have done? To her horror, as she is walking with Will, relief floods the length of her. That she never became Georgy's wife. That she is busy with work and family, free to make her own choices.

"So what do you think?" Will turns to her, bringing Irina back to this street, him.

"About what?" She is at sea.

"You're really going to make a fella ask twice?" He laughs, uneasy, nervous. "I asked if you wanted to come to a party . . . as, well, my date."

Irina's back feels prickly, scratchy. Invisible eyes, invisible men? A reminder that she should return to Moscow House. She must make sure Grand-mère is all right, that Lili has returned from work and Natasha from school, that she tucks Seryozha into bed. Irina imagines saying *yes* to Will but evades.

"Aren't you my superior, in a way?"

"Not exactly. . . ."

"Oh, not exactly?" She laughs. "It would be highly improper if you were."

Will's eyes linger on her. Before Irina can react, he seizes her hand in his very warm grasp and tugs her toward him. "This, too?" His whisper is rough against her cheek.

"Undoubtedly." His mouth quirks up, and she wonders what it would be like to kiss a man with facial hair. Then berates herself. "I must go." She tugs away, starts to walk.

"As you wish, Countess Irina."

She catches a mouthful of damp air on her laugh. Nestles deeply into her coat. Her ugly man's boots thump against the uneven pavement. The homeless lie against the buildings, silent, unmoving. On the other side, an alley and a park, blurred by fog, blending surreally into the misty sky. As though part of the city has been obliterated.

That's when Irina hears the click of footsteps behind her. An exact mirror to her own.

She tells herself it is another person walking home late. But they keep on, not veering, persistent, receding into the distance, then returning, always returning. Irina tastes a dry mouth. She refuses to turn and face one of the Soviet men from the house. Felix, maybe. She redoubles her pace, seeing no one on the streets now, not even the homeless. Her heart thuds painfully as she breaks into a run.

She reaches the gate of Moscow House breathless, her limbs sore and aching.

With one hand on the cold wrought iron, she finally turns. Holds her breath, expecting Felix and his hard blue eyes. The street is empty. Though Irina thinks she sees a flicker behind the corner, a scarf billowing out of place or a shred of a man's coat.

15

Uncle Pasha

LILI HAS BEEN sketching and showing the Americans around Moscow all day. Though cold and tired, she insisted on stopping by the bazaar for a few drawings of former people.

A useful comparison to those lucky enough to work for the ARA, she told Frank, while thinking it a good opportunity to look around for former people she might know.

As Lili steps out of the Cadillac in front of the bazaar gates, she avoids Nikolai's gaze. The entire time he has driven them, he has not glanced at her, not even once, and has barely said a word. What he *did* say was stiff and lifeless, as if uttered by a stranger.

The gates are blurry and undefined at the edges. They rise from the fog, specter-like. Lili thinks of the dead men, the ghosts of her family, and looks around uneasily. The back of her neck prickles. Before, she was convinced the Bolos had no interest in her. Today, with the latest dead body and Auntie's arrest, she isn't so sure.

"Well?" Frank bumps his shoulder against hers. "Will you come to our party?"

Lili is quite sure he is only being friendly. Overfamiliarity and outspokenness seem to be purely American traits and not a sign of romantic interest. But she still flirts with him, and he flirts back, jokingly sighing deeply and feigning annoyance with her.

"Oh, you absolutely must come!" Emma exclaims, momentarily forgetting her apprehensiveness from the motorcar at the thought of the bazaar and the crowds there, the Russians' potential reaction to her and Frank.

Lili respects Emma's decision to go to the bazaar anyway, and Frank is Frank. He doesn't seem to let people's perception of him keep him from doing what he wants to do. Frank and Lili are already friendly, and after a day of Lili and Emma getting to know each other, Emma has become as at ease in Lili's company as she appears to be with the others. Now Lili is happy to see some of Emma's usual good humor peek through.

"Though ARA parties are nothing compared to the ones in New Orleans," Emma is saying. "Oh, the parties there! The jazz, the dancing . . ."

Lili laughs, imagining it all, remembering Uncle Pasha's reminiscences of New Orleans, as Harold offers her a cigarette. "Do countesses smoke?" he asks.

"All they do is smoke." She takes the cigarette, focusing very hard on not lighting herself on fire with it. Now Nikolai's gaze is on her, she can feel it. He leans as casually as ever against the Cadillac, pretending to read from a small leather-bound book. What can he be reading? Lili finally lights the cigarette, taking a drag . . . and coughing—again.

Frank and Harold laugh, shaking their heads at her lack of adeptness. Emma shoots them a scathing look, scolding them loudly for their ungentlemanly behavior.

Lili agrees. But she wants to go to that party. "I'll come to your party."

"Swell!" Emma breaks into a smile.

"Will you be my date?" Frank grins wide, Cheshire Cat–like. Trying to be funny.

Emma shakes her head, smirks, meets Lili's gaze.

And without thinking, Lili bounces up on her tiptoes and presses her lips to Frank's cheek in a big, loud smack of a kiss. Her eyes slide to Nikolai, just for a second.

His book is lowered, and he is looking at her, frowning, angry? Barely registering Emma's cackle, the boys' whoops, Lili quirks her mouth into a smile at him. But Nikolai's gaze is back on his book.

The cigarette turns to ash in her mouth, and she flushes with delayed embarrassment. She imagines Maman's horror at her kissing a man as a joke, or at all; her refrain, *You must behave as a proper young lady of your stature*. For once, Maman would be right. That was impulsive, stupid. Lili throws out the cigarette.

"All right." Emma hooks an arm into Lili's, leaning in close, scenting the air between them with lavender. "Before you bestow any more kisses on these ingrates, shall we go?" A shadow crosses Emma's features as her gaze finds the gate, the bazaar beyond—her fear, Lili supposes.

She gives Emma's arm what she hopes is a reassuring squeeze, for strength, and says, low, "We're together. Let's go."

The open-air bazaar is filled with milling, bustling people who jostle Lili right and left as she leads the Americans down the muddy gravel path between rows of wooden stalls. Stares and whispers follow them, and Lili doesn't know whether it's because of Emma and Frank or that their foreign group looks so out of place here in this rushing Russian throng dressed in plain, rough workers' clothing and tattered former-military uniforms, with their world-weary, dirty countenances.

But curiosity and the desire to make a ruble win out. Boys run up to them in a spray of mud, flecks of dirt flying at Lili. Thankfully, if not dully, her skirt is black, or Irina would throw a fit. Old tsarist medals clink on the boys' chests, their ribbons streaming. Old men are not far, with offers of furs, rugs, tapestries, books, and other antiques. The Americans exclaim over these imperial collectibles in loud, excited tones but refrain from purchasing. According to ARA rules, they aren't allowed. Still, the white-haired aristocratic ladies rise from their old potato crates in hope of a sale.

The jewels at their necks gleam in the smudged, rain-soaked evening light.

Lili stops at an empty spot between a pair of such ladies, the space as good as any to make her drawings. She only wishes Irina were here with her. Lili looks over at Emma and is glad to see her friend glancing around with keen interest, having forgotten her fear, though not her watchfulness. That shadow still veils her face, careful and circumspect, in this entirely foreign, unknown place. After making sure she is all right, Lili tells the Americans to go and explore. They wander away, eyes wide and voices raised, typical foreigners now.

She pulls her sketch pad out of her coat. The pages are damp and curling from the fog. She doesn't have much time; it is about to rain. Slipping a pencil out of her pocket, she presses the tip to the blank page. Blocks out the mouthwatering, savory smells of pirozhki stuffed with meat and potato. The noise, too—the chatter, the aggressive bartering, the squelch of boots in mud. Lili sketches quickly, in broad, careless strokes. The boys with the medals, the white-haired aristocratic ladies with the jewels, other traders with artifacts excavated from a bygone era. A man with a pointy red beard behind busts of Tsar Nicholas and Fabergé eggs in poisonously bright green and pink colors. The girl with chin-length hair selling "fine lace embroidered by former princesses!"

Emma approaches quietly. "Do you recognize any former people?"

Lili told Emma about her project, though not about the house. "I haven't been looking," she says guiltily. She wants to be done with the sketches and is glad to see Emma, her vivaciousness and warmth raising Lili's spirits.

She slips her pencil and sketch pad back into her coat before raising her collar against the damp and taking Emma's arm. A light rain starts to fall. But they don't hurry. They walk slowly, almost leisurely. Resolving to ignore any stares and whispers, Emma tells Lili about the market she visits back in New Orleans, pralines among her favorite purchases, and fresh shrimp, which she uses to make her family's signature gumbo. Lili's stomach rumbles at that; she wishes to try these delicious-sounding foods right here, right now. She takes some photographs with Will's camera to distract herself, and they peer at the offered goods. This time, Lili studies the people in the stalls, wondering if she recognizes a gesture, a face, a voice.

But there is nothing familiar; they are all strangers. And the icy rain brings on a dreadful shiver. Lili pulls down her sleeves, tugs up her collar even higher, to the edge of her jaw. The wool is scratchy, but she'd rather be warm. She presses closer to Emma. Thinks of the motorcar with Nikolai waiting inside. Not thinking of her.

Something catches Lili's eye—a scrap of red, the glint and shine of gold.

In one of the stalls, a man sits under a threadbare red blanket. A black beard covers his worn, stoic face. And on the wooden counter in front of him is a stained oilcloth with an assortment of tarnished gold and silver jewelry, precious stones, and snuffboxes. No diamonds or rare jewels. Not as valuable or glamorous as the jewelry her family used to flaunt but worth bread at least.

"Good evening." Lili addresses the man in Russian.

She thinks there is a spark in those dull gray eyes. But she must have imagined it, for the man doesn't seem to even blink. Lili looks down, examining the jewelry on the oilcloth to mask her awkwardness. She lifts a signet ring at random. Uncle Pasha wore such a ring, as did most of the men in her family. A crest is stamped into the rose gold of this one, faded and hidden behind swirls, vines, and leaflike letters, remnants of some poor noble family erased into obscurity by the Revolution. It is all so damn sad.

"Do you have an uncle, Emma?" Lili asks her friend in English.

"Sure do—Uncle Lawrence, clever to a fault, smile as sweet as sugar for the right person, spry as all hell. Why, the man refuses to sit still. Drives me crazy. But I love him to death."

"I assume you're close?"

"Oh, yes. I left home early. Didn't see much of a point in staying. My mama moved around a lot, looking for work or a new husband. Had a lot of kids, too. And I wanted more out of life. Uncle Lawrence involved me in soup kitchen work and helping poor folks. We would often go together. I miss him something fierce."

Like Lili misses Uncle Pasha. She gives Emma a look of sympathy. "Is that why you are here? Wanting more?"

Emma shrugs. "Will introduced me to ARA work back in the States. It combined doing what I love, helping poor folks, with getting out. Life for people like me in America is . . . hard. Complicated. In Europe, people might stare and whisper, but they don't throw you out. I know Russia's different, and I'm smart about it. Anyway, by the time we left, Will and I had worked together some, and I knew he was the honorable sort. The sort that follows through with what he says. Will said he would make sure I'd be treated fair, respected by him and his men, driven around Moscow if that's what it took—that's how I first met Niko. Now I'm jazzed to be here, that I get to see . . . all this."

Lili has a lot to think about, a lot more to ask Emma. For now, for the hundredth time that day, Lili is damn glad Emma is here and not back in America. Not only because life there really does sound complicated for her but, selfishly, because Lili is making a new friend. She doesn't want to think about Nikolai. But she does think of her uncle, recalls Uncle Pasha traveling to exotic places he would then tell her about in letters he'd send to her dutifully no matter where he was. She aches for another letter from him, to see his words again, so precious now that there are no more of them. She fiddles thoughtfully with the signet ring still in her hand.

"That one has a key inside," the man says in practiced French, startling Lili. His voice is rusty, old before its time. Unmistakably that of a former person.

"What did he say?" Emma whispers. "My French isn't what it used to be, and his sounds different."

Lili translates, absently turning over the ring. The man . . . is familiar. Maybe it is his eyes. She tries to place him and fails. "Est-ce que je vous connais?" she finally asks.

He grips his blanket tightly, as if to assert his anonymity. "Nyet."

Lili places the ring back onto the oilcloth. "Can we go?" she asks Emma, the English comforting on her tongue after the French. The past is rushing back so insistently, Lili feels woozy. She is grateful for her friend's arm, holding her up, not letting her fall.

✦ ✦ ✦

The rain intensifies by the time Nikolai stops the motorcar at the ARA, then at Emma's apartment, before continuing on to Moscow House. Left alone in the back of the Cadillac without Emma, Lili listens to the patter against the roof. That dampness, the rot of dying leaves, finds her even here. She presses her sketch pad to her chest, hard, trying not to think of the spooked Bolsheviks, or the night ahead.

"What were you reading earlier?" she asks instead.

Nikolai's eyes flick to her in the rearview mirror, and she sees the edge of his smile, the first that day. "'A cockcrow rang out,'" he recites. "'The frightened spirits rushed pell-mell for the windows and doors. . . .'"

"Gogol," Lili whispers, unable to suppress her admiration of Nikolai's brilliant memory. Even in their childhood, he recited poetry as if it were a part of him. Warmth blooms deep in her chest before slipping lower, down to her belly, making its home there. "And has Gogol taught you anything new?"

"To fear the living more than the dead."

It is as if the rain-soaked fog has slid into the seat beside her. She thinks of the damn Bolsheviks who have all but taken their house, the Cheka who killed her uncle, exiled and killed the rest of her family. Men did that, not ghosts. Did men also murder those Bolsheviks?

The jolt of the motorcar brings Lili back. Nikolai is expertly weaving between traffic. She gasps as they speed up. Faster and faster, the car lurching and rolling. She sits forward, the better to watch the black ribbon of the road. It flashes with oncoming headlights, then dims. He swerves past another car, barely, and she grips his seat hard.

Nikolai's eyes meet hers in the mirror. To her surprise, they crinkle at the edges. He speeds up, so fast Lili cannot breathe as they rush past the other cars in a blind white blur. She lets out a little shriek and grabs his shoulders. He laughs, gives a shake of his head. Lowers a hand to her arm. It is casual, as he used to do, yet it sends a strange thrill through Lili.

"How did you learn to drive like this?" she asks, still breathless.

"My father," Nikolai replies, and she recalls his family's automobile collection.

Lili wonders where they are now, likely nowhere good, before suppressing the thought. *Stop dwelling*. Forget. Live. She is thankful for Nikolai's driving. The motorcar is an extension of him as much as his poetry. Maybe he is still the Nicky she knew, only he also wants to forget and live. Maybe it is why he drives. To escape a haunted past that isn't so dead. Maybe they aren't, either.

Lili's hands are still on his shoulders. They are surprisingly strong; there is new muscle there. She lowers her face, his curls brushing against her cheek. Nikolai smells of cheap Russian soap, not the expensive, perfumed French kind of before. That and cigarettes. She leans forward a little more, winds her arms around him. He watches her in the mirror, not smiling, not pulling away. His hand slides up her arm, tightens there.

Too soon, the car slows. Moscow House's dome shivers into view.

Nikolai goes rigid, and Lili has the oddest urge to keep holding him. Whatever happened to his family, her house crawling with Bolsheviks must be its own brand of terror for him.

"You can stop here," she whispers, though they are still some distance away.

He hits the brakes, and the heavy automobile grinds to a stop. Nikolai removes his hand. "You should be careful with the Americans, Lil," he says, low.

She disengages from him almost violently, a hard push that sends her body bouncing against the back seat. His stiff voice, the reserve in his face, the tension strung tight between them. He is a stranger again, not her friend, not Nicky.

"They have been calling the Russian women 'Madame Butterflies,' exotic fallen socialites here only for their entertainment. You'd do well to remember that."

"And you'd do well to remember you aren't in any position to tell me that."

"We were friends once. I looked out for you. Nothing has changed."

"Nothing has changed?" Lili repeats, the tucked-away questions rushing back. "Where have you been? Why didn't you find me? It has *all* changed, Nicky. The *world* has changed. You don't know me." The anger, her bruised heart, cuts at her words and makes them jagged. Nikolai abandoned her without any explanation. He doesn't trust her with his past, one she certainly has no wish to unearth. "You are not my friend." This said clumsily.

Nikolai fumbles for the door handle and tumbles out of the Cadillac in a blast of cold, wet air. He jerks open her door and thrusts his head inside. "If I so much as mention it"—his breath catches—"I swear, Lil, I will weep in front of you." He clenches his jaw, looks away. "I have not stopped thinking of you for one minute. Hence the warning."

An angry heat flares up at his ill-timed, condescending warnings. Lili brings her face against his dripping one. And damn her, but her gaze drops to his slightly parted lips, so close she can touch them. But that would be silly. She does *not* want to kiss him.

"They will leave in a few months. If you get into trouble, they will leave you—"

"You're just jealous," she says, vicious, recalling his anger at her kissing Frank.

Nikolai blinks. Steps back into the rainfall.

Lili slides out of the Cadillac, tucking her sketch pad into her coat with shaking hands. She never carries a purse; it only gets in her way. But she wishes she had one now, if only to hide the shaking and her embarrassingly nervous breathing.

"I am your friend, Lili, only your friend. But I see you are a child still."

Why, the snub-nosed brat! "I have managed without your friendship all these years," she shoots back, before whipping around and trudging toward the gate. Her, a child, only a friend! She doesn't need him. But as she walks through the gate, she glances back—and sees his lone figure in the rain. Nikolai hasn't moved.

Rain lashes at Lili's face in cold, wet streaks that leave her shuddering. The hulking shape of the house rises up, forbidding against the blurred black sky. She is glad the fog isn't as thick here. But it lingers, like a mist in a forgotten graveyard.

Her eye catches on a shadow under the oak, heart leaping instantly into her throat. She blinks and wipes at her face, trying to see. *Show yourself!* she almost screams.

The shadow is a figure sketched in gray outlines. A silhouette, and yet a person, a *he* that stands tall and straight. More proof of ghosts, like in the dining room. It is so inhuman, so unnatural, Lili feels her body go numb with the shock. Inexplicably, she steps toward the figure, barely breathing, and it mimics the motion as in a looking glass. Now she can make out the torn, filthy clothing, the bullet hole in the forehead. The whiff of death. Uncle Pasha—real as never before.

It isn't Uncle Pasha, Lil, she reminds herself. *It is his ghost.* But what if this ghost could tell her about his death, that night? She can still hear his words: *We live, Lilichka, then we die. God has willed it so, and we must make our peace with it.*

It occurs to her then: Uncle Pasha might be trying to help her, but what if he needs help, too? What if he is trapped here in the house and needs to be set free? What if he is looking for peace? Even if she has to let in the past, tragedy itself, she would help him.

Up close, the smell is nearly unbearable, like rotting fish left out of the icebox too long. The ghost parts his cracked, dry lips, his mouth a gaping black hole, and raises one blue-tinged hand.

Lilichka... His voice is a current of air. She strains her ears, taking a small step toward him. *I cannot go in*, she thinks he says. *Find...*

She waits. When it doesn't come, "Find what?"

The truth is in the story— Uncle Pasha's ghost wavers. *The key is in my rooms. The story is*— He wavers again. Looks up at the house, eyes widening. He forces out the next part in a rush. *A different time is drawing near.* He is vanishing, the last of his words with him. *The wind of death already chills the heart.*

"Uncle Pasha?" Lili leaps to him.

But he is no longer there. Branches claw at empty air, leaves swirl in an agitated dry rustle not unlike the whisper of a gown against a dead ground. Lili's heart beats hard and fast in her ears. What truth, in what story? And is someone keeping her uncle from the house? Reluctantly, she thinks back to his absence at that dinner. His warning just now—that something is coming. The only clue, a key supposedly found in his rooms.

Lili's clothes are sopping wet. They stick to her skin like the leaves. And rain trickles down her face, her vision blurring. Maybe she is crying. The horror is slithering out, settling into her mind and body, making a home of it. But it isn't midnight, not quite yet. The timing might work differently outside. She could still look for the key, if it is a real clue. Lili pulls open the house's doors—to the heavy, waxy smell of candlelight.

In the hall, long-darkened candelabras blaze up with hungry flames. Though the house has been wired for electricity, they have primarily relied on kerosene or oil lamps since the Revolution. Candlesticks have been painstakingly, irritatingly conserved. The parquet gleams, swept of the Bolsheviks' muddy footprints and cigarettes. There is no sign of them, or of their flag. A blue-and-white Gzhel vase has replaced the ashtray on the antique wooden table. The gilt bronze chandelier gleams like the parquet. Its crystal drops are visible, free of dust.

"What is this?" Lili's voice echoes against the marble. And where are the men?

The crunch under her boots suddenly startles her. Salt and crumbs are scattered along the floor to the darkened nook under the grand staircase, like Hansel and Gretel's trail home from the witch's gingerbread house.

A chewing sound reaches Lili. As if the witch is truly there, feasting on flesh and bone.

Lili is edging toward the stairs, her wet boots squelching, when a red glimmer flashes at her from inside the nook. A blink of eyes, then gone. She expects the witch as she peers inside. Instead, she finds a loaf of bread, half chewed through; a mound of salt; and a discarded towel. A rat, or another animal, could have stolen the bread and dragged it here. But it is hard to explain the salt and towel, reminding her of the old Russian tradition of homecoming.

A few weeks ago, Lili would have taken the bread, even if the rats had it first. Now, after working for the Americans, her mouth twists in disgust at the thought of even touching that loaf, much less finishing it. She leaves it and sprints up the stairs, thinking she will have a look around Uncle Pasha's rooms, then return to the attic.

Lili reaches the landing below the attic, with Uncle Pasha's rooms and Grand-père's sickroom. Here, as downstairs, the sconces on the walls flicker with light. They illuminate the paintings of her ancestors. She feels their dead eyes following her down the hallway to her uncle's rooms. Her skin crawls at the weight in those gazes.

Lili slams her uncle's door closed behind her, body still cold and shaking and somehow separate from her.

These rooms used to be her place of refuge. For a minute, she thinks she will find it again. After all, she would come here day or night, whether to share her latest sketch or unburden herself after a persistent nightmare. Whatever it was, her uncle would usher her inside with one languid wave of his hand and bid her to sit in her favorite settee as they talked it over.

Now candlelight glows against the pink walls. They ripple, almost breathe with her. As Lili walks deeper into the room, the cold touches her heart. This is the first time she's been back here since her uncle's death.

Oddly, as though Uncle Pasha has just stepped out for a moment, there are no sheets on the furniture. The gray maple wood and silk upholstery are not dusty with years of abandonment. And a freshly built fire laps at the grate in the tiled fireplace, crackling and spitting. But it is only when Lili's gaze settles on Uncle Pasha's bed that her body seizes with pure, cold horror, and she opens her mouth in a silent scream.

On the bed, on fresh sheets with his name embroidered into the linen, her uncle's two-piece mint-green evening suit is neatly laid out—along with his pocket watch and cane.

Lili backs away slowly, not daring to make a noise, barely breathing, eyes wide and fixed on the bed. She collides with the door. Fumbles for the knob, suddenly desperate to leave this place. The door finally gives and swings open, and she falls out of the room. She runs straight for the attic, and there, into her sister's arms.

16

The Morning After

LILI FELL INTO a deep, dead kind of sleep with no dreams, not waking until dawn—was it a rooster's ghostly crowing that jolted her?—to find her sister awake. Irina recounted her conversation with their former housekeeper, and Lili finally told her about the night before. She hadn't been able to talk about it then.

Now rain beats against the roof as she and Irina walk the two floors down to Auntie's rooms. The cold is squirmingly damp, which makes Lili moodier than usual. Since they were both up, they agreed to look around not only their aunt's rooms but Uncle Pasha's as well. It is the ideal time, before work and before their family and the Bolos awaken. Unless the scoundrels are cowering in the West Wing, frightened out of their wits.

"Auntie is gone, yet someone is still doing the rituals," she says as they walk. "If it isn't us, Natasha, or Seryozha, it must be Grandmère."

"I don't believe she is physically capable of it, Lil."

"Then it is either the Bolos or the ghosts. And somehow I don't think the bastards are keen on servicing a house of the Sherbatsky-Golitevs."

Lili doesn't know what on earth to expect when she pushes the door to Auntie's rooms open—but all is drab and gray. No lights blaze, no evening clothes are laid out, though it is clean, and the scent of trapped candlelight fills her with unease. "These rooms must also have been . . . tidied up," she whispers. *But by whom?*

"My God," Irina breathes, stepping deeper into the space and looking around. "You weren't overstating."

Auntie's rooms comprise the largest suite in the house, and the most opulent. Crystals drip from darkly gleaming chandeliers twisted into bronzed leaves and vines, aristocratic ladies in airy white gowns pose in portraits of striking Old Russia landscapes. The furniture, fashioned in Parisian workshops and dating back to at least the 1850s, is all dark walnut wood and crimson upholstery as vibrant and alive as blood.

"I wonder if Auntie kept up these rooms the entire time, even when we all moved to smaller rooms." Lili crosses her aunt's receiving room, covered entirely in Persian rugs.

Irina follows. "Knowing her, probably. So, we are looking for any correspondence, notes, or other clues pertaining to that night, Pasha, or the family."

Lili nods, relaxing a little, as she begins to rifle through the tables and cabinets. She opens and closes drawers, mostly cleared out, and searches bookcases, largely decorative. Auntie has never been a reader, preferring prayers and charity—and tormenting Lili.

"What do you think the animal with the red eyes is?" Irina muses, picking up and examining knickknacks at random—this one a fat tortoiseshell pig.

Lili feels a bit like Alice falling down that rabbit hole. "I could tell you, but you will think me silly."

A laugh. "Too late."

Lili scoffs, but the corners of her mouth turn up. She moves on from yet another decorative table, nothing on its surface but shadows of horses imprinted into wood. "It could be an imp, or a gnome, or a chyort of some sort. Gogol wrote of many such spirits coming alive with the Devil-like monster, Viy. Or maybe it is Xenia's doll."

As soon as Auntie was arrested, they hid the vile thing in a trunk.

"Lil?" Irina calls out from an adjoining room.

Lili follows her voice through a small passageway into Auntie's bedroom, as opulent and dramatically crimson as her receiving room. Irina is kneeling by the narrow bed with a rosewood box in her hands. Lili catches a faint whiff of rose water as her sister hands her the box. Inside, there are clay bowls, a lump of wax, a scrap of paper with a bit of verse, a pair of simple rings, and the embarrassingly big ruby-encrusted cross Auntie used to wear like a talisman over her heart.

"And look there." Irina points to the icon corner on its high shelf. The lamp has long gone out, the saints on the icons turned from the room, toward the wall, their wooden backs cracked and streaked with black paint.

"Now, that is more worrying," Lili allows. "Still, why would Auntie leave anything of value here? Why don't we look in Uncle Pasha's rooms?" Though she really doesn't wish to return there after the night before.

Irina nods, rising elegantly, and they make their way back upstairs.

Lili clutches the rosewood box to her chest. She tries not to remember Grand-père's ghostly cough or Aunt Luba's singing. She averts her eyes from her ancestors hanging on the hallway walls. Below them, the marble busts and lamps are dead-still and shrouded in deep purple shadows that drift like a fog.

Footsteps from downstairs are starting to disturb the silence—the Bolos stirring like cockroaches.

In Uncle Pasha's rooms, the only evidence of the night before is that waxy, trapped smell of candlelight. As they begin to comb through the space, Lili feels their uncle everywhere. His soft, fond smile; his melodic voice, his warm embraces. His scent, sandalwood tangled with coffee beans.

"Maybe we should page through the books," Irina suggests, after they've been looking for some time. "But we only have half an hour or so left."

They are in Uncle Pasha's study. His books gleam on the walnut cabinets and maple bookshelves. Lili sweeps her knuckles along their burnt gold lettering, their cracked spines and leather bindings. He transferred the rest of his books to the library, where he would recline in his swampy-green armchair, his *little corner of peace*. "He meant for us to find a key, not a book," Lili replies. "Though the key could be to a book. A story with his truth . . ."

Irina leans against the bookshelves prettily. "Stories *are* also in books, Lil."

"No, that feels wrong."

"Perhaps a diary, then? I used to keep one. Many did, even the imperial family."

Lili had seen Uncle Pasha scribbling on a bit of paper every once in a while. But every time she'd ask him about it, he would demur. *Oh, it is nothing, darling. Only some notes, an old man's reminiscences.* "If he did, he was discreet," Lili says, slowly, still trapped in that moment. They have to be missing something. He said it was here, and it has to be. She returns to Uncle Pasha's writing table, searched already, and presses her palms into it. She breathes in his scent, silently begging him to lead her to the key.

If the damn key would be anywhere, wouldn't it be in a writing table? Though that might be too obvious. . . .

Lili blows out a frustrated breath, feeling for the grooves in the table's wooden surface. She brings her face close to it, curious now. The table is built of dark mahogany unlike the rest of her uncle's furniture. But it wasn't fashioned in France, judging by the design. Lili steps back from the table, considering it. It reminds her of the work of the fashionable St. Petersburg workshop H. Gambs, from the early 1800s. Her memory always serves her right in art and craftsmanship. And if this *is* an H. Gambs writing table, there should be a secret compartment built in behind the drawers. Lili comes around the table, her heart thudding hard now.

She pulls on the gold handle of the left-hand drawer. It slides out easily, revealing the papers—mostly financial statements—she and Irina have already flipped through. Lili claws her way past them, to the back panel. She knocks against it and holds her breath. Hears the answer of hard wood. Releases the held breath in disappointment. *Patience, Lil.* She pulls on the handle of the right-hand drawer next. *Please, please . . .*

Irina is leaning over her shoulder; Lili feels her faint breaths, quickened with excitement like hers. The drawer slides out, and Lili pulls the papers from there eagerly, handing them to Irina before reaching for the back wall.

This time, a hollow sound answers her rap. With a heart threatening to smother her, Lili fiddles with the panel. She pushes into the wood and shakes loose the little door. A scrape of protest, a creak, and it comes away in her hand. She looks at Irina, wide-eyed, as she feels blindly around the secret space. Her hand comes upon a roll of paper and a ring. Lili takes the treasures out reverently, is about to unroll the paper . . .

When Irina snatches it from her. "Whatever is in here will have to wait." She straightens and slips the scroll into Auntie's rosewood box. "We are late for work."

She should be irritated with her sister lording over her, but Lili's eyes are fixed on the ring. A signet ring. And she is suddenly thinking back to the bazaar, to the gray-eyed man with the tarnished jewelry. The signet rings on the oilcloth.

That one has a key inside. She hears his French as if he were beside her.

"What is it?" Irina's perfect brow furrows, a slight ripple of skin.

Lili ignores her, turning the ring over in her hand. The gold gleams like the sun, and she recognizes the Sherbatsky family crest stamped onto the front. A crown with a sword and spear between two lions, along with the motto: *God Shall Provide.* Lili traces the crest, then the rest of the ring, prodding it for any depressions in the gold. There is one—on the inside, behind the crest, subtle yet unmistakable. Her heart skips a beat. She presses her index finger to the cavity, exerting pressure . . . A *click*, and a sharp, jutting object scrapes out. It is a key.

Irina lets out a gasp. "My God, can it be . . . ?" She seizes the ring, examining it. "What does it lead to?"

"Knowing Uncle Pasha, who always thought of everything, the answer is in there." Lili, still blinking at the revelation, points to the rosewood box with the scroll inside. Her hands itch to reach for it, to read its secrets. "Tell you what, Irishka, I will stay and read, while you make an appearance at work." Of course, the attempt fails.

"It languished in a table unread for years. It can wait a few more hours." This said in Irina's imperious elder sister voice. "Besides, I'd like to gather some old clothing and toys to bring to the Hermitage kitchen for the children before work. And there is the ARA party tonight." Saintly Irina makes a motion to lower the ring into the box, to wait there along with their other finds, when Lili rushes to put a hand over it.

She pulls her hand back in embarrassment but manages to force out, "Can I keep the ring, Irishka?"

Her sister looks at her a moment too long. Then she smiles, knowingly, having caught Lili out. "You wish to keep it as a trinket. I thought you hated them."

She does hate them; they remind her too much of a past she would rather stay dead. But this ring is not only a trinket—it is a fragment of her favorite uncle. Irina drops the ring into her palm, and Lili holds it to her chest where her heart beats.

Divining these thoughts with her frighteningly intuitive sisterly power, Irina gives Lili's hand a pat. "I will find you a bit of ribbon so you can wear it just so."

What little comfort Lili finds dissipates as, on their way out of the house, they peer into the nook under the grand staircase—and find the bread and salt gone.

17

The Past and Present Collide at a Party

THE LATEST RECORDS spin on the American gramophones, pounding against Irina's eardrums, a chaotic cacophony of instruments and voices. The ARA's reception room is all shadow and cigarette smoke, talk and laughter and flirting. She glimpses Lili through the haze, swaying to the blaring saxophone alongside Frank and Emma.

A pain is building in her temples from the heat of the fireplace, the long workday.

Irina left Seryozha and Natasha at Madame Trobelska's on the way to work, so at least she isn't worried about them. And she and Lili received their first crate of American food earlier, which they sneaked into the attic before the party. White flour, canned milk, American bacon, macaroni, rice, cocoa, and sugar, all wrapped in bright packaging. But Irina cannot force Auntie from her mind. Perhaps, despite Comrade Suzhensky's warnings, she can still gently inquire about her? What if this puts Seryozha in danger, given the men know who he is?

Irina peers into the haze for familiar faces. Will told her Paulina and Kirill would be at the party, which is what finally convinced her to attend.

A woman materializes out of the crush of people. Dark red hair, eyes that blaze coal black. She offers Irina a fizzing glass with a familiarly coy smile. Instead of a round face and rosy cheeks, angles and deep-grooved lines of worry; instead of priceless, fashionable mink furs, an old vomit-green sweater ill-fitted over a long baggy skirt.

"You didn't recognize me at first, did you?" Paulina Gonchurova's voice is low and husky. She lifts a cigarette to her painted lips and takes a greedy inhale.

Irina blinks, past and present colliding. "How did you recognize *me*?" She accepts the cold glass. Suppresses her longing for a cigarette. For a moment, they watch the spectacle of the party as they once did a ball, in sparkling gowns and diamonds instead of shabby, patched-up skirts and men's boots. Irina takes a sip from the glass. Her mouth bursts with bubbles and the sharp, brut tang of champagne. Imported, French, forgotten. "It is good to see you, Paulina." And it is.

"You, too, Irene." She uses her old, fond name for Irina.

"How is your family?"

Paulina takes a thoughtful drag of her cigarette, lets out a puff of smoke. "My father was killed in February 1917, when the protests first started."

Irina has heard of that time—the gunshots and violence; the angry, hungry people in the streets; the lawlessness. She was in the countryside, pregnant and alone.

"As for my mother . . . well, she died of a broken heart. Only my sister is left."

They make the sign of the cross. "My mother also died of a broken heart," Irina says, recalling Maman's last letter after Papa's death: *It hurts to live, ma chérie. It hurts to breathe.* A few weeks later, they received the missive that she was dead, too. Irina's spirits sink despite the champagne. Not just because of Maman. If Paulina's mother is gone, so is her chance of learning anything useful. "Heavenly Kingdom to them both," Irina whispers.

Paulina stubs her cigarette into a crystal ashtray on the mantelpiece. She grabs Irina's hand and tugs her to the other side of the room. "Have you seen this yet?"

They stumble to a long table that instantly hits Irina with a burst of mouthwatering aromas. Bacon, ham, sausages, and corned beef; yellow and white and blue cheeses; a cascade of fruit and olives and caviar. Irina's eyes widen. She hasn't beheld such a varied spread since the soirées before the Revolution. She grabs a plate and piles it with food, scraping it all clean to the last crumb, for once not caring in the slightest about manners.

Just as she and Paulina are talking about lining up for seconds, they run into Kirill—as ever, the impeccable aristocrat. Though thinner, he is towering, with very dark hair and eyes, and a bearing that makes others feel smaller, and not just in height.

"So, how do you like working for the ARA, Irina?" he asks, after the niceties have been exchanged.

Irina takes a sip of champagne. Her thoughts flicker to Will, not at the party, likely still working. Before she can respond, Paulina glances at her significantly.

"And how do you like the Americans? They are free, no? They live lightly."

"Free," Irina repeats thoughtfully, picturing Will and his bright, carefree smile, his charming informality, even his unshaven face with the beginnings of a beard. "Yes, I suppose they are. Though they work hard."

Paulina laughs, a smoky breath of a sound. Her eyes settle on Harold, who watches her from across the room. "They may work hard, but they live without our ghosts. I can already tell. They are cheerful. Not like us, gloomy and fearful and . . . haunted." She drains the rest of her champagne with a flicker of a smile.

As Paulina dissolves into the crush, Irina brings her glass to her lips. Maybe her family isn't the only one living with the dead. Or maybe Paulina meant it in jest. Irina turns to Kirill, who is sipping his drink quietly. It smells of whiskey. "Can we step outside?" she asks him, raising her voice above the music with a gesture at the door.

Kirill nods wordlessly, and she leads him past the party out into the night.

❖ ❖ ❖

"I am sorry about Andrei, Countess. He was the best man I knew."

Irina leans against the porch's wiry railing, Kirill remaining stiff and rigid by the doors. The night is frosty and so black she cannot see past the steps. There is a needling sensation along her neck. The imprint of a watchful gaze. She takes in a breath, the air cold yet clean and fresh after the party. "You should call me Irina." Her glance wanders as she imagines the likes of Felix turning the corner and hearing the maligned title.

"I meant it, Irina." Kirill turns to face her, his downturned expression one of sorrow. "I was . . . inconsolable."

They cross themselves, whisper the prayer for Andrei's peace. Once, she suspected that Kirill and her cousin were lovers. She never found out the truth. "I am also sorry for your family, Kirill," she says, and they repeat their prayers.

"How is your aunt coping with her loss?" he asks.

It is an opening, at least. "She has accepted his death. But she— was arrested." Irina watches Kirill's face for a reaction. "It happened recently," she goes on, not seeing any on his again-stoic courtier's face, "several days ago, in fact, by the Soviet officials who have requisitioned our house."

"I am sorry to hear it." Is there a tremble in his voice? "Your aunt . . . was always kind to me."

Irina hesitates, debating how much to tell Kirill. "I met our old housekeeper from Petersburg at the ARA kitchen the other day," she says, slowly. "She was surprised my aunt wasn't arrested earlier."

"I confess I am as well."

"Can you tell me why?" Now it is Kirill who hesitates, and Irina gives a self-deprecating laugh. She sips at her champagne, the bubbles buzzing and bursting on her tongue. "Come, Kirill, we have known each other nearly all our lives. Before she was arrested, Auntie was . . . acting strange. I realized, too late, I don't know her as well as I should."

"Don't we all come to this realization?" His sigh streams out white; the melting ice in his glass clinks. "I remember Princess Sablorova grew more erratic, and eccentric, as the Revolution neared. We visited her on leave from the front, and she was, well, distraught. She had always been protective of Andrei. But now she would burst into tears at tea, rush to Andrei and cover him in kisses at dinner, beg him not to leave the rest of the time."

"What did my cousin say?"

"He was worried she was going mad with his absence."

This is not the aunt Irina knows—or knew. Marie had put up an impenetrable front with the family, especially Maman and Grand-mère. She had taken on the role of the stronger sister, daughter, aunt, and woman, not often giving over to emotion, her dry humor never far.

"There is something else." Kirill shifts, the clink of ice faint now, his whiskey drained. "The last time we saw Princess Sablorova, sometime in early 1917, she gave Andrei a necklace in the form of a horseshoe. She said it was an amulet of iron and horsehair. She urged Andrei to wear it in battle for protection. That and a lump of wax over which she had whispered something I couldn't hear."

Irina's heart speeds up. The wax in that rosewood box, and the verse, scribbled on that scrap of paper—like a spell. Or a curse. Could her aunt have been drawn to the occult? It is hard to fathom. Auntie, being devout, swears off any and all of those *superstitions ridicules*.

"That was not the oddest part." Kirill pulls open the doors, the warm, booze-filled air swarming their faces. "Before we left, Princess Sablorova handed Andrei a vial of what she claimed was the blood of a hog, instructing him to drink it down to the dregs right in front of her."

The champagne turns sour in Irina's mouth. "Did he?"

Kirill's teeth glint in the wash of light from the foyer, the doors slamming shut behind them in a whirl of bone-numbing cold. "Andrei was a good little lad. He did everything his maman told him, even drinking her pig's blood."

Her cousin is dead. She shouldn't judge him for humoring Marie.

Yet Irina does. And she wonders how she missed Auntie buying into all that supposedly *ridiculous* superstition.

Irina wishes to tell her sister about her conversation with Kirill straightaway. Yet her feet take her in the opposite direction, to the offices and Will, needing his easy, carefree presence in that moment.

Lamplight pools in front of his office. Irina hesitates, the room darkened, unusually quiet, the rest of the men having left for the party hours earlier. She goes in anyway, the alcohol thrumming through her veins, emboldening her. Or maybe it's just her, finding the confidence and worth she lost in the tangle of years since Georgy and the Revolution. "You invite me to be your date, then miss your own party."

Will glances up from his desk, a tumble of papers and pamphlets with a glass of clear liquid at his side. "Didn't you tell me a date would be improper?"

"Improper, not impossible."

He leans back, running a hand along his scruffy chin as he considers her. *What would it be like to kiss him?* "All right. If you were my date, what would we do?" Desire laces his words, deepening his voice.

Irina knows it well. Many men have desired her, and she enjoyed the attention. Georgy's image from the past cuts in, disapproving, his green gaze possessive. She glides deeper into the office as if to spite his memory. She pauses with curiosity by the photographs tacked onto the back wall. "We would have champagne together," she says distractedly, "then we would dance."

"Apparently, I am missing one hell of a party." Will smirks.

Irina bites back a smile and peers at the pictures, of New York City's towering skyscrapers, the White House, unfamiliar places she assumes are America—a sprawling canyon carved of burnt-orange rock, a thick forest of reddish trees, endless mountains and plains. Seeming, to her, unexplored in the way of all America.

"Have you been to any of those?" Will asks, watching her.

Irina shakes her head. "Only to Paris, once with my mother and once with my father." One filled with garments and grand ballrooms, the other with the streets of Paris, strolling along the Seine, sampling coffees and pastries. Irina's heart beats with the intense desire to see it all again, to experience it anew. The places in Will's photographs, too. The exotic images are an enticing contrast to Moscow's well-worn scenes. "Did you take all these photographs?"

"Yes. I . . . like to travel. See things. I can never quite sit still."

What are these places like? What is America like? And New York—are the skyscrapers as tall as they look? "So you traveled to our sad little corner of the world?"

"It is the unknown frontier, after all. And I don't find you sad."

Irina turns to face him. "How do you find me—us?"

"Alive—mesmerizing—unlike anything I've ever seen," Will whispers. After a pause, he goes on in his normal voice. "I don't think I've ever met anyone as brave as you. And with everything you've been through, you are still kind, and hopeful, and have a wonderful spirit. I don't think I would be, if I were in your shoes."

She turns back to the photographs, this time not helping the smile. The air between them crackles. It isn't only the heat, settling onto her skin like costly velvet. But the places he holds within him, ready to be imparted and imagined. She can ask so many questions. She starts with the obvious. "Where in America are you from?"

Will walks over and points to a photograph of a park and brick buildings divided by a broad street lined with horse-drawn carriages. "New York City, though as you know, I worked in Boston for some years before the ARA."

"Do you miss America?"

"Home is where the heart is, isn't that what they say?" The grin turns into a soft smile. "Yes, I miss it. Particularly New York, my Aunt Mildred most of all. She raised me and so is like a mother to me."

"As our aunt is to us. And your . . . ?"

"My parents died when I was a boy. Automobile accident. Traveled all over the world only to die so senselessly." Will gives a shake of his head, this time smiling easily even as Irina tries to apologize. Instead, he tells her about the "brownstone" where he grew up, the neighborhood around it a quiet, green slice of the bustling city; how he left it for Harvard, then his reporter job; how he still dutifully visits Aunt Mildred, who has a penchant for paintings and peppermint cookies—"Why, the woman exudes peppermint!"

Irina laughs. "She would get on famously with Lili."

"What about your family? You are close with your aunt and sister?"

Irina thought she was close to her aunt; now she isn't so sure. "Erm, yes. My aunt has cared for us since our parents died. And my sister and I have grown closer than ever, especially since working here." Irina smiles, then tells Will about her and Lili's walks to the ARA, filled with talk and laughter; satisfying meals with their "cousins" that are more than just tea, cabbage soup, and moldy black bread; and Grand-mère's stories about how much the hearty Bolos like to eat. Irina skims over the investigations, Auntie's arrest, the specters, her dead family, pressing it all down. With Will, she doesn't wish to remember the darkness. And what would he say if he knew the half of it?

"Have you been to America?" Will thankfully asks, and Irina suppresses her guilt for not telling him the rest.

"I wanted to visit once," she says thoughtfully. "A friend lives in Washington, D.C." Suddenly, she misses Julia more than she has in years, no longer blaming her for leaving. Their choices then spelled either life or death. Now Irina would give anything to see her friend again.

"Has this lot already scared you from visiting?" jokes Will.

"I haven't thought about travel in a long time, even if we could." But she is thinking about it now, seeing Washington, Julia. Will's home. Imagining holding Seryozha and Natasha in her arms, the famous New York City skyline opening before them as in a dream . . . Irina blinks, surprised, having never pictured herself or the children anywhere but in Russia. Yet the image is filled with such ease and freedom, such abandon, that for a moment, Irina aches for it as if it were real. A snapshot of some parallel present, or a hazy future. A place where they, as well as Lili and Auntie, are happy. A place they are safe.

"It doesn't sound like you've thought much about yourself at all," Will says quietly. "Don't get me wrong. I respect the hell out of you for that. But you worry about everybody except yourself. Am I right?"

"That is presumptuous." Irina doesn't wish to admit that he is right. And anyway, how does he know? "Am I not thinking of myself now, being here with you?"

"You tell me." Will holds out his glass, and Irina takes it, their fingers brushing, maybe on purpose.

The alcohol is a sharp, bitter punch on her tongue. She pulls a face. Places the glass on a cabinet.

"You don't fancy gin?" He grins. "I like it. It's pure. No pretense."

Her belly burns, and not only with the alcohol. His mouth is close. The heat unspools lower, between her legs. Irina hasn't desired a man since Georgy. She doesn't remember their first kiss. All she remembers is that sofa, his cigarette-stale breath against her cheek, his bones pressing into her as he . . . At this image, Irina hesitates. She might know about desire, but all she knows about intimacy is Georgy, that night. What if—*I know nothing? What if this is the same?* But no. It isn't, and Will isn't, either. Besides, she is aching to feel *something, anything* but what happened on that night. To replace it, to move on from it— is that the same? She wants to find out.

Irina forces her dead fiancé from her mind. Wraps her arms around Will's neck and crushes her lips to his. His hands find her back. They are large and warm and firm as he pulls her up to his body. She feels him, all of him, his hardness against her thigh. His tongue slips into her mouth and tangles with hers. Will tastes of berries, gin, pure desire. Nothing like Georgy, nothing like that night.

Irina's back is now against the wall, the pressure of their mouths reverberating through their pressing, pushing bodies. Will's other hand plunges into her blouse. His fingertips skim the tops of her breasts before reaching in to cup one breast. A moan escapes her. The spot between her legs zings with heat, and she wants him inside her.

Then her son crashes into her mind, closely followed by Georgy, and Irina breaks away. She is engaging in intimacies with a man in a place of work, *their* place of work. It isn't only the risk of getting caught. Will is more senior than her, her superior for all intents and purposes. If it should sour between them, Irina would be the one forced out. And he could hold that over her. He holds all the power, she none. No, she is as weak as she was with Georgy. The heat curdles, going horribly flat, until all Irina feels is the leftover burn of his scruff on her cheek.

"I must go," she says between breaths. "Forgive me." Shame burns into her now—at her desire, the office and all it means pressing in.

"Irene," Will groans into her neck, using Paulina's name for her.

Irina forces out a laugh, is halfway across the office, when his hand tugs her back. "You think I'll let you walk home alone this late?" Will is smiling, wide and carefree, like himself. Not perturbed in the least at being rebuffed, as Georgy most surely would have been.

The self-recriminations ease a little. She doesn't think Will would assert his power over her like Georgy did. In all his actions, Will has treated her with courtesy, respect, and deference. Irina permits a smile, not wishing to walk home alone, either, not after those footsteps, the thought of Felix. Though she will need to part with Will a few streets from the house, given the Soviet men inside. "Provided you know *that* won't happen again."

"At least, not tonight." Will grins, grabbing his coat from the back of his chair.

"Presumptuous." Irina lifts her chin prudishly, as if she weren't kissing him mere moments ago.

"Yet true."

"Perhaps," she allows. Irina can admit that she fancies Will. Besides his easy, free nature, he is sharp and quick on his feet, handsome in his rough American way. She likes to be around him, to listen to his stories. But she isn't sure this can override her practicality or her responsibilities. Will would necessarily take time away from her family, Seryozha. But he is right: she has denied herself for far too long. The least Irina can do is let the nice American man walk her home; she will see about the rest later. Georgy's face is dredged out of the depths whenever she draws close to Will. What she and Georgy did, what he did to her, is trapping her in the past with him. As in life, Georgy keeps asserting his presence, his entitlement, as if she belongs to him even now.

Irina has a feeling she will need to confront his ghost—and soon.

18

Graveyards Are for Secrets

LILI TUMBLES OUT of the ARA mansion into the blisteringly cold night, already smelling of winter, of sad things and nagging memories. She raises her collar against the vengeful frost. Her surroundings are shifting and spinning from the champagne. A kaleidoscope of black sky and stars, very cold and far away.

She feels Uncle Pasha's ring on its ribbon against her chest, and it sobers her. Irina left the party earlier with Will in tow like a great big hound, the unfortunate lovestruck fool. Lili promised her sister she would return to the house as soon as possible, so they can take advantage of Natasha's and Seryozha's absence to look at their uncle's scroll. Dread blooms in Lili's chest at the thought of the ghosts waiting for her, or the damn Bolos.

She starts to walk toward the house slowly, unexpectedly relishing the silence. The bracing air on her skin, too. It is cleansing after the party.

"Wait!" Nikolai catches up, falls into step beside her. "May I walk with you?" His breaths stream white and smoky into the air.

"I would rather you didn't."

"Come, Lil. We are walking in the same direction. Please?"

"Fine," she grumbles, resolving to ignore him the entire time.

It is late and the city is supposed to be empty. Yet the streets are filled with the homeless, wrapped in ragged old military coats and threadbare blankets, or nothing at all. Several unmoving bodies lie at the foot of the cratered, peeling buildings; alive or dead, it is impossible to tell. Lili finds she is shaking. Nikolai, noticing, unbuttons his coat and drapes it over her own. She tries to protest, but her very bones are stiff, and she gives up, pulling on the coat. The wool smells of him, of cheap soap and cigarettes. It brings some heat back into her body.

"I am sorry . . . for what I said the other day," he says finally. "I . . . forget you are"—he reddens slightly—"a woman now. You can take care of yourself."

Lili hasn't forgiven him yet, but her anger cools. "Thank you."

"Say, do you remember that old graveyard? Your dare?"

She pictures those forbidding gates and the graves beyond, an odd contrast to the warmth and sun; Petersburg's canals, monuments, pastel-colored buildings . . . "Maybe."

"We were reading Gogol, 'A Terrible Vengeance,' about the old sorcerer out for revenge and blood. I found your courage, your daring . . . well, striking. You looked me straight in the eye, without flinching, and said, 'Let's see if the dead will rise and the sorcerer show up.' I was envious. Did I ever tell you I was scared out of my wits?"

"You didn't." Despite herself, Lili laughs.

Nikolai glances away wistfully. "He never did show up. It was just sad and lovely, there in that green, cool oasis. And the dead went on slumbering, unbothered by the traffic and noise of the streets. Though I was frightened, I wanted to stay there forever."

"And now the dead don't slumber."

"Did you see Pavel Sergeyevich again?" Nikolai's gaze is dark.

Despite the two coats, Lili shivers. "Yes, after we motored over to the house last night." She hesitates, then tells Nicky about it. She tugs out the gold ring and shows it to him. "We hope the scroll will have answers."

"And if it doesn't?"

Lili hasn't thought that far ahead, though she should. "We'll search his rooms again, look through the books in the study there. Those in the library as well, two floors of them to be exact." She shakes her head. "Maybe our former servants will know more. Or somebody else . . ." That man from the bazaar flashes into her mind. Familiar, with the kind of rings that led her to the key. She wonders if it really does lead to a diary.

"I would say you should talk to my mother, but she refuses to speak of the past."

Lili nods. It would have been futile either way. Maman rarely confided in Madame Naroshina, seeing her as social competition. And anyway, Lili's family lost touch with the Naroshins shortly before the Revolution.

Suddenly, Lili notices Nikolai is no longer beside her; he is now leaning against a rust-flecked gate.

The dull gold steeple of an abandoned church rises up behind the gate. So does what looks like an old, forgotten graveyard. Ancient tombstones float out of a mist that is rolling in, clinging, blurring Lili's vision. As if she is submerged underwater and beholding the ruins of a drowned, haunted city. Trees sprout ugly roots reminiscent of three-headed dragons, serpentine monsters, one-eyed giants from her and Nicky's tales.

Nikolai pushes open the gate. It creaks on its hinges; dead maple leaves crunch beneath his boots. "I dare you to go in," he says, with a barely contained smile.

Lili casts a quick glance at the street, then at his face, damnably hard to resist.

And without a word, she takes off at a sprint, through the gate and down the gravel path between tombstones. His coat flaps behind her, then tumbles down. She doesn't care. She is thirteen again, running through that old Petersburg graveyard. Lili hears Nikolai's boots pounding the gravel behind her. His breathing, almost at her back; the breathless laugh, near her ear. She imagines his smile, the wide one with teeth she hasn't seen since before.

A tug on her coat, and she is skittering back and into his arms. There is a second of frozen surprise. Then his arms come around her. They are wide and spacious, filled with a depth, a bottomlessness, like the sea when it is warm and inviting.

"Let go of me," Lili howls, laughing. But she doesn't fight him, lets him hold her.

A massive aspen tree spreads its branches above them. It overlooks the graveyard and the town's buildings beyond. The leaves are papery, losing their color. They rustle, thin and veiny, as if the tree is alive with the roaches that crawl out late at night in Moscow House.

Nikolai drops his arms. His breath is in her ear as he recites, "'The whole Dnieper silvered like a wolf's fur in the night . . .'"

Even Lili remembers this part of Gogol's tale. "'A cemetery could be seen,'" she continues, "'. . . no green grass, only the moon.'"

"Except there is no moon tonight, and the stars are as cold and distant as a proud maiden," Nikolai finishes with something of his own. Lili turns to face him, his eyes becoming a lighter golden brown and thoughtful. "I like it here," he says quietly. "It is as it should be. The dead in eternal rest. It makes me peaceful. Do you know, I don't feel haunted here, not even a little?"

Lili has the intense urge to sketch Nicky the way he appears in this moment. She reaches into her coat for her sketch pad and pencil, and draws the outlines of his face—his eyes and nose, his cheekbones, his mouth.

Nikolai stops her hand as her pencil hovers over his sketched mouth.

When she raises her eyes, she finds his gaze intent on her. His hands wrap around hers, filling her with something warm and liquid. Lili hardly feels the cold anymore. She is only vaguely aware of her breathing, the smell of rot and decay on the air.

Nikolai pulls the sketch pad and pencil out of her hands, placing them carefully on the ground. He pauses for a split second. Then he reaches for her waist and lowers his head to rest on her chest. As if to feel the hard, hot pounding of her heart. His hands tighten on her. Bring her body closer, so his chest presses right up against her rib cage.

"I thought you were my friend, Nicky." Lili's smile is sly. "Only my friend."

"I am your friend," he whispers, even as he brings his mouth against her lips.

"Is that all?"

"No." Nikolai's breaths are rapid puffs on her skin. "I was jealous" tumbles out. "I . . . thought you wanted somebody else, not me."

The gravestones peer out from behind him, like watchful eyes. And behind them, the rusty dome of the church with its steeple. A part of Lili, the part that was told to believe in God, senses the wrongness of what they might do. She's never done it, not even close, but knows on some instinctual level what *it* is. Not only an act reserved for the marriage bed, but one that would disturb the peace of a place that is supposed to be holy. But after the horrors she has seen, God is only wishful thinking, the dead just bones and dust.

And the liquid warmth, the coursing blood in her veins, the gravity of the physical pull to another person—she hasn't felt any of it before, this want, this unbearable thirst for somebody else.

Lili is not sure who kisses whom. All she knows is Nikolai's mouth is on hers.

It isn't their first, barely there, chaste kiss. It is hot and *hungry*. They part, panting. Without breaking her gaze, Nikolai unbuttons her coat. Slow, deliberate, button by button. He kisses her again, all heat and pressure and smokiness. Then he slips his cold hands inside her coat and places them on her blouse, just above her waist. Lili is aching for him to touch her, to *really* do it. To feel the imprint of his fingers on her bare skin.

She grabs his hand and clumsily pulls it under and up her blouse. Nikolai stills. But then his fingers brush against her skin. They are hot and feverish, yet reserved, hesitant. Almost stilted in their movement. After more kissing and touching, Lili cannot take it. Despite the anger, the feeling that she has only now gotten her friend back, she wants this. It is as complicated and as simple as that. She reaches for the buckle of his belt.

Nikolai seizes her hand. "No, Lil—"

"I want to," she blurts out. "I want you, in . . . that way." She shakes her head, confused. "In the only way."

A flicker of a sad, wistful smile. "Do you even know what that means?"

"Do *you*?"

His smile turns lofty; he flicks his gaze down. As if she were that little girl again.

Now Lili is angry. *Really* angry. She grabs his face with both hands, still a little clumsy but showing definite improvement, and kisses him so hard his breath hitches. That's when he gives in. Unbuckling his belt, Nikolai lowers his trousers. One swift, practiced movement, and he tugs up her skirt. It bunches at Lili's waist, exposing her legs to the cold. She cannot help but shiver. But then Nikolai is back to kissing her. His hand slides down her stomach, sure now, leaving patches of heat in its wake, and edges into her underwear. As his fingers sink inside her, Lili draws in a sharp breath—at the scalding heat, the mind-numbing intensity of it. Nikolai smiles against her lips, as if hearing the thought, before pushing aside her underwear and briskly lifting her on top of him.

The tree is rough and hard at her back. So is he, beneath her.

One agonizing push—a fissure of pain, followed by the bloom of shocking warmth. Then he is moving inside her, and all she can do is pant and moan and whisper his name over and over. Not Nikolai, but Nicky. Nicky. Lili closes her eyes as he lowers his mouth onto hers. And she lets go of her thoughts, right there in the mist and cold, among the dead, slumbering in a city that no longer sleeps.

19

The Mystery of the Missing Story

LILI BARRELS INTO Moscow House, tearing open her coat breathlessly.

It is all crashing back—the graveyard, Nicky, what she did. And after—her trembling hands pushing down her skirt, her face hot and flushed, avoiding Nikolai's gaze as he fumbled with the buckle of his belt. Then her darting around him and running as fast as her legs could carry her. Lili's cheeks heat with humiliation at her streaking through that graveyard—he is right, she *really* is a child—refusing to face the man she did *it* with, *Nicky*, her childhood friend, dead to her until a few weeks ago.

"Lili!" he had shouted. "Lili! Come back!" *Come back. Comeback.*

She had only sprinted faster, her surroundings a misty blur of tombstones and bare branches and black earth, through the gate, all the way to Moscow House.

As she is about to relive the shame all over again, Lili realizes she is in the entrance hall, and that it is after midnight. Her body tenses just as a strange, dank cold seizes her limbs.

She first becomes aware of the candles and lamps, all lighted, all glimmering like feverish eyes. Then the tomb-like silence. Beneath it, she hears something else, faint snatches of whispered words. And she inhales a whiff of strong black tea. Sees a flash of silver, then more defined, a tray—Dmitri's. Lili opens her mouth to scream, even if it awakens the Bolos, when Cleo shoots down the grand staircase with a shriek. She beats her wings in Lili's face insistently. Hopefully, this means Irina is waiting for her upstairs instead of some kind of trouble.

Lili ignores the darkened nook and bolts up the stairs after Cleo.

Candlelight ripples as she moves, and shadowy figures appear on the walls. They shift and sway, independent of the light now, and she can make out shapes of gowns and hats and feathers and canes. Like her grandparents' guests would have had at the balls of old. Her eyes are wide, panicked, as Lili leaps onto the third landing. The whispering ceases abruptly, as do the figures. A faint singing threads through the air in their place, a lullaby, interspersed with coughing and another sound, a weeping. Long and mournful.

Lili redoubles her pace, not wishing to hear Aunt Luba, Grand-père, or whatever else lives here now.

She bursts into a darkened attic, searching for her family in their cots. She remembers Natasha and Seryozha are away. Hears Grand-mère mutter something in French in her sleep.

In their room, Irina hastens toward Lili as soon as she catches sight of her. "There you are! Where were you?"

The intense flush is back, suffusing the skin on Lili's face and neck with an obscene heat. Her body is sore, especially the lower parts, which ache dully. Or maybe it is the wanting that flares up. Absurdly, she thinks, *He's done that before.* Jealousy, pure and so green she feels nauseous, burns into her at the phantom girls who have doubtless preceded her. She mutters something incoherent, a hot, steaming cup of coffee thrust into her hands before she knows it. "What time is it?" She finds her voice. Takes a sip and tastes the burnt flavor, the cream.

"Nearly three! I was worried about you, Lil. I hope Nikolai gave you a ride."

"That he did." Lili is very aware of her twisted underwear, his wetness still clinging to the worn fabric, and almost cackles maniacally. Instead, she drops onto Irina's cot in her coat and gathers Cleo into the crook of her elbow. The parakeet snuggles in close, all soft feathers and warmth. "Where is the box?" Lili asks, nuzzling Cleo.

Irina grabs Auntie's rosewood box from the table before settling down on the cot beside them. "I spoke with Kirill at the party," she begins, opening the box and taking out the lump of wax. Then she tells Lili the most outlandish, bizarre story about Auntie yet, even succeeding at finally pushing Nicky from her mind.

When her sister is finished, the first reaction to come out is a joke. "Irishka the Reasonable, turning Auntie into some old superstitious crone, a veritable Baba Yaga! Have you found your sense of humor?"

"Amulets, clumps of dried wax, *hog's blood*—you, with your imagination, don't think it strange?"

"This is Bible-toting, proper lady of the House of Sherbatsky *Auntie* we are talking about. So, Auntie may have gone a little mad with Andrei at the front. She may even have tried to protect him with some old superstitions. What does all this have to do with that night, or Uncle Pasha's story? Shouldn't we be looking at that scroll?"

Lili breathes in the stale, sweet scent of vanilla as Irina spreads the sheets of paper out on the coverlet with a lovely roll of her eyes yet with evident resignation. The paper is yellowed, curling at the edges. Lili presses the sheets flat with her trembling hand. Her heart is a thrashing thing with wings, anticipation making her impatient.

20 July 1917. She meets her sister's gaze, heavy with meaning. July Days, when the Bolsheviks had tried and failed to take the capital and the government.

Irina points to the name at the top of the first page. *Dima*. It is the nickname of their butler, Dmitri.

But it is the sight of her uncle's fine, familiar script, the looping scrawl of his letters, that brings tears to Lili's eyes. She listens through this blur as Irina starts to read.

Moscow House

Dear Dima,

I write in secrecy. We have arrived safely in Moscow, but already I have a favor to ask of you.

A loyal lad in our employ has a mother who has recently taken ill in Petrograd. He has managed to secure papers to travel back and forth to see her, agreeing to carry letters for us regarding a matter close to my heart. I have need of a set of twelve chests from my rooms at Peter House.

I am working on my own papers, to collect the chests, as well as to salvage certain valuables and antiques from Peter House of supreme cultural and historical importance to the family and what will be left of Russia once this nightmare is over.

Keep safe, dear Dima, and thank you for your loyalty. We pray Russia shall return to her senses.

Count Pavel Sergeyevich

———

30 July 1917
Peter House

Your Excellency,

I will search for the chests. I can ship them, if necessary. The capital is not safe. There is panic and unrest in the streets after the violence. No government, no police, no rules whatsoever. It is a fallen city, an armed camp at the mercy of a mob out for blood. I am afraid the time for prayers is over. Do not come, dear Count. But if you must, know you will be returning to a very different Petrograd.

Your Faithful Servant
Dima

———

8 August 1917
Moscow House

Dear Dima,

Do not ship the chests. I am still hoping to collect them myself. Our dear poet Anna Akhmatova wrote that our capital may be "savage," but it is "our home," "our city," and "our unintended monument."

Count Pavel Sergeyevich

———

21 August 1917
Moscow House

Dima,

I have not heard from you regarding the chests. Did you find them? They were under my bed when we left the house last spring and bound in the same red leather as the covers inside. These personal papers are dangerous to us in the times we live in. Please respond and set my heart at ease.

Count Pavel Sergeyevich

5 September 1917
Peter House

Your Excellency,

My dearest hope is that you are all keeping well in Moscow.
 I am delighted to relay that the lost chests have been found. A maid had hidden the family's more personal items in the servants' rooms.
 I await your instructions.

Your Faithful Servant
Dima

---

15 September 1917
Moscow House

Dima,

I have finally secured travel papers to Petrograd. I am booked on the next train. I have also managed to secure return papers for you, dear friend. The family cannot wait to see you. Until then, Dima, and watch over Peter House like a hen watching her young. Our possessions are all we have left now.

Count Pavel Sergeyevich

Lili sits back, dazed. "Uncle Pasha traveled to Petrograd in September 1917. I remember because I wanted to go with him." To spend time with her uncle away from the family's constant presence, and to see if she could find out anything about Nicky . . .

Irina nods. "Yes, I remember. It was right before the Bolshevik takeover."

"Right. And he returned with trunks and *chests* filled with Sherbatsky possessions, along with Dmitri." But without word of Nicky. "The chests with Uncle Pasha's personal papers bound in red leather, the story, side by side with the key—"

"Which should lead to his diaries . . ." Irina gives an elegant shake of her head. "It would explain Pasha's eagerness to find them. But where are they?"

Not in his rooms. The image of their uncle rushes in then, as he reclined in that armchair beneath the glass dome on the second floor of the library. Lili would often find him there, shrouded in the sick greenish light from the creeping weeds, with a book open in his lap, surrounded by the paintings, porcelains, and bronzes he and Grand-père had managed to salvage across the Sherbatsky estates.

His favorite place, among his art and his books. His *little corner of peace*.

"The library—" Lili, eloquent as ever, gasps out.

But Irina understands her. "Very well," she says. "But we should wait until morning."

Lili's heart sinks a little at that. She doesn't think she will be able to sleep. Not until they find the chests. But she nods her agreement, her sister reasonable as ever. "Until the damn roosters crow," she says, with a ghost of a smile.

20

The Ghost of Irina's Past

IRINA THINKS SHE hears a scream, the pounding of footsteps, a flurry of frenzied words. She tries to float up and out of sleep, but it is as though her legs are caught in seaweed.

In sleep, Irina is back in her nightmare—in that cold, dark stair behind the secret door. She hears shouts, the mob's hunger, their rage. Her breaths spill out in spurts. The child in her belly kicks, feeling her unease like a second heartbeat. She sees nothing, only the whites of her servant girl's wide eyes. Something hard bangs against their door. *You shall live, you shall live, you shall live*, Irina whispers to the child inside her in a sick refrain.

Finally, she hurtles out of the deep—to the same penetrating blackness. Her hand instinctively slides down to her stomach. Flat, not pregnant. Present, not past. In Moscow, not where Auntie sent her on the eve of the February Revolution.

You shall leave town for the countryside, where you shall have your child. Auntie's voice drifts in from the past.

What about the protests? The resentment of those ragged, hungry women waiting in the breadlines, whispering of official corruption and mismanagement, of revolts, of revolution . . .

If anyone discovers this—Auntie gave her a significant look—*they will not care that he is your intended. Your marriage and our name will be ruined.* A pause. *I shall speak to Pavel. I trust him as no one else. And Luba is ill. She may have the child, but they may not live. Even if they do, she could have twins.*

Twins? Irina was quite at sea in her humiliation.

Auntie whirled on her heel. *Pavel and Luba will adopt your child. It is the only way for you to save face—and keep it in the family.*

And I can take it when—

When you marry the prince? Auntie's features softened, a strange pitying look slipping into the masklike sternness. *I am afraid not.* She eyed her, not unkindly. *I know how you feel.*

How can you? Irina looked up at her aunt, the prickling anger stirring up her nausea. She put a hand to her belly, hard and strange, already protruding, already a baby. *Her* baby. Not Georgy's, not the family's. A piece of her, a life, a son or daughter. The idea of giving him or her up sent a bolt of wild panic racing through Irina. But the consequences—her engagement severed, social ostracism, the family turning away from her . . .

I must also hide the truth. Auntie interrupted her swirling, agitated thoughts. *And with it, myself. A woman is bound in secrets.* She touched Irina's chin before giving one of her stern nods, the one that said, *You understand, yes?*

This was precisely why Irina had turned to Auntie. Like Irina, she is pragmatic, a problem solver solely intent on the problem without judgment. And Irina couldn't bear disappointing Maman, who was told she was sent to another hospital as a nurse, as many were during the war. It was Auntie who kept Irina's secret. Auntie who helped her.

The mob stormed the estate one night in March, looting and destroying all in their wake. By some miracle, they didn't set fire to the place, and Irina and her servant girl emerged from hiding unscathed after the men had abandoned the house. Auntie sent a doctor to Irina when her time came in May, followed by Dmitri, to take her back to the family when she was well enough to travel. By then, revolution had torn their country apart, Pasha's wife and unborn child were dead, and Irina had relinquished Seryozha to her uncle dutifully, fearing the consequences of keeping him more than losing him. Though her very soul screamed for her son, and guilt threatened to cleave her in two.

Irina tosses aside the coverlet and swings her legs over the edge of the cot, taking desperate swallows of the dusty air. Her nightgown sticks to her damp, clammy skin.

She cannot ignore the past like Lili, but she tries very hard not to think about this particular slice of time, dark and nightmarish as it was. Irina sees it only in her dreams. Normally, she can chase the images away when she wakes. But this night, they all come flooding back.

The memories, the searing pain, the guilt. Though her relationship with Seryozha is better than ever, though she has found work and provided for him, though she is his mother in all but name, Irina feels a painful stab in her heart. Not only for giving him up all those years ago, but for not having told him the truth. For allowing Auntie to convince her to keep it in the past. Now that the past is resurfacing, perhaps so should her secret, especially since the Soviet men have learned it and threatened her with it. Either way, Irina must speak to Comrade Suzhensky about her aunt's release. She owes it to Auntie. Right now, though, she needs her strong, indomitable little sister. She needs Lili.

Irina whispers her name—but there is no answer.

With unease tightening her chest, she crosses the room to Lili's cot behind the screen.

In the darkness, Irina makes out white sheets, twisted and thrown aside. Instead of her sister, Xenia's old doll stares up at her with a narrow, melted gaze. Irina's entire body seems to drain of blood. She feels faint, her head dizzy, too light. For on the doll's chipped cheek rests a black cockroach. Irina springs away, skittering backward and nearly falling into the adjoining room. The door isn't closed. It is thrown wide open.

"Grand-mère?" But her grandmother's cot is empty. Panic layers onto the horror.

Irina flings her coat over her nightgown and hastens out of the attic.

On the landing below, she blinks back the light, jarring after the dark. The previously unused sconces and lamps flicker in the hallway. She stops for a second, blinking at them hard, before her ears pick up on a sound. It is a weeping, a lamenting interspersed with wails, sometimes moans. She hears Grand-père's ghostly cough erupt, a door being heaved open with a grunt. Then a cane strikes the parquet, even through the carpet and the weeping.

Irina doesn't wait to see her dead grandfather. She dashes down the grand staircase, several steps at a time. She senses the telltale prickle of being watched on her flesh. As she makes her way downstairs, the prickle intensifies until it is as painful as stabbing thorns. It is the feeling of many eyes cutting to her. Irina reaches the candlelit entrance hall and hears an entire crowd of loud voices abuzz with excited chatter and laughter.

She is expecting to see a room full of people. Instead, they are shadowy pale figures in evening attire, like her dead family in that dining room. Some are clustered near the banister, gesturing and smoking. Others flit into the hall from the foyer in a rush of biting yet stagnant cold air. Irina backs away, not believing her eyes, then believing, caught in the vicious loop. The specters' faces are hazy gray yet alive with an emotion that feels frozen, almost artificial with the burning inhuman light in their dead, unblinking eyes.

Irina thinks a few voices utter her name and a few faces turn toward her.

"Lili! Grand-mère!" she calls out, if only to hear her own voice over the fear. She veers left into the abandoned East Wing. If her sister and grandmother came downstairs, they will be in one of these rooms. A slight twinge of unease twists Irina's stomach. What if she imagined their cots empty?

In the East Wing rooms, the specters lean against lacquered screens, hover by windows, sprawl on sofas and settees, absorbed in their whispering and conversing. A raised hand here, a shrug of a shoulder there; a flash of filmy, oscillating white, there and gone. In the tangle of shadowed figures, Irina glimpses the curve of Maman's neck, the edge of Papa's face, their bodies intertwined on a love seat as she had seen them when they were truly alive.

The uncovered furniture is dusted and gleaming. Irina catches a long-vanished puff of cigarette smoke, a trace of perfume. But beneath it all, that smell of rot and decomposition, of death. She notices something stirring in the corners of the rooms where the candlelight doesn't reach—a pair of spiders, crawling over an old chair with a broken leg; several prickly centipedes, slithering out of a crack in the wall; a large cockroach, scuttling across the thick rug. She recalls the black roach on Xenia's doll. . . . What is happening?

The insects are out in full force, and the specters are stronger, more substantive, more *alive* than ever.

A scream is tearing through her throat. It dies there. Irina feels a pull on her hair, hard and yanking, as if in warning. It forces her to come to a stop—in front of the figure of a man.

At first, Irina thinks it is one of the Soviet men. She is about to rush at him, to ask for his help, even if he thinks her a madwoman. But something about the figure makes her stop. It is the way he stands, almost misaligned, too stiff, the arms dangling at his sides as if he has forgotten how to use them. She swallows her words in horror.

It is another specter, more corporeal than the others. Those have dimmed like the candlelight.

Her eyes find the spectral man's chest—the ghost of a black stain on his ragged Preobrazhensky Regiment officers' uniform, likely where a bullet ripped through; the empty spaces where the epaulettes were. His face is deathly white, a maggot resting on one cheek, his eyes dark instead of green. The closely cropped hair is matted with the same dark old blood, likely from a blow to the head before being shot in the heart by the Reds.

Prince Georgy smiles, an odd, lifeless stretching of the mouth. *Hello, Irina.*

At his echo of a voice, she is chilled to the bone, and her heart shrivels from revulsion. "You are dead. You are dead" comes out of her trembling lips like a refrain.

Have I changed so much? He cocks his head. *You certainly have.*

The last time they saw each other, she was in a perfumed gown of chiffon and lace. Overheated, late to meet her family at the Mariinsky Theatre despite the unrest brewing in the streets of Petrograd. Georgy walked in, unexpectedly home from the front.

Look where we are.

Irina can barely move her head. But she knows they are surrounded by the furniture transferred from that room at Peter House, the Little Reception, where . . .

That vacant, ghastly smile again. *You remember.*

"Go away," she whispers to the specter. But Irina knows why he is here. She called him to life, by remembering, by looking back at their past, and for the first time, by wishing to move on from it—with Will. She holds on to the image of that carefree face, alive like Georgy's is dead. "You are dead. I don't belong to you."

Suddenly, Georgy is in her face. His hands land on her shoulders in a shock of dark shadow and intense cold.

And she is remembering the two of them together on that sofa . . .

He slides an arm around her waist, even as she blushes, says, Georgy, please.

Irina, please, *he echoes, pressing her close and finding her mouth.*

The taste of him, the cigarette he must have had earlier, repulses her. Yet she doesn't pull away. It is more than just the few snatches of kissing she is used to. It is rubbery, wet. His body angles toward her, and she senses its curves and gives, bird light on top of her. A part of her wishes to make him feel better. Another part is afraid to stop. He might not marry her, then. But a secret part of her knows she will never see him again. So she lets him.

Why doesn't Irina remember it? Only the bits and pieces.

The hard cushions against her back. The fumbling, those clammy fingers.

The clumsy rip of her gown. A stab of pain as he pushes inside, that bewildering feeling. Thrusts, groans. Fresh waves of pain reverberating, then numbing. Her eyes closing—until he rolls off her, panting and sweating, a sick man about to die. And it is over.

It is *over*, Irina tells herself. That was the last time she saw or heard from Georgy until the tidings of his death, on some battlefield where the Bolsheviks slaughtered the White army. By then, she had missed her monthly course and knew she was pregnant. Now, as Irina stares into Georgy's ghostly face, she wonders if it is truly over, if he is really gone. Will seems very far away. Maybe she made him up.

Georgy's cold, lifeless arms clasp her to a body more than air, with force in it, and strength. Though no breath or heartbeat. Irina realizes that he is shaking her, hard, and that she is trapped in the skeletal grip not of Georgy, her fiancé, but of a ghostly corpse.

Bang! Bang! *Bangbangbang*.

Irina blinks at the smell of gunpowder, the echo of gunshots in her ears. She draws in a sharp breath. Chokes a little on the smoke. Another pair of arms comes around her. Living, warm, with a real heart beating against her chest. Irina breathes in her sister's scent of powder and citrus. She grasps Lili to her tightly, burying her nails in the fabric of her sister's nightgown and her face in the flesh of her neck as she sobs.

"Enough," a cold voice says.

That's when Irina realizes they aren't alone. She steps away from Lili, wiping at her flushed, tear-stained face, to see Felix—and Grand-mère in her nightgown. She stands unsteadily, staring past them. Her face is ghastly, a waxy, yellowish color. Like a dying bruise.

"Fucking nechistaya sila," Felix mutters, holstering his revolver. His hand shakes.

He must have shot into the air, frightening the spirits. There is no trace of the shadowy figures, or of Georgy. Irina has never been happier to see the hated man.

"What *the fuck* is going on here?" he demands, and Irina is no longer so happy.

"We don't *know*," Lili forces out through her teeth.

"Why were you out of bed?" Irina asks her, ignoring Felix.

Lili glances at their impassive grandmother. "Babushka screamed, waking me. I ran over, but she was gone. So I went after her. I think she was, is, sleepwalking."

"Didn't we agree not to walk the house after midnight, no matter what?"

"What were *you* doing, then? Having a rendezvous with your dead fiancé?"

Irina takes in an irritated breath. This is not the time. But the scream and footsteps from her dream make sense now. She opens her mouth to berate her sister some more.

"Oh, chyort vozmi, women, enough! Now, *how* did you do that? And why is the old dump suddenly so clean? A little upkeep, hm?" Felix barks out a laugh. "Well, be my guest with the cleaning. But stop taking down our flag and stop with the filthy illusions you keep—"

"If it is an illusion, why waste your precious bullets on it?" Irina's hands find her waist.

"I've had enough of your bourgeois superstitions. It is all nonsense. Nonsense, you hear? I am warning you, *desist*. Or you will end up in Butyrka with your mad aunt."

Irina's heart skips a beat. "She is in Butyrka?"

"Never mind." Felix realizes his mistake; his face turns stony, betrays nothing. "Take your old hag of a babushka and return to your designated living quarters."

"I felt his cold touch in the night," Grand-mère suddenly whispers, low and scratchy, eyes burning like two embers. "And his caress of a whisper before he began to weep. At first, I thought it was my Sergei, come to take me away. But no. It was he."

Irina meets Lili's wide-eyed gaze, barely breathing. *Who?*

"He came to me. I saw and heard him. It was a visitation. The end is near."

"Your end will be a lot nearer, hag, if you don't shut your mouth," Felix blusters. But his lips tremble, the scar there flailing. He clutches at his holstered revolver. "Madwomen, lunatics, all of you," he mutters. "Not to mention spies and traitors."

A cold slides over Irina, icy as a bucket of well water. Her grandmother is back to her glassy, impassive, sleepwalking self. But her words still hang in the air, as if suspended.

21

A Family Affair

LILI IS NOT thinking of Grand-mère the next morning, as she probably should. She is thinking of Nicky, as she probably shouldn't.

A part of her itches to talk to him, maybe to repeat what they did. The other part knows he is no longer the boy she knew but someone strange and different. Her feelings for him are no longer just friendly, a desire to be around him, but a desire *for* him, a wanting so deep in her belly that it makes her hot and prickly all over.

Don't be ridiculous, Lil. Even if she wanted to talk to Nicky, she cannot. It is Saturday, and she still doesn't know where he lives. Or if he has a telephone. And anyway, theirs is broken. There she goes again! *Enough. Focus.*

Irina left earlier to collect Natasha and Seryozha from Madame Trobelska's flat. When they return, Irina and Lili plan to look for the chests in the library while the Bolos are out on their errands. Though the cowards have largely kept to their rooms after their second comrade's death and are so spooked they scurry away like cockroaches from light whenever they see Lili or her family.

Lili cannot wait to look for the chests. That, or the horrific doll is driving her from the attic. It is empty, Grand-mère likely in the kitchen, and Lili feels the doll's presence like a cold draft on her skin.

Irina has once more hidden the vile, evil thing in its trunk. But how did it get out? Lili, for one, is convinced Xenia found some way into the attic. Her little sister had a warped sense of humor, believing herself to be the spawn of the flesh-eating Baba Yaga, and she was remarkably determined when she wanted to be.

After a little buckwheat and a cup of fragrant coffee with a splash of cream to fortify herself for the work ahead, Lili makes her way to the library.

The house is quiet and dormant. It mirrors the hovering, slate-gray day outside. The bulbous clouds fly overhead like fat, shapeless monsters about to pounce. Lili tries not to think of Irina trapped in those ghostly arms. Or Georgy's face—the gaping maw, the sightless eyes, the bluish flesh, inhuman in its chilling hollowness.

His arms were so strong, Lil, Irina told her with a shudder. *I felt his nails dig into my skin as he shook me. He, they, could hurt us. If you hadn't showed up with Felix . . .*

Her sister then went on to worry for the children, Grand-mère. All of Russia and the entire world, too. Lili tuned her out. After all, they cannot move out. Even with their ARA wages, there is a severe housing crisis in Moscow, the city hit with a tremendous shortage of affordable and habitable accommodations. Communal housing would be their best option. But they would never abandon their ancestral home, Uncle Pasha's priceless possessions. It is simply not done in families such as theirs.

The West Wing is silent, empty of Bolos. The memory of Georgy's face swims up again. Lili never liked the man, thought him a prig worse than Prince Kirill. She pops a chocolate square into her mouth to chase him away. It is bittersweet on her tongue, worth pilfering from the ARA commissary, her love of sweets silencing any timidity.

Lili pushes the library doors open wider, the familiar smells of old paper and leather rushing at her. Cleo tumbles out with a trill, having flown on ahead. The essence of Uncle Pasha is all over the library. Sitting there by the dimmed fireplace with a book in his lap. Ambling between those ebony bookcases with their dusty, muted tomes . . .

Recalling the two spooked Bolsheviks and their talk of ghostly soldiers, Lili hastens on. She *really* doesn't want to think about Georgy again, or Andrei. She climbs the spindly wrought-iron staircase curling to the second landing, the stairs shaking with her steps. Lili recalls Uncle Pasha dragging the salvaged Sherbatsky possessions he had brought with him from Peter House there. She pauses under the glass dome and tilts her head up.

The glass is mottled, grown over with weeds that have lost their color yet still twist across it like snakes. The daylight here is steeped in a murky greenish light, as if she is at the very bottom of a teacup, or among the ruins of a shipwreck languishing for centuries in the sea. In the shadows, she imagines the sea monsters floating up from her childhood, wrapped in Uncle Pasha's fairy tales and poetry. The Vodyanoy sea king, the Bolotnitsa swamp spirit, other creatures of Old Russia. But it is day, the horror thankfully in hibernation.

"Cleo?" Lili follows the parakeet's answering squawk past her uncle's green armchair, between rows of more ebony bookshelves. Nervousness edges in as Cleo streaks toward the back of the library. If Lili imagined the twelve chests sitting in plain view for her to find, she would be sorely mistaken. Her uncle wouldn't be that obvious.

Trunks and chests are haphazardly stacked along the back wall, piled high among garishly carved chairs and commodes, bronzed frames glaring empty without their canvases, snow-white marble statutes with their heads severed at the necks. It is worse than if they had eyes, reminding Lili of beautiful corpses drained of blood. She pushes away the gruesome image and begins to lift the lids, expecting to see the red leather chests inside. But the trunks are filled with books and pamphlets, the chests crammed with volumes of Dostoevsky, Tolstoy, Pushkin, even Akhmatova. There is nothing between the yellowing pages but dust and mold reeking of mildew and decay.

Either her uncle never brought the relevant chests back from Petrograd, or whatever was inside them was repackaged, possibly hidden somewhere else in the house or entirely elsewhere. If the diaries exist at all. Blood rushes into Lili's face. A scream is building in her chest. All the frustration, the helplessness, is bubbling up to the surface.

She retraces her steps back to Uncle Pasha's armchair and throws herself into it.

She suddenly misses him with a sharp pain that clutches at her heart. All she wants is his arms around her, those expansive arms in which the world shifted and became right again. When she imagines another set of arms, just as expansive, Lili closes her eyes and wishes she could tell Uncle Pasha about Nicky, too. Instead, she falls into a deep, dreamless sleep.

Lili starts. A noise has woken her—footsteps? She listens with her entire body, tense and waiting. There they are again. Small, clumsy, those of a child. *Xenia?* By the light, she can tell it is much later, but certainly not late enough for the ghosts.

"Lili!" a tiny voice trills up from the library's first floor. Not a ghost but Seryozha. Then the stair is shaking with his little footsteps, and he is leaping into Lili's arms.

She catches him up, cold and smelling of fallen, trampled leaves. He squirms, squealing, but she holds on to his skinny body. There is more flesh to it than before. Lili is desperate to hold someone, even her annoying little cousin. She squints at the clock on the mantel; its feline face reads a quarter past five. "What took you so long?" she asks Irina, who has appeared at the top of the stair with Natasha, both rosy faced and in their coats.

"Seryozha wanted to stop by that park he likes all the way across town, and that's after Madame Trobelska plied us with tea and the foulest black bread I've ever had," replies a breathless Irina.

"I was waiting for you. . . ." Lili shakes her head. Seryozha starts to wrestle in her arms, all cold hands and sharp elbows, before worming his way out of her grasp. "I looked for the chests on my own but have found nothing," she adds, tilting her head back and watching the spotty light trickle through the dome.

"Maybe they aren't here." Irina's hands are on her hips. "The men have returned. We should get back to the attic and have a quick supper. Have you seen Grand-mère?"

But Lili is thinking back to what Uncle Pasha's ghost told her, which, admittedly, is not much. She presses his ring to her chest. "No, they *have* to be here." Which means she is missing something. "Natasha, do you know if your papa kept diaries?"

Natasha runs a hand along her father's armchair. "Not that he mentioned."

"Did he mention any other journals or books?"

"No. Just—a book." She reddens. "One book, really."

"Which one?" Lili asks, curious, her hands itching for it already.

Natasha huffs. Reaches into her book bag and hands Lili a small volume.

It is a book of poetry—Anna Akhmatova's. She was against the Revolution, being a noble herself, and a favorite and friend of Uncle Pasha. A slow smile spreads across Lili's face. "You little minx," she whispers wickedly. "Reading naughty bourgeois material. If the men should find you with this little book, we would all be in *big* trouble."

Natasha isn't smiling. Even the freckles on her nose have paled. "I . . . found it among some things Papa left me. Irina was looking at hers, so I decided—"

"You decided what's the harm?" Lili dangles the book in front of Natasha's face.

"Oh, give it back to her," Irina says half-heartedly, distracted by the squeals and chirps—Seryozha racing between the bookshelves after Cleo.

Lili glances down at the book, really not wanting to give it up. She hears her uncle's voice, the one she has suppressed from those dark days. He recited Akhmatova's words like a mantra as gunfire rattled their windows harder than the pounding rain, the screams from the streets piercing the glass even more than the bullets.

Lili had believed the words of Uncle Pasha's ghost to be a warning, but it was poetry. *Anna Akhmatova's* poetry. Then Lili is furiously flipping through the little book, to the remembered poem. The corner of the first page is creased, earmarked, as if especially for her. She reads through it just as furiously. Her eyes widen as they stab into two of the lines: "A different time is drawing near, / The wind of death already chills the heart."

Not a warning, but a location. Lili remembers the books stacked against the back wall. Specifically Akhmatova's, in the same little volumes. And in them, or under them, the story, the truth. In the library after all, only cleverly hidden by her brilliant uncle.

Life is about beauty, dear Lilichka, he used to say. *It is about poetry.*

Lili rushes to the back wall, ignoring Irina's and Natasha's cries for her to return the damn book. She begins with the trunks she left splayed open. "Look for Akhmatova's volumes," she throws over her shoulder.

"How do you know?" Irina asks from behind her, grabbing hold of Seryozha as he barrels by.

"Papa loved poetry, Akhmatova in particular," Natasha says, striding over to Lili. She begins to swing open the lids of the chests nearby, pulling the books out one by one.

Lili picks up a trunk, her arms straining with the weight of it, before dropping it to the floor. She unclasps the lid with shaking hands, coughing, waving aside the dust and staleness. She glimpses *Anna Akhmatova*, and her heart gives a hot thud. Her sister's and cousin's skirts skim her back as they lean over, pulling the little volumes of poetry out of the trunk, Cleo fluttering excitedly above them.

"Lili!" exclaims Irina, pointing to Lili's hands—and in them, the journal bound in bloodred leather with a delicate gold clasp on the side. In the trunk, there are many more such books. And on each cover, three letters, also in gold: *PSS*. Pavel Sergeyevich Sherbatsky.

"Papa's diaries," Natasha breathes.

Lili's fingers tremble as she fumbles to fit the ring's key into the clasp. The lock clicks, and Uncle Pasha's diary falls open. His words, the story he wanted her to find.

Just then, a scream punctures the air, and everything grows very, very still.

The hair on Lili's arms rises at the unnatural stillness. As if the house has shuddered, then ceased to breathe. She looks at the others with wide eyes, then shoves the diary back into the trunk and rushes toward the stairs.

At first, all she can hear is the sound of her rapid breaths, the whir of Cleo's tiny wings against the heavy air, Irina and her cousins behind her. As they sprint out of the library and through the West Wing, Lili starts to hear brisk footsteps ahead, the murmur of men's voices, a spot of light spilling out from the hall.

A group of Bolsheviks is gathered below the railing to the grand staircase's second landing. A few oil lamps have been lit. Yet the hall is shadowed with misty gray twilight. Something red glitters at her from beneath the stairs—a pair of eyes? No, just the reflection of lamplight. In it, she can see that the Bolsheviks have replaced the missing flag. But it is dripping with black paint. Like the backs of those icons in Auntie's rooms.

Lili can hardly breathe, hardly think, as she pushes past the men, already knowing that scream, at the root of it, the voice she has known all her life.

Yet Lili cannot stifle her cry.

In the middle of the circle of hunched and staring men, Grand-mère lies unmoving on the parquet. A deep red stain spreads beneath her head. Her mouth is twisted in shock, her eyes staring up, both frozen like her body. The limbs are splayed unnaturally. The neck is angled wrong, looking broken. *She* is broken. Dead.

Grand-mère *is dead*.

Lili covers her mouth, the scream ripping out through her fingers anyway. She senses more than sees Irina brush past her. Hears her sister begin to scream. A rush of hot air and piercing sound and anguish. Then higher, thinner screams, those of her cousins. And all Lili can do is wrap her arms around her shuddering middle and try to breathe.

22

Unclean Spirits

THEY WILL KILL us echoes in Irina's mind. Though it is not yet midnight, she glances around the entrance hall for the spirits, for Georgy. She pictures his dead face, the empty, vengeful look. Now the spirits have proven they can kill not only the Soviet men but them. Irina tightens her arms around a drowsy, wrung-out Seryozha, rocking him back and forth.

She tries not to look at Grand-mère. A dirty sheet has been thrown over her body, blood blooming through the fabric in spurts of poppy red. She focuses on her family instead. Natasha sits at Irina's feet with her eyes closed. Lili leans against the doorframe to the East Wing with a glassy gaze. Cleo is in hiding, having narrowly escaped the men earlier. What are they going to do? The walls and ceilings of the house seem to bear down on Irina, the scrape of the lantern from the foyer unsettling her, as she tries to *think*.

There is a low murmur coming from the group of men, Comrade Suzhensky nodding at something Felix says. The other men avert their gazes, muttering. *Nechistaya sila. Haunted. Cursed.* Irina thought Soviet men didn't believe in old Russian superstitions, certainly not unclean spirits. But this is the third death in Moscow House since they moved in. Maybe even their minds are wandering to dark places.

Men hurry past—the police, Cheka, other officials. Their eyes slide to Irina, curious, then away just as quickly. As if the supernatural is a pox passed on by a bare glance.

Irina shifts her son in her sore arms. They have been waiting for an hour, if not two. The children are falling asleep on their feet. And it is traumatic for them to stay in the room with their grandmother's body, the place where she died. It all comes crashing back: Grand-mère is dead. She will never again laugh with Irina, share those enchanting stories of the glory days, cook for her. Love her. Irina will never be a granddaughter again, or a child. Even in this last hour or two, she has felt her age settle on her like another layer of clothing.

Though the very air seems soaked in blood, Irina breathes deeply through her tears. There will be time for grief later. She needs to think about their situation soberly. Another death, poor Grand-mère's, may mean that not only are they in danger but the deaths are related. If so, Auntie cannot have anything to do with them. Either way, Irina must speak to the men as soon as possible. "Can you hold Seryozha?" she asks her sister.

Lili snaps out of her daze and nods. Seryozha barely makes a sound as Lili takes him. Irina strokes his soft cheek, willing herself to be strong.

"May I speak to you, Comrade Suzhensky?" she asks the Old Bolshevik on her approach. *Back straight. Chin up.* She must remember who she is. Grand-mère would wish it.

Comrade Suzhensky appears scattered with stress and weariness. He glances at his men. They avert their gazes, shift their feet. Even still, the Old Bolshevik gives Irina a nod. Felix steps toward them, as if to follow, but Comrade Suzhensky raises a hand, and he falls back. Rage flashes through those ice-cold eyes; Irina feels it in her bones as Comrade Suzhensky takes her aside. "Sad business this, Irina Alexandrovna. I am very sorry for your loss."

She dips her head in acknowledgment. "Can the children be allowed to go up? Or will there be additional questions?" Those were brief, interspersed with cries and tears, and she doubts they were helpful. Still, she will do all in her power to shield the children from any more.

Comrade Suzhensky's face loses some of its glazed cast, and he looks at Irina almost pityingly. He draws closer, his cologne strong, and lowers his voice. "I must tell you, Irina Alexandrovna, there is talk of moving out, even of tearing down the house." She is about to protest such injustice, but he keeps speaking. "Perhaps your babushka had a heart attack and fell. Perhaps her death is not connected to Boriska's, or Tolya's, though that, as you know, has been ruled an accident. Regardless, there will be a lengthy investigation, and not by me. It might take time, given our administrative, erm, hurdles. If I am no longer here, you may come see me in my offices."

"Thank you." Despite herself, Irina's voice quavers. First Auntie, then Grand-mère, now the men. She never thought she would wish for the men to stay. But if they leave, Irina will be alone in a haunted house with an eighteen-year-old girl and two children. Unless Auntie is released. Irina lifts her chin higher. "Where is my aunt?"

"Remember what we agreed on, Irina Alexandrovna."

"She did not kill anyone. My grandmother's death is proof of it." Irina hesitates for a split second, then takes the risk. "Would you put in a word for her? *Please*, Comrade Suzhensky."

He looks at her steadily. "I will tell you what, Irina Alexandrovna. I will inquire again, and we will see. If need be, this time, you may appeal to Comrade Kamenev."

Irina nods numbly, all of a sudden drained and wishing to be anywhere but in this house. She thinks of the ARA offices, the hive of activity and good humor. Will. Something tugs at her. She likes him, all else nonsense and noise, so what has she been waiting for? She glances at Grand-mère's prone form under the sheet. Her body. Dead. Life is short. A well of grief opens inside Irina then, piercing her through the heart. The pain is so intense, so bottomless, that she wants to feel something, anything, else. But no. She must stay with her family, share in their grief, keep them safe. She has one request left. "Would you allow a funeral for my grandmother?"

"Sir!" Felix bursts out upon hearing it. "You cannot be serious! Someone is vandalizing our property! Just look at that flag, the black paint all over it!"

Like those icons in Auntie's rooms. But Auntie is gone, the perpetrator still here.

"Under any other circumstances the answer would be no, Irina Alexandrovna," Comrade Suzhensky says, ignoring Felix. "But Countess Katerina Sherbatskaya was a kind, honorable woman who helped us greatly. You may choose a cemetery for her, and my men will help arrange a *small*"—a warning glance—"*very small* funeral."

Back in the attic, Irina holds vigil over her son and cousin, who instantly fall asleep on her cot. The house is quiet, grieving. Only the men's voices carry from downstairs, and the scrawl of Lili's pencil. She sits next to the sleeping children, one hand sketching, the other gently stroking Seryozha's back. Cleo perches on her shoulder, silent yet watchful.

"Go, Irishka," she says, startling Irina.

Irina shifts on the hard floor, resting her chin on the coverlet. Lili cannot know of what, or who, she is thinking. "Go where?"

"To see Will. I am not a child, Irina." Lili doesn't glance up from her sketch pad. "You don't need to give up your life for us. I can look after them just as well as you."

Irina watches Lili, suddenly seeing a woman in her little sister's place. Not so little anymore. Maybe Irina should trust her more. For Lili is right. Irina has again suppressed any and every urge in favor of her responsibilities. And that well of grief is threatening to swallow her whole. What will happen if it does? Will has the uncanny ability to push away the sorrow, her Russianness and responsibilities. She can be herself with him.

Even thinking of him now replaces the bloody image of her grandmother.

Irina wonders what it would be like to kiss him again. To do what she had with Georgy, but with someone she likes, who cares and is considerate of her.

Their faces are still close; her eyes drop to his lips. "Now, will you kiss me or not?"

Will laughs and shakes his head. But he grasps her face with his warm hands, bringing her in even closer, until there is only a sliver of space between them. His eyes are very blue as he finally catches her mouth in his. Irina tastes gin, him. At first, the kiss is no more than a brush of their lips. But the pressure intensifies and heats, sparking desire deep and low in her belly. He traces a hand along her neck and collarbone to her breasts, gripping her waist and pressing her tightly to his chest. The bloody image of Grand-mère fades. So does the grief, Georgy.

Irina breaks away, unsteady, breathing hard. She needs more. She needs to forget. To replace the old with the new. She takes Will's hand and leads him to the bed.

After, Irina reaches for her clothing. Already the recriminations of leaving the children are rushing in, sharp and jagged edged, along with the searing pain of losing Grand-mère. She needs to return to the house.

"Irene." His voice stops Irina.

Will is propped on his elbow, watching her. The lamplight wavers on his face, which is drawn, uncharacteristically serious. The sheets are a tangle of linen, bringing back images of them together—him letting her straddle him, her completely in control, his intensity yet gentleness, his kisses tender yet passionate. As considerate in bed as in life, leaving her crying out in pleasure at the end. This, *Will*, is no Georgy. The sheets barely cover his nakedness, and the hungry ache of desire hits Irina all over again, nothing to do with her grief.

"Will you tell me what is happening?" Will isn't smiling.

Irina snatches her blouse and skirt off the parquet. "My grandmother . . . had an accident" comes out in a rush. "She is dead."

"Oh, Irene." Before she knows it, his strong arms come around her.

23

The Beauty of Books and Cookies

THE MORNING OF Grand-mère's funeral dawns with clouds hastening smokelike across a peculiarly white sky. Lili sits on her cot in a black skirt borrowed from Irina, naturally too big for her. She strokes Cleo's wings, fiddling with Uncle Pasha's ring on its ribbon.

Since Grand-mère's death over a week ago, Lili has avoided the library. The price of letting in the past seems to be death. And if she starts to read Uncle Pasha's diaries, there will be more of it, rushing back, *taking* her back. Leading to more death.

Even if Lili wanted to, the Bolo bastards have been damnably vigilant.

And on top of this, she hates that the ARA has excused them from work. She cannot work on her project, *and* she is stuck in this stifling attic with her weepy cousins and unbearable sister. Except for Irina's visit to Will, which went well judging by her slight smile upon her return, Irina has been reminding Lili of Auntie. Sweeping about eerily in her black gowns, issuing her commands and instructions. At home in her usual irritating elder sister role. After all, burials are meant to happen within three days of death. Yet due to the preparations and negotiations with the Bolos, it has taken longer, frustrating Irina. Lili doesn't care about the reason. She doesn't like it. Any of it.

Irina appears in the doorway with red-rimmed eyes and another severe black gown. "Someone is here for you." Her mouth is not pinched in its usual frown of late, but quirked into almost *a smile*. Cleo twitters excitedly, beating her wings hummingbird-like.

Lili slides off the bed with a huff. "Do I want to know?"

"Be nice to him," warns her sister, evasive as ever.

Lili's skin prickles hotly. Can Irina mean Nikolai, *here*? Lili has tried not to think about him, or his weeklong silence, since . . . that night. But then, she hasn't tried to find him, either. Shame still burns into her at what she did. She wanted to live, and she did. So perhaps there is no shame in it. Still. Nicky represents that same past, unpredictable, dangerous, deadly. Her new, strange feelings for him are, too.

Lili makes her way downstairs with a heart that is beating damnably funny. The house has been unusually quiet, though they have kept to the attic. On the second landing, she shivers. She has tried hard to ignore Grand-mère's death, to put up walls against the past, and this place makes it more real.

Suddenly, "You cannot be serious." Nikolai's voice.

"This house belongs to the Soviet government. I decide who sets foot in it." Felix, that brute of a Bolo, is standing before the door, barring Nikolai's entrance.

Nikolai's eyes cut to her. "Lil, he won't let me through. I—"

"What is happening, Comrade?" She tries for cool and collected as she crosses the entrance hall to the foyer. "We live here, too, and we have a right to guests."

"Suzhensky may not see it, but I do," Felix spits out, voice and gaze dripping venom. "You are trying to kill us all, colluding with other former persons and Americans to bring it about. You will get what you deserve. In the meantime, you will not scheme under this roof." He folds his arms over his chest, rooting himself in place. "You have five minutes to speak outside. Then I will call over my tovarischi, and that princely face will not be so handsome when we are done with him."

Nikolai's jaw twitches. "Just try, and we will see whose face is worse for wear."

"Is that a challenge?" Well, this could spin out of control in a minute.

"Enough, boys." Lili grasps Nikolai's elbow and marches him out of the house.

She lets go as soon as they are outside. She flexes and unflexes her hand, the fingers that gripped him itching for something to do. Lili senses the house behind her. She decides to ignore the looming courtyard, the oak with Uncle Pasha's grave. "You really shouldn't bait him like that," she says, with a laugh. But she notices how pale he is, his eyes skittering to the windows, where she is sure Felix is watching. This cannot be easy for Nicky, given what likely happened to his family. Lili wonders why he is here.

"I am sure *you* bait him—them—all the time."

"I don't always make the best decisions."

Nikolai glances at the house again. He takes her by the arm, away from the window. "I only heard today" is said in a rush. His face is so close that Lili can see a new hollowness in it. "They had me drive to Petrograd on ARA business the day after . . . I saw you last. I cannot imagine what you must think of me. I tried phoning, but—"

"Our telephone doesn't work." Her heart thumps, funny, strange. He was away, not ignoring her. Still, that changes nothing. *Leave him in the past where he belongs.* It is too dangerous. And she cannot bear to think of anything happening to him.

"I tried to send a message, a letter—" He stops. Looks back at the house. "I am so sorry about your grandmother, Lilichka. I wanted to see you, come to the funeral—"

"You shouldn't be here, Nicky." Her face heats up. *Stop calling him that!*

"Lil—" He lifts his hands up to her face, changes his mind, steps back.

"Thank you for coming." She forces a smile. "If I stay out here any longer, the bastard will let me know in no uncertain terms." A tight laugh. "As for the funeral, it is something I need to do myself. But thank you, really, I mean it."

Lili expects him to play the wounded lover from the stories. But Nikolai paid attention to propriety more than she did. Even now, he schools his handsomely refined features into the perfect expression of polite solicitude, as if she has merely turned him down for a dance at a ball. "I understand," he says in a voice betraying nothing. "Will you please pass along my condolences to your sister and family? My mother's also."

That smile is back, cutting into the flesh of her face. "Of course." Lili wants to keep talking to him, wants her friend from all those years ago. But it isn't only the danger that prevents her. She doesn't know what to say or how to behave around Nikolai, convinced that if she doesn't make space between them, she will lose him. And maybe there is a way for them to be friends in the present without the past, without falling back into old patterns.

"Oh—" Nikolai reaches into his back pocket and pulls out a small parcel wrapped in brown paper. He hands it to her, reddening. "From, erm, Petrograd. You used to like these."

Lili cannot help herself; she tears into the parcel, glimpsing her favorite gingerbread cookies. She feels very, very warm inside. "Where did you find them?"

His mouth quirks up. He starts to turn away, then stops. Beneath the mask of elegance and manners, a vulnerability glimmers. It is unexpectedly disarming. "If you change your mind"—the rasp in his voice sets her heart thudding—"I will be at our place."

The graveyard where . . . Lili steps toward him, about to call out his name, *Nicky*. Maybe she was too hasty, the danger an excuse. Maybe he isn't her past but her future. And this undefinable thing between them is better than friendship, is real and possible.

But Nikolai is already hastening through the gate and out of sight.

Lili drops down onto the steps. She is shaky, confused. Her insides are turned upside down, twisting her up until she feels sick. That intent look, so capably hidden yet still there. Like him. She pulls out her pencil and paper to sketch. Then tosses them aside. Turns back to the parcel with the gingerbread cookies inside. And as she pops one cookie into her mouth, savoring its sweet and spicy flavor, she thinks of Nicky despite herself.

As is typical for such occasions, the rain begins to fall as soon as they start for the cemetery chosen for Grand-mère's final resting place.

After Lili polished off the gingerbread cookies—down to the last one, she isn't ashamed to admit—the walls went back up. Way up. And now, she forces herself to focus only on her footsteps, her breathing, the feel of her sketch pad in her coat. It is a damn good comfort, as is Uncle Pasha's ring against her heart.

Irina floats out of the rain in front of Lili, a black-clothed figure, with Natasha and Seryozha on either side of her. And in the distance, at the head of their woefully small party, the wooden coffin looms, wreathed and held up by several Bolsheviks more favorably disposed to them. It is a pitiful sight in all its impoverished simplicity. A strangely lonesome, bare procession for a countess of the illustrious Sherbatsky bloodline.

The graveyard is as bare as their party. A lone priest waits there, tall and bent, all in black. It smells of overturned earth, of rain and sad things. The prayers are read and sung, the coffin is sealed and lowered. The grainy soil is wet against Lili's fingers as she glances down at Grand-mère's new dwelling. Deep underground, where no rain can reach it. No sun or warmth, either. She lets the soil drop onto the coffin and watches it spatter. Thinks dimly how Grand-mère hated dirt. Irina wails. Her cousins weep. The men doff their hats. The grave is filled.

Lili seems to float above her body. Not really there at all.

After the service is over, their party turns homeward. But Lili cannot stand the thought of seeing her family's grief so fully on display there, of tiptoeing around the spooked men, who eye them and whisper and, for once, keep to their rooms. Their absence makes the halls and corridors subterranean in their sepulchral silence.

Lili needs to float down, to speak to someone not her family.

She mutters something to Irina about needing air and walks through town to that old graveyard. Morbid and strange though it may be, it *is* their place. She pulls open the gate, which groans in the twilit stillness, and takes the gravel path between the tombstones. Even before she glimpses the aspen tree overlooking the graveyard, Lili sees his figure leaning against a grave with a book in his hand. It stopped raining some time ago, but a clinging coldness hangs on the air, which isn't misty so much as dense and heavy.

At her approach, Nikolai looks up. He slides the book into his back pocket before lighting a cigarette and handing it to her.

Lili accepts it without a word as she perches on the grave beside his. It is cracked, the cross long rotted, the weeds long dead. Above, the aspen spreads its branches like a wizened old man his wasted arms. The leaves are faded and dying and crunching beneath their boots. Her gaze lingers on the place where they took each other so openly, so damn brazenly. The shame of it is curiously gone. Neither of them speaks of it. And as if by some tacit agreement, they don't touch each other, either. Lili doesn't need a man to kiss, but a man who will sit beside her and listen. She needs her friend. She needs Nicky.

The fucking past. What to do with it? Maybe the answer isn't to put up walls and ignore it, nor is it to completely let it in. Maybe it is to use it to make a better present for herself, her family, Nicky. But to do that, Lili needs to face the past, starting with Grand-mère's death. She takes a long drag from her cigarette and lowers her head as the smoke streams out, thickening the air around them. Finally, she lets out a sigh.

Then she starts to talk about Grand-mère. Her metal-tasting boiled water and soups. Her embraces, scented with ripe roses and a trace of wistfulness. Her stories of sparkling ladies and grand palaces and jewels that dazzled. Her conviction that no matter Lili's disposition to unladylike things, she is still a grand lady from a grand house.

And through it all, she feels Nicky close beside her, listening.

❖ ❖ ❖

Upon her return to Moscow House, Lili goes straight to the second floor of the library. She feels bruised and tender from the memories of her grandmother. Still, she pulls Uncle Pasha's ring off its ribbon, and she uses the key to unlock the first diary. Then the next, and the next. Each of the locks clicks open with the Sherbatsky family crest as if by magic.

The library makes space for her in its depths, a silent, shifting presence. It seems to intuit that Lili needs it. Maybe the ghosts do, too. For reading Uncle Pasha's story might lead to her setting him and all the dead free, giving them peace. And if anybody stands in her way, she will learn to fight them. Irina treats her as an annoying little sister because, well, she can be. But after witnessing Georgy's attack on Irina, followed by Grand-mère's senseless death—no accident—Lili will not let any damn ghost or Bolo take her family and home. Even if it is haunted—for now.

24

Office Politics

OCTOBER 1921

"How long do you plan on wearing those ugly black gowns, Irishka?" asks Lili.

"I am in mourning," Irina replies pertly. "As are you. Or should be."

"I'm in this hideous black skirt, aren't I?"

Irina gives a shake of her head. Incorrigible, that is what her sister is.

It is their first day back on the job, and the ARA offices are largely deserted. For this reason, Mr. Carroll agreed for Irina to assist Lili with her former people project.

Now they are on their way to the Hermitage kitchen to see Ludmila Dmitriyevna. Not only to prod the woman about Auntie, but for Lili to make sketches and photographs of her work. And to deliver the heavy bag of children's clothes and toys Irina is carrying.

Will's camera glints from within Lili's bag—borrowed from Irina, of course. Irina cannot help but think of him, wondering where he was that morning. She hasn't seen the American since the night of Grand-mère's death. He almost attended the funeral, but she didn't wish to antagonize the Soviet men by inviting an American to a funeral they weren't even supposed to have. Now all Irina wishes is to return to Will's warm bed. This time, she wouldn't rush to leave it. The day is fine, though, and she resolves to enjoy it.

They are passing through a blustery park, the trees aflame with already brilliant reddish-yellow leaves. They cascade down, petal-like, in ripples of gold that dazzle Irina's tired eyes. The burning, brisk smell in the air further invigorates her. "How are Pasha's diaries coming along?" she asks over the crunch of the leaves.

Lili averts her gaze. "There are so many of them, Irishka, each with so many entries that recount his life in such minute detail, his study of history and his military work with the Semenovsky Life Guards Regiment . . ."

"You need to be more targeted in your search," Irina says, suspecting that Lili is reading the diaries in their entirety. Her sister adored Pasha and would do anything to learn more about him. But they are out of time.

After Georgy and Grand-mère, Irina cannot help but assume the deaths in the house are related to one another and the spirits. Though she doesn't yet have evidence for this. The fact is, with each death, the spirits are more corporeal and alive. And the family is in greater danger. She shudders, imagining Georgy's cold, skeletal embrace. They need answers—and next steps. Whatever they are, Irina must keep her family safe.

The sudden, very intense urge *to leave* hits her. Not only the house but Moscow. That image of her and the children, with the New York City skyline opening before them . . . No, it isn't possible. The house is their sole remaining inheritance. Even if Irina could entertain leaving it, it is impossible to obtain travel papers. So, then, they stay. In the meantime, she will not take any chances with the children.

She and Lili left Seryozha with Madame Trobelska again, and Natasha is to join him there after school.

"You should focus your efforts on the entries around the night the Cheka came to Moscow House," Irina adds. "And keep an eye out for any mention of Auntie or her superstitions."

"There you go again with your orders." Lili blows out a puff of air, pushing her hair back from her face. "And that is easier said than done, Irishka."

"Maybe, but you have to try. There will be plenty of time to read Pasha's life story—later." Then, "Unless he meant the diaries to be a distraction."

Lili shakes her head vehemently. "He wouldn't do that."

"Not Pasha—but his ghost."

"Do you think they are all dangerous?"

Irina considers this. Papa, Grand-père, and Pasha haven't harmed them, protecting, even helping them. But she doesn't know enough about the spiritual world to say definitively that they are harmless. "I wish I knew, Lil."

The Hermitage slides into view in all its abandoned glory. So do Lili's posters, tacked onto the windows, their colors bright, their children happy. The sweet smell of corn wafts into the street. Irina shakes off the sudden wave of sadness at the deplorable state of the Tavern. She takes Lili by the arm, giving it a squeeze, and they walk inside together.

Irina spots Luda right away. Their former housekeeper is wiping down one of the tables zealously, with real feeling, after what must have been the morning rush. She brightens upon seeing Irina's bag of goods for the children and accepts it gratefully. Following the usual niceties, as Lili starts to take photographs with Will's camera, Luda gives her sister a long look. She asks if Lili remembers her parting gift—a rat in a bread basket—which Lili argues was really a small, harmless mouse. Then, that it was Nicky's joke, not hers.

Irina sighs deeply. She stands entirely corrected: Lili is still a child. Irina hurries to explain to the poor woman, who is quite flustered—"It was a rat, I tell you!" she nearly shrieks—about Lili's ARA project. After a not-so-promising pause, Luda finally obliges, though reluctantly. She tells Irina, and only Irina, it is out of respect for the dead

Countess Katerina Sherbatskaya that she will help them at all. Irina sees her opportunity and takes it:

"Ludmila Dmitriyevna, before Lili starts on her project, may we ask you about our aunt?"

Luda huffs, not bothering to hide her irritation. "I knew you would be back about that." She turns toward the counter. "Eh, Galya!"

There is a crash, followed by a muffled curse, and a woman Irina's age materializes. She is slight, blonde, with a quick smile and a pixie-like appearance that belies her age. Though Irina doesn't remember her face, she does remember noting her name on her list.

Galya executes a perfect curtsy before sitting beside Luda across from Irina and Lili. "When Ludmila Dmitriyevna said she saw you—alive!—I said my prayers. And I haven't prayed since the Revolution!"

Luda gives Galya a sharp look. "Galina Antonovna assisted in Moscow House's kitchen from time to time."

Irina doesn't remember this, either, as she barely made it out of bed during that time, and kitchen assistants rarely showed themselves to the family. She glances at Lili, now lost to her sketching. She will need to do this herself. Irina decides to start with their former housekeeper first.

"You said you were surprised that our aunt is still alive," Irina says slowly. "What did you mean by that?"

"Peter House was . . . in turmoil back then. I would constantly hear explosive, sometimes violent arguments on the other side of the door to Little Reception."

"Arguments?" Irina blinks. Her family was known for their almost stoic approach to life. To her knowledge, that never changed, not even during the Revolution.

Luda nods curtly. "As I understand it, your aunt wished to leave Russia while the rest of the family wished to stay. She would scream about how Russia was dead, how the Bolsheviks were taking over, how she hated those that pushed families like yours from power. She would rail against your grandfather, your uncles, the entire family. But especially against Count Pavel Sherbatsky."

"Uncle Pasha?" Lili looks up from her sketch, wrinkles her nose. "That is . . . odd."

"Yes, she trusted him," Irina agrees, remembering how Pasha was the only family member Auntie had gone to with Irina's secret. *I trust him as no one else.*

"Well, you know how siblings are. One moment you trust each other, the next . . ." Luda exhales a breath of air almost dramatically, as though all that nonsense is the privilege of the rich, and only they have time to bicker.

Irina and Lili have never been such siblings. Either they are close or they are distant. Irina doesn't remember them ever raising their voices at each other. The same goes for Maman, Pasha, and Auntie. For the first time, Irina doubts Luda. What can she really know? Perhaps she is making up lies about the family. Perhaps she resents them. Still, Luda seems respectable and respectful, especially of Grand-père and Pasha. She might be misremembering.

"Sometime in the spring of 1917—I remember because you were away"—Luda's gaze darts to Irina—"Princess Sablorova had a particularly nasty argument with the family. She bellowed that they and Count Pavel were killing you children, that the only way to save you was to take you out of the country. It all changed after that. *She* changed."

A chill creeps over Irina's skin. Though the sun streaming in is warm.

"Princess Sablorova would dissolve into bitter tears. Start screaming at Count Pavel—at dinner, at a family meeting, around the house. Throw objects at him, shatter priceless heirlooms. One time, she broke a vase dating back to Peter the Great's reign! Imagine that! I had never seen your dear uncle so upset. Pale as a corpse. I was afraid for him, especially when there was a shouting match . . . one of the ugliest things I've ever witnessed. In the end, I heard her say, very distinctly, *I wish you dead, Pasha.* This was right before the family removed to the countryside, then to Moscow. I stayed on at Peter House and was let go when the funds ran out."

Irina's body aches from the chill at Luda's words. During the Revolution, the three siblings and their children moved into Peter House. Irina and Lili don't often speak of that time, as much from the pain as from Irina's fear of questions about her whereabouts. But the woman Luda is describing is nothing like the composed, statuesque woman Irina knows from the past and mostly the present. She turns to Lili. "Do you remember any of this?"

Lili has abandoned her sketch. She shakes her head. "If it happened, it was not around us. Auntie never lost her composure, remaining the ice queen. She would bring us sweets when none were to be had in Petrograd. One time"—Lili giggles—"*ice cream*! I liked her a little more after that. She did do her best for us, for me."

"Yes, I believe she did. Her Andrei and you children were her world," Luda says, turning to Galya, who has been silent, her liveliness dimmed a little. "Galya knows more about your aunt in Moscow. She wrote to me for advice when Princess Sablorova started requesting strange things from the kitchen. I told Galya, 'Give the princess what she wants, or you'll be out of a job!'"

"Strange things?" Irina thinks back to the items Auntie gave Andrei for protection.

Galya hesitates. At Luda's nod, she says, "Not long after we received news of Prince Andrei's death, in the spring of 1918, Princess Sablorova requested an entire loaf of bread, uncut, along with a mound of salt. Odd, given there was no bread to be had. I was forced to go out to a pastry shop and buy one at an exorbitant price."

Lili worries at her sketch pad, meeting Irina's gaze, as if she, too, is thinking of the bread and salt below the grand staircase. "What else, Galina Antonovna?" Irina presses.

"A maid told me she found remains of dinners and suppers in the princess's evening bags. A chicken leg here, a half-consumed piece of fish there. A crust of black bread. The strangest request was for blood."

"What kind?" Irina recalls Kirill's mention of hog's blood.

"Mostly pig's blood. Sometimes that of a rabbit or a cow. Once, a horse."

Lili snorts. "How did you find animal anything in Revolutionary Moscow?"

"The butcher obliged us, though it was hard to come by. Princess Sablorova would ask for other things, too. Raw chicken legs, coffee beans. A sieve. Pitchers of water. Melted wax."

Irina's heart thuds fast and hard in her ears. The blood, the wax, the other items in the rosewood box . . . There can be no doubt Auntie was dabbling in the occult, in old Russian superstitions. But what does this have to do with the night Pasha died and the spirits?

Lili leans forward. "Did my uncle say anything about my aunt when he returned to Petrograd for the Sherbatsky possessions in the autumn of 1917?"

"Not that I recall, but your dear uncle was much changed." Luda exchanges a look with Galya and presses her lips into a thin line. "He was so scrawny! Kept glancing about, scattered as never before. Jumping at the slightest noise. I thought he was ill. Do you remember Svetlana Vasilyevna?" she suddenly asks.

It is the third name on her list. *Sveta! Where are you, girl?* "Was she Auntie's maid?"

Luda gives a short nod. "In Moscow. She was the one who found the leftovers and is now a housekeeper at Aara." *ARA* is drawn out in the Russian way.

Irina cannot visualize Svetlana, but she remembers her. She nods gratefully at the women. "Thank you—both of you," she says, before standing and pulling her sister toward the door, where a brisk draft swirls.

"Do you believe them?" Lili whispers, clutching her sketch pad to her chest.

"If Kirill hadn't told me about Auntie giving those things to Andrei, I may not have," Irina replies in an undertone. "But I believe Kirill. And there might be a truth to all this that we don't yet know. I'll find out where Svetlana works back at the offices."

"I'll stay and work on my project," Lili decides, then hesitates. "Will you wait for me at the ARA?"

Irina touches her cheek. "Of course, Lil. I will not return to the house without you."

Irina easily finds Svetlana's name on the latest payroll—and her assignment. Along with Paulina, she is supposed to be at the Pink House, the men having nicknamed the various ARA buildings around Moscow based on the colors of their façades. Irina will need to visit both women. But not today.

The hours pass swift and sure-footed. A few times, Irina hurries past Will's office, catching a glimpse of him leaning back in his chair with the telephone receiver held to his ear. Each time, his gaze flicks to hers, and he flashes her a knowing, self-assured smile that sets her stomach flipping and flaring with heat. As she is speaking on the telephone to some petty Soviet official regarding a lost shipment—Will was right, she isn't as afraid as before—Irina starts to fantasize. Of Will slipping those strong, rough hands over her body, pressing her against that wall . . . *Focus, Irina*, she tells herself, not once but twice.

By the time the offices empty and the sun finally winks out, Irina cannot stand it anymore. Her sister isn't back yet, so she has a little time. She walks over to Will's office slowly, not wishing to appear too eager. Suddenly, Will's hands grasp her waist, his gin-soaked breath on the skin of her neck. He draws her against his body firmly, tightly, so Irina feels his chest at her back, all the muscles and heat and heart of him. Her eyes widen at the hardness she can sense through his trousers. "William, for shame, we are at work!"

"Everybody has left. It's just you and me, Goliteva." With a deft movement, he spins her to face him and leans in for a long, hot kiss.

"What if someone returns?" Irina says, breathless, cheeks smarting from the scrape of his beard.

"Oh, they are already on their second cocktail." Laughing, Will tugs her into his office and throws himself into his chair. As she steps up to him, his eyes darken until they are the color of the ocean, deep and bottomless, swollen with a tempest.

Irina eases into his lap, letting her legs fall on either side of his waist. Will grips her hips and pulls her on top of him hungrily. His hands slide over her body with an urgency that crackles through the entire length of her. Irina's blood rushes in her veins, pounds out of control, as he slowly skims his fingers up her belly, along her sternum, up and up. She leans back, suppressing the moan sitting hot as a coal in her mouth. His hand stops at the severe neckline of her gown, his light breath grazing the tops of her breasts, which press and strain against her corset.

"Oh, Irene," Will groans, pressing his hardness against the layers of gown caught between them. "I am mad for you. Absolutely, totally mad for you." Then he is pushing against the layers, plucking them back, until he is directly beneath, driving into her through the thin cotton of her underclothes.

Irina arches her back in response, clenching her teeth against that moan so hard they ache. Her mourning, the office, the risk of getting caught, none of it matters anymore. In fact, the clandestine secrecy of the act only hardens the urgency, the heat, the unbearable need. By the time Will is inside her, she no longer cares if they are seen.

She only wants the feeling to last.

25

A Creature of Shadow

THE ENTRANCE HALL is slick with candlelight—the first time since Grand-mère's death. The ruined flag has been discarded and not replaced. Half-opened suitcases and valises are scattered all over, the dragging of heavy objects and men's frenzied voices carrying from the West Wing.

"Come on, Lil." Irina pulls her sister toward the noise. Though she hopes she doesn't show it, panic is building in her chest. Are the men leaving?

The noises and voices grow louder as they pass through the flickering rooms. The expectant heaviness in the air weighs down Irina's insides with dread, with foreboding.

Suddenly, a cold draft rushes through the rooms. Irina claps a palm over her flying hair and finds Lili's hand. The flesh there is cold with sweat. They look, wide-eyed, at each other—as canvases bang against walls, carpets and tapestries billow, chandelier crystals chime, statues crash to the floor, and furniture is overturned. Something moves from behind a fireplace screen. It isn't yet midnight. Still, Irina thinks, *A specter?* But it is a darting, dashing kind of movement. The very parquet seems to shift along with the draft.

Irina draws back in disgust when she sees shiny reddish-black cockroaches streaming in from the fireplace.

And the screen at the grate is filled with black holes. As if moths have eaten through the silk. Irina peers around the room, noticing holes in the fabric of the other furniture, too. And there is a musty, earthy, damp smell. The house may be old, but it has never smelled it. Like a crypt, deep underground, cavernous and very strange.

Lili lets out a little shriek. "Are those *roaches*?"

"Yes. Let's keep moving. We need to see Comrade Suzhensky."

They continue on, gripping each other's hands. Irina imagines Georgy's pale, blue face, as if his memory is drawn out by the smell of Will on her skin. Her sister tugs on her arm, and all thoughts of Georgy flee.

A small hairy shape stands before them in the next doorway. Irina glimpses the gleam of overgrown white hair and a long charcoal-black cloak that blends with the shadows like spider silk. The face, if it has one, is part hidden below a wide-brimmed hat, not worn at least since the times of Catherine the Great. The rest is covered with a similarly white beard that seems to reach the floor. But it is the flash of its eyes that makes Irina seize with pure, very cold fear. They are the deep scarlet of freshly spilled blood.

Lili leaps toward the creature. "Don't you dare run away from me, you little rascal!"

Its screech is so piercing that Irina's hands fly to her ears. Then, in a whirl of shadow and evaporating light, it vanishes. In its place, a glistening black snake gives a violent, tongue-thrashing hiss. Lili jerks backward.

In a blink, the snake is gone, too.

Lili glances at Irina, mirroring her bewilderment. "It *is* an imp." She chews on her bottom lip in thought. "Could be a gnome, though. Regardless, a spirit, one that can appear before midnight, maybe with twilight . . ."

"I revise my previous statement of it being an animal. But let's deal with it later, all right?" Irina pulls her sister forward, into the next room and toward the study—away from the creature-turned-snake, whatever it was.

They reach the hallway, a chaotic tumble of luggage and other belongings. The men brush past, not seeing Irina or Lili in their flurry of activity. Shutting trunks with loud bangs that make Irina flinch; dragging cases overflowing with clothing and books, leaving dark marks on the wood; ripping down posters, nails protruding from the walls like ugly parting gifts.

Among the milling men, Irina makes out Felix and perhaps a dozen or so of his loyal comrades. They are gathered in a tight group, the only men not packing or cleaning. Instead, they laugh and throw imperious glances at the others. Ever since Grand-mère's funeral, Felix's group has been inseparable, stalking the house like a pack of hungry Siberian wolves, as severe faced and falsely righteous and vengeful as Felix himself.

In that moment, he turns in Irina's direction. The harsh blue of his eyes burns into her like a flame. "This isn't over," Felix mouths, making her almost stumble into Lili.

The door to the study is ajar. A crackling sound drifts out, along with the acrid, stifling smell of real flames.

Irina hurries in, with Lili at her heels, if only to escape the hated man.

Like the hallway, the study has been turned upside down. Paper litters all surfaces, even the floor. Comrade Suzhensky is bent over the fireplace, throwing paper and pamphlets into the flames. They are blisteringly hot, the room close and stuffy, a shocking contrast to the cold draft in the other rooms. Smoke coils from behind the grate, blurring the study's edges, the air hazy and nightmarish. Especially with cockroaches crawling all over the paper. As if the house has grown too swollen with darkness to keep such things inside its walls. So it is releasing and giving the dark free rein to roam, to be seen.

"Comrade Suzhensky?" Irina's throat is already dry from the smoke.

The poor man practically jumps at her voice. His wispy white hair, which Irina now sees is a wig, sits askew atop a bald head shiny with perspiration. "Oh, it is only you, Irina Alexandrovna."

Irina exchanges an uneasy glance with Lili, saying, "We hope you aren't leaving." But it is obvious they are.

"We will not spend another night here," wheezes Comrade Suzhensky. His face is flushed purple. Dark circles puff out under his bulging, bloodshot eyes. "Not another night."

A phantom laugh bursts out of nowhere, a bloom of sound there and gone.

The chill erupts in pox-like goose bumps all over Irina's skin. It grows unnaturally, unearthly quiet. And cold, despite the fire. Is it midnight already?

Comrade Suzhensky stills with a stack of paper clutched in one meaty, shaking fist. "I have had enough. I am an old man, Irina Alexandrovna, my heart is weak." He gives Irina, then Lili, a long look. "My advice is to find another place to live. This house is cursed with nechistaya sila, the same I used to see at my babushka's old farmhouse. I have requested for Princess Sablorova to be released. I cannot do more. If you wish, you may visit me at my offices." Suddenly, jerkily, he falls forward, as if shoved from behind.

Irina draws in a sharp breath, reaching for Lili. A spirit . . . ?

Comrade Suzhensky's gaze is frantic as it sweeps the study for the source of the shove. He steadies his bulk on the edge of the table before pushing a stack of papers, a few books, and a bottle of cognac into his briefcase. He shuts it with two efficient snaps, swiping it off the table and hurrying toward the door. "Do think about what I said, Irina Alexandrovna," he says, and is gone.

"Well, I never thought I'd see the damn day." Lili peers after him gleefully.

Even with Felix's fresh threat, Irina thinks, *Now we are truly alone.* Out of the corner of her eye, wide gray lips curve into a laughing smile, appearing and disappearing just as quickly. And with them, the sudden sharp scent of pipe smoke.

"I heard you are leaving on an inspection of the Pink House," Irina says as she walks into Will's office the next day. While Lili is out sketching with Frank, Irina intends to speak to Auntie's former maid and hopefully see Paulina.

A shutter clicks, and a bright flash blinds Irina momentarily. She blinks, makes out Will's camera aimed at her. Another click, another flash, and she tilts her head up, not smiling, as she has been taught. Will snakes a hand toward Irina and tugs her to him, managing a kiss on the corner of her mouth before she reels back, scolding him.

"I cannot resist." He laughs, slinging the camera onto his shoulder and asking Irina the question she wants to hear. "Would you like to join me on my travels across Moscow?"

They walk along the blustery streets, stopping by an old woman street peddler to buy pirozhki with cabbage and potatoes, as well as sunflower seeds. The day is overcast, but the wind isn't cold. It carries the scent of dying leaves, which whirl on the gusts, rustling and whispering. Irina bites into a pirozhok. The pastry is piping hot, steaming with the flavorful aromas of dough and filling. Will slips an arm around her waist. And though their coats are bulky, she is warmed inside out. Irina smiles up at him, for once perfectly content. She slips a few pirozhki and a handful of seeds into her bag for Seryozha and Natasha at his urging, wishing she could tell Will about her son. *Really* tell him. Perhaps she will, and soon. Before Felix can carry out his threat.

Irina refuses to look around, afraid to catch those blue eyes watching.

She hurries to suggest they take a tram to the Pink House. She hears the distant clang of its bells and grinding metal over the murmurs of the staring, grim-faced passersby. But Will flags down a droshky, and they clamber into the carriage. There, as always, Irina is taken back to the sounds and smells of Old Russia. The *clip-clop, clip-clop* of the horses, their sweet, musty scent underneath the stink and soot of the motorcars. She and Will talk about the carriages that fly through New York's cobbled streets, how different autumn is there, still summery warm and golden in October.

The horses are quick and limber, the driver bent on earning his coin as mercilessly fast as possible. As they rush down the wide, faceless boulevards past the speeding cars, Irina even allows Will a kiss—one feverish, breathless press of the lips. Then, as if no time has passed, they are before the Pink House at 8 Bolshoi Znamensky Lane. Irina's cold cheeks are ruddy from the thrashing wind as they alight from the carriage and face the sprawling mansion.

As they are walking inside, Irina realizes she has been here before. It is the former residence of Sergei Shchukin, known for his art collections displaying bold, contemporary paintings all the rage in Paris. Irina used to come to his viewings and soirées with Maman and Auntie. Unlike the Hermitage Restaurant, the mansion remains untouched by time, on the outside as well as the inside. Each room they walk through is the same as in her memory: the dizzyingly high ceilings painted with exotic birds and naked airy women in high relief, bronzed chandeliers blazing with light, the famous paintings hung frame to frame over the gaudy patterned wallpaper.

As at headquarters, the offices of the former Shchukin mansion take up several reception rooms, though it mostly serves as a residence for the ARA chiefs.

Irina inspects the office and its staff along with Will. It consists of several Russians and a dozen or so Americans. When they are done, Paulina beckons to Irina with a wave and a wink. She hops onto her desk, crossing her trousered legs and leaning forward as Irina approaches.

"So, why rouse yourself to come to our neck of the woods, Irene?"

Paulina offers her a cigarette, which Irina politely declines. She may crave it, especially when smoke drifts to her so tantalizingly. But she is a mother and must set a good example. Already Irina is irresponsibly engaging in an affair with a man who is her superior of sorts and certainly not her husband. She will not add smoking to it.

Inadvertently, her gaze flicks to Will, and Paulina's pert little face narrows sharply.

"Ah, you and the bearded American . . ."

"No," Irina says, too defensively. It has been a long time since they've traded secrets. "I . . . only wished to leave the office for the day."

"Is that all?" A puff of smoke is blown playfully in her direction. "I say have your fun. You deserve it after—" Paulina stops, taking a pull from her cigarette and scattering ash all over her desk. "Georgy was not a bad man, was he?" Her eyes have softened, become the liquid black of spilled ink.

Irina leans against a neighboring desk. "No," she says, before she can think. He wasn't, was he? He was not a liar, a thief, or a murderer. But he was selfish and entitled, possessive of all he owned, including her. And he abandoned her. Irina decides on honesty. "He wasn't good, either." She doesn't elaborate.

"You don't have to tell me. I am sleeping with my own American."

Irina's eyes widen. She lowers her voice. "Harold?"

Paulina's tight red curls bounce as she nods. "With any luck, he will fall in love and take me and my sister to America."

Irina feels an ugliness at her words. "You don't . . . love him?"

While she has imagined America with the children, Will has never been part of that picture. His absence suddenly seems wrong. He is wonderful, and the sex is, as the Americans say, *swell*. More than that, Irina feels *seen*, empowered in a way she hasn't been before. Maybe a little free, like him. She feels wanted and adored, instead of used and abandoned. But is that love? Can she see herself marrying him? Irina glances at Will, at his relaxed smile as he takes a photograph. Can she see herself marrying at all? Now that she is her family's sole caretaker, has worked to provide for them, Irina isn't so sure. Only that she would never sleep with Will as a passport to America.

"Harry is entertaining enough," Paulina is saying. "He passes the time. But I don't think I like him, or any man. They are valuable for my purposes, that is all." Her gaze flicks up to Irina. "After all, they are using us, too, no? The wealthy, powerful American men lording over us poor, subordinate Russian women."

Irina tries to think if Paulina was romantically involved before the Revolution, but she doesn't remember. She decides not to ask, switching subjects if only to get Paulina's words out of her head. How reminiscent they are of her own thoughts from before. "How do you like working at the Pink House? It is still like an art gallery, no?"

"Yes, I hate it. The Monets, Picassos, and Matisses only remind me of Sergei Ivanovich's soirées . . ." Paulina lowers her voice. "The men here aren't as they are on Spiridonovka. They are filthy beasts, stubbing out their cigarettes on any surface in sight, laughing at the Matisse canvases with the naked dancers, trashing everything. I wonder what Trotsky's wretched wife will say when she finds out. The head of the so-called Museum Division of the People's Commissariat for Enlightenment would blush with fury at how these men flirt with us, acting like kings, like her own husband, the famous Leon Trotsky. Harold is a saint in comparison."

"I am looking for a former maid," Irina offers, feeling the need to likewise share something with Paulina.

She only laughs. "Why, are you in need of one?"

"My aunt has been arrested, and I have . . . questions."

Paulina takes a thoughtful drag. "I don't remember your aunt."

"She didn't live with us when you and your mother would visit."

Another thoughtful drag. "They hated each other, didn't they?"

Irina blinks. "Who?"

"Your mother and aunt. They weren't close, were they?"

"I . . . believed them to be. Why?"

Paulina shrugs. "Truthfully, I have blocked out that time. But I remember my mother saying something about it. That there was a tension between the sisters, maybe the siblings. Eh, I don't remember. Just that they never saw eye to eye. And that your aunt was envious of your mother for being in love with her husband. Doing whatever he told her to do." Paulina leans back. "I didn't realize I knew that. But there you have it. And before you ask, no, I don't remember anything else. Nor do I want to."

Irina nods, but the tight uneasiness in her chest doesn't loosen. She does not remember Maman or any of her siblings being anything but courteous to one another. At least in front of her. And apparently Lili also. Now multiple people have cast doubt on this.

Irina chats a little more with Paulina. Then, seeing Will still at his photographs, she makes her excuses. Before they go their separate ways, Paulina mentions that she might find Auntie's maid in the Pink Drawing Room, dusting the Soviet people's Matisses. And that is where Irina goes.

Irina now remembers Svetlana as a charming woman in her midthirties with generous curves and cheeks as round and scarlet as ripe apples. She sees a slip of that woman in the Pink Drawing Room. All angles and sunken face the waxy lily-white of the ill.

"Galya told me you would be coming by."

Irina blinks, summons her manners. "Yes, it is good to see you, Svetlana, dear."

Svetlana ushers her to a Rococo-style sofa, with pink dried-looking roses patterning the silk. A large canvas hangs over them, a Matisse, with figures dancing nakedly and with abandon. Svetlana hacks out a rattling cough; it leaves blood on her lips. Irina smells it, sharp, sickening, like that hospital. Consumption, she knows at once.

Pity stabs at her; she hasn't even tried to find out how their former staff has fared.

"I only started in the autumn of 1917, some months after your move to Moscow that summer. I met Andrei one time before he left Moscow House to join the White army. Most of the winter was waiting for letters from dear Andryusha. Princess Sablorova would send me to the post office every day, no matter how cold or snowy the streets." Svetlana sniffs, furtively rubs at her bloodied lip. "Princess

Sablorova didn't speak much. At least, not to me, and not that I heard. But then, I left each night for my parents' flat or other work."

That unbearably squalid winter still warming them with hope the Bolsheviks would fall . . . Irina remembers her canopied bed, the swollen gray sky outside, the trays of tasteless suppers, there being shortages of everything and prolonged power cuts. She was listless, aching from phantom pains, tortured by living under the same roof as her son and not being able to see him. Most days, she couldn't rise from bed. Irina was the ghost.

"Then we received the news of Prince Andrei's death in the spring." Svetlana's voice is brittle, from either illness or the darkness of those times.

That keening wail that had broken through to Irina . . . Yet she lay there, numb, entirely lost to her own sorrow, oblivious to anyone else's. Even if it was Auntie, for once needing Irina. For Irina had known the news on an instinctive level. She will regret her inaction for the rest of her life. She pushes away the stale guilt, the memory.

"A week or so later, Princess Sablorova went out. That alone was strange. You remember we rarely did. But that night, I came to her door to see if she needed anything before I left, and she was not there. Neither could we find her. A few nights later, it happened again. Then, the odd requests came, mostly from the kitchen. Several days after that, she locked herself in her rooms and refused to come out. To take trays of food or other sustenance. To answer our entreaties. I left for the night. The next morning, she answered my knock, pale and withdrawn. An iron tang wafted toward me from her rooms. I believe it was blood. I saw a few drops on her collar."

A fit of coughing overtakes Svetlana, so like Grand-père's, the ghost of which Irina and Lili heard last night—only more distinct, more real, than ever.

Svetlana presses a hand to her mouth. Her fingers come away bright with blood. She is wheezing slightly as she continues. "I asked her, 'Princess Sablorova, are you all right?' I was frightened for her. Thought she might try to harm herself. She gave me a smile that turned my heart to ice. Then asked for a tub of water and a cloth to wash up. Usually, I would help her with this. But she said no, very sharply. I withdrew, afraid I had displeased her. I brought what she asked for and left. That night, it was the same. The next morning, too. For three days and three nights we lived in this uncertainty. After the third night, when I came to her door in the morning, she had deep purple shadows under her eyes. It was then she asked that I bring her a fern branch, a pine bough, and a batch of Dmitri's very strong tea. Princess Sablorova was very specific on this point."

More superstitions—maybe some kind of . . . ritual? "Did you bring her the items?"

"Yes. She locked herself in her rooms for the rest of that day. I knocked and called her name. But she ignored me. Through the closed door, I heard her restless step as she paced, talking to herself, or someone else. She kept saying, 'Where are you?' Then, 'I shall bring you back. I shall find a way.' Even the heavy crinkle of her black skirts could be heard. That is how violently she moved. As if possessed by some nechistaya sila."

Irina suddenly has the intense urge to stop listening, to leave this sick woman and this gaudy house. "But she came out eventually. . . ."

"We had to break down the door and sedate her. She had a fit, screaming at the top of her lungs. Weeping. Raving. Even when sedated, she kept muttering nonsense."

Irina thinks she remembers the screams. But when she asked Maman about it, all her mother said was not to worry. Irina then fell back asleep. The guilt prickles at her again, unhelpfully. She leans closer to Svetlana. "What kind of nonsense?"

"How she failed. How it didn't work, and he is gone forever. I assumed she was talking about Andrei. That is all I know. I left your family's employ right after that."

Irina nods. After a short pause, she thanks Svetlana and scribbles the name of Auntie's doctor for her on a scrap of paper. Irina then finds Will, and he engages a droshky to take her back to headquarters before continuing with his inspection of the other ARA offices. She feels none of the warmth of the previous ride. Will is gone, her conversation with Paulina as fresh in her mind as a nightmare. And Irina thought she saw a man looking suspiciously like Felix among the crowd—as Will was paying the driver.

Something else niggles at her.

Auntie has always been the composed, rational member of the family. This makes the fits stand out all the more. The first was the one Svetlana described. The last was when the Soviet men had moved in. And there was another in between, half a year after Andrei's death—a few days following the Cheka visit and Grand-père breathing his last. Irina and the children were kept from their grandfather's corpse. But she heard it whispered, by Dmitri or Maman, that Auntie was taking Grand-père's death hard, that she sat with his body into the long hours of the night. Apparently, praying. And that she finally broke down on the third night, screaming and weeping. She was ill for months after that. Irina's rooms were on the other side of the house, and she didn't hear any of it. All she remembers is her own grief—for her son, for Grand-père and Pasha.

If she had asked questions, the truth was kept from her.

Now she considers: Could Auntie's fits have been brought on? If so, by what—or *whom*? Could it have been Auntie herself? Their servants had left by then, all except the now deceased Dmitri and a nurse, Masha, who had taken care of Seryozha and Grand-père. She died along with Xenia of scarlet fever. If the three fits are related, Auntie would have asked either Dmitri or Masha to gather the protection charms and blood. For the most recent fit, Auntie would have collected those items herself.

Irina wonders if the items *were* for a ritual and, if so, what it was for.

26

Word Time Travel

"YOU . . . CAME." LILI stares at Nikolai, who stands expectantly on Moscow House's threshold with a black umbrella shadowing his face.

Though, of course, she told him to come the night before. With mounting distress and humiliation, she recalls colliding with Nikolai upon rounding the corner of the ARA. A soaked gray twilight blotted out the day, and her hands were shaking at the thought of returning to the house alone. It was the first time Lili had seen him since Grandmère's death. She tried to ignore the fluttery, unmoored sensation that clutched at her.

Then Lili blurted it all out—that she didn't wish to go back to a house emptied of Bolsheviks, though they *were* bastards; that she is drowning in Uncle Pasha's diaries; that she's scared to disappoint Irina. It isn't that Lili needs help. She needs her friend. Someone to tell her if she is sinking too deeply into her uncle's story.

Now Nikolai's mouth appears out of shadow, curved into a smirk. The rain pounds hard against the canvas. "Have you changed your mind?"

Lili presses back, beastly awkward, as he walks past. She cannot sense the cold through the hot humiliation burning through her like brush fire. Rain lashes at her, the rotting leaves scented with decay, with death. She hurries to pull the doors closed, dripping wet already. She was planning on spending her Saturday with Uncle Pasha's diaries, having entirely forgotten about Nicky.

Nikolai's lips are cold as he leans in to kiss first one cheek, then the other. He lingers there a beat too long before yanking his umbrella closed in a burst of raindrops. "So, how are you, Lil, really?"

"Fine, Nikolai," she says evenly. She hates pity, his especially.

"Do you know"—his gaze sweeps the entrance hall—"I haven't been here in years."

"Really?" Lili feigns surprise. But it's been at least since before the Revolution. "Are you hungry? Would you like some tea?" Russian hospitality has been drilled into her since birth.

Nikolai smirks. "You don't have to stand on ceremony with me, Lil."

"Er, all right." She wishes Cleo could offset her awkwardness. But it is a rainy, dark day, and her parakeet is still asleep in the rafters. Lili settles on cool and aloof as she leads Nikolai through the newly abandoned West Wing toward the library.

A dusty gray light curls along the edges of the curtains. Lili's skin is hot and spiky. This time, from being watched—and not by Nikolai. Darkness spills into the corners of the rooms, shadows rustling against the walls. The imp creature? Or the ghosts, restless for night? Watery black spots have sprung up on the wallpaper, a fungus or growth of some sort. And a damp, cloying feeling. Lili almost smells the dying leaves again. She doesn't remember ever seeing mold in the house, except in the trunks with the books. She'll need to ask Irina about it.

On the library's second landing, Lili shows Nikolai Uncle Pasha's diaries.

She arranged them in chronological order along the stair's railing, setting aside those from the 1917 February Revolution to the night the Cheka came. That's when her world fell apart, and that's where she wants to begin.

She tells Nikolai what to look for, and they each grab a diary. He settles onto the floor against the bookshelves, casual, at ease with reading together as they used to. Lili has the strangest urge to curl up beside Nicky. Instead, she snuggles into Uncle Pasha's armchair. Nestles deep into the scratchy wool of her coat. She keeps it on; it is ghastly cold, especially now that she is static.

On 2 March 1917, Uncle Pasha writes: *The streets of former St. Petersburg are still restless after the women's demands for bread on the morning of 23 February turned into a full-scale revolution.* Lili skips several paragraphs—after all, she lived it—until:

Marie has moved in with us, along with her husband and son. Their house has been taken over by an angry mob. So here we are again, under one roof like children.

Tonight, I was afraid when Marie did not return with the whitewashed dusk. We avoid the streets at night. She finally whirled in like the unseasonal blizzard outside. Not herself. Her hair was undone, her eyes wild, bloodshot, strange.

"What happened, Marie?" I demanded in rapid French. "Were you attacked?" Many noblewomen in town have been set on by marauding men.

"No," she whispered. She tore viciously at her snow-covered coat.

"Then what is it? Shall I get Aleksei for you?"

Her eyes went horribly wide. Then she lunged at me, beating my chest with two iron spoons in one hand and a lump of what looked like melted, dried wax in the other. "Where is Andrei?" she cried out, trembling all over. "Where is my boy?"

"In his rooms," I said, having seen her son for supper followed by cigars and cards, as was our custom. "Marie, are you well?"

"She told me . . . My God. She told me—he shall die. My boy shall die." Marie let out a keening, anguished wail that made the flesh on my bones crawl.

"Who told you?"

But my logical, composed sister was now raving. Something about the spoons having holes, an ill omen, death. Her fingers trailed marks on my shirt, a velvety scarlet red. Blood. It was all over her, even on the georgette crepe of her frock.

Before I could speak, Marie rushed from the room. But her eyes stayed with me.

The raving, the strange objects, the blood. Many at court availed themselves of the dark arts, of prophesies and mystics, of witches and tellers of fortunes. Even the German woman, the so-called empress. The only good news is her mystic friend is dead. The few times I met him, Rasputin frightened me. His eyes were like Marie's.

Can she be dabbling in the occult? Or influenced by someone who is? I know most of it is harmless. But I don't like it. I have never liked it. It, Rasputin, his unearthly miracle cures, brought about Russia's ruin. No, I do not trust it.

An invitation from Viktor soon distracted me and, despite the late hour, I trudged to the Mariinsky for a lovely concert. Viktor held my hand in the darkness of our box. If not for the torn-down golden eagles, the mud and evil-smelling cigarettes, and the jeers of the new <u>citizens</u>, I would have been content.

I hope Irina is safe in the countryside. For now, sleep—and perhaps I shall awaken from this living nightmare, this hell on earth, this Russia I no longer recognize.

Lili looks up, fingering Uncle Pasha's ring on its ribbon, carefully thinking of the past. "Do you remember a man named Viktor? I think . . . he was my uncle's lover."

Nikolai tips his head back in thought. "There *was* a man, with your uncle or watching him, always watching. Yes, I remember it now—him."

Lili searches deep in her memory, comes up empty, gives up. She has known many men who preferred other men—especially in Uncle

Pasha's artistic circles—and though she has never found such relationships anything but normal and right, society back then had forced them into hiding. Did Uncle Pasha hide, too? He doesn't mention Viktor's surname, or patronymic, leaving the man cloaked in infuriating shadow.

"Why was Irina in the countryside during the Revolution?" asks Nikolai.

"Working at some hospital, I think. We . . . don't really talk about it." Lili blows out a breath. "You and I used to read about magic, prophesies, fortune tellers, the dead. But it is Irina who suspected Auntie's interest in the occult. My uncle apparently thought the same."

"He also pointed out that many ladies of their set were superstitious."

Nikolai is right, Lili thinks. Maybe Auntie dabbled with divination or fortune-telling or some other superstition, maybe even with something darker, mysticism or magic. But what did that have to do with the ghosts or the night Uncle Pasha died? After all, men had stormed their house and murdered her uncle before arresting Papa and Uncle Aleksei. The superstitions Galya described may have been innocent enough. And Luda, well, Lili doesn't trust her at all. Not after the old bag remembered an innocent joke and twisted it into something sinister and ugly. Unexpected laughter bubbles up. "Say, Nicky, do you remember when we slipped that mouse into our old housekeeper's bread basket?"

"Yes. But I remember it as a rat. A big, fat one."

Maybe the old bag wasn't exaggerating after all. Lili laughs, wishing she could throw her arms around Nicky, suddenly transforming into the boy she knew. But that would be wrong. They are pretending nothing happened between them. Which is what she needs, her friend without the complications. "See, this is why I like you," she blurts, realizing her mistake too late. "As a friend . . . as anyone." She hates how his curls tangle over his brow and how his shirtsleeves are pulled up to his very elbows, revealing the black hair curling over his skin. She drops her eyes, but not before glimpsing his wicked smile.

"Do you wish for company in that chair?" he quips.

"Not without another box of gingerbread cookies."

"Shall I motor over to Petrograd, then?"

"No." Lili tries not to smile. "Let's keep reading." Her cheeks are on fire from embarrassment. If he sat beside her, even without the cookies, she would let him.

After what seems an eternity, Nikolai glances up from the diary in his lap.

"This entry is from late April 1917. Pavel Sergeyevich talks about how he and your aunt had an argument in the Little Reception room of Peter House. Shall I read it?"

April 1917, Lili thinks, and lets herself remember that time—her family removing from Peter House that May in great haste and traveling to their country estate. Then fleeing to Moscow House amid the unrest a month or two later. She suppresses the shred of memory she's kept buried—the strained ride in their automobiles after almost not finding gasoline, the vicious people spitting and cursing at them as they passed. Luda told Lili and Irina of arguments between Auntie and Uncle Pasha right before that, and in this very room. Perhaps the old bag was right about more than just the rat.

"Do read the entry, Nicky." Lili cannot keep his nickname from her lips. It is like the splash of warm, aromatic tea on her tongue, with deliciously dark cherries. Especially when he reads.

Marie has not been the same. Tonight, her eyes again glistened bright and unnatural. Almost untethered. Especially when Papa mentioned the end of our estate income. There will no longer be adequate funds to maintain our expenses. I was bone tired, darling Luba beside me, big with child yet small and gray with sickness. Still, I had to speak.

"We must remove to Moscow," I said, explaining it is quieter there and will allow us to weather the storm while Russia's fragile democracy takes root.

It was Marie who attacked me. She said I was out of my mind. Called up images of the tsar under house arrest with his family, others like us dead in the streets. She begged Papa to think of her poor son and our poor children. To leave as many are doing.

I stood my ground and said, very clearly, "We shall not leave Russia." Naturally, the family sided with me. Marie was suggesting we abandon our houses, possessions, who we are. The priceless paintings and sculptures and tapestries alone, much less the antique furniture, decorative arts, and other treasures! No, it is unthinkable. Simply unthinkable.

"You are more worried about your possessions than your children," Marie spat out.

And in her eye, I saw not only that untethering but hatred, pure and simple. A part of me was convinced that she would take up a blade and tear through me right then and there. But I drove the point home. "Without their legacy, our children have nothing and are nothing. Besides, we need to carry our name with dignity. That means no fleeing."

"I agree," said Alexander. "To love, and to country!" Everybody in the room smiled and nodded, in the thrall of the charming Alexander Golitev.

Marie was shaking her head so hard I thought it would swivel off her neck.

"We shall go to Moscow," our patriarch ruled, "following a visit to the countryside. We have spent every summer there for decades. This year shall be no different. Tradition is the only way to transcend the evil attempting to bring us down."

"But look around you, Papa," Marie cried out. "Russia is different, we are different. We will die if we stay here. And the children—"

I did not hear the rest. I walked out.

Not quite the scene of screaming and madness Luda had described; rather, a difference of opinion. Auntie wished to leave Russia, and Uncle Pasha and the family wished to stay.

"There is more." Nicky breaks into her thoughts. "Should I keep reading?"

"Yes," Lili decides after a minute. Though she promises that as soon as this is all over, she will read Uncle Pasha's diaries in their entirety, cover to cover, word by word.

"In May 1917, before your family left Petrograd, your uncle writes—"

Preparations for our departure are underway.

I worry for Irina. And for Luba, smaller and grayer than ever. I sometimes fear she will not make it. And for the first time, I see the age in Papa, in the slower way he thinks and moves. But as with all else, I shall put my trust in God.

Marie has been quiet. The edgy, wild look in her eye has dimmed. She is, as ever, her dignified self. But every once in a while, that look flashes back into her eyes like lightning. It blinds me for a disorienting moment. And I question if I saw it at all. Is it a ruse to make me think her mad when she is really thinking, scheming, waiting?

Her presence is a heavy thing. It steals the air out of any room. As if Marie means to suffocate me. And like a noxious perfume, it lingers long after she is gone. She watches me from under her thick black brows when she thinks I am not looking. But she rarely meets my eyes. Though hers I feel everywhere, like those of a predator stalking her prey. You may think me mad. I am not. Marie is not, either.

I am counting down the days to my last meeting with Viktor. Then he will leave.

He has asked me to come with him, but of course I said <u>No</u>.

"It is the same the rest of that month and early summer in the countryside," Nicky says, flipping through the diary. "Except for your

Aunt Luba's death, Seryozha's birth, and your uncle's parting from Viktor."

No shouting matches or shattering of priceless heirlooms. Nothing to suggest the kind of explosive behavior Luda had spoken of. But there *was* tension. Either Lili didn't notice it at the time or the family hid it well. They were courtiers, after all. They could hide anything—even hatred. "What about later that summer and autumn, our arrival at Moscow House and Andrei's decision to join the White army? Auntie *was* upset...."

But Lili and the other children hadn't been privy to those discussions, if there had been any. All she remembers is her cousin announcing his decision one evening at dinner, with his characteristically eager smile and a toast, Uncle Aleksei smiling pleasantly, her aunt staring back tight-lipped and ghastly pale, both evidently already informed of their son's news.

"There is an entry from November 1917, and two from December 1917. Would you like me to read them?" Nicky asks dutifully, and Lili nods, letting Uncle Pasha's words wash over her.

3 November 1917

I cannot sleep. What a day, for the end to come so senselessly. Oh, Russia, you are truly lost now, your descent into anarchy all but assured. Today we rose to the news the Bolsheviks have taken over Moscow by blasting into the Kremlin.

We have been trapped in the house since 28 October. Shooting, machine-gun fire, and explosions surrounded us. There are bullets in our courtyard. The house feels more like a besieged fortress. All we have left to eat are potatoes. All the windows are covered. The telephone lines are dead, the lights have gone out. There are barely any newspapers. Only rumors.

A counteroffensive, a civil war, with ours called the Whites and theirs the Reds.

We stayed in the dining room long after Irina and the children left following dinner. My niece is still not herself, tired and withdrawn, though her ordeal was nearly five months ago. She almost fainted when Andrei, our dear boy, stated his intention of joining the Whites. Marie already knew. Still, I had expected her to rail at me, to blame me for her son's decision, to again press her case for leaving Moscow and Russia.

But I only felt invisible hands wrapping around my throat. I tell you, it was difficult to draw breath. Her eyes fixed on me. Steady, unshakable. Hard and black as onyx. Bewitched. I thought I saw flames flickering in the irises. The Devil himself staring out. And her expression twisted into such anguish, such hatred, that my words fail me. Or maybe it is my heart. It has a funny way of beating these days, too fast, with too many skipped beats, drowning in blood like our homeland.

———

2 December 1917

We are afraid of any man with a gun. The Bolshevik Red Guards have set upon the city like bloodthirsty hounds. We avoid going out as much as possible, shutter the windows and doors until Moscow House resembles a tomb we are buried alive in.

At times, we have only tallow candles for light and a little firewood for heat on the intensely cold, long nights. But I refuse to burn anything in the house.

Marie is everywhere. Her presence has turned accusing. As if to say, <u>It is your fault. And if anything happens to him, it will be on you.</u> Andrei left in November. There has been little word from him since. A line or two, hastily scrawled on a scrap of paper, delivered by some White soldier passing through Moscow. That is all.

Does Marie still blame us for not leaving? Is she plotting to steal the children from us under cover of night? Or does she plot more nefarious plans? She looks so calculating, so intent, filled with such hatred that I fear she shall go as far as to kill me—with her hands as much as her dark arts.

Maybe she is the one entombing us in this house. Cursing it like the witch in <u>Sleeping Beauty</u> to one hundred years of sleep. Only, we will not live that long.

I can only unburden myself in these pages. I try to speak to Papa, but the silence of his rooms is listening. I try to catch Maman at her washing or baking, but the walls echo back. I try to speak to my brothers-in-law, or Anna, but the windows have eyes. I feel itchy, as if I cannot quite find my place, as if my body is poised midflight, away from here. Maybe into Viktor's arms, which I dream of every night.

But enough! Enough. At least I can open the window and breathe in that Russian air, the air I was born to breathe. The air I shall die breathing. I know it as certainly as death itself. I am where I should be—home.

---

7 December 1917

Frightening news from Petrograd: there is now an official komissiya dedicated to combating counterrevolution. They are calling it the Cheka. People like us are required to register, some to be interrogated. God help us if Marie was right all along.

Outside, rain lashes at the window in slanting streaks as if to bury Lili and Nikolai in the same house Uncle Pasha envisioned as a tomb. It even smells like a grave with that damp, wet stink of rot and fungus and deterioration. Beyond the rain, twilight steals into the slate-gray, swollen sky.

Lili is unmoored, emptied, the diary entries hollowing her out by transporting her to that cold, dark winter nearly four years ago. To the past. This time, she lets it all in.

She hops from the armchair and starts to pace. "I remember the waiting, the sitting around, the looking out the windows, everybody grave and fearful. I kept busy, reproducing portraits of royals and our dead ancestors, or else reading with Irina when she wasn't tired. We were told her hospital work had led to a breakdown. I took care of Xenia, even baby Seryozha when Nurse Masha needed a break. But I remember the unending snow, the tense silences, the mobs in the streets, the rifles Papa and my uncles would take up to keep watch."

"What about your aunt?" Nikolai asks. "Do you . . . well, believe there was anything to Pavel Sergeyevich's fears? Or to what Luda said?"

Lili gives a laugh. "What did he fear? That she was *there*, that she was watching him? Well, she has been doing that all my life. Much more so than my mother. And she didn't kill my uncle. We know this." A prickly anger unexpectedly sluices through the numb cold. Why is *she* the one telling *him* about *her* family? "What about you, Nicky?" She captures his gaze and holds it.

His face darkens, his eyes becoming opaque, unfathomable. "Don't you think your uncle and what happened to him is more important at the moment?"

Lili crosses her arms. "We can only talk about my family, is that it? You haven't told me—anything. What happened to you and your family, how you ended up in Moscow, why you—didn't let me know. I thought you were dead. But you just didn't trust me."

A flash of white-hot anger. "You are the one who didn't want anything to do with the past. Now you do. Well, I don't. It isn't that I don't trust you, Lili, it's that I'm not ready to go back there. Can't you understand that?"

Lili's anger burns out, drops into the pit of her stomach in a hard knot of remorse. She notices how weary he is, the hollowness in his face somehow more pronounced with the stubble on his cheeks.

"That is why I didn't look you up." A corner of his mouth lifts in a smirk. "And why you didn't look me up, either."

He is right, the bastard. She didn't ask questions after Uncle Pasha's trip to Petrograd. She chose to assume that, like the past, Nicky was dead. It was easier that way. One burial of what had been, then only the present. "Why are you here now?" Lili asks curiously.

"Isn't it obvious?" Nikolai averts his gaze, scrubs the back of his neck. "You, we, are different," he says. Then he approaches her, tentatively, and lifts his hands to her face. If he expects her to jerk away, she doesn't. He traces her features lightly with his fingers. "Now, instead of running, or making excuses, or God knows what else, can you—sit with me?" He crosses the room to the armchair, watching her all the while.

It is fair, what he said. Lili cannot force Nikolai to share a painful past that she has only recently started to explore. But they are here, in Uncle Pasha's library, reading his story together, as if he meant them to. This has to be enough. For now.

"You just want to sit with me?" Lili teases.

A small, playful smile glimmers on his lips, but he says nothing.

Lili heaves a sigh. But she cannot resist, and Nikolai knows it.

She walks over to him and, after a beat of hesitation, sits in his lap. She is awkward, all elbows and frightful angles. A hopeless child. No real experience, no damn grace, certainly no femininity. And as Lili throws her arms around his neck, she almost grazes his nose with an elbow. But she forgets any awkwardness when she notices how very cold and lonely he looks. Maybe instead of speaking, all Nicky needs is simple human contact.

So Lili tightens her arms around his shoulders and pushes her face against the flesh of his neck. The stray curls there brush against her cheeks. He tips his head back, forcing her to meet his gaze. His face is bare, open, totally unguarded. And in that moment, she thinks maybe what he needs is *her*.

Before she can talk herself out of it, Lili leans down and clumsily catches his mouth in hers. She swears she almost missed. But she feels Nicky's fingers trail her neck to grip her face, pulling her in ever closer, ever deeper. Kissing her back.

27

Red Raids and More Time Travel

AS LILI WALKS into ARA headquarters on Monday, she can tell something is very wrong.

Paper is strewn all over the offices, posters of the old, severe President Harding and Chief Herbert Hoover torn from the walls. The usually cheerful, polished men rush past with shirts half-buttoned and faces flushed and blotchy. Their whispers simmer hotly, blowing over to Lili in wisps. *Raid* and *ransacked. Bolos. Fuckers.*

So, the bastards have managed to force their way in even here. Lili feels bristly, bleary, violated. As if the last safe place is no longer so. She meets Irina's gaze grimly. Though the Soviet government theoretically isn't supposed to trespass on American property, it is still Moscow. Now the ARA offices are as topsy-turvy and nightmarish as Russia herself. A shadowed, fucked-up kind of Wonderland Lili doesn't even recognize.

But it is when she glimpses her desk that her hands turn cold and clammy. "Bastards," she whispers. The word has no force behind it, no spine whatsoever.

On the wall behind her and Frank's desks, where they had painstakingly assembled the photographs, drawings, sketches, and bits of typewritten and handwritten notes on the ARA's former people employees, only the glare of empty wallpaper can be seen. All else has been ripped down and scattered carelessly over the parquet.

Weeks of work, of traveling all over town for that one more sketch, of scouring the payroll for people like them, hearing their stories, their tragedies, their triumphs . . .

Irina crosses the room to speak to Will, whose face is as dark and thunderous as the other men's, while Lili approaches the wall. Frank is on his knees there with a wastebasket. He doesn't look up.

"And we had just said we were almost ready to submit your story."

It is probably the first time Lili hasn't seen his face light up with that bright, white-toothed smile. It makes her sad.

She kneels beside him and starts to pick up the photographs and pictures of Luda, Galya, Paulina, Kirill, others. Of Moscow, too—30 Spiridonovka, the Hermitage and its queues of children, the bazaar with the white-haired aristocratic ladies selling their jewels. Some are torn, others smudged, several besmirched with fingerprints. Only a few are left untouched. It occurs to Lili that whoever did this, likely the Bolos, now knows exactly which former people work for the ARA, though they probably already did. Her fingers tremble as she sorts the paper into piles, the one for Frank's wastebasket making her cheeks flush hotly with an entirely futile, stupid anger.

"Don't fret, Francis. We will piece it all back together and return for the rest." Lili rolls back on her heels and pulls out her sketch pad and pencil, attempting to order her thoughts and calm her trembling fingers. "What do they think happened?" she asks in a low voice.

Frank shrugs. "We arrived to find the offices like this. Last night we were out late. They must have come then. Since we headed straight upstairs, we didn't notice. Not until this morning. The Cheka, probably. The Bolos have been more brazen lately. We've caught them following us about town, and we think a few agents have been stationed on Spiridonovka, watching the mansion and us. Will and Carroll and others have been on their telephones all morning. But the Bolos are denying everything, swearing up and down the raid wasn't them."

The heat in Lili's cheeks explodes all over her skin. "It is bullshit."

A project that is supposed to be her *fight for* something, for people like her and their story, has turned dangerous.

"Right." A corner of his mouth quirks up in wry amusement.

The heat eases. She puts aside her sketch pad and pencil. "And here I thought it was you, in a wild moment of Jekyll and Hyde madness," she jokes, and Frank finally laughs.

"There you are!"

A pale and harried Nikolai is hurrying toward them.

And her hard-won ease is turned on its head, becoming as topsy-turvy as the offices. Lili feels prickly, as though her very insides are itching. That kiss in the library smashes back into her head—its heat setting her entire body aflame, their tongues tangling, his stubble leaving a sting on her cheek she can still feel.

That was all they did before Lili walked Nicky back to the entrance hall, painfully awkward as ever. She doesn't even remember meeting his eye, though she might have mumbled a hasty *Thank you*. He smirked, asked if it was for the help with the diaries or the kiss. She doesn't remember much after that, only his warm lips on her cheeks and the wink of one dark eye followed by the slam of the doors.

She hefted some of the diaries up to the attic but didn't have the heart to return to them by herself, as Irina was occupied with their cousins. So Lili went to the park with her family instead, Seryozha insisting on it with his irritatingly childish whine. Though it was gloomy outside, and the rain did not let up the entire time.

Now Lili feels Nicky's cold hands on her arms as he helps her up. His gaze scans her face, each feature, every shadow and freckle. "Are you all right, Lil?" he asks, glancing at Frank. "Both of you. I heard the Bolsheviks raided headquarters, and I rushed over. The bastards. I cannot believe they would—"

"We weren't here when it happened." Lili is painfully aware of Frank curiously, openly studying them. She clears her throat. "I'm all right, Nicky." Their intimacy feels strange in front of people. As if the itch scratching at her insides is turning bizarrely from heat to discomfort, wicked rose thorns breaking violently through skin.

The Haunting of Moscow House

"Do the Bolos still live with you?" Frank slices through the awkwardness.

Lili shakes her head. "They left. Too afraid of the ghosts." She smiles a little at that.

"Ghosts? All right, well, whatever gets the job done, I guess. But you should still be careful. They'll be watching you even more than before. You, too, Niko."

Lili dimly recalls Irina saying something about an investigation into Moscow House, only not by Comrade Suzhensky. Lili doubts the ARA raid had anything to do with that. After all, there are whispers all over Moscow about Lenin growing uneasy with the so-called *humanitarian* ARA. More than once, judging by the telltale prickle on the nape of her neck, she has caught someone following her, too. "I am always careful." Lili winks.

With a polite nod at Frank, Nicky turns to her. "Would you like a ride home tonight? I can stay and read with you . . . if you wish it." He is uncharacteristically twitchy, fidgeting, raking his hair back. His curls catch at the collar of his coat and sweep into his eyes, which—she notices, shivering—are darkened with something feverish and restless.

Frank is watching them sidelong. Still. Lili has to say, *do*, something. She wants to scream, *Yes! Come over, stay, kiss me again.* Rashly she reaches over and brushes the curls from Nicky's forehead. His skin burns, and not with illness. She jerks her hand back, fingers tingling. "I'd . . . like that. As long as you don't mind the ghosts."

Nikolai gives her a small, relieved smile. "I never did." He hesitates, starts to turn, changes his mind. Steps toward her and presses his lips to her cheek. "See you tonight."

Lili's face is probably red as a tomato. She retraces her steps back to the wall and Frank. "Don't you dare say a word," she warns, without glancing up.

"Lili's got a boyfriend," Frank whispers, singsong.

She has rarely heard the word. But she knows what it means. "I do not!" Lili almost screeches, tempers her voice. "Nicky—Nikolai is a friend, that is all."

Not even she believes that, her mind crashing back to those darkened eyes, the feel of his warm lips, his smoky, sweet taste. Her insides turn as wobbly as holodets meat jelly at the thought. Lili doesn't want the complications, but she can no longer resist this new physical charge between them. She will not. They can be friends who kiss, she decides. The heated, wobbly feeling stays, drops down to her belly like a hot ember. Lili is ready to jump out of her skin, hot and itchy, waiting for twilight to slip into the sky.

It finally does, and she is the one who kisses him.

She does so against the Cadillac, her body instinctively lining up to fit his as she pulls down his face. Lili ignores his surprise before their lips meet. She loses herself in the slick, flame-like heat, the pressure that robs her of breath. Despite the bitter cold, the snow waiting on the air, it burns through her from lips to lower belly. They break apart, still breathing the same air, unwilling to look away. And Lili knows she is in trouble. That this feeling, this big, hot, expansive thing within her, might just be what people call love.

Has it—that charge, the energy, the *love*—always been there between them, simmering just beneath their skin? No, they can never return to being friends or children. But then, Lili realizes, they left friendship and childhood behind a long time ago. And not just in that graveyard. They lost it during the Revolution by staring death in the face as if it were as there and alive as the ghosts in Moscow House.

Nicky takes her face in his hands and traces her features, contemplative, and Lili thinks he might be thinking the same. Something stops her from saying it aloud. Maybe she isn't ready. A little of the cold, the tension, slips back in. With it, the awareness they are outdoors in the rapidly approaching darkness, vulnerable to prying eyes . . . and tongues.

"We should go," Nicky says, low and gravelly, again seeming to hear her thoughts. He glances around. "It isn't safe out here."

They motor over to Moscow House, where they park a little farther down the street. All the while, Lili is aware of the silence, the strain in the air, the possible eyes following them. They walk quickly along the street and into the house.

It is all candlelight and shining marble and a suffocating heaviness that bears down on Lili from the ceiling, the walls, any and every glimmering surface.

"This wasn't here the other day." Nikolai points to the wall above the grand staircase—the same wet black spots, the fungus, has sprung up there, too.

Lili peers around the hall, seeing the hint of blackness blooming mushroomlike on the other walls as well, along with wet streaks. The wallpaper is peeling back, revealing yellowed white paint, itself peeling in ghastly patches. She can *smell* its rot and decay. "Come on," Lili says, uneasily, "let's go up to the attic." It is dark by now, and she would rather not take any chances. The ghosts may not show until midnight, but the creature might.

As soon as she opens the attic door, Cleo swoops down, a twitchy, fast-moving shadow in the dark. Feathers brush against Lili's face as she strokes the little parakeet.

"Where are Irina and the children?" A flick, then the strike of a match and a light flares up, its rusty orange glow illuminating Nicky's dark features. His eyebrows seem heavier, the curve of his lower lip more pronounced.

Those lips will be the death of her if the ghosts aren't, Lili thinks wryly. Out loud, she says, "They were supposed to be back, but Irina mentioned she might be held up at the ARA, given the Bolo raid. If so, she would have left my cousins at their friend's. I think Madame Trobelska is growing frustrated with the arrangement."

Lili leads Nicky into her and Irina's room, followed by a tittering Cleo.

He places the candle on the table by the window, and she presses down the image of Uncle Pasha standing on his grave just outside.

"So, this is where you live . . . and sleep." Nikolai gives her a narrow, deeply intimate look that makes her blush furiously. "And you can leave your cousins with my mother anytime. There isn't a day when she doesn't lament the loss of the old world, me being married by now and her with a brood of grandchildren."

Lili laughs but feels warm and tingly inside. "Thank you, Irina will appreciate it." She had left the diaries lined up in a neat row on the table. Now she selects one for herself and one for Nicky. Their fingers brush inadvertently, sparking heat between them and a stab of longing through her belly. "I . . . appreciate it, too."

"I know," he says, hesitating for a minute, then tugging her to him and catching his mouth in hers for a kiss that sets every one of her nerve endings on fire with pure want. He lets go, too soon. "I would do anything for you, Lil—anything." Nicky's voice is rough with emotion.

"I know," she whispers, the words *I would, too*, maybe *I love you*, on her tongue. Lili is itching to kiss him again, his mouth tantalizingly close. But the idea of doing what they did in the graveyard feels wrong here. And the Bolo raid is making both of them tense. She can feel it in his jerky movements, the rigid set of his shoulders.

So Lili takes his hand and leads him to her cot. "Will you sit with me, Nicky?"

His laugh is husky. "Will you? No running?"

"No running." It feels as though they are talking about something more, and she likes it.

"All right," he says.

Lili senses the touch of his hands on her shoulders as he helps her out of her coat before they sit together on the cot. At first, they are horridly stilted and awkward. But the gravity between them draws them closer until they relax into each other. For once, Lili is glad it is bitterly cold. She throws a thick wool blanket over them and feels the thrill of his body, his head leaning against hers, his breathing a little ragged but evening out.

Cleo drops into her lap, and she pulls her in tightly. "Do you mind reading, Nicky?" Lili asks.

He reaches an arm around her shoulders, and she shifts so that her cheek is pressed against his chest. Then he takes up a diary and begins to read in that wonderfully deep voice of his, so faithfully evoking Uncle Pasha.

3 March 1918

Today is sure to be one of the darkest days of my life.

We received the dreaded news that our dear, brave boy is gone. Andryusha was killed in action a few days before. I realized it as soon as I heard the keening wail. I paced with sweaty palms, unsure what to do. Go to her rooms, and risk Marie's wrath, the blame for her son's death? For it <u>is</u> my fault. But even knowing it would cost Andrei's life, I would still not have left. Somebody needs to defend our world, and our brave boy did. I could never take that from him. Or my pride in his sacrifice.

Toward nightfall, I decided to go to Marie's rooms.

The wail had weakened, becoming a pathetic moan interspersed with stifled sobs.

I have never seen my sister so indisposed. Marie lay in the grand bed with her hair unmade, falling in black waves over a damp white nightgown. She wore no dressing gown, no rouge on her cheeks. And there was a sour, stale smell to her rooms. The family was gathered around her solemnly, as if to pay their last respects. The children were not present, not even Irina, which was only right. They did not need to witness such grief.

Marie met my gaze with a lift of her head from the pillow. Her eyes—good God. They shone <u>witchlike</u>. An orange flame flickered in the irises that could have been from the candles. Or from the fires of Hell. "<u>You!</u>" she screamed. "You murdered my son!"

"He did not kill Andrei, ma chérie," Aleksei hurried to whisper in French.

"He did! He did!" Marie shrieked. "It is because of him and his pride, his obsession with his possessions and this house, that we never left. That we are still here. And that my boy, my only son, is dead!" Then she roared, "Out, all of you! Leave me!"

"Please, ma chérie, be reasonable," Aleksei tried weakly.

"Out of my sight! Especially him—a brother to me no longer."

I should not have gone to her rooms. I had known she would blame me. Not only for her son's death, but for not leaving Russia. So she truly hates me. Has disowned me. Yet my heart is frightfully calm, as if Andryusha himself is standing beside me.

---

10 March 1918

We have been watching Marie closely, fearful she will try to harm herself, or take her own life. She has not yet left her bed. I was banished from her rooms for several days, but somebody was needed to watch over her during the night. Since her outburst, Marie has not spoken to or even glanced at me. Every time I step into that sour room, she turns her back to me. I take a seat at her bedside anyway and begin to read from whatever book is in my lap. From Pushkin and Lermontov to Akhmatova. Poetry has always been my language when words have failed me. Though sadly, it is our relations that have failed.

---

13 March 1918

This night was the strangest of my life. I am still numb from the frost. And my throat and limbs ache, a sure sign of a cold. But now I am certain Marie is dabbling in the occult, in the dark arts and magic. For I saw her with a real teller of fortunes.

Tonight was my turn to watch over Marie. I came to her rooms promptly at 9 o'clock, as instructed by a harried, white-faced Aleksei. But when I tugged on the handle, the door did not open. It was locked. I had a moment of fleeting panic, knocking, calling out my sister's name, hearing nothing but unnerving silence on the other side.

Suddenly, the door was flung open. I toppled forward, Marie sidestepping me just in time. Her face was a mask again, those dark eyes the only indication of any unrest in her soul. Despite her fever, they blazed with that strange orange light.

"Marie?" I was still lying on her threshold, bewildered at her impeccably dressed hair and sleek black gown, at her scent of rose water washing over me.

"I am going out" is all she said.

Outside, it was a whirling white maelstrom. Though spring, the snow does not let up. As on that night one year ago. "Now? It isn't safe, and you are ill."

Marie stepped over me, pausing just outside the door. "Do not follow me, Pasha."

Dazed, I rolled to my feet and let her go down the stairs without a word. But I could not in good conscience do as she asked. I ran to my rooms, grabbed my coat and galoshes, and hurried after her.

She did not notice me, as she was already a receding blur when I stepped out of the house. But I could see her footsteps in the snow, and I followed, creeping along the snow-packed streets like a spirit.

The streets were empty, somehow still dark even with the large-flaked snow. As if we were trapped in the German snow globe I once brought back for Lili.

I realized we were heading toward the town center before I glimpsed the red wall, the Kremlin's spires, the peaks of St. Basil's rich, colorful orbs. I have not really looked at them in a long while.

They now remind me of all we have lost, a true symbol of Red Russia.

It was near Resurrection Gate that Marie stopped abruptly.

I hid myself behind a tree, praying to God and all the Saints that she would not see me.

But she dipped under the arch of the building on the left-hand side of the gate. I squinted, shuffled closer. Another woman appeared from inside a little wooden stall. There used to be a small market here. I didn't know it was still active, and at this time of night.

A little oil lamp burned at the front of the stall, otherwise hung with black cloth.

My hands and feet were falling numb, my clothes becoming sodden. A treacherous wind blew off Red Square. I waited like this for God only knows how long. When Marie finally reappeared, I was dripping wet, shuddering so hard my teeth clattered. I was barely able to stumble away as Marie swept past me back in the direction of Moscow House. Meanwhile, I crept up to the stall. Only the apprehension simmering in my chest warmed me. I hesitated before reluctantly walking up to the burning oil lamp.

The black material billowed, as if stitched out of the wings or skins of bats. A woman poked her head out. This close, I could see her clearly, and I leaped back. She was ghastly. Her long black hair was streaked an unearthly silver, like slivers of cold moonlight trapped in unholy darkness. A scarf covered the top of her head, dyed scarlet red, as if dipped in blood. But it was her eyes that pinned me where I stood. <u>Untethered</u>. Like Rasputin's had been. Like Marie's have started to be.

The woman smiled, and I recoiled. Half her teeth were blackened or missing. "Yes?" She was likely in her midsixties yet had a sprightly, lethal way about her, even her voice. A cigarette dangled from her mouth, comically hideous.

"Who are you? What is this place?" I croaked out.

"Vera." A puff of smoke. "Shall I tell your fortune, Count Sherbatsky?"

Horror took hold of me so completely that I bolted from the evil hag and her cursed stall without a word. I reached into my collar as I ran, not caring if the cold air rushed in, and grasped the gold cross at my chest. The one Viktor had given me for my last birthday that we had celebrated together. Then I uttered prayers to God and the Saints as furiously as if my life depended on it—for it most surely did—all the way back to Moscow House and my rooms, where I collapsed half dead in my bed.

14 March 1918

She is planning something. Something dark and forbidden. Something the hag must have revealed to her. Or the Devil himself. For perhaps they are one and the same. Nechistaya sila.

I have not felt at peace in my library for a long time. But it is still a place I drift to naturally each day. I was picking up a history I had written on the Sherbatsky clan, being in the middle of preparing a project on the family for the Bolsheviks, when I stopped. I had caught a whiff of rose water.

Marie was sitting in my favorite velvet green armchair.

The blood in my veins seemed to freeze, along with my heart.

She was bent over several dusty, old-looking tomes spread out across her lap. The sight was so peculiar, so unlike the Marie I knew, that for a moment I forgot my shock and horror at her sitting in my chair. Or the library, in which she barely sets foot.

When she heard the creak of the floorboards at my approach, Marie whipped her head up. That witchy gaze zeroed in, nailing me in place as though into a coffin.

Her lips spread slowly in a smile that was not really a smile. It was a stretching of the mouth, a gash splitting open like a wound. Once, I knew a clown that took his own life. That very night, I saw him at the circus, and he had smiled this way. All teeth and gums, the glint of bone, something in it unhinged yet profoundly knowing.

I dashed out of the library, buzzing with the question, <u>What can she be reading?</u> I had glimpsed a charcoal sketch of a snake on the opened page. Not just any snake—a viper. Are we living with one?

What is Marie planning? What is she capable of?

15 March 1918

Good God! I am back in my rooms, sick not only in body but in heart. I have come from Marie's. And God help us all. I am clutching Viktor's cross in my left hand as I write this, my knuckles whitened, the edges of the cross cutting into my skin.

Marie has not let anyone inside her rooms, not even Aleksei. I am ill, as I had predicted upon returning from that ill-fated excursion to Red Square and the fortune-telling hag. But I have kept an eye on Marie's door, unable to rest. Finally, she whirled into the hallway and down the stairs. She had her coat on over another funerary gown. Another excursion, I supposed. This time, I did not follow her.

Instead, I crept into her rooms, surprised she had left them open.

I went straight to the receiving room, hoping she had taken the books from the library and left them on her writing table. I was right. There were the same tomes, glaring up at me. I flipped through their fragile, yellowing pages. Some were spread open, others bookmarked or with their pages folded at the corners. I read those passages carefully, though I could barely stand upright. Marie's rosewater scent was everywhere, thick and cloying, smothering me.

It is all children's tales, fairy stories, I told myself. Spirits forgotten not only with the Revolution but with the modernity born of this century. A ghost reaching back through the generations of our family's ancestors, to the very beginning of our bloodlines, personifying our fathers and grandfathers, the heads of our family, the house itself. Laughable! Ridiculous! According to the Church, nothing but superstition. The tales we tell our children. And yet. Was it not superstition that brought Russia down?

There was something feverish in Marie's markings. Words, entire phrases and paragraphs, circled not once but many times, and with a red pen that seemed to bleed. I refuse to copy here what I saw in those pages. I need to know what it means first. And what Marie means to do with it. Where she went this night. I left the books in the exact same attitudes I found them in, noting titles, authors, other identifying features to locate them later. Once I do, I shall hide them somewhere safe. In case I—or anyone after me—has need of them. But not now. I cannot risk Marie finding out what I know.

I just realized: today is the Ides of March. My fingers tremble, aching like the rest of me. The only consolation is that I have had word of Viktor. He is back in Moscow.

Stupid man. Stupid, lovely, wonderful man. He has returned. With travel papers—for us, for me, to Paris. Our favorite place in the world. I have yet to respond. That there will be no Paris for me. That I shall not leave. Not even now. No, Moscow House is my destiny and my end. It is my tomb. Whether my death be in a day, a week, a month, but no more than a year. If not my heart, which beats with a sick little kick and skip to it, then it will be Marie, my own darling younger sister. The viper in our nest.

———

19 March 1918

I believe Marie is attempting to resurrect a spirit long dead in the house. A very old spirit. The first ancestor of our family's bloodline.

Marie has locked herself in her rooms again. For days, she opens her door only to her maid and a kitchen girl. The family is staying away, convinced she is back to her demanding self. They are wrong. Marie is carrying out her plans. I see tray after silver tray brought to her door. I glimpsed a glass pitcher of bright red liquid—the scarlet of that fortune-telling hag's scarf, or Marie's pen. I caught its iron-tinged, metallic tang. Blood.

I tried to ask around to be sure. Stopped her little maid, went down to the kitchens. But everyone fears Marie. She must have warned them to keep silent.

There is something I read in one of the tomes—that one can make a sacrifice to this spirit to appease it. To help awaken it from a deep sleep. Such dark arts necessarily use blood for sacrifice. I do not refer to the spirit by name, not daring to write it out. I read that speaking his name can awaken him, too. And when you see him, death is around the corner.

I realized I am not <u>ready</u> to die just yet. I have been thinking of dearest Lili, of innocent Natasha and Xenia, of sweet Seryozha, of beautiful, kind Irina. No, I shall not write his name. And I know where I shall take those books. To the only safe place left—to Viktor, his smoke-gray eyes my only consolation.

Even now, in my rooms, Marie is everywhere, as though she is watching me through the walls that separate us.

My theory is the purpose of awakening the spirit is to kill us. Murder by a mundane object such as a knife or a pistol would be too easy. No. Marie wishes for us, for me, to suffer.

God save us from her unholy, Devil-sanctioned darkness.

---

24 March 1918

Praise be to God! Whatever Marie has been trying to do, whatever sacrifice to whatever demonic spirit, it has failed. For here we are, alive and whole and well. She has taken to her bed since yesterday in a fever that has left her raving. She had a fit, screaming, muttering unholy things, perhaps incantations or curses, nearly jumping out the window. Poor Aleksei had to nail it shut so she cannot open it. Now Marie is the one in a coffin, and I am back in my armchair, free of her watchful presence—for now.

All the servants have left us except dear, loyal Dmitri and Masha. I wait for this month to end, for April to arrive with its cleansing spring showers. Yet isn't April a doomed month? I have heard it said it portends tragic things. My hand is shaking too hard. I can write no more.

28

Coming Together

"I THINK I KNOW what's happening!" Lili exclaims, rushing over just as Irina is walking into the attic, Seryozha and Natasha stumbling in her wake. Their burst of laughter and chatter is much too raucous for Irina's aching head and empty stomach.

Last night, by the time she and Will had finished their telephone calls, tidied up after the raid, and completed their other ARA duties, it was too late to return to Moscow House. She spent the next hours on a hard-cushioned sofa in the offices, managing to catch only a shred of sleep before collecting the children from Madame Trobelska's that morning. *Do what you need to do, Irene*, Will had said, letting Irina take the day for herself. He kissed her tenderly, deeply, when they had privacy. Though the conversation with Paulina was still trapped in her head, Irina leaned into the kiss, into its warmth and Will. More and more she wished to tell him about her son.

All this quite flies out of her head when Nikolai appears in their doorway—sheepishly. "Good morning, Irina." He smiles, without teeth, and blushes furiously.

There is a painful moment of discomfort before Lili bursts into jarring laughter. She steals a glance at Nikolai, who turns even more red, if that is possible. "Oh, Irishka, Nicky and I read Uncle Pasha's diaries. I didn't exactly think it would be safe for him to walk through the house after midnight. Nothing untoward happened, I swear it!"

As long as that is the whole truth. Irina looks between them suspiciously, slipping into her role of prim and proper elder sister. Though, since Georgy, what right has she had to propriety?

"Where is my doll?" Seryozha screeches at the top of his lungs, as Natasha mutters something snarky in reply, and Cleo swoops down, whistling and squawking at them all.

Irina cannot think with all this noise. "Quiet!" she finally shrills, and everybody immediately falls silent. She bends toward Seryozha, aiming to appear conciliatory. "If you go read with Cleo and Natasha, I'll have a treat for all three of you after." Thankfully, they flounce off, appeased for now.

Once Irina is in her and Lili's room, with the door firmly shut, she cuts a straight line to the stove and places a copper pot of water on the burner. Her stomach is contracting emptily, and she is too drowsy to handle whatever this is without coffee. She fumbles for the box of matches and lights one, holding it to the burner and watching the flame catch on the wick in a spark of blue. Then she finally turns to face Lili and Nikolai. "Explain, please."

Lili doesn't need further encouragement. She is ready to burst. "Uncle Pasha was convinced Auntie was working on a sacrifice *to a spirit*," she rattles off, in a loud, eager voice. "I believe it was to awaken the Domovoy."

"Domovoy," Irina repeats, thinking back to the chyort spirits of Old Russia, folk beliefs she had only heard whispered by servants and reduced to fairy tales. "The house spirit?"

"Yes, and I believe she succeeded. It's the imp we've seen around the house."

Irina understands none of it. "I need more, Lil. This is too much, much too fast."

Lili crosses the room, disappearing behind the screen only to reappear with her book of fairy tales in hand. "There aren't too many stories written down about the Domovoy, but there is one in this book.

I've read it to Seryozha. I didn't make the connection until last night, when we read the entries, and Uncle Pasha referred to an ancestral spirit that is part of the house. Most of the time, he isn't referred to by name. There are books with more that Uncle Pasha planned to give to Viktor for safekeeping."

Irina furrows her brow. Her mind is coming up blank. "Who?"

"We think"—Lili glances at Nicky, who holds her gaze and nods—"Viktor was Uncle Pasha's closest confidant—and his lover."

Irina opens her mouth. Closes it. "But Luba . . ."

"It was kept secret. I don't know if Aunt Luba knew."

"All right." Irina pushes away all the questions but one. "Say this Viktor does have the books you mention. How will you find him?" She ignores the simmering on the stove and steps closer to her sister, whose eyes, she realizes, are shining with tears.

Lili dashes a hand across her face, swallows, masters herself. "I have seen him. Not only before, but at the bazaar. He was selling signet rings like Uncle Pasha's with the key. But I didn't know who the man was then, though I think he recognized me. The more we read about him, the more I remembered. It was his eyes. Gray, and kind. I need to return to the bazaar to see him again . . . and to get the books."

They are motionless and so silent that Irina can hear the now bubbling water, Natasha's playful voice through the door. Finally, she goes to the stove. She is glad of the space and time to process the revelations tumbling out of that murky, shuttered past. Irina has wondered about Pasha and Luba. Their relations were warm and friendly yet seemed empty of true passion. At least, Irina had never felt it. On some instinctual level, she thinks she has always known. Pasha's gaze lingering on other men, commenting on their looks and bearing; his bohemian friends from the theaters and art studios across Petersburg; his spending countless nights on the town without Luba.

The existence of a fairy-tale creature from Old Russian lore is harder to grasp.

When Irina returns with three cups of coffee and a can of ARA milk, which she splashes into the cups, Lili is facing the window. Irina hands Nicky his cup, places Lili's on the table. Lowers into the chair with her own cup in hand. Its warmth seeps into her cold, stiff fingers, the comforting burnt scent winding its way into her.

"There is more," Nicky says, with a glance at Lili. "Pavel Sergeyevich followed your aunt to a fortune teller named Vera after Andrei died. We think this Vera might be the one who told your aunt about the sacrifice. Back then, Vera had a stall near Resurrection Gate."

Irina thinks back to the women they've spoken to. "The timing does coincide with the oddities Auntie had requested from her maid and the kitchen, indicating when she tried the sacrifice. Assuming her attempts coincide with her fits, she tried several times before succeeding, since we didn't see . . . the imp until recently. She tried once when Andrei died, once after the Cheka came, and once when the Soviet men moved in. But what was the sacrifice *for*? That is to say, if the sacrifice was meant to awaken the Domovoy, to what end?"

Lili turns back. Her eyes are red rimmed but dry. "Uncle Pasha believed it was to murder him. Maybe us, too." She goes on, "All the arguments, all the tension, all the blame—for staying in Russia and for Andrei's death."

"No," Irina says, with a firm shake of her head. "She wouldn't do that."

Lili doesn't touch her coffee. "You were always her greatest defender."

"I *know* Auntie. And I *know* she is not capable of it."

"There is an alternative." Nikolai pauses, taking a gulp of his coffee. "In the stories and fairy tales, there are people . . . who bring the dead back to life."

"Necromancy," Lili says, in a fearful whisper that chills Irina's blood.

"Or resurrection. What if your aunt . . . wished to bring Andrei back from the dead?"

"But what about the Domovoy?" Irina shakes her head. The

coffee is cooling, the tension building back up inside her, coiling her body like a tight spring. "Or the night Pasha died? Remember, Auntie wished to re-create it with that dinner. To change it."

"She could have intended to bring back your whole family," Nikolai points out.

"And the Soviet men? Who killed them? Or was that a coincidence?"

"What does black magic often require?"

"Blood." Lili's chest rises and falls rapidly. "The Domovoy, or the ghosts, could have killed the men, maybe Grand-mère. But if Auntie hated and blamed Uncle Pasha and the family as much as he seemed to think, then why would she attempt to bring them back? Why go through that, now of all times?"

"Why indeed," Irina echoes. "I saw Paulina when I stopped by the Pink House the other day. She mentioned . . . tension between Auntie and Maman." Irina swallows down her coffee to the dregs, wishing she had better answers. "Maybe we will know more when you go see Viktor and I find Vera. And we should finish reading Pasha's entries. We *will* get answers, Lil. And we will save this house." *And each other.* They have to.

For the first time, she is glad Auntie is away. Though Irina doesn't believe her aunt to be dangerous, she has a feeling this search would be significantly more complicated with her around. Auntie has never given up her secrets easily, or at all.

"Yes, maybe there's a way to reverse Auntie's sacrifice, or somehow force the ghosts to leave. I know it is what Uncle Pasha would want." Lili picks up her coffee thoughtfully. She puts the cup back down almost as quickly. "There is something else. That fungus on the walls, I think it's spreading."

Irina was afraid of that. She has also noticed the black mold. They will need to try to get rid of it. The room falls into silence, and she senses their conversation is at an end. Finally, she allows her eyes to drift to Lili and Nicky. "Anything else I should know?"

Both flush borscht red, then actually *giggle* like children. Nicky glances over at Lili, and Lili glances over at Nicky. But they say nothing. With a pang, Irina recalls the last time she saw Georgy alive. She never told him her true feelings, or lack thereof. How used and abandoned she felt after what happened between them. She also thinks of her own secret, still untold, still waiting. And she doesn't wish any of it for Lili.

"Will you . . ." Irina pauses, thinking how best to phrase it. "Promise me that you'll say what you need to say to each other. And for God's sake, be careful."

Lili drops her gaze. But she bobs her head. "All right, Irishka. We promise."

Soon Nicky makes his excuses and leaves. Then it is a breakfast of hot cocoa, hard-boiled eggs, bacon, cheese, and an assortment of sweets from the ARA commissary—biscuits, blood-orange crinkles, cookies with honey and peppermint.

Lili grabs Irina's hand across their trunk-turned-table and gives it a brief squeeze. "Thank you, Irishka," she mouths. She grins, grabs another cookie, and pops it into her mouth.

"Eat up," Irina tells her grimly. "That fungus won't clean itself, you know." But she is content, even smiling. She realizes they both are.

29

Revelations

LILI IS BEING followed.

She knows this because of the chilling silence. The skies are soaked in a gauzelike fog that hovers over the empty buildings eerily, and Lili tastes snow when she sticks out her tongue the way she used to do in Petersburg with Nicky. This early, not even a tram or droshky clatters by. That's why the footsteps striking the pavement behind her are that much more stupidly obvious. They have been in pursuit of Lili since she left Moscow House. And they haven't so much as paused, taking boulevard after boulevard with her, irritatingly purposeful.

By now, every muscle in her body is taut and poised for flight. As if Lili would sprout wings and soar away like the woman-headed Alkonost bird from the fairy tales. She almost snaps the pencil in her pocket in half. She darts a look back—and sees a man not in typical Cheka dark leather but in an anonymous, double-breasted black overcoat. Some agent, investigating either Moscow House or the Americans.

He tips his hat back, and his gaze cuts into hers. Cool and shockingly direct.

Clearly, he wishes for Lili to know she is being followed, and she wishes she could scream. Full-throated and *loud*, if only to shock the hell out of the bastard.

Instead, Lili keeps walking as if she hasn't seen him at all. Past the bazaar where she was intending to stop in to see Viktor before work, and along the streets. She will tire the spying snake out. Better that than bringing trouble to Viktor's doorstep.

Somewhere in the tangle of streets, tramlines, and little domed churches, it starts to snow. At first, only flurries eddy against Lili's cheeks. They are featherlight, yet pinpricks of such intense cold that she has to burrow deeper into her threadbare coat. The snow intensifies, spins and whirls, grows fat and wet, melting ice on her skin. It is blurring the already hazy air and drowning everything out. Lili blinks back the snowflakes. The cold is profound, with a damp quality to it. Her feet are soaked in minutes. She thinks of the tales that say blizzards are caused by devils on earth. Yet the snow may be a hidden blessing. When she risks a glance back, the man is gone.

Lili swallows. Takes a raspy inhale, her throat and lungs seeming to shrink. She keeps on like this for a little longer. Now she is trembling so hard her teeth are chattering. Lili forces herself to think of something warm—Nicky's arms encircling her, the heat of their kisses, falling asleep together in an actual bed.

One last look behind her—no man, no footsteps—and Lili is safe. Her breath rattles in a throat quickly becoming sore and achy. But she retraces her steps back to the bazaar and Uncle Pasha's Viktor.

Lili locates his stall—it is there, he hasn't left—and approaches it without hesitation.

At first, she doesn't see him and panics for a second. Then she notices a mound of old furs in the corner, a shape underneath, worn boots peeking out below.

"You lied to me," Lili declares. "I know you are Viktor. And you know I'm Count Pavel Sergeyevich's niece."

The furs are tugged back, and the man rises to stand tall and straight-backed like her uncle. Only, he is in plain rough clothing, with a scraggly black beard and lank hair. His wrinkles are much too deep for a man probably in his early forties. Lili knows they are marks of suffering, of sorrow. But his eyes are the same as she remembers from Uncle Pasha's soirées and diaries: gray like smoke, like the clouds carrying the snowfall.

"It is an honor to finally meet you, Countess Liliya Goliteva. Your uncle spoke of you most of all," Viktor says in Russian, his voice entirely unlike his appearance. It flows like water in a stream, smooth and refined.

Lili exhales a relieved breath but glances around. The bazaar is as empty as the streets, except for several stray merchants. She smells their cheap cigarettes, hears the stamping of their boots against snow, their words: *Dead, absolutely dead today.* "Is there somewhere we can speak? I was followed, though I think I lost him."

Viktor's gaze sweeps over the stalls expertly. He gives a quick nod and gestures for Lili to come around his stall. There is a door there, and she enters the little cabin just as Viktor is snapping a faded curtain over the front, giving them privacy. "I have waited a long time for you," he says. The scratch of a match, and a flame bursts to life big and bright. He shields the candle with his hand. Lowers it onto a crate by two wooden stools.

"But you pretended not to know me," she points out, sitting on a stool, shivering. Her clothing is wet and heavy on her, and it seems colder in here than even outside.

"Pasha told me you would come, but that I should be sure you knew me first."

Lili leans back against the wall, dazed. "But how did he *know*? And how did we not see you here earlier?" She stops, forces herself to slow down. "You and my uncle were . . ."

A pained look pulls at Viktor's face, kneading his skin, turning him into an old man who might have been handsome once. "We were, may God forgive us."

"For what?"

"For deceiving your aunt." There is a jaggedness to his voice. "She was a good, kind woman. She did not deserve it. Or us."

"She didn't know?"

"She knew."

Lili swallows back more questions to get to the heart of the matter. How Viktor ended up here, seemingly waiting for her. "You returned to Moscow for him."

"I did, with travel papers for us both. But you knew your uncle. Brilliant, beautiful, headstrong to a fault. Once he decided to stay, it was done. And he was unwilling to leave you and the children. So I stayed, lived on the fickle goodwill of distant relatives here in Moscow. And after . . . he died—" A flash of white-hot pain seizes Viktor's features. His voice drops low, becoming wan, like a new moon. "I went to stay with a sister in the countryside. The rest of my family is . . . dead or in exile. I used to be Prince Viktor Vadimovich Oblomov."

The Oblomov aristocratic clan is nearly as ancient as the Sherbatsky-Golitev family. "Why return to this hellhole?" If not for Moscow House, Lili would surely be in the countryside.

Viktor smiles faintly. "I had a dream one night. Of him."

A shiver catches up Lili, full-bodied, her reddened fingers not spared.

"So I packed up my family's possessions—it was auspicious, really, as we had need of additional funds—and left. With a little money, I was able to afford this stall, slowly selling off my artworks, books, jewelry, and other heirlooms while living at a boardinghouse. I heard this bazaar is popular among former people. I was hoping you would find me here. When you did, I had to bide my time until you read Pasha's diaries and would know me."

"You knew about the diaries?" Lili's heart plummets possessively; she did not.

"I knew he kept them. But he never spoke of them, not until the end. The second to last time I saw Pasha, he told me he would hide these writings, but in a way that would allow you to find them, his *story*."

"Did, well, Uncle Pasha tell you anything else?"

"I did not see him much at the end." Viktor grimaces. "I confess I was angry with him. The time Pasha told me about the diaries—it must have been in the spring of 1918—he was raving. He had changed much before then, becoming withdrawn, moody as never before. Twitchy, too. But this time, he raved about his sister, Marie, about how she was a witch inspired by the Devil, on the cusp of awakening some ancient spirit with black magic. I tried very hard to shake Pasha out of it. He also had a persistent cough that lingered worryingly, and he looked ghastly, pasty and bleary. I smelled spirits on him. I asked Pasha if he had been drinking, and he laughed, told me he was to die soon, so it mattered not. That's when he told me about the diaries and handed me a set of books. He only said, *She will know. She will discover the truth, about Marie and everything else*."

Lili's heart warms at her uncle believing in her enough to trust her with his story. "Did you believe him?"

A laugh breaks through the pained mask of Viktor's face. "Pasha was the dreamer, not me. The Church tells us not to believe in spirits. So I never have. I thought him paranoid, locked away as he was in that house, imagining horrors where there were none. But now . . . now I believe there was a grain of truth to what he said."

"But the Cheka killed Uncle Pasha, not my aunt or the spirit."

Viktor gives her a small smile. "Destroying someone in our world comes in many forms, Lili." He pauses, reflects. "Have you wondered why the Cheka came at that particular moment? Though your uncle and grandfather were working peacefully with the Soviet government, and your grandmother knew a member of the Politburo?"

But the cursed Cheka is apart from even those institutions. Anyone can be a suspect. Still. "Are you implying that my aunt had something to do with it?"

"I am only suggesting that it is plausible for someone to have informed on your family. Many did so back then, and it did not matter if they were friends, or family."

Lili's body remembers her wet clothing, finds the shiver on her skin. The watchfulness, the rage, the blame, the vengeance. *Could* it have been Auntie? She wished to change the course of that last dinner, to atone. Nicky proposed she had resurrected the family. Could it have been due to guilt, even regret, at informing on her blood?

Viktor strides over to a pile of wooden crates at the back of the stall. There is the cracking open of lids, some rifling, before he returns with a stack of books.

The dust hits Lili's sore throat, and she dissolves into a fit of coughing. But she accepts the books and presses them to her chest, feeling their hard edges poking through her coat. "Thank you," she whispers. Then, "You said you saw my uncle one last time?"

"Yes, early that summer. Pasha had not returned any of my notes or letters. He, well, didn't wish for the family to know about me, us. Still, I stayed on in Moscow. I was elated when I finally heard from him. We met at a small park between our places. Pasha looked even more ghastly, the bones stark in his face and body, even through his coat. No longer twitchy, but . . . absent. He held my hand. Said nothing. I thought I would give him space. Then I heard what happened . . . oh, Lili, you cannot imagine the pain, the regret. It very nearly swallowed me whole. There was much that had gone unsaid on that bench."

The shiver prickles along Lili's spine. Her sister had said the same. She thinks of Nicky, of the words that sat on her tongue unsaid. But does she know what she wants? Certainly not marriage. Maybe something entirely new. Something untouched by the past. Lili only knows that warm, expansive, big feeling in her chest at the thought of Nicky, of a life with him. Perhaps not the fairy-tale endings they used to read, but an ending nevertheless, one that would find them beside each other for whatever came next.

For a brief moment, Lili considers telling Viktor about Uncle Pasha's ghost. But it isn't the Pasha they knew, not really. The life in him isn't natural or real. And he wouldn't wish for Viktor to remember him that way. Lili fumbles with the ribbon at her throat. The diaries are unlocked, and in her possession. She assumes this man has nothing left of her uncle. She tugs at the ring, pulling it off its ribbon before offering it to Viktor.

"This was my uncle's. It holds the key to his story, which you helped me find. He would wish for you to have it."

Lili trudges back to Moscow House, work be damned. She is cold and empty, the talk with Viktor having wrung her inside out. It is early afternoon by the time she gets back to the attic and spreads Uncle Pasha's books before her on the table.

Irina is at the ARA, ideally not worrying over her; Natasha at school; and Seryozha at Madame Naroshina's. It is only Cleo, twittering and whistling excitedly, glad of the company for once. Lili tries to give her parakeet a smile. She wipes her nose instead, proceeding to hack out coughs that are dry and painful in her chest. She steadies herself, looks down at the books—and the drawings there of a cloaked, humanlike creature.

Lili thinks it is very like the imp she and Irina saw in the West Wing.

In some drawings, he is a man with a long white beard, like Uncle Pasha's tales of holy fools in Old Russia. In others, he is a hairy animal, bent and apelike on a stove or pech. In all, his eyes are large and flashing. Lili recalls the many times those bloodred eyes flashed at her from within the house's shadows.

The next drawing is of a snake with a zigzag pattern, dark brown on caramel reptile skin. Even she knows it is a viper, one of the deadliest snakes in Russia. Uncle Pasha described Auntie looking at such a picture. Lili examines it, then the book's forest-green cover, as if it is concealing the snake within its twisting ivy and greens.

Cleo gives a screech, fluffing her wings uneasily. Her beady eyes sweep the room.

Is it Lili's imagination, or are the walls peeling? No, overhead, there is a hint of the moldy black spots. And more spiderwebs than she remembers. "You feel that, too?"

Cleo's eyes fix on the wall behind the screen. Lili's throat goes perfectly numb. Something is rustling, *rooting* inside the wall. At first, she thinks, *The imp*. Then, *The vile doll*. The next minute, it is gone. All is still and silent and sleepy. Lili gives Cleo a nervous shrug, receives a fluff of wings in reply, and turns back to the book.

Its pages are brittle, flipped too many times, written all over. Of course, Auntie's handwriting is unreadable. But to the left of the viper, there is a block of text that is very much readable:

> The Domovoy often takes the form of a snake, watching over hearth and home and family. Kill the snake, and you shall destroy your health, your good fortune, and your house.

Lili sits back. She saw that snake in the house, sometimes shadows shaped like snakes. She turns the book over. *Spirits of Old Russia* is written on the spine in ghostly white letters. She picks up another book—*Creatures of Myth and Fairy Tale*. It is earmarked to a page with a depiction of a creature on a pech with black fur thick as a wooly carpet.

> The Domovoy caresses when he speaks. But he can be tempestuous and gloomy like the sky when he feels neglected or displeased. He dwells near the threshold or stove. Sometimes, on a pine or fir branch in the yard, if it is green and with enough needles to sustain him. If you catch a glimpse of the Domovoy, it is a poor omen. If you wish to appease or awaken him, make a sacrifice.

Lili hastens to pick up a crinkled leaflet from within the book's pages—*A Guide to Running Your Household (Spiritually)*. Under the heading *Domovoy*, she reads the lines of text underlined and circled in the same bloodred as the imp's eyes.

1. Speak softly and respectfully yet forcefully.

2. Think about him, feed him, and keep him happy.

3. If you have neglected or forgotten him, bring in a pine bough for him and decorate it with offerings.

4. Leave offerings in all places in the house he could live.

Lili lifts her eyes to Cleo's. "We are in trouble, my girl," she says, and Cleo gurgles her assent. For they have broken what seems the only rule that matters by neglecting their Domovoy *for years*. What if it turned him malevolent, even murderous, so he went as far as to kill two men and one defenseless old lady? Though it also seems possible to appease him by making offerings. There is mention of a *sacrifice*, but nothing about how to do it. If it is even the same sacrifice done by Auntie. Cleo beats her wings at the next book. It is a slim volume and called simply *Know Your House and Its Dangers*.

A strip of leather bookmarks the page discussing the Domovoy, who apparently warns of trouble's approach, weeps before any death in the family, and pulls on hair to warn of abuse. But the Domovoy also exhibits poltergeist-like reactions and general noise, even screeches and moans, and causes disorder and mayhem in the house. The noise, the messes, the ghostly happenings . . . And didn't Grand-mère mention the Domovoy appearing to her the night before she died, like the girl in that tale feeling his cold touch? Lili remembers hearing the weeping before bad things happened, before the deaths in the house. Her fingers tremble on the next page—and the illustration of a Domovoy with its hairy hands wrapped around a throat.

> While not by its nature malevolent, in Kharkov Province, a Domovoy was reported to have flung a pot of scalding hot porridge at his master, killing him instantly. Numerous reports elsewhere attest to a Domovoy strangling his sleep-

> ing master or mistress in their beds, sometimes in dark passageways. Be warned that he is a dark, capricious trickster with a good memory for neglect.

A Domovoy *is* able to kill, then. How swell for them all. Lili moves on to the last book, *Explaining Spirits*, and the underlined text there.

> His name comes from the word dom, or *house*.
>
> He is of the house. In the very walls of the house.
>
> Its protector, its ancestral spirit, its god.
>
> Master of the House. Dedushka. *Grandfather*.

In the very walls of the house. Lili pictures the Domovoy crawling through the rotting walls of Moscow House like a great big centipede, just behind the black fungus they haven't been able to scrub away. Lili cannot still her hands, now slick with a very cold, clinging sweat. Whether or not Auntie informed on the family or brought back the ghosts matters little. She awakened the Domovoy after years upon years of neglect, succeeding in bringing him to life. And if the Domovoy has turned malevolent, even murderous, who's to say he will stop? And which one of them will be next? By now, Lili is shaking, cold, ill. But there remains one last thing for her to read.

There aren't many diary entries after March 1918 and before the night the Cheka killed Uncle Pasha. Most are random, consisting of a word or two on current events, the weather, Grand-père's declining health. But a few touch on Auntie recovering from her illness and resuming her watchfulness over Uncle Pasha—and the rest of the family.

In an entry from September 1918, he writes:

The Sovnarkóm has officially endorsed the Red Terror, a counter-revolution, <u>floods of bourgeois blood</u>. Tonight, we men huddled together in a sad party before the samovar and post-dinner liquors left untouched. We spoke of what to do, me holding strong and proud as ever, the others beginning to waver, to crack, to let in the poison of regret.

As Aleksei was dissolving into his cowardly hysterics, my eyes grazed a figure, just behind the door. It was cloaked in shadow. But I saw her clearly. Marie. Her dark eyes were fixed on us, more alert and decided than ever. Her magic may have failed, but she is still scheming. I am convinced she is about to make her next move.

In another entry, also from that September, Uncle Pasha writes:

I have curbed my honesty when it comes to politics. I trust no one, not even my dear Viktor, whom I have refused to see for months now. But tonight, Aleksei and I got into a row. Every incendiary word is burned into my mind.

"Better to be ruled by the Germans," he threw at me. "They are our best hope for overthrowing the Bolsheviks."

I drew back in horror. My own brother-in-law. "What you suggest is treason."

"I care not. Marie was right. We should have left when we had the chance."

"It is un-Russian of you. The Bolsheviks need to be overthrown, but I would rather a Red Russia than a German one. She may be bruised and beaten, but at least she is ours." I spat the words at him, wishing I could do much more.

That is when I glimpsed Marie, hovering behind a big-bellied vase. Her eyes glittered strangely. One moment, with a flash of hardness, maybe hatred; the next, back to their steady watchfulness. And, perhaps, an edge of a smile. Oh, I feel so cold. Death must be near. She must be close to deciding what to do with me, how to kill me, and when.

The Haunting of Moscow House

Lili strokes Cleo's warm, downy wings, and her little parakeet snuggles into her hand. The Red Terror led to a rush of investigations, arrests, and imprisonments, the Cheka cinching its power. And throughout it all, Auntie continued to watch, and to listen. The conversation in the last entry would have been more than enough grounds for arrest, as if it were needed. Anything could be grounds for arrest—misinformation, even lies.

What if Viktor is right, and Auntie informed on Uncle Pasha and the family? If that is the case, Auntie is responsible for their deaths. And if she felt the least bit of guilt over it, she could have made the decision to resurrect the dead, somehow using the Domovoy, who then came back with a vengeance, killing the men in the house and Grand-mère. A convincing theory, but just that. What really happened remains cloaked in infuriating shadow. And what it means, if it is possible to reverse Auntie's sacrifice or banish the Domovoy and the ghosts. Lili can only hope there is a way, and that this fortune teller knows it. Their family and the house depend on it.

Lili turns the page, the last one in the last diary. The last entry.

She exhales a slow, painful breath, trying not to cough. She snuggles Cleo closer and presses the diary to her chest. To bring Uncle Pasha to her very heart. Lili inhales his warm, woody sandalwood scent, pale and dim yet clinging to the pages. She wishes she could speak to him, even with the bullet hole in his head, even under the oak tree where he lies dead and buried. She looks down at the lined paper, at the date hastily scrawled there. Cold, hard realization shudders through her.

Uncle Pasha's final diary entry was written on the day—mere hours—before the Cheka burst into Moscow House and murdered him in cold blood.

It all tumbles back then. The gleam of those revolvers. The violence of that shot. The burst of blood. A vibrant, terrifying red. The long hours of that dark, sleepless night. The men digging into the cold, frozen earth with their shovels the next morning.

23 November 1918

The air is sick today. It is the quiet, the way the creaks and groans of the house have settled into an expectant hush that curdles inside me, like soured milk. The eyes that have been watching me are strangely closed. This quiet portends tragedy. Is Marie about to strike at me? If so, I am ready.

I spent time with each of the children today. Then I went to the nursery. There, as nowhere else, the anxiety and fears are silenced. I can hear myself think. My heartbeat slows to its regular, comfortable rhythm, and I am myself.

Seryozha was taking his afternoon sleep. His cheeks should be plump and rosy, yet they are pale and sunken. Still, he is a handsome boy. Dear Irina tells me he looks like a Dolgonog, with his full head of dark hair and dark eyes. But to me, he is the spitting image of Irina, he looks like a Sherbatsky. And I like to think he looks like me, too, like the son I never had with Luba. But enough. Enough! Such pain is not meant for this page. It only lives in my heart. As does the pain of Viktor, who writes no more.

Yes, enough. I must rest my pen now, put on a brave face, and dress for dinner. I shall finish the rest of the entry when I am back. But oho! It is late. Goodnight. Goodnight.

I shall write tomorrow.

At that, Lili swallows a sob and pushes aside the diary.

She feels faint, sick, struggles to breathe past the pain in her throat and the nausea clutching at her. She dashes to the washbasin, her stomach roiling, *heaving*. Just in time. Then it all comes out, watery and acidic, leaving her throat even more achy.

Lili leans over the basin, taking furious gulps of air. Seryozha is Irina's *son*? Her sister was in the countryside not working at a hospital but having *a child*? And after all these years, not so much as a word? If she didn't know the intimate fact that Irina is a mother, the boy she thought a cousin *her nephew*, then Lili doesn't know her sister at all, and the bond between them is only a front. There is no force behind it, no depth—indeed, no truth—the very concept of their sisterhood reduced to blood and not much else.

Lili is aware that she is being utterly selfish, even horrid. Her mind skims over the why and how, what her sister had to go through to keep up the charade, in front of not only her but Seryozha. She is too swollen with hot, irrational anger at her sister. And at herself for not having seen it. There is a pain, deep in her heart, piercing, ego consuming, that makes her want to lash out at Irina. To demand why she never told Lili about her son, why she kept such a big secret, when all Lili has ever wished for was to be her equal, her friend, her *sister*.

But Irina has always been too good for her, too many years older, too experienced and smart. She has never trusted Lili, not with the past or present, not even with Will. Like Nicky. And suddenly, Lili is irrationally, horribly angry with him, too. The two people closest to her do not trust her, believe her to be but a child.

That is all Lili can think as she wipes her mouth with the back of her hand and, ignoring Cleo's frantic screeches, bounds down the stairs and out into the snowy late afternoon. She needs to confront her sister before her anger boils over and there is nothing left but hurt and betrayal and overwhelming loneliness.

30

Lili Goes Missing

"KIRILL HAS BEEN arrested!" Paulina bursts into the room, Emma hastening in after her.

Irina's heart gives a dreadful thump. Kirill, her cousin's closest friend, their childhood playmate, the polite, gentle man she met at the ARA party. And if Kirill has been arrested, what does it mean for the rest of the ARA's former people? What does it mean for Irina and Lili?

Irina moves toward Paulina and grabs hold of her cold, trembling hands. Paulina's face is drained of color, melted snow trickling from her skin and clothing and gathering on the parquet in puddles.

"What *happened*?" Irina asks, peering into her face.

Paulina shakes her head, for once scattered. "I was late after my break—can you believe I chose today to linger over food? I returned at three, and everyone was in an uproar, yelling, phoning, cursing. The entire office was turned upside down. Kirill and another Russian employee, Vlad, had been rounded up not ten minutes before."

Emma nods brusquely. "I was there. A group of men stormed in, arrested Kirill and Vlad, and left, all without a word." Her arms, lavender scented, all-encompassing, come around Irina and Paulina in a tight embrace.

Irina smells crisp, sharp air; feels wet snow, which seeps into her blouse in seconds. But she is grateful to be held. She is so very numb, stung as she is by shock, by fear. *Who was it?* Irina almost asks. But she knows. Who else bursts in at all hours? Arresting and destroying people without charges, often without grounds or explanations?

Paulina meets her gaze, and Irina has never seen her friend look so small, so helpless, her own fear mirrored back at her. "I cannot be arrested. My sister . . ."

Irina's mind flashes to her own sister, her son and cousin. And Auntie, still not at home, despite Comrade Suzhensky's promise. She has hesitated to make further inquiries about her aunt, given the revelations at the house. Instantly, Irina feels a stab of regret at that, and she presses it down. She smooths an errant curl from Paulina's cheek. "Do not worry, my dear. I will care for your sister if anything should happen." And she means it.

Irina realizes men are pressing in on all sides, crowding the three of them, asking questions with no answers, tossing about jagged-edged yet ineffectual swears. Striking matches and lighting cigarettes. Casting uneasy glances toward the doors.

"The Blue House has also been infiltrated," Will calls from his office. A few minutes later, he appears, the skin beneath his beard even whiter than the previous day.

The men quiet, their exhales the only sounds in the room. Smoke gathers thick and gray in the air, drifting and swirling between them, making Irina's mouth water.

"No arrests yet," Will adds, "but the rooms were searched overnight. Nothing obvious, not like the Pink House or here. But their chief informed me that nothing is in its place, documents rifled through and disturbed."

"Fuck those bastards." Harold shakes his head. Hands a cigarette to Paulina, who lets go of Irina to shakily bring the cigarette to her lips. There is no color in them.

Irina brushes past the men toward Will. His gaze is distant, mired in thought. Despite the fear, she tries to keep her chin up, her back straight, herself calm. "Why?" she finally forces out. "Have they said—anything?"

"We haven't been able to reach anyone of consequence. But the Bolos are worried, suspicious. The more the people need us, our aid and food, the more they attempt to undermine us, starting with the press and these searches. It is all meant to get in our heads. They've sent a few letters to the chiefs in the past several days, complaining we are only hiring from the former bourgeoisie, whom they claim are 'enemies of the state,' all with a 'counterrevolutionary past' and 'anti-Soviet spirit.'"

Irina hasn't had time to read the newspapers. She holds herself very, very still. But her insides are churning, spiking her breathing and her heart. "What is this, the Red Terror all over again?" Her mind is racing, thinking of Seryozha back at Madame Naroshina's, Natasha at school, Lili—where *is* Lili? Irina sucks in a breath of air; there isn't enough of it. "Will." She turns to him, suddenly faint and dizzy with panic. "Lili—I haven't seen her since this morning . . . What if—?" *Has she been arrested?* Due to their class, their ARA work, possibly the investigation into Moscow House . . .

Will swivels to face her, his expression losing its thoughtfulness. His eyes are a very soft cerulean blue. He wavers momentarily, glancing about, before placing his hands on her shoulders. They are heavy and warm. Reassuring. "Do not worry, Irene. There might be another explanation. Did she mention any plans this morning? We can ask Frank. She may have gone out for some sketches. Though, in this weather . . ."

Irina's breaths are reduced to frenzied spurts. Her thoughts are muddled, fuzzy at the edges. Did Lili intend to go see Uncle Pasha's friend? When, and where? Irina imagines Maman's recriminations, even Grand-mère's, her role as elder sister drilled into her from birth. She becomes aware of Will's hands, now stroking her arms, up and down, down and up, massaging concentric circles into her skin through her blouse. The motion brings back a little clarity. "The bazaar. S-she might have gone there."

He nods. "And the snow is bad. So she could have been delayed or decided to return home. Either way, don't jump to conclusions."

Irina tries to swallow down the bloodcurdling panic just as Will pushes something into her hand—a bottle wrapped in *Pravda* newspaper. "Drink this."

Without a word, she takes a swig. The vodka is bitter and violent as it hits her mouth, then her throat. It expands tentacles of blurry, melting warmth into her chest and stomach. Another swallow. She nods her thanks before handing the bottle back to Will, who takes a long, generous drink and passes it on to Frank. The men's hushed whispers and shuffling, their coiling, mouthwatering cigarette smoke, finally return to Irina.

Will leans in, so close she breathes in pure alcohol, feels the prickle of his beard on her skin. "I'll make some telephone calls," he says, low. "Go find your sister. And—" He averts his gaze. "Be careful, Irene." A quick, chaste kiss on her cheek, and he is gone.

The snow outside is a vortex of whirling white, ushering in a bleary, bluish night that only disorients Irina. Or maybe it is the fear and the vodka, a dreadful combination.

She forces herself to a stop, casts a glance about apprehensively. Gulps several deep breaths of the frosty air. It hits her throat with the same violent punch as the vodka. She catches sight of the Cadillacs. Snow has encased the automobiles in a soft, glittering white, like ladies' gowns at the balls of old. Irina hurries over, suddenly thinking of Nikolai and how much easier—not to mention faster—her search would be by motorcar.

"Nicky?" she calls, instantly hearing his muffled voice in answer, then the crunch and creak of snow, and his snowy figure emerges out of the whiteness.

"Irina?" Nikolai squints at her through the fatly falling flakes.

"Oh, Nicky, thank God."

His lips don't quirk in their charming smile. "What happened." It isn't a question.

"They are arresting Russian employees—" For a minute, she cannot go on, realizing her fears are coming true. She thinks back to her

ARA interview, the risk Mr. Carroll spoke of. Now here it is, looking her in the face like the Bolsheviks' Nagant revolvers.

"Where is Lili?" Nikolai's voice has shed any pretense at politeness.

Irina is shaking her head, again dissolving into that well of deep, dark panic. "I don't know, Nicky. She never showed up to work. My God, what if—?"

"It's all right, Irina." He masters himself, taking her by the arm. Not rough, but not gentle, either. "Come, I'll motor you over to the house."

Once they reach Moscow House, he leaves the Cadillac half parked on the curb of their street. Night has descended, quiet with the snowfall yet tense and waiting. The snow hasn't slowed; if anything, it has grown more persistent on the ride over. Irina fumbles in her purse for the key. But Nikolai places a restraining hand on her arm, and she stops. With his other hand, he pulls a Browning pistol out of his coat pocket. Papa had owned the same one. She hears the click of the bullet, sliding into place, and sees his nod.

Suppressing her fear, Irina unlocks the doors and pushes them open. Except for the candlelight, there is nothing and no one.

Not even in the attic, which is empty, dark, somehow *unlived in*, Cleo nowhere to be seen. Irina lights a candle and walks through to her and Lili's room. Her eyes settle on the books. Dusty tomes cover the table's previously bare surface. Some are thrown face up, pages damp and bristling from some unseen breath of air; others are lying face down, spines creased and cracked, left open too long. The pages are filled with illustrations—of a creature with flashing eyes. Irina freezes in place. The same, or very nearly, as the one from the West Wing. Her gaze drags toward one of Pasha's diaries, flung open on top of the books. She steps toward it, and the very blood in her veins turns to ice.

Dear Irina tells me he looks like a Dolgonog

he is the spitting image of Irina

like the son I never had

Irina drops the diary. It lands with a soft thud on the books. She covers her mouth with her hands. There isn't enough air; it is a little like choking on nothing.

"Well, it looks like she found the books, maybe Viktor—" Nikolai's eyes sweep over Irina, instantly noticing her distress. "What is it? Are you all right?"

Irina shakes her head. Holds out Pasha's diary.

Nikolai walks over and takes the little red-leather journal. His face sharpens in understanding as he reads. Yet he doesn't pepper her with questions. He only asks, "Where do you think she could have gone?"

Irina doesn't know. Only that her sister has to be angry with her after learning about Seryozha. Lili could have dashed back to the bazaar, to the ARA, out for a walk to clear her head—but in this snow? Suddenly, Irina recalls her own promise to visit the fortune teller. "Maybe she went to Red Square, thinking I was there to meet Vera. I told her I would go after work. Lili . . . can be impulsive."

"You're telling me. I'll motor you over, then return to headquarters. Maybe she is there. If anything is amiss, I'll come back and wait for you in the same place."

Irina nods numbly. She hates herself for telling Lili to say what she needs to Nicky. It was hypocritical, so incredibly high-handed. For Irina hasn't followed her own advice with the people in her life. And now, it might be too late, at least for Lili. What if she was arrested, like Papa, Aleksei, and Auntie, never to be seen again, believing Irina didn't trust in her own sister?

The image of her and the children coming upon New York City crashes back into Irina—the sprawling, glittering skyline on the horizon, the sea breeze on her cheek. What if it is too late for that, too? But no, it is ridiculous. A dream, a parallel life, a fairy tale. They belong here in Russia. They belong in Moscow House. That is their reality. Their only reality. Fairy tales do not exist. At least, not anymore.

31

The Problem with Déjà Vu

"THERE YOU ARE!"

Will is waiting for her when Lili crosses the threshold of 30 Spiridonovka. She has never seen him angry, but his ruddy face, flaring nostrils, and what can only be described as a thunderous expression give him away fairly easily. Lili cannot bring herself to care. Her throat is painfully sore, her nose swollen, her clothes soaked through.

"Your sister is beside herself with worry!"

Lili crosses her arms. "Yes, Irina has always been good at that." She feels a selfish, savage kind of glee. At least she can still frighten her sister.

"Where have you been? Do we need to speak about your start time, Goliteva?"

"There's a snowstorm outside, if you haven't noticed, William. Where is Irina?"

"She went out looking for you!"

Lili notices something palpably wrong in the air. A tense current hums underneath it. As on the day of the Bolo raid. A few harried, white-faced men rush past, puffing at their cigarettes more furiously than usual. A cloud of acrid smoke hangs over the place, burning Lili's nose and throat. Even in the hall, she hears the frazzled ring of telephones and men's curses; notices Paulina and Emma in the distance, nodding at something Harold says. Strange. The women are rarely at headquarters. Will follows her gaze, his flush draining.

"Kirill and another Russian were arrested today," he says, no longer angry, only weary.

A bolt of shock races through Lili as she recalls the footsteps, the man in pursuit. That is a better excuse than the snowfall. "The Cheka followed me this morning, all the way from the house to the bazaar, where I . . . had to make some sketches. That's why I didn't come in earlier. I was frightened and ended up returning home instead."

The rest of the hardness loosens in Will's face. "I told Irina this was a possibility."

Lili has so many questions. But none of them are important, not right now. She is thinking of her project, ripped down and nearly destroyed during the Bolo raid. If the Cheka is now targeting the ARA's Russian employees—specifically, former people—her project might have given them additional names, ammunition, kindling to their suspicions and paranoia. Since then, she and Frank have tried to use aliases, unless the former people have expressly given them permission to use their real names. Still, there are photographs, images of people, some of the names . . . "Will there be more arrests, you think?"

Will meets her gaze. His is a tumble of dark blue emotion, not comforting at all. "We don't know. We have been calling various officials, trying to learn anything we can about the arrests and why they were carried out. But nothing so far. We will keep trying. But—maybe you should go home for now, Lil. It isn't safe here."

Lili nods, her throat suddenly the least of her concerns. "I will, thank you, William. But I need to do something first." Will motions for her to get on with it, and she sweeps through the office rooms toward her desk—and the board of ARA former people she has re-created with Frank. The sketches, photographs, and notes painstakingly fixed up, put back together, in some cases completely redone. And now she must tear it all back down, hide what she can, and toss the rest into the wastebasket.

Lili's heart nearly smothers her as she hurries over to Frank. "Do you have a crate or a box?"

"What? Why?" He faces her with wide eyes. "What's wrong?"

"I don't want the Cheka getting their hands on this again." Lili dashes to the board and begins to pull down her sketches and photographs, the notes typewritten by Frank, all those familiar faces, streets, and words sinking into the darkness of a crate that Frank has hastily swiped from under a spare desk. "If anything happens to me . . ."

Frank meets her gaze levelly. "I will take care of it. Assemble the material, write and submit the article."

Lili nods gratefully. "Thank you, Frank. I . . . need you to add one more person to our project. Though he doesn't work for us, I met Prince Viktor Oblomov earlier today. His story will contrast nicely with those of the former people employed by the ARA." Lili recalls how she belatedly asked Viktor if she could include him in her project. He agreed, requesting her not to use his name or take his photograph. She quickly relays these details to Frank as they fill the crate with whirling white scraps of paper not unlike the snow outside.

In many ways, the *bang!* of the front doors, usually too far to reach them in this distant room, doesn't surprise Lili. Still, she cannot help the jolt of horror and rush of déjà vu when, a few minutes later, Comrade Yakov Peters marches in, followed by Felix and a stream of leather-clad men. It is as on that November night nearly three years ago. But the problem with déjà vu is it is utterly useless.

It did not warn her, and it certainly won't save her.

Lili hastens to push the crate under a nearby desk as Frank strides over to Comrade Peters. Will and Harold rush into the room and to Frank's side, followed more discreetly by Emma and Paulina, who remain quietly by the doors. Lili doesn't wish to make herself seen. But she also doesn't wish to hide. She settles for her usual state of awkwardness, arms limp at her sides, heart fluttering against her rib cage like a trapped bird from the fairy tales. It is fitting that Comrade Peters is looking more like the skeletal villain Koshey the Deathless.

"You and your agency have no right to be here," Will declares. "This is American territory as far as you are concerned. I suggest you gentlemen take your leave."

Comrade Peters smiles. "This building is not owned by the United States, Mr. Hardwick. It remains under the purview of Comrade Trotsky and the People's Commissariat for Enlightenment. The Cheka may arrest any Russian citizen we please."

He turns his sharp, beady gaze on Lili, who tastes a dry, very sore throat. She smells the melting snow on these men, damp and bitter, and the reek of her own sweaty nerves. And she senses the itchy prickle of another gaze.

Felix is smiling at her, smug and self-satisfied, relieved to be delivering on threats that have bit at them so ineffectually all these weeks. Vile, horrible man! Still. No matter what he and the Cheka are here for, Lili tells herself to be strong. Like she knows Irina would be.

"Your actions, sir, are in direct violation of the Riga Agreement," Will insists. "I must once more ask you to leave, or be forced to appeal to the Soviet government and the Politburo."

Comrade Peters chuckles. He looks over at Felix and his men, who shake their heads and cast amused glances at one another between laughs. "You may take it up with whomever you please," says Comrade Peters. "The Riga Agreement doesn't interfere with the Soviet republic's discretionary custody of Russian personnel. I have three arrest warrants burning a hole in my pocket for three such persons, and I won't be leaving without them."

"Who is it?" demands Harold, crossing his arms as Lili's heart gives a hot, violent thump.

Comrade Peters smiles pleasantly. "Paulina Gonchurova, Prince Nikolai Naroshin, and"—his eyes slide to Lili—"Countess Liliya Goliteva."

Everything in Lili tightens, blackens for a moment, nearly goes out. She is aware only of the pull and release of her breaths, scratchy and rasping to her ears.

"What is the basis for the arrests?" She hears Will's incredulous voice, but it is floating up to her as if underwater, distorted, warbled by a new time and space that has sprung up.

They don't need a reason! Lili wants to shout. She has a fleeting thought of Nicky. Her anger at him burns away into a flood of warm relief. At least he isn't here.

"A special order. Based on our intelligence, you and your American colleagues have been drawing anti-Soviet elements into your organization, ostensibly here for humanitarianism but in actuality to engage in espionage and gather information on the Soviet state so you can topple it. Counterrevolution, my dear Mr. Hardwick."

Will barks out a laugh. "Your special order is bullshit. It is your paranoia, another attempt to discredit us with the Soviet people. And under Article 3 of the Riga Agreement, the ARA has 'complete freedom' in 'securing Russian and other personnel.' Regardless, that is not a basis. It is not a charge."

Lili meets Felix's hard stare. It is unlikely that, with Paulina, Kirill, and the other Russian targeted, the arrests are related to the investigation into Moscow House. Still, Felix *is* here. Though Irina isn't under arrest. Lili is relieved at that, too. The thought of Irina, the head of their household and the caretaker not only of their cousin but of her own son, locked up in a cell, leaving the children alone and helpless, is unbearable.

"Article 3 doesn't stand if you are hiring criminals and political enemies of the state. It is in organizing your staff that you may be preparing to replace us. But I prefer to leave all that to politics, Mr. Hardwick. My task is to place the aforementioned anti-Soviet elements into custody to be investigated and questioned further for their promotion of counterrevolution and their engagement in counterrevolutionary activities. There are your charges."

"These"—Will sweeps his gaze over the room and Lili—"are not criminals or counterrevolutionaries. They are aid workers, employees of the American Relief Administration, and damn good ones."

"The warrants have been written and signed. All that is left is to execute them." Comrade Peters smiles a little at his pun. "I mean, to take the suspects into custody—by force, if necessary." He crooks a finger at Felix, who nods at their men, and the revolvers are raised. "I do not have arrest warrants for you, Mr. Hardwick, or your compatriots, but give me time and that might be arranged under Article 25 of your Riga Agreement."

Will's face darkens, and he grows very quiet. In fact, Lili doesn't think she's ever seen him so menacingly still. "You wouldn't dare, and Daddy Lenin wouldn't let you. We would be out of this hellhole so fast you wouldn't even be able to pick up your telephone and call one of those meetings or commissions you Soviets are so fond of."

Oh, for God's sake. And Lili doesn't much think about God. Even she sees this is a lost battle. After all, whether or not they work for the Americans, the Russian employees are subject to the Cheka. And if the Cheka, with Comrade Peters at its helm, decides or is told to make an arrest, even Americans are powerless to stop it. This confrontation is sure to escalate. Lili steels herself. And before she can change her mind, she moves forward.

She ignores the Americans' furious whispers and walks right up to Comrade Peters, thrusting her wrists in his face with a pointed glare at that beast of a man Felix. "Well, Comrades?" Lili forces an edge of a smile, like her own very sharp brand of blade. She is a Sherbatsky-Golitev. A countess. She will give herself up only with her chin held high and one of Irina's haughty stares. "What are you waiting for?"

Felix's gaze settles on Paulina, who shrinks back. He smirks. "We are waiting for the third name on our list. Where is Prince Nikolai Naroshin?"

Lili is barely aware of Will biting out something along the lines of "Fuck you."

Her hands are shaking with a furious cold that seems to reach every part and cell of her. It is the metal clamping around her wrists, hard, heavy, final. Lili believed she had seen it all with Uncle Pasha's murder, Papa's and Uncle Aleksei's arrests. But to her extreme shame, she feels a spike of bloodcurdling, bone-rattling horror at the thought of the interrogations and prison cells awaiting her. It must be the stupid déjà vu.

Now her heart is racing. A wave of dizziness sweeps over her, until she is weak and woozy and almost glad of the hands that seize and drag her, along with Paulina, through the rooms of the office wing and into the foyer of the mansion.

Lili can just make out the Americans' panicked footsteps somewhere behind them. "You will hear from us," she hears Will bellow. "This will not stand. You have no right—*no right*—"

A disorienting moment of shifting night and whirling snow before Lili is assaulted by the smells of gasoline, old leather, a wall of raw Russian tobacco smoke. She is shoved into the black motorcar so efficiently her head spins. The dizziness returns. She is alone, likely purposely separated from Paulina. Lili knows where she is being conveyed—where all former people eventually end up—and there is not a damn thing she can do about it.

32

The Fortune Teller of Red Square

The Kremlin's familiar brick walls look redder and bloodier in light of the arrests. Through the unraveling veil of panic and fear, Irina hears the frenzied click of her boots on the slick cobblestones. Every few seconds, she glances back. Thinks she hears the echo of footsteps, only to turn and see nothing but vast whiteness blanketing the town.

The walls press in a little closer, the toylike, candyesque St. Basil's Cathedral very nearly blotted out beyond Resurrection Gate.

Irina stops, but there is no Lili, and no fortune teller, either. Didn't her sister say Pasha followed Auntie to this gate? There are few stalls, all boarded up, possibly abandoned.

"Are you looking for somebody?" comes a low, rasping voice.

Irina spins on her heel. The snow is falling thick and wet. She expects a Cheka agent. Instead, beneath the white powder covering everything, she sees a tattered coat and faded handkerchief haphazardly thrown over long, wavy hair with silver-gray streaks. The bewilderment and tension ease a little. Not an agent, but a woman. She is tall, older, with a hooked nose. She puffs on a cigarette, which, in this weather, is an impressive feat. The woman watches her with large, luminous eyes like a black cat. The words stick to Irina's throat. She forces them out.

"I . . . am looking for someone named Vera. She used to own a stall here a few years back." Irina says nothing about fortune-telling; such superstitious, tsarist nonsense can land one in prison. "My aunt knew her. She came to see her here often."

"Everything is boarded up, as you see."

The bitter cold is biting viciously into Irina's skin, stiffening her limbs as she waits.

"The snow is only expected to grow worse. You should return home."

Irina is about to push the matter—but the woman hurries on. As she brushes past, the woman pushes a scrap of paper into Irina's hand before fading into the snowfall. Irina casts a glance about, then unfurls the paper with stiff, cold fingers. On it is a building number and a street. An address. She looks after the woman, intrigued yet torn. What if she will miss Lili? But she decides the encounter is too fortuitous to pass up and hastens to follow.

Irina comes to a run-down apartment building. The deep quiet is punctured only by the growl of some poor hungry dog, or the plaintive wail of a child.

Inside, Irina climbs a set of concrete stairs that reeks of beets and cabbage, filth and piss.

Finally, she approaches the door with the number six on it. There she hesitates, her mind catching up to her body. What if this is a trap? But unlike the Cheka or its informants, the woman has no new coat or boots, is scruffy and hungry. Irina thinks of Auntie's black magic, the horrific sacrifice that woke up the red-eyed creature. Irina has never bought into magic, or fortune-telling. But now, standing in this desolate building, in front of this dirty door, she believes. Her throat tightens in fear. Is this . . . dangerous? Does it fly in the face of God? Is it of the Devil, as many believe? But then she thinks of the spirits at Moscow House and knows she has no choice. Irina must speak to this woman and find out what she knows, if the sacrifice can be reversed or the dead cast away.

Irina summons her self-possession and knocks.

The door swings open with a loud, teeth-grinding scrape, and the woman appears. A few hairs stick out from the neckline of her coat, remnants of a fur collar. "You have something of your aunt in you—Irina Alexandrovna."

"And you are Vera," Irina says, stepping back as Vera thrusts her head out and peers into the hallway.

"We live in dangerous times, Irina Alexandrovna, do we not?" When Vera smiles, her blackened teeth slide into view, as tiny and sharp as an animal's. Some are missing altogether, nothing but empty, rubbery gums.

Inside, Irina is assaulted by stale air, by mold and decay not unlike that of Moscow House. The one-room flat is dim, shrouded in black hangings reminding her of silken bats with expansive wings. It is spare, except for a small walnut table near the crude stove with an oil lamp in place of a samovar. "Were you waiting for me by the gate?"

That raspy laugh again. "I still sell my wares there. And snow is good for business. I tend to linger after shutting down. How did you hear of me?"

"We found your name in some of my uncle's writings."

"Ah, Count Pavel Sherbatsky. Is he alive? What about your aunt?"

"My uncle is dead, my aunt alive. Though she has recently been arrested."

"Say no more. I don't want to know," Vera says, shaking her head. She grabs Irina by the elbow, her yellow nails witchy long and curving, and pulls her to the table. "Why don't you warm yourself by my stove?" Irina lowers onto a hard stool, and Vera settles into a wooden chair across from her. "You must know who I am."

Irina glances around the little flat, noticing something red and gory on the kitchen counter—meat, by the look of it. Over the sink hangs a wet, dripping mess—a carcass of some dead animal with blood and entrails spilling out. A shudder of disgust heaves through her, especially as she inhales the smells beneath the staleness, of rotting meat, the butcher's. Irina does her best to ignore it. She is in the right place. She will get her answers.

She is surer of this than ever when she notices the icons facing away in their corner, their backs covered in the same black paint she and Lili saw in Auntie's rooms. And on a peeling dresser, there are clay bowls and glass jars with beeswax. Auntie likely used such items for fortune-telling, maybe at Vera's instructions.

The woman is watching her with those feline eyes, so sharp they cut like blades.

"Why are your icons turned to the wall?" Irina asks curiously.

Vera raises an eyebrow, evidently surprised by the question. She smiles her black smile. "What I do is made possible by nechistaya sila. I wouldn't wish to frighten it away with icons." When she marks Irina's aghast expression, her smile contracts into a grimace. "That is what people say anyway."

It is now or never. There is no space for fear. Irina says it all in a rush, concluding, "I'd like to know what you told my aunt when she came to see you in March 1918—if you told her about the sacrifice, the Domovoy, how it is all done, and, well, what the dead have to do with it."

"While I understand your predicament, Irina Alexandrovna," Vera says, at length, "I cannot help you. I do not divulge sessions with my clients to anyone."

"But you are a fortune teller," Irina blurts, "not a doctor."

"I prefer the term *diviner*, confidentiality the fundamental tenet of divination. Well"—she leans forward—"not unless there is an obvious and significant risk to the requesting party's life."

Besides specters, a vengeful dead fiancé, and three people dead, all already communicated? No, no risk to life whatsoever. Irina bites down the retort, but barely.

The catlike eyes narrow. "Show me your palm."

Irina hesitates, just for a second, before extending her arm.

Vera's hands are rough and calloused, but they are also warm and strong and capable. She turns over Irina's hand expertly and peers at the network of crisscrossing lines there. "This line, running across your palm closest to your fingers, is for love," murmurs Vera. "If it ends in a *V*, you'll be lucky in love, and you'll marry well." She traces the line where it vanishes into Irina's flesh, no *V* visible. Only the line, striking out on its own.

Irina swallows, hard, flashing back to handsome, kind, wonderful Will. Does she believe Vera? Is that why Irina doesn't see Will in that daydream of her and the children in New York? She doesn't know. There is only the surprising feeling of her insides sinking.

"The second line is your trade," continues Vera. "Yours starts out faint and weak but then grows, becoming bold and strong and lasting to the end. This means you'll find a worthy pursuit. The final is your lifeline. It—"

Irina glances down at her palm, at the callus there. "Oh, it's from all the cleaning and scrubbing."

"That may be, but the callus is preventing me from seeing your lifeline. It is . . . an impediment." Vera studies Irina, black gaze penetrating, as if she can see under Irina's skin, flay her open. "You are cloaked in darkness, Irina Alexandrovna. It's touched you. Marked you. Now it won't release you. Not easily, anyway."

Vera drops Irina's hand, and it is cold despite the crackling stove. Irina waits, to see if this means her life is at risk, and if Vera will help her.

"Many come to me because they miss their dead," Vera says, slowly. "Most clients want nothing more than to contact their dead. But a few want more—to do the unnatural, the abnormal, and bring their dead back to life."

Irina works hard to keep her face perfectly still. "Was my aunt one of those clients? And what about the Domovoy?" Vera gives her a stern look, and Irina relents. "Forgive me. Do you help these clients?"

"No." The word is clipped, final. "That isn't my trade. I cannot bring back the dead, nor would I want to. But there are practitioners with certain supernatural powers who know this dark art—sorcerers."

"Sorcerers," Irina repeats, feeling the sudden urge to laugh. Either that or cry.

"Haven't you read Gogol?"

"Of course. But it is fiction. A fantasy." Like her dreams of the world, of America and New York.

"And what, pray tell, is fantasy based on but life? Why would Gogol write about sorcerers if he weren't open to their influence, if he didn't seek them out, like your aunt?"

"My aunt? She sought out a . . . sorcerer?"

"She might have—I don't know." Vera rises and walks over to a small stack of books. She pulls out a green volume with *Nikolai Gogol* on the spine in silver lettering. Tearing out a page, she scribbles something there and hands it to Irina.

Viy is printed at the top, followed by the most horrific part of the tale—a beautiful maiden rising from her coffin and walking through a church with her dead eyes closed and her dead arms open. Irina shivers, drops the page. The story is about a witch who returns from the dead to torment a man who flew with her through the night, then did unspeakable acts to her. On her deathbed, she wills him to sit and pray over her corpse for three nights. Each night, she reanimates and sends devilish creatures after him, ultimately frightening him to death. Between the title and the text, Vera has written the name *Daniil*. And under it, an address, here in Moscow.

Irina swallows down her fear and picks up the page.

"I gave your aunt the same name when she came to me that spring, distraught over her son's death. She was so grief-stricken, I told her that her son could be brought back, though not by me. I warned her the dead are shades of themselves. They may be well-meaning, but it is more likely death will twist them into something other, something dark and strange. I'll let Daniil know to expect you."

"Wait." Irina is unable to suppress the tremor in her voice. "How *do* you bring back the dead?" The pieces are shifting together into a horrific puzzle, a nightmare . . .

"You already know." Vera's gaze is steady. "A sacrifice to awaken the Domovoy, who in turn can be asked to awaken the dead of the house."

Irina blinks at Vera, realizing that Nicky was right—Auntie's sacrifice was to bring back their dead family.

Irina is unable to quiet her thoughts as she retraces her steps back to Resurrection Gate. The wall and square beyond glow a lurid red through the blizzard. She holds her breath. No Cadillac, no Nicky, certainly no Lili. She releases her breath, wondering if she should return to the ARA or to Moscow House.

Suddenly, the squeal of tires, and a snow-covered motorcar comes crunching doggedly through the snowdrifts, blinking its white headlamps at her. And Irina knows it is Nicky, their fears come to pass—even before she sees the Cadillac and his stricken face through the glass.

33

A Long, Dark Night

A HUSH FALLS OVER the office as Will finishes recounting Lili's and Paulina's arrests.

Irina clutches her mug of hot cocoa so hard her fingers burn. She is at her desk, Will, Harold, Frank, and Emma gathered around her. Cold knots in the pit of her stomach, stirring up her nausea. Her sister and friends—arrested. And she wasn't even there. She is supposed to care for Lili, being the eldest and most responsible.

You had one task, Irina imagines Maman saying. *Incompétente!* And she is.

What to do? Get Lili released. Find the Domovoy, then the sorcerer. Decide what to do about the spirits. Oh, and collect the children from Madame Naroshina's. But the *have to*s are wooly, fuzzy things, filling her head with frenzied fears, cottony questions with no answers. She keeps worrying at the callus on the palm of her hand.

An impediment. Cloaked in darkness.

What if the darkness isn't the spirits but these arrests, and she is next? She wishes she could take her sister's place, but who would care for Seryozha and Natasha then? Irina is in the best position to seek answers, to appeal to Comrade Suzhensky if she has to and to Lev Kamenev if all else fails. But neither guarantees anything. Auntie is still gone, after all. No, there must be something else Irina can do. Something *the Americans* can do. Despite the Soviet government pretending otherwise, it is the Americans that hold the power here in Moscow.

Nikolai appears pale and slight in the doorway. As if he has aged backward in a matter of hours, once more becoming the little boy Irina used to know.

"You shouldn't be here, Niko," Will says. "They have a warrant out for your arrest. They might come back."

Irina slams her mug down on the desk and looks pointedly at Will. Any feelings for him fall away. All that exists is getting her sister back. "What have you done to help release the Russians?" Mr. Carroll told her the ARA would mitigate their risk. Now the ARA needs to uphold their side of the bargain. "The arrests were carried out because of the ARA work. So, I repeat, what have you done toward their release?"

Will blinks at her, stunned, searching for words. He lets out a very weary sigh. "We have been phoning all the officials we know, even Politburo members. But they aren't answering our telephone calls."

"Have you gone to see them?"

"No." Will winces, has the decency to look ashamed. Her words have hit their mark. He lets out another sigh. "You're right."

"Please help us," Nikolai says, in a voice that breaks Irina's heart.

"They will." Emma rests a hand on his arm, turning to Will. "Won't you?"

"The fucking Bolos won't get away with it," Harold says instead, cavalier.

Frank sees through the ineffectual boast. "Carroll is on inspection in Siberia. I doubt we can do anything without him, or the other chiefs, who are all with him."

But Irina is thinking back to something Will said about the Soviet government's desperation for ARA aid. Even she knows the famine shows no signs of slowing. If the Americans should withhold their aid, or threaten to, it is possible Lili and the other Russians would be released due to the application of a little pressure. Irina needs only to convince Will to act, with or without the chiefs. "I might have an idea," she says slowly, carefully.

"By all means, Irene." Will's lips twitch despite the seriousness of the situation.

She ignores it. "Order a stop on an ARA relief shipment to Moscow—foodstuffs, clothing, medical supplies—and threaten to cut supplies everywhere else across Russia."

Will gives a bark of a laugh. "You're joking. Carroll will never go for it."

"He will once he finds out the Soviet secret police has been ransacking his offices, getting their hands on his documents, spying on his American staff . . ."

"Irrespective of the arrests."

"Irrespective of the arrests but including them. Draft a letter of complaint to the Soviet government outlining your demands for resuming operations. No searches, no spying. Then insist the ARA employees be released and permitted to return to work immediately."

Harold flashes her a knowing smile. "A threat."

"An empty one," Will warns sternly, with none of his bright, casual attitude.

Irina understands—after all, if this is not handled properly, he risks much, maybe even his job. She doesn't wish to bring trouble to his door. But she also needs to get Lili and their friends out. "An empty threat," she agrees quickly. "Aren't you tired of the Bolos hampering ARA operations? Following you? Watching you and the offices? Raiding? They will never agree to a shutdown. As you said, they need American help."

"Their actions *are* a clear provocation and infringement of the Riga Agreement," Frank puts in, with a meaningful look at Will.

Irina holds herself stiffly. Yet her heart batters her rib cage, waiting, hoping, still a little resentful. The irrational anger at the ARA, at Will, lingering.

"I will need to run it by Carroll and hope he agrees," Will says, finally. "He will be outraged to hear of all this, especially the arrests, having little patience with the Bolos these days. But will he risk the mission? I don't know. I can try to telegraph several offices in Siberia to see if they can get a message to him. It will take time, and I'm afraid my hands are tied until then." His eyes seem to say many more things to Irina. *Sorry*, for one.

The anger has burned through her. "I understand, William. Thank you." And she means it. But it doesn't keep a feeling of utter bleakness, of hopelessness, from stealing in. Irina has no idea if this plan will work, empty threat or no, if Mr. Carroll will even go for it. A glance out the window, at the snow billowing against the glass. She cannot even collect the children or return to the house. Speaking of. "Come stay with us, Nicky," she says, with a glance at him. "Returning to your flat given the situation might be dangerous."

He nods numbly. And Irina's heart breaks a little more—for him, Lili, all of them.

"Well, I doubt they will be coming back tonight, not with this snowfall," Will says, with his own glance at the snow. "Why don't we all get a few hours of sleep, and you two can leave first thing in the morning?"

It is a good plan, and their group disperses to find a bed or sofa for the night. Irina doesn't hesitate to walk right up to Will's room. And he doesn't hesitate to let her in.

"I am so sorry, Irene," he rushes to say, as soon as the door falls closed behind her. "You must think me beastly—for not doing more. I will do *all* I can for you and Lili, do you hear me?"

His hands are on Irina's shoulders, their warmth radiating through her despite the cold. And suddenly, with Lili gone and the Cheka once more persecuting them, Irina not imagining Will in her future doesn't matter. Nor does the fact that they work together. He is here for her, as he has been the entire time. Whatever happens, if Vera is right or not, Irina will tell Will what she can. She slips out of his arms. "I would like you to sit, William."

"All . . . right," he says slowly, clearly uneasy. But he takes a seat on the bed, looking up at her, waiting.

Irina takes a deep breath and lets it out along with the truth. "Seryozha is not my cousin."

A beat of silence. "Who is he, then?" But there is understanding in those blue depths.

This is it. The moment she might lose him. "He is my son. Only my aunt and Lili know. Oh, and the Cheka."

A pause that seems to last an eternity. Then, very quietly, "Who is the father?"

"He is dead." *And haunting me.* "We . . . were engaged to be married. He—wasn't a good man, I don't think. In any case, I didn't love him. And he died before I found out about the baby. He never knew."

Will nods, just as slowly. "Okay."

"I wanted to tell you, but I've kept this secret so long . . . I—forgive me. I—"

Before Irina knows it, Will is taking her in his arms. No questions, no recriminations. And everything fades away. Only his embrace is left, unrestrained, its warmth as infinite as the sky on one of Petersburg's white nights. "Oh, Irene, what you must have gone through— are still going through! I am so, so sorry."

Irina closes her eyes, her body and head too light and giddy with relief. She knows Will's arms cannot protect her. She's going to do that on her own. But she feels heard, and that is everything. "I thought—you would be angry. Me with a child, not telling you, keeping such a secret, *lying*—"

"Irene," he stops her, putting his hand to her lips. "We aren't teenagers. We both have a past. And you *have* told me." He tips his head back, the corners of his mouth lifting. "I admit it isn't the most conventional, or straightforward, approach to dating. But I know what it is for an unmarried woman to be with a child on her own. And I have always respected my aunt for it. Most men don't think like me. But then, most men don't have an Aunt Mildred in their life, or you."

Irina wishes for some of that relief to come back, but she isn't done. "You should sit back down."

"More secrets?" Will smirks. But as before, he dutifully retreats to the bed.

Irina tells him about the dead Soviet men then, the other men moving out, the investigation. "We don't know what is happening," she concludes truthfully. After all, she doesn't know whether the spirits are doing the murdering or the creature. "The head official at the house believes us to be innocent, which we are," she hastens to add. "He thinks it is the house . . ."

Irina cannot finish. Will's eyes are a very pale blue, containing such feeling and such incredible compassion that it is as though she is completely unburdened. Not only of her secret but of the secrets of Moscow House, too, though Will doesn't and won't know the worst of them.

"I'm sorry you didn't feel like you could tell me any of this, Irene," he says, genuinely sorry. "Do you think the men's deaths were accidental?"

She tilts her head. "I don't know. But I agree with Comrade Suzhensky that something isn't right with the house. I'm afraid for the children. All of us."

"They will be back, you know."

And Will knows only of the human danger. If he knew the rest . . . But Irina simply says, "They already have come back," thinking of her sister.

A beat of silence, then Will is up again. The floorboards creak beneath his nicely polished shoes as he paces the room. "You have options, Irina," he says finally. "You don't have to be at the Bolos' mercy, fear that at any moment they will return, take your house all over again, or burn it this time. No, let's find you somewhere else to live. And if all else fails, we can come up with an insurance policy."

"An insurance policy?" It is too much American speak for her. "Speak plainly, William."

"I have a contact here in Moscow. An old Harvard buddy who's been living in Russia since before the Revolution. He owes me a favor. He can prepare travel papers for you."

Irina stills. "To where?"

"Well, anywhere you like. Europe—America, if you wish it."

Europe, America. These are places Irina didn't think she would actually ever see. She believed that image of her and the children a dream, a ridiculous fantasy. A fairy tale. She thinks of her son, cousin, Lili. What if they could all escape—the house, the Cheka, Russia? She pauses on that carefree picture of them somewhere else, in New York maybe. Yet neither the image nor Will's words can ever be.

Irina knows she will never leave her sister or the house behind.

"That is not an option for me, William," she says firmly, driving away the offer and the image, squashing the fairy tale like another roach at Moscow House.

"But Irene—think of your son, your cousin, yourself. If the Bolos come back with an arrest warrant for you—what will happen? To you, to them? What if the children are also arrested? The Bolos aren't above that. As I said, the papers would only be an insurance policy..." Will's voice fades. He looks away, clenching his jaw, that strong American jaw. "I don't want anything to happen to you, all right?" His whisper is strained and rough.

The warm room turns cold. "I cannot think about travel papers, even in theory, even as an eventuality, with my sister in prison. I am sorry, William. But thank you . . . for thinking of us, of me." Irina reaches out to him then, wrapping her arms around his neck, wishing more than anything that he know she is grateful.

And as she knew they would, his arms curl around her without a word. The night is too long and too dark. At least with Will, she doesn't have to face it alone. Irina knows he will never let that happen.

34

Irina Finds a Little Strength Before Finding a Surprise

IRINA TRUDGES THROUGH the uncleared drifts of snow, gripping Seryozha's cold little hand, Natasha pressing in close on her other side. Irina can feel her trembling, even through their coats. And she feels rather than sees Nikolai, who they agreed would walk a little distance behind them so as not to draw attention. He is wearing the garments the Americans lent him, an inconspicuous black coat and a matching bowler hat that shades his face from view.

Not many are in the streets this early, and it is hard to see through the white. Irina is glad of this, as it will make it harder for them to be followed.

They are a grim little party, not speaking, not even glancing at one another. All of them, Irina is sure, are thinking of Lili—where she is, how she is, what is in store for her, and them.

Snow frosts the still-leafy tree branches in ivory, steeping the town in a powdery, fairy-tale-like glitter. Snowflakes drift from the bleary, colorless sky, but they are mere specks, dry and featherlight against Irina's skin.

The cold bleakness from the night before rushes back, and so do the doubts. She walked out of Will's room confident in her plan. But though he promised to do all he could for her sister, what if it still will not work, or the Soviet officials refuse to listen? What if she cannot keep her family and Nicky safe? The callus itches.

Irina collected the children from Madame Naroshina's earlier that morning, telling the worried mother only what she needed to know about Nikolai's arrest warrant in case the Cheka darkened her door. Then Irina retraced her steps back to the ARA for Nikolai. Now the four of them are on their way to Moscow House, to deliberate on what to do next. But Irina knows it is all up to her. What they do, as well as keeping up their spirits.

So she starts to talk. About what they will eat when they reach home—cold chicken and soft white rolls and canned vegetables, provided by Will from the ARA commissary; what the children wish to do that day—play in the snow, read, or draw. Irina's heart fills with such warmth, such a profound sense of *home*, that she even looks forward to seeing the old house. Nothing, no sofa or bed, even Will's, is as satisfyingly *home* as her own house, their attic, the place of their refuge and life, all the little moments it's composed of—Lili hopping into Irina's bed with her, sketching and chatting; the children, cuddling up to them and reading fairy tales about handsome tsareviches and beautiful, clever maidens building their happily-ever-afters for themselves, by themselves.

Irina realizes this is what she needs to fight for. The feeling of home, of family, of *belonging*. And no matter the doubt, she needs to try to make that happily-ever-after happen for them—one way or another. Irina inhales a breath of the bracing, snowy air and is refreshed. Strong. Ready for whatever is to come.

That turns out to be a fat rat on the porch of Moscow House. Irina draws back in disgust, shooing the foul rodent away before Seryozha tries to chase it. The entrance doors are unlocked, and she is sure she locked them.

"What is it?" Nikolai asks, on guard, the first words he has spoken all day.

At the rush of air from the hastily closed doors behind them, the lantern swings above their heads, emitting that unsettling, bone-chilling *creeaakk*. It flickers in and out, an eye winking. Irina peers into the dim foyer, the hall suffused in daylight shadows. Uneasiness clings to her, nipping and prodding, darkening what lightness she was able to find. There is a distinct whiff of rose water beneath the decay, like shriveled dead roses.

Cleo swoops down, beating her wings. "What is wrong, Cleo?" Irina tries to understand the squawking and screeching. She wishes her sister were here.

"It's Auntie!" Seryozha points to the grand staircase.

Everything in Irina tightens. A shadow skims the wall—tall, with a feathered hat, a full skirt, and a confident step—before Auntie appears at the top of the stairs. Even from the threshold, Irina can tell she is smiling. Before Irina can pull him back, Seryozha drops her hand and barrels forward with gleeful squeals and chatter, Natasha at his heels. Irina exchanges an uneasy glance with Nikolai before remembering the strength she has found.

She draws herself to her full height, back straight, gaze steady. "Hello, Marie."

Auntie has reached the bottom of the stairs, the exact spot Grand-mère fell to her bloody death, and kneels to embrace both children. Her eyes snap to Irina. "Released from Butyrka and not even a kiss on the cheek from my eldest niece?"

Irina turns to Nikolai. "Would you take the children up to the attic while I speak to my aunt?"

"Of course," he replies, with a respectful yet short nod at Auntie. He crouches before Seryozha. "Hello, Count Sergei. Why don't we go upstairs and play with your toy soldiers? I hear there is a great battle coming, and they will need their commander. . . ."

Irina can tell her son is instantly won over. He is already moving past Auntie and climbing the stairs with sparkling eyes. Natasha and Nikolai follow, Cleo soaring overhead. They cast their last glances at Irina, who faces her aunt squarely. "We know everything," she says, once they are alone, though her statement is only half true.

"And what is that?"

"You brought back the dead, woke up an ancient spirit, put our lives in danger. Why did you do it? Why couldn't you just accept they were gone?" The words are tearing out of Irina faster than she can think. "Did you kill those men? And Grand-mère—do you know that she is dead?"

"I heard." Auntie's features soften. She steps closer, her dead rose smell assaulting Irina. Her dusty black gown is from the last century, with peaked balloon sleeves and a bodice of glossy silk. "The rest is nonsense."

Irina flushes with a hot rage that sparks deep in her chest and radiates to all the cold, lonely parts of her. Does Auntie dare to lie even now? "Answer me."

She doesn't. "Where have you been?"

"You have the gall to ask me where *I've* been?" The rage pushes into Irina's voice, making it shake. "We know what you did, Marie. Now admit it and let us make it right. I cannot leave the children alone in a house full of specters, Georgy is back and very angry, an ancient creature is running around—and Lili has been arrested."

Auntie's small smile falls away. "I did what I had to." Then, "I am not worried for Liliya. You shall go see Comrade Suzhensky. After all, that is how I was released."

"It is an entirely separate situation." Irina gives a shake of her head. "Lili and I have been working for an American organization, the ARA. The Soviet officials aren't pleased."

"Then why weren't you arrested?" asks Auntie, clever as ever.

That, and Auntie's release, could indeed be due to Comrade Suzhensky. He does have a soft spot for Irina. Maybe he respects that she takes care of her family, or that she has held her ground with him.

Or maybe he simply finds her attractive. He is a man, after all. And if she appeals to him again, he might just help her—again.

"Good work ridding us of the Bolshevik swine. I didn't think you had it in you."

Irina scoffs. "Your spirits frightened them away." She squares her shoulders and places her hands firmly on her waist. *Do* not *back down. Or let her manipulate you.* "Auntie, this is dangerous. Don't you care about us? If you do, help me to drive the spirits away . . . return this place to how it was. We don't have to lose the house, or each other. Help us. We need you," Irina adds for good measure, knowing how her aunt likes to be needed.

But she is unflappable. "Return to what? A poor, ignored half existence with everyone dead or dying, the house shutting down, abandoned room by room? That is not a life. We shall go back to how it was before," she whispers. "They will help us."

Irina is becoming aware of a glint in her aunt's eyes, glittery, inciting, maybe unhinged. She peers closer and realizes Auntie is trembling, her cheekbones sticking out alarmingly in a face as pallid and dead as the spirits'. She looks feverish, somehow disconnected from reality. "Are you all right?" Irina asks. "*Who* will help us?"

"You will understand soon."

"Understand what?" Irina springs to her aunt, who is already turning toward the stairs. "Tell me! Don't you dare turn your back on me, Marie!"

"Shouldn't you be focused on your sister?"

A scream of frustration is building in Irina's throat, but she presses it down. Auntie isn't willing to speak, or admit anything, with the exception of those half-veiled, maddeningly vague remarks. Yet they are enough to indicate that Irina and Lili's theories about her are, if not right, then very close indeed. Irina will try again to talk some semblance of sense into her aunt. If she cannot, she will attempt to stop the spirits herself. Inconveniently, she recalls Pasha's fears and her own regarding Auntie's use of black, ungodly, unnatural magic, and shudders.

For now, Irina begrudgingly admits her aunt is right. She needs to pay the Old Bolshevik a visit. That is, after she makes sure Nikolai and the children are safe in the attic. Though Irina suspects Auntie has occupied her own rooms. And she wouldn't harm Seryozha or Natasha—or Prince Naroshin, for that matter. Would she?

"Irina Alexandrovna! Oh, what a delightful surprise!" Comrade Suzhensky is breathless with excitement as he ushers her into his cozy little office. Though she waited for hours in the antechamber before being allowed in by an aloof, grim-faced secretary.

Irina notices that his face is more youthful and jovial than she has ever seen it. He steps to a silver cart on which glint and glimmer crystal carafes with liquors in a dazzling array of colors, from amber to dark cherry.

The Old Bolshevik motions to the cart and its treasures grandly. "Cognac?"

"Thank you." It cannot hurt, might even help. "Comrade Suzhensky—"

"Is your dear aunt back in the bosom of your dear family?" He practically vibrates good cheer and, Irina hopes, goodwill.

Cognac is poured into two slender glasses, its aromas rushing at her—those of peaches, dried apricots, figs, oak. Then the cold glass is in her hand, and Irina is taking a surprisingly greedy swallow. The liquor tastes as decadent as it smells. It loosens her a little. "Thank you, Comrade Suzhensky. I heard my aunt's release was entirely due to your efforts." *To our very sad, extreme detriment*.

"Oh, you give me too much credit. Comrade Kamenev has immense respect for your family. Now, what is it that I can do for you, Irina Alexandrovna?"

"My sister and several friends were arrested. I wish to inquire after them."

Comrade Suzhensky's face shutters. "I know nothing of that situation."

"So there *is* a situation?"

"I have not heard anything." But his eyes blink once, twice, *three* times.

Irina thinks fast. He cannot say, though he wishes to. What else can she ask to learn more? "Will you . . . m-make inquiries? I am so worried for them." She gives a silly little laugh, for the benefit of whomever is listening, likely the secretary.

"Unfortunately, Irina Alexandrovna, whatever has befallen your sister and friends is not part of any of my investigations." Again—he blinks three times. "But I know they are well taken care of by our glorious state, in the usual, most convenient place."

Irina's heart gives a thud. *Usual place* . . . Butyrka. It has to be.

"It is nice weather, don't you think, Irina Alexandrovna? I love a snowy winter."

Confused, "Why, yes, Comrade, what Soviet citizen doesn't?"

"Indeed. I take a walk every morning. But my favorite time is when the snow is nice and packed. A few days after a snowfall, I would say."

Irina's heart skips a beat. She nods, doesn't dare mouth *Thank you*. In a few days, he might have answers. At the very least, he will speak to her. They tip their heads back and drink.

The snow has tapered off. An eerie quiet hangs on the air that sets Irina on edge. She casts glances over her shoulder to see if she is being followed. But it is a still, empty night. No one is in the streets, not even the homeless. Perhaps they are hiding in the abandoned buildings. The cold is so intense that if not for the cognac sitting warm in her belly like a fat cat on the pech, Irina would have frozen in her threadbare coat.

It is the kind of cold that steals into muscle and sinew, cartilage and bone.

Even as Irina steps into Moscow House to the flare of candlelight, brighter and hotter and waxier than ever, the cold stays. Auntie or the

Domovoy, maybe both, are preparing for midnight and the appearance of the spirits. Before she returns to the attic, Irina needs to try to draw out the imp. She has been considering how to do this, thinking back to Pasha's books and something she saw there. Her eyes seek out the nook under the grand staircase where Lili found bread and salt. Their former servants had also delivered bread and salt to Auntie.

Irina veers toward the kitchen, where she and Lili have moved back most of their food. She shudders in the hallway where Boriska died.

It is dark in the kitchen, and Irina tries to keep her mind occupied to banish the fear. She pats the counter for the candle and matchbox she knows are there, brushing against something furry. Her fingers tremble as she grasps the box, succeeding in pulling out a match and scratching it to life. A few roaches scurry away. The flame catches onto the wick, the candle flickering uncertainly before bathing her surroundings in an otherworldly orange light. The space becomes cavernous, the tiled stove monstrous. Saucepans gleam on their hooks like watchful eyes.

You are a grown woman, Irina chastises herself. *And a reasonable one.* Mostly.

She pulls a loaf of black bread from a cupboard and cuts it into slices. Her stomach grumbles, and she pops a sliver of crust into her mouth, stale yet hearty. She pours a mound of salt, finds an old, patterned tea towel behind a sack of turnips. She ignores the cold, prickling feeling she isn't alone, though midnight is still hours away.

Irina hurries back into the entrance hall, where she gingerly places the towel, bread, and salt inside the nook. She settles in for the wait, leaning against the nearest wall with her eyes on the staircase. She prays the imp doesn't take long. But all of Russia is hungry. An old, neglected spirit must be, too.

Is Irina frightened? She was before. Now she only wishes to get it over with.

The candlelight ripples like water over the room's polished surfaces, softening its edges, blurring the ugly black spots of mold. Irina slept poorly the night before, winked in and out without falling into real sleep. Now the candlelight lulls her into drowsiness. Her eyelids flutter closed despite herself. It seems a mere instant, and she gasps awake. Something has woken her. Something cold and slick and revolting.

Irina blinks away the sleep, struggling to get her bearings, get her fuzzy mind to focus.

Someone is leaning over her. She can see the outlines of them. Two figures. Oscillating, almost floating on the air like shreds of escaped smoke. Then taking physical shape.

Do you think she is dead?

If she were, we would know it.

Irina blinks at the swell of Maman's black hair, the violet in the eyes. At Papa's smile, real, with the glint of teeth. The specters are tangible, with alarming color to them, and solid depth. Their faces are shaded with bluish shadows hinting at bruises and frostbite. Part of Irina burns to speak to her parents. But by the unnatural angle of their bodies, the empty, dead look in their eyes, she knows they aren't her parents. Not really.

Irina must get to the attic. But she cannot move, her limbs cramping from cold and shock. She glances toward the nook—the bread and salt are gone. Irina releases an outraged hiss. The Domovoy must have sneaked by and stolen the bundle. *How* could she have been so foolish? Now she is stuck between her dead parents.

She has no choice. She has to try to get past them. As quietly and as slowly as possible, Irina starts to shuffle along the wall. It is damp and porous. She flinches at the thought of the mold touching any part of her.

Maman's and Papa's speech comes out warbled, as though they are all trapped underwater.

Irina redoubles her shuffling. Her ears fill with voices and footfalls, her nose with perfume below the decay. Flashes of cold nip at her skin as other spirits brush past, whirling in and out of her vision, along with garments that seem to be alive with fluttering moths. Irina slips past her parents, who are absorbed in their discussion.

She reaches the bottom of the staircase and leaps to her feet, sprinting up the marble steps. She feels, rather than hears, a pair of childlike footsteps behind her. A turn of her stiff neck, and she glimpses her youngest sister with her skirt of gold. The dead girl meets her gaze—and smiles.

Irina stumbles. The smile is made of perfectly sharp, blackened teeth.

She pumps her legs harder, faster, even as she hears piano music. Then the hum of a lullaby, winding from the abandoned nursery. Irina stops despite her good sense telling her to *run*. She strains her eyes into the hallway's greasy light. The humming shifts, draws closer. It is louder, a real sound with words she doesn't quite recognize. A glimpse of a grayish, ghostly Luba, rounding the corner with her big belly, and Irina bolts up the stairs.

She springs onto the landing with Grand-père's rooms, nearly stopping again.

The singing has been replaced by a hacking cough, with rasp and phlegm and blood to it. And her name, wheezy and rough with illness but clear—her dead Grand-père calling for her.

A door handle rattles. Then a door slams open, its hinges creaking from disuse. The death knell–like strike of a cane, and the specter of Grand-père appears. *Irina!*

Turning from the ghastly sight, pressing her hands over her ears, Irina forces herself to focus on not stopping; on getting her legs, growing heavy and tired, to keep pushing forward. She flings open the attic door and pounds up the stairs.

Irina, she hears behind her. But it isn't Grand-père's voice. Nor is it Xenia chasing her. No, it is *his* voice. *Him* doing the chasing. *His* face, in all its horribly handsome peevishness, that she glimpses in the darkness. Georgy, with the dirty scarlet stain blotting out his chest and his eyes glowing a shocking poisonous green.

Irina is numb with cold, her breaths worryingly shallow. She cannot inhale a full breath and her chest is exploding. Her vision blackens, wavers. She is using the last of her strength.

Where are you going, Irina? No matter where it is, my darling, I will find you.

"I don't want you to find me!" Irina screams. "Go away, leave me alone!"

Just as she feels cold, stiff fingers wrap around her ankle, clamp on it hard, the door at the top of the stairwell is thrown open with a violent *bang!* and Nikolai appears, brandishing his pistol. Georgy lets out a shadow of a laugh. But his dead fingers unclamp. Irina still feels their chilling imprint as she pounds up the rest of the stairs. Then she is sobbing so hard she doesn't know if she—cool, collected, reasonable Irina—will ever stop.

35

In a Butyrka Cell

"I REQUIRE MORE PAPER, Comrade," Lili says to the guard at the cell door, tracing the deep grooves of the pencil in her pocket, wishing to keep sketching, writing, anything to keep her mind busy and away from where she is or what will happen next.

"What am I, your grocery?" returns the guard.

Lili is undaunted. "I have the right to paper if I wish it."

"Wish all you like, but you won't get it from me, *Countess*." His mouth quirks into a mocking smile that has her clenching her jaw. "And anyway, why do you need paper? Shouldn't you be listening to the holy word of your God?"

His eyes flick to the group in the far corner of the cell, all former people in ragged old finery, reciting prayers. An aged general stands over them, reading the Gospels out loud in his powerful, deep voice, commanding his flock to peace the way Lili imagines he used to command armies to battle.

She wonders if peace is possible in this stark place, this cold and soulless prison that has witnessed such suffering and death. Uncle Aleksei and Papa have both passed through, have seen and lived it, have stood in the very place she stands now. Has Auntie been here, too? If so, where is she now? A tremor goes through Lili at the possibilities. The group repeats the general's prayers in hushed tones, their arms crossed and eyes distant, visibly transported to faraway places. Maybe to their homes and families. Or to the past, their own version of peace. Their Thrice-Tenth Kingdom, the fantastical fairy-tale land at the edge of the world.

Lili prefers to stay firmly rooted in the present. She is already ill in body. Why drag her spirit and heart into it? The breath rattles in her throat, the cough dry and trapped in her lungs. She is glad her nose can't smell the unwashed bodies, or the horrible fish soup, braised cabbage, and runny millet that pass for food.

Nothing will distract her from her goal—to survive.

Her eyes travel to Kirill, who has stopped his incessant pacing and now sits sullenly at the edge of the praying circle. With what relief they greeted each other when Lili was first deposited here. As for Paulina, she was separated from Lili back at Lubyanka, where they spent two sleepless days and nights being questioned.

Lili closes her burning eyes against the memory of that place, colder and more soulless than the present one—the series of officials who paraded in and out of her interrogation room, where she was held after being plucked from a cell of other former people; and the questions: *What is your work at Aara?* They drew out the word. *Who do you really work for? Are you a spy? Are you promoting counterrevolution? You are, aren't you? Come now, what are your intentions? Have you betrayed your country? You have, haven't you? Confess.*

Confess. No, Lili will not think of it, though her tired, ill body aches and groans. Neither will she think of her family, Uncle Pasha, and that gunshot. Therefore, the pen, the paper, the sketches and words. Only the present, and her imagination. Lili fantasizes she is an imprisoned maiden from the fairy tales, this guard Baba Yaga or else Koshey the Deathless. Then she nearly laughs, right in this guard's hateful face.

"I find writing or sketching a more worthy pursuit, don't you think?" Lili says to the guard, earning her a curious look. "You Soviets don't believe in God. So, then, why would you think listening to the Gospels would do anything for me?"

He smirks. Yet his eyes spark with interest. "Writing or even sketching will not do anything for you, either, little countess." Surprisingly, his voice is not teasing, only sad. It makes his face a little less hateful. "Your letters aren't going through, you see."

Lili's brow furrows. "*Your* meaning mine, or all of ours?"

"Yours—and that of the tall, snooty one."

"Prince Kirill." Lili adds the title to see if the guard will get angry. He doesn't. This further emboldens her. "Because we work for the Americans, the ARA?"

He casts a glance around, then gives the briefest of nods.

"Do you think we will get out of here?"

"*We* meaning . . . ?"

Lili gives a shrug. "I don't know. Any of us."

"You never know." But his eyes skitter away, in guilt or indifference, she cannot tell. "I'll get you that paper, little countess, but it might take some time."

Something within Lili gives at that, a small kindness for a girl with not much of a present and apparently no future, either. When she smiles at the guard, it is genuine. She thanks him, very softly, then retreats to the tiny window. For perhaps the first time since arriving in this cell, Lili sits—on the cold floor, directly beneath the window, in a pool of unexpected light. Through it, she can see the spire of a silvery white church, a long-lost, forgotten symbol of Old Russia. It is so beautiful Lili wishes she could sketch it.

She gives in and thinks of home. Not of Moscow House but of Irina, her nephew Seryozha, her cousin Natasha, her ARA friends and former people project, little Cleo. And finally, Nicky.

Lili hopes he was able to avoid arrest, shudders at the memory of his name on those cold, official lips. She doesn't know what will happen to her, or if she will ever leave prison. And while she still believes she is too young to think of the hazy future, of any kind of forever, Lili knows if she were to see Nicky again, she would find the words to tell him how she feels. Nothing grandiose, of course. No silly, sweeping gestures or honeyed words. Just that she wants something new with him, only him, and that she will gladly sit with him anytime he asks. Maybe Lili will even tell Nicky that she likes him, that a fairy-tale ending isn't out of the realm of possibility for them. Though the flush flames hot on her cheeks at that. Maybe not so far. She is too much of a damn coward.

Lili closes her eyes, blocking out that church spire, the whispers and prayers, and she daydreams. Motoring around Moscow with Nicky in the Cadillac or poring over Uncle Pasha's diaries together in the library. All those moments as they fought, kissed, had sex, fought again. Kissed again. Each look, touch, laugh, or smile.

And to Lili's surprise, for the first time in days, she relinquishes her surroundings and drifts into sleep.

36

Frozen Snow, Frosted Moonlight

THE LAST SEVERAL days have passed in endless ARA petitions and telephone calls to Soviet officials while waiting for a response from Mr. Carroll; sleepless vigils at Moscow House, watching over the children and her aunt; and praying for Lili to come home.

It is morning, and Irina is pacing a small, snowy park, waiting for Comrade Suzhensky. He didn't tell her where they would meet, but she assumed it would be somewhere near, but not too near, his offices. The more minutes that trickle by, the more her toes grow numb and her cheeks bruise with cold, and the more she doubts.

It is no longer snowing. The snow is frozen under a glassy layer of ice and frost.

Finally, through the whiteness, Irina makes out a corpulent, black-coated figure striding toward her. Comrade Suzhensky jerks his chin toward a bench under an oak tree whose colorful leaves glimmer through the icy snow like jewels. She warms a little with relief and hurries to the bench, lowering onto the cold, hard wood.

Irina directs her gaze forward, just as she hears Comrade Suzhensky's creaky footsteps and glimpses as he drops onto the other end of the bench. He is the straight-faced, somber official today.

"Your sister is being held in Butyrka," he mutters, not sparing her a glance, "along with Prince Kirill Serpukhov. Paulina Gonchurova is still detained at Lubyanka."

Irina expected as much. "Are they all right?" She matches his voice. Sweeps a glance over the park, as lovely and romantic as a fairy-tale wood, entirely at odds with their conversation.

"According to my sources, yes. Though your sister is ill."

Irina's heart seems to freeze in her chest, like the dead leaves in ice. "Ill?"

"A cold, they say."

"Is there any indication of or plans for release?"

"I'm afraid not. They wish to make an example of them to frighten other Soviet citizens from working for Aara. This could mean forcing them to sign damning statements, admitting to harboring anti-Soviet sympathies and engaging in counterrevolution and espionage for the Americans, or"—Comrade Suzhensky clears his throat—"charging them with treason and . . ." His voice fades into the snow.

More questioning, possibly torture; a long trial and false testimonies; and an even longer imprisonment, exile, execution . . . the possibilities are truly endless—and hopeless. Irina takes in a shaky breath, the air coiling sharp and cold in her mouth. "What can I do? Should I go see Kamenev? What can I *do*, Comrade Suzhensky?" Her whisper is fierce and grating. "I *have* to do something—anything."

There is such a long silence that Irina thinks he may not answer. But he does, in a whisper that is nearly erased by the town awakening, by the trams, the droshkies, the distant murmur of automobiles and passersby. "Go to Comrade Kamenev. I will visit him also. Then convince your American friends to intervene, and not just with telephone calls. Only that can help you now."

Irina wants to cry, *I have already done that—and nothing!* But Comrade Suzhensky is already rising. "Where is your aunt?" he asks suddenly.

"My aunt?" Irina blinks, taken aback. "At home, of course."

"Be careful, Irina Alexandrovna." Some of his old warmth bleeds through. "She has betrayed your family once. She may do so again."

"Betrayed—w-what? What are you suggest—?" The air in Irina's mouth turns sour, almost rotten, as if she is back at the house and inhaling the mold.

"That is why you were allowed to stay on at Moscow House."

Irina opens her mouth to ask more, but Comrade Suzhensky is already hastening away, his figure reducing to a dark, nebulous blot not unlike an ink stain on one of Lili's blank sheets of sketch paper. Her aunt betrayed her family? But how, when? The answer, though, is obvious. When the Cheka burst into Moscow House in November 1918, killing Pasha and arresting Papa and Aleksei. At the hard, jarring certainty of the realization, Irina feels all the loveliness drain out of the little park until it is an empty, skeletal graveyard, ugly in its cold and desolation.

Back in the attic, Irina sheds her coat beside their little stove and shoves her numb, swollen feet toward the warmth. Her skin is damp from the thawing snow. Or maybe it's the house. She presses Seryozha to her chest even as she trembles. At the feel of his squirming little body, Irina has the overwhelming urge to tell him, right there and then, that she is his mother. Despite the words bubbling up, she hedges. There will be a better time.

Besides, Nikolai is waiting for an account of the morning's events. Natasha hands her a steaming, blistering hot cup of coffee with a splash of milk, just as Irina likes it. She sips at the coffee as she tells Nicky about the park with Comrade Suzhensky, then her follow-up meeting with Comrade Kamenev.

Cleo flutters uneasily up in the rafters, making throaty, garbled noises. As if to interject into Irina's story with a remark, or an expletive.

As calmly and dispassionately as she could, pressing down her tears and rubbing discreetly at Maman's brooch in the folds of her coat, Irina explained to Kamenev what happened at the ARA and respectfully yet resolutely asked for his help. Like Suzhensky, he claimed with a serene, official smile that the matter is quite out of his control, insisting her sister and friends are being well treated. She nearly believed him.

Irina recalls Kamenev's parting words as he escorted her out of his office: *Though I cannot help with your friends' releases, I shall make inquiries after your sister and take up her cause out of respect for your venerable babushka.*

Yet Irina is no closer to getting her sister released than she was on that long, dark night of her arrest. And now she doesn't know what to think of her aunt. Neither, apparently, does Nicky.

"Do you . . . think she informed on your family?"

"I don't know what else her betrayal can mean. She knew enough, not that the Cheka needs specifics for any arrest. And she certainly had enough anger toward Pasha and the rest of the family. If she did do it, then she is responsible for their deaths. But then why bring them back?"

"Maybe she didn't mean to. Or regretted informing on them."

"Maybe." Now Irina is thinking about more than her dead family. How did the Cheka know about Seryozha? Could her aunt have told them?

"Is . . . Lili all right—truly?" Nikolai's whisper cuts into Irina, all other thoughts fleeing. His pale face has thinned alarmingly, his eyes turned fearful. Haunted.

"She is all right, Nicky." But of course her sister isn't all right. She is imprisoned, ill, though the last part Irina doesn't tell Nikolai. He is carrying enough guilt and worry.

"Then why haven't we heard from her?"

"Maybe she doesn't have pen or paper. Maybe she—"

"She would find pen and paper, Irina. It is the first thing she does anywhere. It is a bad sign we haven't received a letter from her. Regardless of what these officials tell you."

"We will get her back," Irina persists through his doubt. "My aunt didn't write the entire time she was in prison. Yet here she is. I will return to Kamenev tomorrow before work, then keep trying to convince Will to agree to my plan. We *have* to have hope, Nicky."

Seryozha squirms from under Irina's arm, nearly upsetting her coffee, which splashes a little onto her hand. "I want to play! Can Nicky play with me?"

"Why don't you play with Cleo?" Irina glances up at the rafters pleadingly.

Cleo twitters in reply, ruffling her feathers, visibly annoyed to be sidelined out of such a crucial conversation. But she dives down and playfully flaps a wing at Seryozha. She shoots into the adjoining room, and he races after her, giggling and squealing.

"What if I lost her, just as we've found each other . . . ?" Nikolai says in a low, rough voice, Natasha quietly withdrawing into the other room. "I wish it had been me."

Irina shakes her head. "Do *not* say that, Nicky. She wouldn't want it."

"I never thanked you, did I?" His gaze is a light brown in this moment, warm with gratitude.

Irina reaches for his hand and squeezes his cold fingers. "And you don't have to."

He squeezes back, lets go. "Has your aunt been any more forthcoming?"

Irina sips at her cooling coffee. She leans back in her chair and looks up at the rafters, hung with more cobwebs than usual and streaked with faint wet stains. There is a smell to the attic, too, a waterlogged, damp reek of ancient wood damaged by water. As if the house is rotting from the inside out. She forces her mind back to Marie. Whenever Irina starts to question her aunt, Marie simply smiles a quiet little smile, veiled in Mona Lisa–like secrets. Or lets loose a puzzling litany of requests, schemes, or complaints.

The last time Irina saw her, Marie was flitting about her rooms like the moths that have moved in there with her, tugging on gowns, hats, gloves, shoes—as if preparing for some fashionable ball or soirée. That scent of dead roses lingered. Black mold sprouted through her bloodred wallpaper, the gilded chandeliers and candelabras swathed in gossamer spiderwebs. Irina asked Marie what she was doing, but her aunt only went on about finding the perfect garments for the perfect night. She twirled before a full-length mirror, mottled black and layered with virulent dust. The grimy glass distorted her image, spun it into deformed shapes, her into some fairy-tale monster.

"You must get ready," Marie sang out. "No trousers or moth-eaten gowns."

"Everything is moth-eaten." Irina crossed her arms, losing patience, her cheeks flushing with a lick of heat even in the cold. "What are you going on about, Marie?"

She whirled toward Irina, her eyes bulging in a face that still hadn't regained any color or life. "Why, we are to have a ball, Irina. And then they shall be back, really and truly back. Alive as you and me, to stay—forever."

"They *are* back, Marie. We don't need a ball to tell us that."

She shook her head furiously, her black hair as loose and unfettered as her eyes. "We did not remember them as we should have, so they are not as alive as they should be. The blood was not enough. Now I see what I must do. A grander gesture, a true revival of the past."

"Did you kill the men?" Irina tried again, approaching her. "How did you do the sacrifice? Did you go see the sorcerer?" She placed a hand on Marie's shoulder, all bone and sharp angles. "We'll be arrested if you throw a ball here. Do you hear me, Marie? We need to cast away the spirits, the Domovoy, before someone else is hurt."

Now, as she recounts her aunt flouncing about in her undergarments, Irina actually *laughs*. The kind of laughter that bursts out hard and loud. Even Nicky laughs with her.

"Do you really think she would throw a ball?" he asks between breaths.

"And invite who?" Irina smirks. "I'll watch her, of course. But the telephone is broken, the post is unreliable at best. She hasn't left her rooms, or the house. I've had to carry meals up to her on a tray like a servant. . . ."

The laughter dies on Irina's lips at the realization that her aunt is truly a lost cause and will provide no useful information. That means

Irina will have to visit the sorcerer. She pulls the page of Gogol's "Viy" from her skirt pocket and hands it wordlessly to Nikolai. She waits quietly for him to read it.

His eyes sweep over the page, understanding coalescing in their depths. "No, Irina."

"Yes. Tonight." Or she will talk herself out of it. "I need to keep busy, Nicky. Find out if the sacrifice can be reversed—or the spirits cast away. Our home is all we have." Will's advice resurfaces. Finding other housing, arranging for travel papers . . . No, those aren't options. Not real ones. They will stay and fight for Moscow House.

"You have each other, just as I have Lili, you, my mother. *That* is home." Nikolai lowers his head, utters a curse under his breath. "Very well. I'll go with you."

"No, we cannot leave the children with my aunt, and you should not leave the house."

While Lili is in prison, Irina *will* keep what is left of her family safe, Nicky included.

Based on the scribbled address, Daniil the sorcerer lives on the grounds of a sprawling cemetery some distance away from the town center. Irina presses down the spike of fear at the thought of visiting an empty cemetery at night, alone, before returning to Moscow House for more horror. But like a silent viper, ghostly as the spirits, the fear only tightens about her throat. Even as they go and play with Seryozha, read poetry with Natasha, share an intimate supper of hot potatoes and aromatic rye bread with butter and pickles that Irina cannot taste.

The silent cemetery spreads in front of Irina like a vast underworld city frosted by moonlight and snow. It is a cold, clear night, but as soon as she steps through the gate, a mist curls toward her. Not unlike a nightmare, blooming to life in the free fall of sleep.

Irina, you are a reasonable, modern woman and have been through much worse, she tells herself.

Her breaths steam out into the night, filled with the trace of turned-over, damp earth and leaves long rotted. And though she is reasonable, she has since learned the dead don't always slumber as they should.

Darkened poplars sway like skeletons on either side of her, the path she's on a snowless black ribbon of pavement cutting into rows of tombstones and crypts. Occasionally, a magpie calls out, breaking the silence.

Irina tries to ignore the calls, the oppressive air. She slows to a stop, taking out the page from "Viy" and peering down at it. But there is only the sorcerer's name and the cemetery address; the rest is the text of the tale, the young man praying over the dead girl on her slab of funereal stone.

Irina shivers, imagining ghostly arms winding around her neck. Smothering her. *That is enough of that.* She thrusts the paper back into her pocket if only to chase away the chilling image. But there must be some clue in the tale or perhaps in the author himself. After all, Vera said Gogol was in tune with the supernatural. Irina wonders if the story of "Viy" relates to the sacrifice to the Domovoy and the resurrection of the dead.

She wishes that Lili were here. She would know what to do. *Think, Irina.*

If the address led her to the cemetery, Irina reasons, the sorcerer must live here. Maybe he is a caretaker or gravedigger, or a religious man of some kind. After all, the mystic Rasputin has been described as a monk.

Irina forces herself down the path, on guard for any building resembling a dwelling or work shed.

Overhead, the moon floats out from behind shreds of torn cloud. It is so big and yellow and low that it bathes the snowy graves in an eerie, ethereal light. Her heart shrivels in fear. What is she doing looking for *a sorcerer*?

Just as Irina is about to turn back, she glimpses an izba in the distance. It is built in the old style, with rough-hewn logs. An old man appears in its doorway and starts toward her.

"You must be Countess Irina Goliteva," he says in a strong voice, holding out his hand. "Vera told me you would come, and here you are."

Irina is still a little disoriented. But she takes his hand, roughened from work and very warm. "And you must be Daniil."

"Come, Countess." Daniil motions with a brisk nod. "Let us rest from the cold awhile. My hut is just there."

She hesitates for a second before following the old man.

"How do you live here?"

"Oh, very simply, Countess. I help in the cemetery, and they allow me to stay."

"Please, there is no need for formality."

"I insist. I am of the old ways." He pulls open the hut door.

There is a burst of heat, but Irina only stares at Daniil. He doesn't seem like a sorcerer, certainly not like a Rasputin, unholy and dark. But Daniil also doesn't look the part of a former person. No, he appears to be an ordinary Russian man, with tangled gray hair and beard and thick, bushy eyebrows. He wears a shabby patched-up coat and trousers over a pair of felt boots and galoshes.

The izba is likewise simple, with a traditional pech standing across from a rickety table. It is surprisingly inviting, smelling of broth and herbs and garlic. Irina sees the fragrant bulbs strung up by the door.

"This feels like a real home," she says wistfully.

She accepts the stool Daniil offers her, as well as a steaming cup of mint and berry tea. Without shedding his coat, he sits on an old rough-hewn bench and looks up at her expectantly. Irina replaces the cup and takes a deep breath. She tells Daniil about the spirits, the Domovoy, her aunt, sparing nothing. After she is finished, he is quiet.

Finally, Daniil raises his eyes to hers. "Out of all that I do, the business of bringing back the dead is my least favorite. Do you know why?"

"It is unnatural." The cold from the cemetery slips back into Irina's heart.

He nods. "However, there are times that this act is justified by desperation. Your aunt sought me out in the spring of 1918, following the news of her son's demise at the front. Her loss affected her deeply and threatened to destroy her. It is . . . difficult to bring back the dead. But once done, it is nearly impossible to reverse. Once the sacrifice awakens the Domovoy, and he awakens the other spirits, they are no longer interested in sleep."

"Yes, I know about the Domovoy, and the sacrifice. But *nearly impossible* means there is still a chance, does it not? I attempted to draw him out with bread and salt—"

"Irina Alexandrovna, I shall be direct with you." Beneath his gray felt hat, Daniil's gaze is sharp. "Only the dying can see the Domovoy. Or else those marked for uncertainty, for great change. Change that upends entire lives."

She swallows, hard. "I have seen him. So has my sister."

Daniil draws back. He crosses himself. "Then you *have* been marked."

The callus on her palm seems to itch and burn. Irina fidgets. The page in her pocket rustles. And she forces herself to keep talking and asking questions, as dwelling on the impossibilities is utterly useless. Besides, she needs to know more about the sacrifice and what it entails. "Why 'Viy'?"

A shadow flits across Daniil's windswept features. "Nikolai Gogol awakened his Domovoy like your aunt did hers. That's why 'Viy' has fragments of the real sacrifice in it."

The cold in her heart is back. "And the real sacrifice . . . ?"

"One must sit over a dead body for three nights. If one survives, the Domovoy will awaken. When he does, one must ask to be his master or mistress. Only then can he be commanded to bring the house's dead back to life."

Irina feels so very cold. She thinks back to what their former servants have said, Pasha's diaries, the fits. Marie tried the sacrifice to bring Andrei back after learning of his death, but it didn't work. This explains the odd requests, the animal blood, and the fit that left her ill for weeks. She attempted the sacrifice again, this time with a dead body, right after the Cheka killed Pasha and arrested Papa and

Aleksei. It is why she was found with Grand-père after he died. For some reason, she failed again and had her second fit. It was only after the Soviet men moved into the house that Auntie's sacrifice succeeded, awakening the Domovoy and their dead family.

But did she use a dead person for the sacrifice? If so, why did it succeed when it had failed with Grand-père?

Is it possible that Marie killed those Soviet men after all? Several days ago, Irina wouldn't have believed it. But since learning of her aunt's supposed betrayal, she isn't so certain. And why would Marie wish to bring back the family? There are so many questions, still unresolved, still cloaked in secrecy and lies. One niggles at her most.

"Does the person making the sacrifice need to . . . kill?"

Daniil pauses. "Not necessarily. The dead may be recently deceased."

This explains Auntie using Grand-père's body, but not why the sacrifice didn't work then. Most recently, when the sacrifice did work, the first dead Soviet man *might* have met with some accident, and Marie could simply have found him, then used his body for the sacrifice and left the remains for Irina to find three days later. It is possible, but . . . what about the other man who was killed, or Grand-mère, who died when Marie was in prison? Perhaps they *were* just accidents. Either that or someone else killed the men and Grand-mère. Perhaps it was the spirits, and they survive on more than just memories. Irina thinks how to phrase this without sounding unhinged.

"Do the spirits need . . . blood to stay alive?" she forces out, her mouth dry and cottony.

Daniil's eyes flare with a strange light, a glint not unlike the one Irina has seen in her aunt's gaze. Hollow, wild, terrifying. "Not just to stay alive—but to be more realized, more corporeal and real."

This is consistent with what Marie has said. But. "Does this mean the spirits might become—as flesh and blood as you and me?"

The peculiar light in Daniil's eyes dims. "They are dead, so no. But they might return to their physical forms, as they were when they died—as long as, like the Domovoy, they don't venture past the house and its yard."

"How do you reverse the sacrifice?"

"Well, the Domovoy is already awake, so all you need to do is draw him out and ask to be his mistress. This is easier said than done." Daniil gathers several items into the crook of his elbow before placing a dried fern branch and a white linen cloth on the table in front of Irina. "First, introduce yourself and hang your most worn pair of shoes in the yard. Then brew a strong batch of tea with this fern, then pour a handful of salt onto a slice of bread and wrap it in this cloth. Afterward, place both in your front hall or yard, depending on where your Domovoy dwells, and bow to the four directions, whispering phrases of honor, compliment, and apology for neglect."

"Is there a particular time of day that is better?"

"After darkness falls and before the first sign of dawn. But midnight, the unholy hour, is best. For added power, bring in a pine bough from your yard and hang it with additional offerings—whatever you have that you would like to give to your Domovoy. When, *if*, he agrees for you to be his new mistress, order him back to sleep, along with the other spirits. But the longer and more corporeal they are, the harder this will all be."

"We only—ask?" Irina is puzzled.

"Respectfully. In a quiet yet firm voice. Never presume or demand. If he agrees, it is binding, and he will be forced to submit. But the difficult part is getting him to agree." Daniil shifts before Irina uncomfortably. "You said you have a sister. . . ."

"I do, but"—she sighs deeply—"a few days ago, she was taken by . . . them."

Daniil's grizzly eyebrows knit together in understanding and seemingly genuine sorrow. "I hope she returns to you, Irina Alexandrovna. Not only for your sake, but for the sacrifice. It is stronger if it is bound in family ties, you and your sister bound in blood, calling on your family's first ancestor. Other family members might work as well. But the bond of siblings, of sisterhood, is always the strongest, the most powerful magic in this and in life."

Irina thinks of her aunt, naively preparing for her phantom ball; her cousin, still young and innocent, already orphaned; her little son, believing both his parents dead, unaware of the truth. And the only sister Irina has left, in prison with little hope of release. Again she wishes Lili were here, with an ache that makes her physically ill.

Irina is ashamed at the ruins she has left their sisterhood in, how she refused to trust Lili or take her seriously. And now, what Irina wouldn't give for her sister's particular brand of toughness, her knowledge so conducive to their predicament, her sly smile and jokes. What Irina wouldn't give for her sisterly advice and wisdom. Or simply to talk together as they used to, to laugh and stroll together about town.

Irina clenches her jaw. She *will* get Lili back. And when she does, she will embrace her sister fiercely and tell her everything. Then they will get rid of these spirits for good—together.

When Irina returns to Moscow House, she expects the same phantom soirée.

Instead, in a distant room of the East Wing, she catches a glimpse of her dead parents swaying to a soft, barely there tune played on the grand piano by ghostly hands. It is likely Andrei. What a brilliant piano player he was, with those long, elegant, almost skeletal fingers.

As in life, her parents are unaware of all but each other, their ravaged, still-shaded bodies intertwined.

On the landing below the attic, Grand-père's tall shadow leans in to look at a painting of some dead ancestor or royal, then vanishes when he sees Irina. She can hear Luba's spirit singing to her unborn child, her lullaby threading and unthreading through the halls with their eerily flickering candlelight.

For one mad moment, Irina thinks maybe she could get used to the apparitions. But then her eyes fill with the gold of a skirt, her ears with malevolent giggles. Then *his* voice, always his nightmarish voice in the end.

Irina. Darling. You know what I want. Poisonous green eyes flash at her from the dark.

Then all she can do is run the rest of the way to the attic as someone pulls on her hair, as if in warning, and that cold, dead grasp is back on her ankle. This time, it isn't dragging her down but reminding her.

You cannot outrun me, Georgy's voice echoes even when Irina is in the safety of the attic.

The entire house feels like a tomb, with skeletons of the past rising from their coffins and walking its halls and corridors, even slithering into the only haven they have managed to find. No, the spirits must go. Or Irina and her family will be buried alive in Moscow House with them. That, or die from the damp and mold.

37

Reunions

NOVEMBER 1921
Several Weeks Later

WHEN SHE STEPPED into the motorcar, Lili didn't know if she was being transferred to another prison or to her execution. Never in the world did she expect to be released.

But that is what happened, though she still doesn't believe her luck. Or fate, if that is what it was. She stands dumbly on Spiridonovka Street, blinking up at the ARA mansion, taking in the icy air in gasps, too fast, as if she hasn't breathed in a very long time. Lili doesn't even mind the foul smells of the street. Her throat, though no longer sore, aches with the cold. She doesn't much mind that, either.

She barely notices as the motorcar behind her purrs awake like a great big mechanical cat. She wishes she could stroke it, or give the Bolos inside a salute or something. But before Lili can do such an admittedly stupid thing, it slinks sleekly and quietly down the street and out of sight. A menacing kitty cat, a Red demon inside.

The November skies are pewter gray. A cold wetness seeps into her threadbare clothing, the same she was arrested in. And it is so bright with the snow that for a second, Lili hears only the slam of the doors.

Then, she sees him—out of all people, Nicky. His head is tilted down as he fiddles with a pair of keys, likely to the Cadillac. How very thin he looks, with that frown cutting such deep, permanent lines into his skin, which is unnaturally pale and bruised with shadows. Lili wouldn't want to sketch him right now, not like this. So she just watches him, not believing she is standing on this sidewalk, so close to him, both of them free.

Finally, he looks up. His keys fall to the wet asphalt with a clang.

"Come on, Nicky." Lili manages a laugh, remembering her old self a little. "Shouldn't you welcome me home, or do you intend to stand there without a word?"

Nikolai says nothing; he races down the stairs two steps at a time. And before Lili knows it, he is pulling her into his arms—as she imagined in that cold, lonely cell, when the possibility of coming home, of being free, was a distant, almost impossibility. He draws back only to take her face in his hands, pressing his cold, damp forehead to hers, so close his breath surges against her lips in a vaporous cloud. "It is you? Truly?"

Lili laughs. "It's me." *I think.* Though there is a strange heaviness knotting her chest, a souvenir from Butyrka, she is sure. A reminder of how close she came. Or some device the evil Bolos have surgically sewn in, so she never runs right again.

"The Americans told us it was safe to return to the offices—they received assurances from the Soviet officials. They were hoping this would be followed by releases, but I refused to believe it. Not until I saw you with my own two eyes, Lil."

"I *am* here. They—let me go. They never arrested you, did they?"

"No, thanks to your sister. She let me stay at Moscow House."

Her throat has suddenly swelled again, become clotted, this time with the urge to cry. Nicky brushes a hand over her face, and Lili feels the light touch of his fingertips on her nose, cheeks, chin, finally her lips. As if to make sure they are all there, that none of them have been stolen or somehow replaced. "Nicky." She takes his hands in her shaking, clumsy ones. His eyes, when they shift to her, are startlingly hollow and very dark. "I thought about you," she starts, "in prison, and—"

"I'm just glad you're all right. That is what matters, that you're here—"

"I like you." Lili blinks at the mortifying admission. She rehearsed this speech, and yet it has come out thorny and thoroughly dispassionate. "Not just as a friend, as—well—" God must exist, with a wicked sense of humor. She clears her throat, dropping her eyes to her dirty boots. Her whole face is *on fire* with humiliation.

"Will you ever cease to surprise me, Lil?" Nikolai asks, drawing her gaze back to him. And he is *smiling*. "I like you, too." His voice is low and rough with emotion. His arm curls around her waist, brings some heat into her damp clothes and very cold skin. "You know, not just as a friend," he adds. The corners of his mouth quirk up in amusement before he presses her to his chest, hard, as if to make his point.

Her nervousness drains away. Lili wraps her arms around his neck, nestling into the spot between his neck and clavicle, where his hair curls against her cheeks. She breathes in that smell of him, of cigarettes and cheap soap and Nicky, all Nicky. "Good, because I was away so long, I thought you might have found somebody else."

"Yes, she is a very lovely girl. We are married, with a child on the way."

"Nicky!" Lili draws back, swatting him. "Too soon."

"You started it." But he isn't smiling anymore, not even a little. Nicky grasps her tightly, all impatience and urgent heat, and catches her mouth deep in his. It is the kind of kiss that is breathless, just a little bit rugged and tumbling, like his voice.

Inside, Lili rushes into her sister's arms.

It is in the crook of Irina's shoulder, in the perfumed hair reminding her of home, that the mind-numbing fear of that cell crashes back in. Lili's eyes start to sting. And before she knows it, sobs are tearing through her throat. She gasps for breath as the hot tears come, hard and fast and very wet. All she can do is cling to her sister.

"You're all right, my darling," Irina whispers over and over, combing her fingers through what must be a hive on Lili's head. "All is well, thank God."

There is the pounding of small feet—not Xenia, this isn't Moscow House—but Seryozha. He wriggles into the sliver of space between them, shouting Lili's name.

Irina laughs. "We will speak later." She grows serious. "But you should know, Marie is back."

A chill winds through Lili, even as she releases her sister and picks up her naughty nephew. "Lili!" he trills in his high little voice. "I knew you'd be back. No one believed me! Why are you crying? Aren't you happy?"

Auntie has been forgotten again, and Lili cannot speak—the damn swollen throat again. She presses the boy to her so hard that he squirms. Natasha leans in for a lengthy, warm embrace. Yet it still doesn't feel real. Not until another pair of arms, worryingly thin and smelling sharply of cigarettes, are thrown around her neck. Lili cries out in surprise when she sees Paulina's face. What they've been through has bonded them. Lili kisses Paulina on both cheeks with enthusiasm just as Kirill's long arms come around them both.

Lili steps back, taking in their faces—like Nicky's, much paler and thinner, but with a brightness that sparks a sudden warmth in her chest. "When did you two get out? Were you at Lubyanka the entire time, Paulina?"

"Just now," they both say. "And yes," Paulina adds shortly. "I think I will sleep under the open sky for the rest of my days, no matter how cold. Fuck walls. Fuck enclosed spaces."

"I don't know, those famous Russian winters are worse than I imagined."

Lili turns to see Will extending his hand to her for a handshake. That warmth is back. She has a feeling he is the reason she was released. Ignoring formality, Lili launches herself into his arms. "Thank you," she whispers, this time keeping the tears well in.

Will shakes his head. "It was your sister's brilliant plan, threatening the Bolos with stopping ARA shipments. And Phil Carroll agreed, the crazy bastard. Then it took mere days for them to capitulate. This is after who knows how many telephone calls, demands, and, oh, yes, Irina's meetings with Soviet officials. It was all her. If not . . ."

A transfer, or an execution. Lili shudders. But she doesn't have time to think of the *if*. The rest of their friends are now crowding in—Harold calling for shots of vodka to celebrate their return, Emma laughing that all three are in sore need of baths (that, at least, is accurate), and Frank asking for Lili to look at their wall when she is ready. The story of the ARA former people, he tells her, has been reassembled by the *entire* office, and they can write the article together whenever she likes and submit it. Lili smiles at him gratefully, feeling the sting of those damn tears again. She meets her sister's gaze over the others and mouths a "Thank you" that will never be enough.

Then she walks up to Nicky, and she kisses him, right there, right in front of everyone. Several glances wink at them, a few laughs and cheers, a whoop—from Harold. Then . . . nothing. Nikolai throws an arm around her shoulders with a shrug and a laugh. Apparently, they were that obvious and surprised exactly no one.

After a multicourse dinner of cold zakuski and hot vegetable soup followed by a mouthwatering roast venison with potatoes and beet salad, Emma hustles Lili, Paulina, and Kirill upstairs. She has drawn them baths in their own bedrooms for the night. Emma takes particular relish in telling Lili—with a sly smile—that Irina has a room with Seryozha and Natasha, leaving Lili with her own private room. If not for the hot flush, Lili would have replied with some ridiculous retort. But as none comes in the crucial moment, she only stares after Emma, awkwardly pressing her towel to her chest.

Lili's damp skin is still tingling from the steaming water and her thorough scrubbing when she shrugs on the dressing gown Emma has left for her. Leaving the dripping lavatory as is, Lili drifts drowsily into the bedroom. She halts abruptly, a burst of adrenaline shooting through her.

Nicky is leaning casually against the door, watching her with a small, teasing smile and a bowl of vanilla ice cream in hand. "Is it all right that I'm here?"

Lili smirks, reaches for the bowl. "Since you came with ice cream."

He laughs and shakes his head, dropping his gaze—shyly, she thinks.

They sit together on the bed, side by side yet awkward, quietly sharing the dessert. It is creamy and decadent on her tongue. She is generous to be sharing it at all. Nicky places the now empty bowl on a nearby table and sits back down, the two of them stealing glances at each other, uncertain. So Lili leans in and kisses him.

Twilight has turned the inside of the room a very dark, very murky blue. As if the two of them are swimming in the sea, or falling through some hazy wonderland of muted colors and soft edges. A land explored only through touch . . . Nicky's arms enveloping her, his mouth on her skin, her neck, her shoulder, naked in the moonlight. Then finding her mouth in the blue light, drawing her into a fathomless depth with no bottom and no end.

By the time they lie together on the bed, there is nothing between them, no clothing, no barriers, no secrets—no doubts. His thumb grazes her cheek, then her lower lip, kissing her so hard and so long that she turns dizzy. Need flares hot and deep inside Lili, kindling like a flame in her heart, then racing through her body and setting it on fire with pure desire. All those days in that prison, the months of not being sure, not understanding, have led them here. The warmth of his arms, the fresh linen of the bed, such a contrast to the tree in that old graveyard.

Lili presses her lips to his, forgetting that cell and the graveyard, until all that is left is to have him, all of him. To finally be with Nicky with everything out in the open.

"Lil?" Nicky whispers a little later.

She is *really* not up for conversation, content to float in her half-sleep haze. But the floor is hard beneath her back, rousing her more than she wants. They ended up on the carpet, the sheets from the bed tangled about their legs. Lili snuggles into Nikolai's chest, her cheek brushing against the silky black hair curling and uncurling over skin still damp from earlier. "Yes, Nicky?" She runs a hand through it, thinking that if he is about to ask her for another go, she will gladly, slightly eagerly, agree.

But that isn't where he goes. "When you were arrested, I promised myself I would tell you about . . . me, about what happened to my family."

Lili puts a hand to his lips, the stubble under his lower lip prickly against her skin. "You don't have to tell me, Nicky. Really." After everything she—they—have gone through, the past that doesn't pertain to the two of them now matters very little to her. This thing between them, *that* is what matters. The rest is, well, in the past.

"Please let me tell you, Lili," Nicky insists. He takes in a deep breath, and she turns to face him. "When the provisional government fell in October '17, my brothers said we should leave, as everyone was, as your aunt wanted to. But my parents were oblivious. That day, they went to a ballet at the Mariinsky, and we went for a walk along the Neva. The whole of Petrograd seemed to be out. Yet it was tense. The fog was rolling in off the water in a salty mist that touched my cheek with a cold nothing to do with the weather. Mika said—" Nicky flicks a glance at her. "Do you remember Mikhail and Lev?"

Lili gives a tiny nod, though Nikolai's brothers were older, then in their late twenties and frequently away on military business.

"Mika said the town felt sick. 'Yes,' Lev agreed. 'I don't see any hired ladies of my acquaintance.' I asked them why. And Mika said, 'Why, brother, they have the uncanny ability to smell danger on the air like hounds smell blood.'"

Lili shivers, having heard of the Winter Palace's bombardment that very night.

"That evening," Nikolai says quietly, as if hearing her thoughts, "the air filled with shots—rifle, pistol, machine gun, you name it— and armored cars raced through the streets. We barely escaped the shooting. Papa was killed during that first wave of interrogations soon after the Cheka was founded. Near the Bolshevik house on Gorokhovaya, you could hear the cracking of the rifles. Many in town spoke of a trench dug along the walls of that house, where people like my father were taken out and shot."

"What happened to Mika and Lev?" Lili asks in a hesitant voice.

"Arrested, tried, sent into exile at some camp. My mother believes they are still alive, that any day they will walk through the door of our squalid little flat, and we can all pretend life will go on as before. Though how they would even know we are in Moscow, much less where we live, is a mystery. We only came here this past summer." Nikolai is dry-eyed, but he feels cold and rigid against her. "I . . . don't like to remember it, Lil. When I do, I relive it all over again. It is why I drive. At the wheel, there is nothing but the engine under me and the road ahead. No past or future." He ducks his head shyly. "And I have time to read, to think about words and stories, to dream."

Lili takes Nikolai in her arms, wrapping her legs around his waist tightly, pressing her entire body into his, hoping the heat and *love* there, for that is what it is, can heal all the broken, lost parts of him. And yet, can they truly heal after what they have lived through? And isn't that why the ghosts are back? The sacrifice, yes, but the ghosts wouldn't have returned unless there was space there for them among the living, among Lili and her family, to let them and the past in, maybe in hope of healing it and themselves.

But she doesn't wish to think about ghosts. So she kisses Nicky, nice and slow and tender, until his hands slip to her waist, and he hardens against her belly. Then she takes him in her hand and guides him inside her, and they start to breathlessly push against each other, desperate for closeness. Desperate to feel alive, too.

Sometime later, as dawn paints the room a soft, fuzzy gray, there is a brisk knock at their door. And Lili knows whatever time they had is over. Nikolai helps her into a fresh set of clothes provided by Irina the night before. For a moment, he clasps her by the waist, dropping his head against her stomach. Lili feels, rather than hears, Nicky take in a deep, very pained breath. He draws back and wraps her hands in his, peering up into her face. His eyes are large and dark, and they flash with real fear.

"I am afraid for you, Lil," he says, in a whisper.

She hasn't spoken to her sister yet, but Lili is aware they must return to Moscow House after work to deal with the ghosts, the Domovoy, Auntie, whatever happened in Lili's absence. She swallows, tracing the outline of Nicky's cheek. His stubble prickles her skin. She pushes down the fear that has leaped into her own heart.

Out loud, she says, with some of her old teasing, "When did you become such a coward, Nicky?" But her laugh is strained.

He doesn't laugh. Or even smile. "Can I ask you to do something for me?"

Lili nods, waiting, uneasy, cold despite his still-warm touch.

"Survive," he says, quite seriously, and she knows that whatever is happening at Moscow House must be bad indeed.

38

What Will It Take?

LILI'S ARM IS threaded through Irina's as they trudge down Moscow's snowy, twilit boulevards. Like their walks to the bazaar, it is their chance to speak to each other freely and without restraint. The air is almost warm with her sister there beside her, and Lili almost looks forward to seeing Moscow House.

That day, Irina left Seryozha and Natasha in Madame Naroshina's very capable, eager hands before setting off on an inspection of several kitchens, hospitals, and children's homes. Meanwhile, Lili worked with Frank on their former people article. After a quick supper of leftovers and a cup of coffee each to prepare for the night ahead, they finally left the ARA. Lili traces the edges of her fresh sketch pad, her new pencil, glad she picked both up at the commissary.

Overhead, a pink-orange glow simmers in the sky. It suffuses the town's domes and spires in misty pastels. A toy city swathed in layers of time and myth and fairy tale. But, as in the fairy tale, with a fierce red lining, as if of spilled blood.

As they walk, Irina tells Lili about the country estate where she waited out the term of her pregnancy, endured the violent storming by the revolutionaries, watched Uncle Pasha take her son. She tells

Lili about Georgy, too, of his demands to forget all that is Irina, how he took advantage of her. Finally, about how much she likes Will.

"I am deeply sorry for not trusting in you, Lil," Irina says, voice taut with emotion. "For—pushing you away. Maman, everyone, taught me to think of you as a younger sister, not as a friend. I . . . didn't realize we already were. And if not for the Revolution . . ."

"You would've become Madame Dolgonogaya." Energetic, capable, clever Irina, destined for such a life with such a selfish, entitled man . . . No, Lili wouldn't wish such a fate on any woman, much less her beloved sister. "I pushed you away, too" drifts out on the exhale. "I didn't make it easy for you with my *at times* childish behavior."

Irina squeezes her arm, and they walk on a little without words, totally at home in their silence. Only the crunch and creak of the snow can be heard. In the distance, the occasional rumble of a tram, the *clip-clop* of horses, the growl of a motorcar. "I am happy for you and Nicky," Irina says cautiously.

There is an influx of heat into Lili's cheeks. Her first instinct *is* to make a joke, to laugh it away. "Thank you," she says instead. "I . . . realized so much in that cell. I like him, Irishka. I think I always have. I just didn't know it. Anyway, I took your advice, and I told him. He was . . . happy. We are happy, I think."

"I know you are. With him, you always have been. Maman . . . oh, she would be thrilled. And Grand-mère, too." Irina's smile goes from wistful to sad to tentative. "Are you still cross with me about Seryozha?"

"No. I only wish you could've told me sooner. You should tell him and Natasha, Irishka. They will want to know. Secrets are dreadful things. They fester like—poisoned apples." Lili's thoughts flit to Auntie, all those dark revelations transforming her into the Evil Queen from "Snow White" in Lili's mind.

"I will tell them," Irina says, slipping an arm around Lili's shoulders and giving her a warm, lingering kiss on the cheek. "I am so relieved to have you back. I still don't believe it, still think I'm trapped in that nightmare of you in that place, us in the house with . . ." Irina takes a deep, shuddering breath. "I should tell you about what happened when you were away."

The smell of rot, of something spoiled, hits Lili as they cross the threshold of the house and walk into the entrance hall. It is so revoltingly sweet and damp that it turns her stomach. The tension in the air vibrates up her spine, as if she has drawn too close to a gramophone. Or an orchestra at a ball.

But the only real noise is the heavy tread of Auntie's footsteps, even through the house's layers. In the dim candlelight, Lili notices the mottled, water-stained walls. The mold, worse than ever. The black spots are blotchy, greenish, *moving*. She backs away in disgust. Giant prickly centipedes latch onto the moldy walls like barnacles to a sinking ship. Spiderwebs shroud the chandelier's bronze vines, drip down with its crystal, stretch into the corners of the room, alive with a flitting and flickering—of moths. The house, a vast marble tomb.

"My God," Irina breathes. "It was not this bad a few days ago."

A burst of chirping, and Cleo flies into Lili's open arms in a warm tangle of feathers, claws, and beak. Lili strokes her parakeet affectionately, whispering how happy she is to see her, how she has missed her. "Is Auntie in her rooms?" she asks eventually, Cleo chirping, this time in the affirmative. "Can you tell us if she leaves them?"

Another chirp, and Cleo is soaring through the hall and up the stairs.

Lili is only beginning to suspect the true depth of her aunt's depravity, her dabbling in black magic, her informing on the family. But Lili has never imagined her committing *murder*. Either way, they need Auntie out of the way when they try to draw out the Domovoy. Then they can decide what to do with her—ideally, before she can inform, or kill, again.

Irina touches Lili's arm. "We should begin. It is past ten o'clock." Only two hours until midnight.

Lili helps her sister light the rest of the candles and lamps. The centipedes and moths scatter with the bloom of brightness, the scent of wax thick and greasy.

While Irina retreats to the attic to brew the tea with the fern branch, as well as to collect Daniil's items and two pairs of their oldest, most worn boots, Lili fetches a loaf of bread and a bag of salt from the kitchen.

Back in the hall, the creak of the grand staircase almost makes her drop her bundle. But it is only Irina, descending the steps with her own arms full and a small, encouraging smile that sets Lili at ease. They walk out the doors into the still, cold night. Lili takes a deep breath of it, the tension and waxy air draining out of her limbs.

Then she hurries to a pine tree by the back wall of the property. Its needles are a dull straw yellow, long dried, dead. But she breaks off a branch and returns to Irina. With a nod at each other, they walk to the oak tree with Uncle Pasha's grave. Lili feels the cold and dampness of this place seep into her. Like Irina, she fastens her pair of boots from the attic to a branch by their laces, so they hang directly across the entrance to Moscow House.

It occurs to Lili the house is like a temple, the Domovoy its god. "Let's bow to the house," she says suddenly. At Irina's questioning look: "I read the Domovoy is god of the home. Well, we bow in church, don't we?"

Understanding sparks in Irina's eyes. "Good thinking, Lil."

They face the house together and bow before it as though before a fiery gold iconoclast with all the saints of the Orthodox faith. The candlelight inside flickers in response like eyes blinking.

Encouraged, they return to the hall and make their last preparations with the fern tea, the pine bough, the slice of bread and salt wrapped in the sorcerer's white linen cloth. They hang the bough with offerings that Irina brought from the attic: a pair of Auntie's diamond earrings, Georgy's engagement ring—good riddance—and packages of macaroni and rice from the latest ARA crate.

After placing the offerings into the nook under the grand staircase, they bow north, east, south, west. And they whisper the words they agreed on: "Dedushka, we honor you. You are the best Domovoy, our lord, our grandfather, our protective spirit. We are sorry for neglecting and displeasing you." They place bread and salt on the threshold and in the yard, then step back inside. Only a few candles and lamps are now lit, theirs having been snuffed out. The silence curdles the blood. It is sullen as though the house itself is brooding, waiting.

For what? What do it and the damn Domovoy want? *What will it take?*

Lili cannot stand it anymore. "Come out, you imp!"

In reply, a shattering screech.

"What are you *doing*?" Irina mouths, just as a crash comes from behind them, making Lili nearly jump out of her skin with the influx of raw, very cold fear.

A stooped, dark shape scurries across the hall—the Domovoy. He lifts his head and glares at them with his bloodred gaze. Lili dashes after the spirit, just as he dives into the nook.

"Did it . . . work?" Irina asks, peering over Lili's shoulder.

Lili crouches down, the parquet hard on her knees and thick with dust. She swears as a few cockroaches and a small army of black beetles stream out of the nook. Lili, still prickly and reeling from the insects, barely hears Irina's scream behind her. The offerings are gone. So is the imp. Leaving, as ever, no trace. Not even the spiderwebs are disturbed.

"I don't *understand*," Irina says, out of sorts, hair askew. "He *appeared* to us."

"But he didn't give us a chance to ask him to replace Auntie. So it didn't work." Lili tips her head back, trying to breathe through the hot frustration clawing at her chest. They are left with a mad aunt planning a ball in Soviet Russia, an imp loose in their haunted house who cares not a fig for their sacrifices, and ghosts about to make their nightly appearance. "No, this will *not* stand. Come back, imp—come back this instant!" Lili's voice rises to a shout. "You owe us this much after our sacrifices! The food we've wasted on you!"

Instead, actual *bodies* blink to life all around them. Bluish, dirt- and bloodstained, in ancient garments that release puffs of dust and moths. At once, the lamps and candles flare bright and hot. The house's silent tension explodes—into knocks, slamming doors, clinking glass, talk and laughter, all jarringly loud and *real*, with such slick, unnatural cold that Lili grabs her sister's hand and holds on tight for dear life as they sprint up the stairs.

In the attic, it is cold, too. They immediately light a candle and turn up the stove.

A *click!* and Lili spins on her heel, knowing instinctively what has happened before she runs up to the door and tugs—pointlessly—on the brass handle. Locked!

She pounds on the door. No answer. She keeps pounding, hard, the backs of her fists starting to smart with a sharp, stabbing pain.

Irina runs up to her, pressing an ear to the door. "Marie, is that you? Open this door immediately. Do you hear me? Goddamn it, Marie, open up!"

But the door remains infuriatingly locked; Auntie, if it is her, silent on the other side. Then footfalls, receding.

Lili turns to stare, wide-eyed, at her sister. An errant moth flits between them.

They have been locked inside the attic like a pair of naughty schoolgirls. And where is Cleo? She was supposed to warn them about this very thing. Now they cannot keep their aunt from doing whatever she damn well pleases. Suddenly, Lili wishes she could spirit herself back to the ARA mansion, to that twilight-soaked room, to Nicky and their twisting sheets and heated embraces. But the memory of the hardness in his eyes, the tightness of his jaw, jolts her back. She needs to focus, to be afraid—to survive.

39

Conversations Long Overdue

22-23 NOVEMBER 1921

IRINA GRASPS HER sister by the waist as Lili thrusts her head out the window and leans over the ledge. "We can climb down!" she calls out, voice muffled.

"It is *four flights*," Irina nearly screams, entirely unlike her normally restrained self. They have been trapped in the attic since the night before, an entire day having elapsed. There is a cough starting deep in her chest, from all the dust and damp and decay.

Irina can tell by the flood of bright yellow light on the snow outside that the electric lights have been turned on. They haven't been used since before the Revolution. It appears Marie's ball is happening whether they like it or not. Irina refuses to call her *aunt* anymore. She hears the rise and swell of sweeping yet spotty orchestral music from the ballroom, inhales the waxy, overpowering smell of candlelight even here, these many floors up. Now the question is: Will they be informed on by neighbors, or by some Cheka agent tasked with watching Moscow House?

Thank the Lord the children are safe at Madame Naroshina's. Irina wonders how they are, what they are doing this very minute. Will's offer rushes back, as it has all these long, uncertain hours. Before this, the possibility of leaving Russia was a passing thought, a dream, too far and cold, like starlight. Now it is a real possibility. A choice. The map from her youth rustles on the table as if in assent, the world illustrated there a promise. Is Irina entombing her family like Grand-père and Pasha? Is she choosing the house over her children, as Marie accused? Irina needs to find a way out of this attic and then . . . maybe she will know.

"Well, if you don't think we can climb down, what do we do?" Lili is back in the room, and Irina lets go of her waist. "Do you know what day it is—or will be?" Lili's voice shakes.

"The twenty-second of November." As soon as the words are out, Irina knows. There hasn't been a moment she hasn't remembered. Yet overnight, she seems to have forgotten. "Yes." For at the stroke of midnight, it will be the twenty-third of November, three years to the day since the Cheka's first visit to Moscow House.

"Auntie must have planned the ball to take place tonight. Maybe it will help the ghosts to become more alive. Or, as alive as they can be."

Irina shivers. Thinks she hears, *You cannot outrun me.* She shakes her head, that voice, out. "Daniil said the more alive the dead are, the harder to reverse the sacrifice. We need to stop Marie before that happens or, God forbid, the Cheka comes. Perhaps we missed something when we tried to draw out the Domovoy. . . ." Irina has been replaying Daniil's instructions, the steps they took. But it seems they did it all to the letter. "Maybe we just need to try again. And again. It took Marie three times, a significant number in the fairy tales. And—" Irina pauses, not wishing to think on this possibility. "If we need to, as our last resort, Seryozha and Natasha can help."

"All right." Lili leans toward the still-open window, shudders, and reaches to close it. "I am worried about Cleo. What if Auntie—?" She stills, her eyes fixing on something. "He is back, Irishka."

A chill sweeps through Irina that has nothing to do with the bitter air. Through the dark night, she glimpses a ghost of a man under the oak. Pasha is tilting his head up and looking directly at them. It must be close to midnight already, yet since he is outside, the rules might be different. The window creaks open a little wider, sending a fresh burst of frigid, wintry air at her. An icy breeze slides past them into the attic like another ghost.

Pasha's spirit flickers. No, he is *moving*—dropping to his knees, throwing his hands into the air and his head back, as if to cry out to the very Heavens.

"What does he want?" Lili asks, frustrated. "What can he *mean*?"

Irina becomes aware of the heavy silence behind them. The nape of her neck stings—with a new kind of chill, with foreboding.

She hears a series of clicks, a key turning in the lock. Then the scratch of the door as it swings open. She meets Lili's wide-eyed gaze, and they lurch into the adjoining room.

The attic door is ajar—and the Domovoy is peeking out from behind it. Shock jolts through Irina. This is closer than they have ever seen the wizened little spirit. The brim of his hat is lifted slightly, jauntily, his face still impossible to capture. Except for one scarlet eye, which winks at them. And his mouth stretches into a grin.

Lili lunges at the spirit, and all Irina can do is leap after them both—through the door, down the two sets of stairs, alight with dozens of candles and lamps, even electric lights.

The steps groan under Irina's boots, roaches and beetles scattering. She pushes aside the disgust sitting thick and cloying in her throat. Or maybe she has swallowed a moth. She tries to think. The Domovoy unlocked the attic door—was it at Marie's behest? Irina shivers. Maybe Marie wishes for them to come to the ball.

Irina notices the bone-chilling cold of the hall first. The windows are thrown open, frosty night streaming in. The Domovoy has disappeared. But it is the jarring sight of Seryozha and Natasha that freezes Irina in place before she reaches the foot of the stairs. Not just that they aren't supposed to be here, but that they are in Georgy's arms.

Irina grabs Lili's hand, the callus on her palm giving a painful twinge. "Am I imagining it," she whispers, eyes fixed on the trio, "or is that Seryozha and Natasha with Georgy?"

"It's them," Lili confirms grimly. "How did they—?"

All at once, it crashes into Irina. "Marie learned they were at Madame Naroshina's and collected them while we were locked away." Irina tightens her grip on Lili, wishing for some of her toughness and attitude before stepping down—toward Georgy and the children.

They are white-faced and trembling, their eyes pleading, as they stand obediently in those ghostly arms. Yet Georgy is physically nearly as substantive, and solid, as they are. There is flesh to him, even the faint pulsing of blood in the hollow of his throat. And his eyes are that poisonous green, the bloodstain on his chest red and slick, as if with real blood. It is after midnight now, and the ball, being a ritual of the past, must have breathed new life into the spirits. If more human blood should be spilled, the spirits will be impossible to stop.

"Release them this instant, Georgy." Irina's voice is deliberately stern, as if speaking to a petulant child. He has always been one, after all.

"Not before you tell them," he says, his own voice loud and clear and haughty.

Yet the smell of rot wafts over from him to Irina, sweet and sickening. And she knows that despite appearances, Georgy is as dead as the house. She feels the black spots of mold mushrooming through the walls; centipedes spangling the shedding, peeling paint; the water stains from some phantom flood expanding, its dampness trapped in her throat. "Tell them what?" she murmurs. But she knows. The sickness turns into dread.

"Oh, for goodness' sake" comes from Lili, before she lets loose a string of curses so obscene that if not for her dead fiancé, Irina would surely have reprimanded her, sisterhood or no. "Let them go, you dead bastard!" And Lili lunges at Georgy.

Before she can reach him, he says, lazily, "I would not do that if I were you." He pats Seryozha's head and plants a kiss on Natasha's cheek. The boy is looking at Georgy with wide, frozen eyes, Natasha beside him as deathly still as Irina. Tears slide silently down her cheeks. Georgy's gaze settles on the window. "That glass may break into tiny fragments and fly at us. Or that chandelier overhead might come crashing down."

Irina tugs Lili behind her. She will not lose her sister again. "What do you want, Georgy?"

"I want my son—and you. I want us to be together as a family."

Seryozha swivels his head to Georgy. "Me?" he says, very small. "Your s-son?"

Natasha's gaze flicks between them uncertainly. "What is he saying, Irina?"

Irina keeps her eyes trained on Georgy, trying not to react to his words. The words that contain in them the power to destroy her future with her son and cousin. "You are asking us to die for you. Do you truly wish to doom your son to such a short life?"

"Why not finally tell the truth?" Georgy baits.

Irina is desperate to believe he has been warped by death. But she knows *this* is the lie. She recalls the cruel glint in his eye, the entitlement. And she feels profoundly sorry for Georgy. Not that he is dead but that he had no chance to grow or change. She can. By banishing him from her life forever. But first. Irina takes a deep breath, gathering the words. They burn with regret, withheld for far too long. "I am your mother, Seryozha, and this is—*was* your father."

She barely notices Georgy's glare behind her son's pained look, the quiver of his lip. She steps closer. But to her horror, he presses deeper into Georgy's embrace.

A shriek tears through the hall, and Irina whips around—to see a small, wiry figure with streaming white hair hurtling toward them. Irina grabs Lili, shielding her with her body. But the figure dives straight for Georgy. He releases Seryozha and Natasha with a hiss, and they scramble away. The figure springs onto Georgy like a wispy white spider. In the tangle of ghostly limbs, Irina glimpses a face she has known all her life—Grand-mère.

"Irishka." Lili tugs at her hand. "Seryozha and Natasha—they're gone."

Irina looks around wildly before hurrying to the East Wing doorway, from whence music winds like the cold breeze. She catches a glimpse of a small foot, disappearing around the corner of a distant room. She throws a hasty, grateful "Merci, Grand-mère" over her shoulder, then breaks into a sprint after the children.

Irina cannot breathe for the perfume and tobacco smoke clotting the air. Nearly corporeal spirits lounge lazily on settees and sofas, chatter loudly near windows and alcoves. She reminds herself it is 1921, the party not real. As she runs, she sees hints of the deadness underneath the spark of life. The corpse-like flesh of the specters is hidden just barely by filthy, ragged clothing releasing puffs of moths and errant flies that buzz in her ears. And the old bloodstains and bruises, the shadowy eyes and veiled expressions—like Georgy, like the house, all dead, all ghost.

The ballroom is ablaze in a nightmarish orange flicker from dozens of candelabras. As in the rest of the house, the floor-to-ceiling windows are thrown open to let in a night so dense and black there isn't a glimmer of a star. And definitely no moon. The moth-eaten drapery dances on the icy breeze as Igor Stravinsky's notes slip spottily through the room. They fade in and out, unfolding and expanding before exploding into a furious, almost primal swell of strings and rhythm. The same nearly corporeal bodies fill the room and flit on the dance floor, dancing a chaotic version of a quadrille, then a waltz, then back again.

Irina turns back to see Lili standing a few paces behind her, entirely dazed at the sight of the ballroom. "Get the items for the Domovoy," she says urgently above the swelling music. "We need to try to draw him out again. I will look for the children." Before her sister can reply, Irina is hastening farther into the room, praying to catch a glimpse of her boy and girl.

Irina is only met with dead, hollow faces. As she brushes past ghostly limbs or oddly frozen garments, intense cold burns into her. The air is marshy, damp, sick with rot. So she tries to imagine

Seryozha's toothy smiles and pranks, Natasha's clever jokes, Lili's swagger and her *Irishka!*, Will's stories and ocean-blue eyes . . .

Someone seizes her hand suddenly, and Irina is violently sent skittering—toward a dead man.

She swallows, hard, her panic rising as she recalls Georgy's slick grip. With a shaky exhale, Irina tugs her hand back and springs away, deeper into the ballroom, until she is skirting the dance floor. But it is a little like wading against a very strong river current. The spirits push and pull at her, her skin becoming numb with cold.

"Hello, darling" comes a voice, strong and real. Achingly familiar and dear.

Irina cannot help but stop. "Papa?"

Her dead parents stand in front of her—Maman with those vacant violet eyes and Papa with his smile, his arms about Maman's tiny, very solid, very real waist. "You are unhappy, dearest," Papa says. "Care for a dance?"

Irina stands very still, taking in her parents in horror, their realness, even the veins under their skin pulsing with unnatural life. For one vulnerable second, she remembers her desire to be with them, missing Papa's intent gaze as he listened to her, Maman's warm smile when Irina pleased her. But a tug on her skirts, and she is looking down into the pale rash-swept face of Xenia, who twirls maniacally at her feet with the vile old doll in her arms.

Xenia's smile is a motionless thing, as if she died with it on her lips. Her eyes, like their parents', glint with a dark edge, a deadness. This is a warped, nightmare version of her family.

Irina's callus throbs as if in warning. She manages to dart past Xenia and her parents, a slippery fish among sharks. She will not fall for Marie's rosy, pink-hued dream of them. But what if Seryozha and Natasha do? Would the spirits kill them or lead them to their deaths? Unfamiliar spirits are now shoving Irina forward with stiff fingers and long, clawlike nails—into a pair of cold arms that wrap rigidly about her neck. As if to smother her.

"Come, my darling," Georgy says, leaning into her. "Let us go."

This close, despite the influx of blood, his flesh is stiff and so dead. A maggot threads through his lower lip. Irina draws back in revulsion. "I'm not going anywhere with you." She spits into his face as she never had the pleasure of doing in life. "Even if you were alive, I still wouldn't go with you. I never loved you—I never will."

His eyes flash a virulent chartreuse green with rage, his arms tightening and dragging her—struggling—toward a giant candelabra blazing wildly at the back of the ballroom.

She screams, but the Stravinsky swells, snatched up by the whirling wind, and her scream is lost. Irina realizes she is being backed into the flames. They are dangerously close, hot and scorching against her skin, almost unbearable. But her son and cousin flash into her mind, and Irina thrusts her hands out. Then, with all her strength, using all the pain and suffering this man has caused her, she pushes Georgy—hard. Blinking in surprise, he stumbles away. His mouth stretches into an indignant roar, but the flames have caught onto his old uniform.

At the burst of bright light, Irina shuts her eyes.

When she opens them again, Georgy is gone, and the rest of the dead have fallen back.

With what little energy is left in her legs, Irina sprints to the source of the music, to the interior wall of the ballroom, with the mirrors and the heavy busts of marble and bronze cupids and goddesses. Her ancestors stare out of the massive oil paintings above with dead eyes. Below the paintings, Irina glimpses Pasha's old gramophone. The dusty horn quakes with the Stravinsky, softer now, as if making space for her. Even still, the music is not a comfort but a tumble of strings and drums, the song of mayhem, of chaos. Or maybe it is Marie, sweeping suddenly in front of Seryozha and Natasha—as if to protect them from Irina.

"Let them go, Marie," Irina says steadily, lifting her chin as if she were as unflappable as Marie, trying not to inhale that dead rose scent.

"They wish to stay, Irina," Marie returns with a faint smile. She is wearing the blackest, most elaborate evening gown Irina has ever seen, a feathery silk creation she recognizes as a Georges Doeuillet, with metal and rhinestones that clink with every movement. Marie is a starved crow of jutting bones and sagging skin, the gown a shroud on a woman already dead.

"If they stay, they will die." Irina edges closer. "Seryozha"—she directs her gaze on her son—"I am your mother, and I love you. I wanted to tell—"

"Then why didn't you?" he bursts out.

Irina kneels, the parquet cold even through her skirt. "I was afraid." She dares a glance at her cousin before ignoring Marie and leaning toward both children. "You see, Seryozhinka, your papa and I were engaged to be married a long time ago. But then the Great War happened, followed by the Revolution and Civil War. Your papa—not the spirit of him, but him as he was—was very brave and fought in the wars. He didn't know about you. Back then, it was . . . difficult to have a baby without being married, do you see? And so your Uncle Pasha adopted you, so you would have a good, honorable life."

Her son's brow furrows; he doesn't quite understand. But his face has lost its hard edges, its red spots of anger. It is downcast and very, very small.

Irina turns to Natasha. "And you are my cousin, more like a sister, and I love you. In time, I . . ." Irina's eyes well up despite the fear, the music, Marie. "I hope you'll forgive me. I tried to do what was right and least disruptive—"

"Irina lied to you," Marie interrupts, glancing from Natasha to Seryozha. "You cannot trust her. You belong here with your family in your home. You shall not take them from me, Irina," she says, stubbornly. Yet her look is fearful, caught.

"You sound like Pasha," Irina says, sadly. "But you have only brought death into this house. And you have poisoned it with your hatred."

Marie is shaking her head furiously. "No, I brought them back, and the past, and now we can all live together, as we would have if not for the Revolution."

"We cannot have it back. They are gone. This—is not them."

"It *is* them," Marie hisses, pressing Seryozha to her tightly, possessively.

"They are dead, just like the old world." Irina steps forward, as careful as with a cagey beast, but Marie only clutches at her son and cousin tighter.

Seryozha lets out a cry, and Marie turns to him placidly. "Do not listen, mon cher. She does not believe as we do. Come, children, let us find your evening clothes."

"It hurts! You're hurting me!" Seryozha's cry cuts into Irina's heart. He strains against Marie, hard, until he wriggles out of her grasp—and rushes to Irina.

Her son leaps into her arms, cold and trembling, just as Natasha also dashes from Marie's side to hide behind Irina. She is weak with relief, but knows it isn't the end.

"Andryusha!" Marie stamps her foot. "Come back here!"

Irina shivers, tightening one arm around Seryozha, the other bringing Natasha in closer. "This is Seryozha." But her whisper is drowned out by the music. "Why did you resort to this?" Irina tries again, raising her voice. "Killing those men? Grand-mère? When you are the reason the Cheka came to this house in the first place."

"You know?" Marie's lips blanch, and she rushes to her explanations, her justifications. "I . . . made a mistake. They weren't supposed to die. I only wished to frighten them, to show them the inside of a prison cell, so they understood their Russia could not be saved. I . . . lost my only son, Irina. My beloved, lovely boy. I didn't wish the same fate for you, your sister, Natashenka. Seryozhinka. And I was so angry at the family. For not listening to me. For not saving my son, all of you, when they had the chance. Still, I didn't intend for them to die. The bastards promised they would be released. Then we would leave Russia. Settle somewhere else, somewhere new."

"What you did led to their deaths. And the deaths of those innocent men, too."

"Those men were *not* innocent," Marie says hotly. "They paid for their crimes. Their blood brought back the family, my Andryusha. You don't think I know it was my fault they died? All this, why I didn't just bring back Andrei, is my atonement."

"Do you also regret telling the Cheka about Seryozha?" Irina shoots back at her.

Shock flashes across Marie's face. "N-no, I would never. All I have done since that night three years ago is to atone. To protect you children as best I could. You do believe me, don't you, Irina?"

Marie's shock seems genuine, but Irina will never again believe or trust her. "All of it was for you, to assuage your own guilt. Why did you even wait three years?"

"I tried, before, but I was too weak. When Andryusha died, I used animal blood for the sacrifice. I couldn't stand the thought of human blood. Then, when your grandfather died, I tried the sacrifice with his body. But I couldn't do it. It was not until the Bolshevik vermin tried to steal my house that I found the strength to do what I had to. I only killed the first man. The Domovoy took care of the rest."

The house sways, caught up in a violent gust of wind. The candles flicker before flaring brighter. The Stravinsky blares on. Irina realizes there are cracks zigzagging through the walls behind Marie. Here, too, the faded paint is peeling to reveal glaring plaster, water stained and dotted with the moldy black spots, some stirring to reveal centipedes, beetles, spiders, and other insects that make Irina's flesh crawl.

"I do not like to kill," Marie says, voice and face thoughtful. "I did not kill your grandmother. Neither did the Domovoy. I was told she saw the dead family. Clutched at her chest. Then at the railing, too late. She fell, Irina. Her heart failed her. It wasn't me. It was an accident." She closes her eyes, seeming more like a corpse than ever.

No, if not for her, Grand-mère would still be alive. Irina recalls her grandmother's spirit attacking Georgy, protecting Irina even in death. But it is too late for Marie. There are some things that a person cannot come back from. Marie may have been their aunt, their matriarch and adoptive mother, but she has brought to life a past dead and illegal to remember in Soviet Russia, with Soviet men living in their very house. And she informed on the family, leading to the deaths of not only Pasha, Aleksei, and Papa, but also Maman, who followed Papa into exile.

"Vera told me this would happen," Marie says now in a small voice that Irina barely hears. "S-she told me this would be my fate. The spoon had iced over with a hole, you see. A short life. An impending death. And here it is, hastening toward me. Oh, I can feel it. The flames . . . 'You shall die,' she said. 'Too soon, the walls of your last house shall fall all around you in a blaze that will devour your body and your soul.'"

Irina turns from Marie. She will deal with her later, perhaps appeal to Comrade Suzhensky. Now she is searching for Lili. They need to draw out the Domovoy—together with the children, despite Irina's trepidations—before it is too late.

40

One More Ball

LILI DASHES INTO the ballroom breathlessly, the items for the Domovoy bundled under one arm.

She left the offerings for the imp, hoping the little bastard was more appreciative this time. The ghosts were trapped in their own world, maybe the one destroyed by the Bolsheviks, so they didn't interfere. But fear is a sly fox of an emotion, stealing even into Lili.

The ballroom doors behind her groan open, then slam closed heavily.

Lili whirls—to face Nikolai. Hatless, hair windblown and curling, coat flapping in the draft. She gasps in surprise. "Nicky! What are you doing here? You shouldn't be—"

Nikolai grasps her face in both hands, his eyes almost the black of his hair, urgent, very agitated. His gaze is fixed behind her—at the ghosts returned to such vivid, devastating life. Likely, the memory of his papa and brothers also. Then his words are rushing at her over the ghosts' chatter and laughter, the waxing and waning of the Stravinsky. "Lili, what is happening? Did your aunt—? My mother is missing. She hasn't been back to the flat since yesterday. The children, either. I thought you might know . . ."

White-hot realization crackles through Lili. "Madame Naroshina might be here. Auntie locked us in the attic the night before. She collected the children from your flat—"

"—and maybe my mother also." Nikolai's eyes are blacker than night. "My God, Lil, I have to find her. I cannot—" *Lose the last person in my life.*

"You won't," Lili says firmly, not letting him give voice to her own fears. She presses the bundle securely against her arm. She needs to find her sister so that all this can go away. So that Nicky can find his mother, she can find Cleo, and the house can return to its version of normal. "Go look for Madame Naroshina, and I will find Irina to try to get the Domovoy's attention."

"It didn't work the night before." It's not a question. "I . . . cannot leave you, Lil."

The doors burst open, this time with a violence that unnerves the chandelier. Its crystal drops clink and jangle, like crushed glass underfoot. Lili is vaguely aware the music and the ghosts have quieted. What she sees makes her rigid with remembered fear. The déjà vu steals in along with the cold. And she is back in that sterile cell, the naked walls closing in, the spire of the white church a sick reminder of the past imprisoning her.

"Well, what do we have here?" A familiarly hard voice cuts into her fear. "Former people, throwing an imperial ball in Soviet Russia. Perhaps they are also engaging in degenerate dancing, the foxtrot or some other Western dance."

Lili meets that ice-cold blue gaze before shaking her head at Nikolai. He stills, not turning, his eyes fixing to hers. "It's Felix and his comrades," she whispers.

Felix thrusts his right arm into the air. The steely silver of a Nagant revolver flashes in his hand. The earsplitting *crack!* of a single gunshot rings out.

Lili is spinning back into the past, to the time and place of that other gunshot, the ghost of which hasn't stopped ringing in her head for these three long years. *Bang!* The stain of tea, crushed caviar, blood. Now Lili is once more staring down the muzzles of those hated revolvers. *No, Lil*, she tells herself fiercely. *It isn't the same. Nor are you.* She shakes herself out of the cell, out of the past, out of that bottomless well of fear and pain.

Though her ears still ring, and there is the sulfuric smell of gunfire on her tongue, she forces out, "Go and find your mother, Nicky."

Lili's hands are no longer trembling. Nor is she afraid of these small men with their toylike guns. She has survived the murder of her favorite uncle, the rest of her family's arrests and deaths, her own arrest and stint in prison. Yet she is still here. Though Comrade Peters is not. Lili notes there are fewer men than she initially thought. No more than a dozen, Felix included. And she recognizes their faces. It isn't the Cheka, nor is it a sanctioned raid. Of course it isn't. Soviet officials believe if they arrest Lili or any of the other Russians again, the Americans will pull their ARA aid from Russia and leave.

It is only Felix and his cronies, back for their second helping of the nechistaya sila they don't believe in. And it hits Lili: the men think the ghosts are *living* former people. The fools must not have looked close enough or denied what is so laughingly blatant. She can sense the ghosts by the cold blooming into her back, radiating out, the hair rising on her arms. The gunshot has caught their attention, which is unfortunate for Felix and his men. But fortunate for her. She feels a smile spread slowly over her lips.

Nikolai gives her one last questioning look, and Lili nods before he strides into the crowd of ghosts.

The cold twists, becomes dead still. It curdles the blood in her veins, spiking her pulse. She turns her head very slowly—to the wall of ghosts behind her, all staring at the men with wide, chillingly empty eyes. Some lick their blue lips hungrily.

"—glad we have their attention." Felix is laughing.

Lili lets her smile widen even further. "You really shouldn't have come back."

She should be a little scared, of the men and the ghosts. But given how the men tried to steal and destroy the house, she has a feeling the ghosts will not care much about her. Neither will the men when they have the dead to worry over. At least, she hopes.

"Lili Goliteva. I knew you and your vampiric family were up to something. I just didn't know it was this good. Comrade Peters will be interested to hear you are hosting former people and throwing balls. No one will care about a few . . . incidental deaths."

"You are absolutely right, Felix Ivanovich."

He blinks, visibly stunned. His comrades stop laughing, cock their revolvers.

"The thing is, though, it won't be *their* deaths." Lili points behind her. She can tell by the prickling at her back, the ice cold and dread, that the ghosts have edged closer.

Felix, still confused, fumbles for words. "Whose, then?" he spits out finally.

Poor bastard. "Why, yours, Comrade."

"What is she saying?" A swarthy older man steps forward.

"You said this would be easy and safe." Another man's gaze flicks fearfully between Lili and Felix. "That they would be unarmed and harmless."

"Oh, it isn't that, Comrades. It's just, well, you haven't looked at the former people as closely as you should. For you see, Felix Ivanovich, they are already dead."

Felix turns as unnaturally white as the ghosts. One of his comrades lets out a strangled noise. Lili can *feel* and *smell* the ghosts now as they shuffle up to her. She notices the intentness in their shadowed eyes; hears *It's them*, an echo of a laugh.

Before Lili dives into the ghostly crowd, she glimpses Auntie, shutting the ballroom doors.

Then it is like plunging into a body of ice water. Dread seeps into Lili along with the swampy dampness. She tries to take little sips of air, the rot and aged perfumes turning her stomach. Several screams, followed by the scuff of boots against parquet as the men try to run. More screams, faint and otherworldly. Are the ghosts attacking the men? She has, after all, seen Georgy's strength on two occasions. Lili doesn't look back.

Her ears fill with gunfire. *Ratatatat!* A bullet whizzes by her ear, too close. She ducks, just in time. Prays Irina and the children are safe, Nicky and his mother, Cleo.

Lili breaks into a sprint just as the gunfire ceases, only to be replaced by the chilling sounds of bones breaking, of anguished moans, of death.

Lili's body is numb by the time that she glimpses Irina with her nephew and cousin. This deep in the ballroom, there are fewer ghosts; most of them have pushed past her to the doors and the men. Lili is bursting to tell her sister—she has realized what Uncle Pasha tried to show them.

"The Domovoy appears only when he's needed!" Lili shouts to Irina over the Stravinsky and the screams. Lili saw her uncle in such grim straits but once, when Aunt Luba went into labor and he was told to pray for her soul. She saw him kneel then in the same way he did outside their window, with his arms raised desperately to the Heavens. And Lili understood. It isn't the number of times that one tries to draw out the Domovoy, or how, or even the manner of offerings, but one's need for the spirit.

"I would call our need fairly dire, wouldn't you?" Irina shouts back.

"Oh!" Natasha's eyes are bright with excitement. "We get to help?"

"It would appear so." Despite the situation, Lili winks at her cousin.

"Come, children," Irina says sternly, and gathers Seryozha and Natasha close before taking each of their hands. "They know," said in an undertone.

Lili nods—it's about damn time—and reaches for the children's other hands to complete their circle. Only, when she tries to take

Seryozha's hand, there is Xenia's old doll. The demon's smile seems to be melting, becoming so diabolical, Lili's flesh crawls.

"Xenia!" Seryozha suddenly calls out, peering around Lili. "Where did she go?"

The ghosts glide past like shreds of torn, rotting cloud.

"Throw away the vile thing, and take my hand," Lili orders the spoiled boy.

Irina's gaze shudders down to the doll. "Seryozha!"

Clearly, Lili needs to take matters into her own hands. She rips the doll out of her nephew's stubborn grip and, despite his red-faced protestations, winds her arm all the way back and tosses the doll as far as possible. Hopefully, out the damn window. Then she barks out "*Bow*" on instinct, and bows in all the directions to the imp. "Protect us, Dedushka," Lili whispers as she does so.

Irina follows her lead. She bows reverently. "Protect us, Dedushka."

Seryozha is still red-faced and screaming for the doll, and for Xenia's horrid ghost, but Natasha pulls him into a bow with her, repeating Lili's words.

"We have given you offerings, Dedushka," Lili says, trying to speak from the heart, from the need for the spirit that she channels from the chaotic music, the alarming screams, the house groaning with the violent wind. "We have hung our favorite shoes, brewed your favorite tea, shared with you our bread and salt, even decorated a pine bough for you with more offerings. We have honored and complimented you. Apologized for our neglect of you over the years. We know you have a different mistress, but listen to us, Dedushka, please. Help and protect us. These ghosts mean us and the house harm."

To Lili's surprise, the Domovoy shivers to life inside their circle mere moments later. This is good, but now for the hard part. "Good evening, Dedushka," she says as evenly as possible, and the others follow.

"Good evening." His voice is scratchy; she thinks it carries entire centuries.

"Thank you for protecting us," Irina whispers, glancing at the children.

Natasha and Seryozha are struck totally and completely dumb, their eyes as big as saucers. If not for the seriousness of the situation and Lili's fear, she would definitely have made some teasing remark by now.

"I try to protect those of the house that know me," he returns with a glimmer of a smile.

The screams and music grow louder, more desperate, and Lili knows this is their chance, maybe their only chance. "Dedushka," she says over the noise, "will you allow us to be your mistresses?"

His red eyes glint, hard as rubies. "I already have a mistress."

"If she remains your mistress," Irina says, reasonable as ever, "we will die, and the house will die. And there will be no one left for you to protect."

"But you shall order me back to sleep."

"The ghosts," Lili counters, quickly, jaggedly, earning a questioning look from Irina. She isn't completely lying, just playing with words like she plays with color and charcoal. All they have to do is convince the imp to agree. No one said it has to be fair, and the implication that he may stay awake and alive is too irresistible for him.

The Domovoy thinks this over. "Very well," he says at length, though uneasily.

Lili is careful not to look at Irina, who she is quite sure doesn't approve of her reasoning. But now that the Domovoy is under their control, they can ask him to order the ghosts back to sleep. But first. "Dedushka, do you know where Madame Naroshina is? Or Cleo?"

"I don't know who Madame Naroshina is, but the bird is in your aunt's armoire." He flicks his wrist, once, before lowering his hand into his robe's shadowy folds. "There, I have let your bird out. But I cannot force the dead back to sleep. Life runs through them too insistently now. They will not listen." He glances to the front of the ballroom, to the whirl of shadow and limbs, screams and laughter. "Blood has been spilled."

The wind blows icily across Lili's cheeks. She swears under her breath as Irina meets her grim gaze and presses Natasha and Seryozha to her tightly. The children squeeze their eyes shut—just as a crash comes hurtling from the front of the ballroom.

Out of the corner of her eye, Lili glimpses a flicker, an orange stain unfurling in a spark of blue-white. Flames. A fire. No, a *blaze*. She follows its ripple to the nearest window. The silk damask is almost entirely consumed. A candelabra must have caught onto the billowing drapery, and the gusts of wind have further fanned the flames.

She hears Irina's and the children's gasps, smells the burning on the air, the flames growing hotter and brighter. "Can you try to put out the fire, Dedushka?" Lili asks the Domovoy.

"I can try." His red eyes flick to Seryozha and Natasha. "But you should take them out of the house—in case . . ." *I fail.*

The flames give another spark, then a mad hiss. The house groans. The ceiling starts to crumble, pieces of moldy, waterlogged plaster showering down with a crash.

Lili will try to save Moscow House—for Uncle Pasha, who loved it, its history and treasures. But she will not trade her life or those of her family for the house. She will not trade the present for the past. She wants Nicky, her family, and her job in the present. Herself now.

"He's right." Lili looks pointedly at Irina, who, judging by her glance toward the doors, is coming to the same conclusion. "You should take them somewhere safe," Lili says gently, placing a hand on Natasha's very cold arm, stroking Seryozha's silky hair, missing both naughty, silly children already. "Where is Auntie?"

A long, crackling silence. "She is past saving," her sister says, finally.

Lili cannot believe her ears. Irina, their aunt's staunchest advocate, all but telling Lili to leave Auntie behind? "All right," Lili returns, uneasily. Auntie *is* the Evil Queen, the one who started the horror and likely killed those men, informed on their family, committed other terrors Lili may not know of. She knows only one thing: that she trusts Irina, and that if her sister believes their aunt is past saving, then she is. "I am sure you will tell me later."

"Aren't you coming?" Irina's voice pitches.

Lili shakes her head. "Nicky is here, and his mother. I need to find them first." And Cleo, who she hopes has been freed and is on her way to the ballroom.

"I think Georgy is gone for good—it turns out that flames destroy the spirits. Keep this in mind, all right?" Irina throws over her shoulder, as she sweeps a now pale, terrified Seryozha into her arms and a trembling Natasha to her side. All three look back at Lili. "I better see you on the other side, Lil, or I will never forgive you." This is said with a wryness entirely out of Irina's character.

Then her sister, cousin, and nephew are gone, swallowed up by the smoke surging at Lili like a noxious black cloud heavy with thunder and disaster. When she glances around, the Domovoy has also vanished. A fat cockroach scampers by. Then a long, hairy centipede with countless legs, followed by several black widows, a beetle or two, and a stream of ants. The mice and rats scuttle after the insects. Not a good sign. Lili wishes she would hear the ghostly crow of a rooster, a sign that morning is coming. But it is only past midnight on the anniversary of the worst day of her life, and the party is only just beginning.

41

You Reap What You Sow

IRINA KEEPS TO the mirrored wall as she edges toward the ballroom doors.

She cannot see through the billowing black smoke. Her eyes and throat sting from the haze and ash, the flames searing her face. Seryozha has buried his own face in the crook of her shoulder. She holds his head with one hand, glancing back to Natasha. Her cousin has fastened a torn strip of skirt around her mouth. Irina wishes she thought of that. But it is too late. They cannot stop now, need to make it out before the flames block the doors.

She feels a twinge of regret for leaving her sister behind. But she knows Lili; once her mind is made up, there is nothing Irina can do. She must trust her sister to save herself.

And Marie? Irina waits for the regret, but it doesn't come. It appears as though the fire will decide all: whether the house will withstand the flames, and whether Vera's prophecy will come true. Despite the heat, Irina shivers. The *blaze* piece was accurate. Will the walls of Moscow House fall next? Will Marie die as they do? The saying *You reap what you sow* flashes through Irina's mind. She chases it away. She may wish for justice to find Marie, but she prefers to leave it in God's hands.

Irina makes out figures past the smoke, though not whether they are man or spirit. Her head aches from the music, thumping against her eardrums louder and more chaotically. But the screams are dying down, except for the occasional phantom laugh. The smoke tightens around her throat like an invisible hand, stealing into her lungs, making it hard to draw breath through the painful rasps.

"I cannot breathe," Seryozha says, small, muffled.

"We are almost there, my darling." And Irina almost believes it.

She feels a wetness under her boot—too late. She slips, one knee smashing into the parquet so hard that intense pain explodes there, dazing her for a split second.

A thin arm winds around her waist as Natasha pulls her up. Irina steadies herself, tightening her hold on Seryozha. The floor is wet with puddles of a dark and sticky liquid, congealing already, scarlet as—blood. She looks back at Natasha, whose eyes are also on the blood. The spirits have killed, are now more alive than ever.

Irina and the children must keep going, must make it to the doors. . . .

That's when something crashes into them. For a moment, Irina is suspended in the brutal force of the blow. The impact knocks Seryozha out of her arms and to the floor with a wet thud, though she doesn't see it. She slams into the mirror, her shoulder shattering into the glass.

Her head spins. The smoke twists sickeningly, as in a nightmare.

Irina blinks, disoriented. Pain blooms in her shoulder, belatedly in her side. It is throbbing so violently that she clutches at her waist, forcing herself to breathe through the pain.

Distantly, she hears Seryozha's voice, Natasha's strangled cry, her name.

Irina tries to push up, look up, but something presses into her back. It is hard and heavy, like a sack of stones weighing her down. And her hands and arms are so cold and so wet with blood, which is slick on her blouse, seeping into all parts of her. Irina wiggles below the weight, tilts her head very slightly to the side . . . Her insides plummet to the floor with the blood.

Felix is looming over Irina, one boot wedged into her back to prevent her moving. He smiles as their eyes meet and shoves his revolver against her temple.

"Let us go," she says, with as much authority as she can summon.

She sees his other arm is wrapped around Natasha's throat. But her cousin's gaze is steady. And Seryozha stands tall, not crying or cowering. Pride flares deep in her chest.

"I told you that your family will fall," Felix says above the crackle of the flames, the blaring of the music. "And you will, along with your children. You are all traitors to the motherland, enemies of the Soviet republic and her people. You demeaned us for centuries. Now you're finally getting what you deserve—justice."

"You must have been a sad, lonely boy indeed to hate us this much." Irina glances behind Felix at the smoke-wreathed ballroom, the crumbling ceiling, the wall of soot-stained mirrors. Georgy's threat about the glass flying at them comes back to her. There's something in it. . . . Irina forces her muddled, aching mind to *think*.

"You know nothing about me or my childhood." Felix digs his boot into her shoulder blade; she cries out in pain. "I was close to putting an end to your sister once and for all, but you had to interfere. Now you are back under my boot, where your kind belongs."

Think! She is mistress of the Domovoy, reasons Irina, and the Domovoy is master of the house. So if she wishes for the wall of mirrors to fragment or a part of the ceiling to crumble, will the spirit help her? Felix is now squeezing the revolver's trigger. "*Dedushka. I need you*," she whispers to the air.

"What did you say, bitch?" Felix demands, spittle flying.

"Can you break the mirror and send the fragments at this man?" More loudly.

"Madness must run in the family, eh?" Felix grins, tightening his hand on Natasha's neck. She gives a little indignant noise of protestation. "Any last words?"

Irina's heart is pounding so hard against her rib cage, the edges of her vision dim. Where is the Domovoy? Felix laughs, once more squeezing the trigger, and she thinks that even if the house spirit comes, it might be too late. She might already be dead. Irina closes her eyes, fumbling for her prayers, when she hears a sound. It is so slight that, at first, she cannot place it. She hears it again—a *crack!*—and she understands.

The mirror is splintering with what she imagines are jagged, violent lines. And the glass is fragmenting into glinting shards so sharp they can pierce through flesh like a blade through rotting fruit.

"*Get down!*" Irina shouts, taking advantage of Felix's boot loosening from her back in a moment of surprise.

Then she lunges for Natasha and Seryozha. Felix, stunned, releases Natasha's throat, and the children huddle low to the blood-slick parquet, Irina covering them with as much of her body as she can.

If Felix makes a sound, she doesn't hear it. Only the violent crush of glass, and the spray of blood on her back and arms. Their breathing rasps in her ears. But the revolver and boot are gone. Slowly, Irina lifts her head. Glittering fragments and blood fill the edges of her vision, and she knows Felix is dead. She rises on wobbly legs, her boots slipping and sliding on the bloody floor. She averts her gaze from the man's remains, helping Natasha and Seryozha up. Natasha covers her mouth, smothering her scream.

"It is better not to look," Irina says grimly.

Despite the still-throbbing pain in her shoulder and side, she allows her son to climb back into her arms. Then she and Natasha limp past the motionless body, now reduced to nothing but glass shards and blood.

You reap what you sow echoes in her mind as they pull open the heavy ballroom doors and stagger through Moscow House, a minefield of specters caught in their wild party, oblivious to them and the flames. The house shifts, as if to keep them inside. But they are already stumbling out into the bitter black night.

Before the entrance doors of Moscow House shut on them, Irina glimpses the Domovoy.

His fiery red eyes cut to hers—and, bizarrely, give her a wink.

Maybe he knows that she intends to come back, hopefully before the fire spreads. To protect the house and keep a roof over their heads. To find another way to cast out the spirits. To save her sister at all costs.

42

Blood and Flame

Trails of smoke envelop Lili like an enchanted fog, prickling and somehow alive. In the flames beyond, she thinks she can make out the shape of the three-headed dragon of legend—the flickers of blue and red in its slick scales, the bright orange gush spewing from its many mouths. She blinks, and there is nothing. Only her imagination. Lili wishes she could sink into a fairy-tale land and leave all this behind.

Acrid haze and ash burn into her. The air is stagnant. Rotting like the ghosts. But she keeps shouting. "Nicky! Madame Naroshina! Cleo!" Then, "Dedushka!"

The ghosts float above the floor in their mad dance to the now jarring music, puppets animated into horrifying reality. They are jerky in their steps and turns, their joints still stiff with death, which they cannot shed no matter how much more alive they appear.

Two figures materialize out of the crush.

"Lilichka," Papa says in his gentle voice, the one she remembers so well.

Don't do it, Lil. But Lili looks into his face. She hasn't seen it since his arrest, and she cannot help but be mesmerized by each feature in its flesh. And each abnormality. The bluish skin and shadowed eyes, the hint of the rash on his very tangible neck.

"Come here." Papa opens his arms. At his side, Maman smiles at her.

How wrong it is, Lili thinks. *Maman never smiled at you in life, except if you were utterly miserable.* And how strained this smile, how leering!

But Lili's legs carry her to Papa of their own volition, and she steps into that frozen yet solid and very real embrace like a sleepwalker. She feels the tight press of his skeletal arm on her back, as if he means to snuff the life out of her. Lili cannot move. She is trapped in those arms, Papa's body a cool tombstone against hers. Her thoughts become very, very quiet. As they did when the river's current would carry her downstream in its cool, wet grasp, like Ophelia floating into a dreamy death sleep.

The next thing Lili knows, she is raising her hands to Papa's bird-thin shoulders, and they are whirling through the cold and smoke. A skirt flutters against her legs—Xenia and her vile doll. Lili lifts her eyes and makes out Grand-père and Aunt Luba and Uncle Aleksei, watching and smiling beside Maman. Dmitri walks by with a ghostly tray of champagne flutes balancing precariously above the faint outline of his head.

"May I have this dance?" says a deep, familiar voice.

Lili's heart swells despite herself. He is young and handsome, even as a ghost, even with the chalk-white skin and the glaring dark red stain in his neck where he must have been shot by the Reds. Andrei flashes Papa a smile. Then it is her cousin's arms of air, and they are off, twirling across the dance floor with the other ghosts. Real, alive, their faces flushed with new color, their movements more fluid. Less dead somehow.

A movement flickers in the corner of her eye. The wave of a hand—at a window.

Lili wants to keep floating. But a voice inside her vibrates: *Stop being dim, Lil. Wake up.* Wake up. When they sweep to the window, she peers out.

The hand waves at her insistently, and she peers harder.

Uncle Pasha hovers just outside, almost blending into the billowing curtains. His mouth opens and closes, says something Lili cannot hear—not past Andrei's voice in her ear, whispering how glad he is to see her, and the music swelling to new heights.

Uncle Pasha is shouting now. His neck strains, his upper body nearly thrusting into the house, but not quite.

"*What is it?*" Lili mouths, body instinctively resisting the dance, muscles taut with exertion to stop it, heels attempting to find purchase, failing.

Her cousin's arm tightens on her back, his hand grasping hers roughly, and she is whirling away from the window and Uncle Pasha. Lili digs her boots into the parquet with the last of her strength, but she only slides deeper into Andrei's arms. She tries to call for her uncle, but her voice fails to carry.

"Dedushka, help me!" she manages, calling for the imp again, truly needing him now, just as a figure hurls over the windowsill like a spinning top and rushes at her.

Andrei is wrenched back with one violent pull. The wet patches of ice-cold on her body instantly thaw. Uncle Pasha is wrangling with Andrei. The ghosts turn as one, blazing a flashing silver with rage. Their gazes flare with a repulsive dark glitter, a hatred, and a hunger. Lili backs away from them as Papa and Uncle Aleksei stride toward her. Her blood runs cold. She whirls around and throws herself in the opposite direction.

Lili remembers she is supposed to be looking for Nicky and his mother. And where is Cleo? It is very hard to see, to think, to *breathe*. The smoke presses into her throat, making her choke and gasp painfully for air. But it is sucked out of the room by the ghosts and the escalating inferno, unable to be stopped even by the Domovoy.

A horrific monster indeed, spellbound by rage and vengeance. Like Auntie.

Lili nearly screams in frustration. She sees only flickers of unfamiliar ghostly faces. And certainly no damn doors. *Good work, Lil.* The voice inside her is back, bristling with accusations. *Now you have no way out.* She spins on her heel, squints into the smoke, makes out a tall, angular figure.

It is a woman, in a black gown resembling a gash of darkness, with bejeweled hands raised high above her head. Auntie? Lili scrambles over to her on instinct. But just as quickly, she jerks back. There is a bright spark of silver, and a sticky wetness sprays Lili's cheeks. She brings a hand to her face. Her fingers come away bloody. Another spark, and she glimpses the blade in Auntie's hands. No, not a blade—a shard of glass. Blood is spurting from Auntie's palms, and a body lies motionless at her satin-slippered feet, cockroaches crawling all over it.

"Auntie?" Lili wheezes, Irina's words floating back to her. *She is past saving.*

Her aunt smiles. "Horror may sometimes be for love, Liliya. But this horror, my horror, is for vengeance. Those men with their big ideas and even bigger stomachs took everything from me. Now I shall do the same to them. It will end in this house, in this blaze, tonight."

Lili says something, but she cannot hear her own words. There seems to be nothing past the Stravinsky, the wind and flames. Not even Auntie or the ghosts.

The Stravinsky cuts out, the record slashed into silence. But for the roar of the flames, it grows very, very quiet. Only a groan or gasp here and there, a peal of a laugh or cry, blooming to life, then vanishing. The glass in the windows and mirrors starts to splinter and crack. The hot flames billow closer, suffocating like ghostly fingers.

Lili is burning up. Her skin smarts, *stings*. Droplets of perspiration trickle down her forehead and slip into her eyes. She hacks out cough after cough that rock through her, spitting out ash. Her mind is hazy, and she feels heavy, almost bone weary.

You must escape, Lili. The voice is not hers but Uncle Pasha's. It envelops her in warmth, in love. How strange, as the ghosts bring such cold and darkness.

"It's too late," Lili whispers past the scratch in her throat as she drops to the floor, right into a puddle of fresh blood. Its sticky wetness seeps into her trousers. Beside her, a stray cockroach flails on its back. "I couldn't find Nicky or his mother. Or Cleo. All I wanted was . . . to free you, Uncle Pasha, to give you peace. I failed at that, too, failed at keeping this house safe for you. Now it will all burn down. Every last brick."

Uncle Pasha's ghost steps out of the flickering wall of flame. *You did not fail.* His voice is fainter than those of the other ghosts. *You uncovered your aunt's darkness and betrayal, averted the same disaster that befell me, Aleksei, your parents.*

"This *is* disaster!" Lili throws her hands up. She suddenly really doesn't want to die. She wants Nicky, her family. She wants to publish her ARA article so the world knows about people like her. She wants a future worth something despite the Revolution.

The house groans. A piece of ceiling or plaster from the wall crumbles down. Fragments of glass shatter against the parquet. Lili flinches, doesn't move.

Go. The house is not worth your life. A sigh on the air. *I understand that now.*

"Would you have done it differently?"

A subtle shake of the head. *I belong here. There was no future left for me out there. But it will give me peace if you save yourself, Lilichka, and leave your aunt here with me.*

A future, a life free from the ghosts of their past. Is it really possible? "I met Viktor. I gave him your ring." Lili shifts in the blood, thinking. "Where have you been, Uncle Pasha?"

Your aunt did not let me in the house. You asked the Domovoy for help, and he let me in. She knew that I knew all. Even still, I had to save you. All of you.

Lili coughs out a laugh; it hurts. "Uncle Pasha, when will you stop trying to save me?" Even in death, he is still *here*, for her, for her family. Maybe saving the house wasn't the point. Maybe she had to confront their past, then move on from it and *live*. She was at sea, a silly little fool.

I will never stop, not even when I am gone. You must stand now, Lilichka.

Despite the weakness, the wooziness, the *sadness*, she pushes up to her feet. She steadies herself, barely, head dizzy and body sore and uncooperative. Smoke travels into her mouth, nose, eyes. Lili blinks. Uncle Pasha has vanished. She wants to cry. Instead, she starts to shuffle forward, step by slippery step, until a shriek slashes through the smoke. Then feathers brush against her face, and there is a furious beating of wings.

A pluck on her sleeve, a fierce nip, before the shrieks intensify.

"Cleo!" Lili cannot believe her parakeet has finally found her.

Someone pulls on her hand. The skin is not cold, not the dead flesh of the ghosts, but warm, rough, familiar. *Lil*. Then, more defined, "Lili." A red-faced Nicky is tugging urgently on her hand, Cleo thrashing her wings at them both to hurry. The rest of his words rush at her. "—must go. Do you hear? Can you walk? Lili?" *Lili*.

She nods. "W-what about your mother?"

"Mother is out and safe. Come *on*, Lil."

Lili glances back for Uncle Pasha, Auntie, any of her family—but no one, nothing.

Nicky grasps her hand as they veer to the wall of mirrors, now jagged fragments of glass dripping fat drops of blood. The fallen glass crunches under Lili's boots. The flames unfurl before them, searing hot, twisting into the monstrous shapes of zmeys and serpents rearing up—and blocking their path to the doors.

"*Dedushka, help us pass through the flames and ghosts*," Lili whispers to the air. "*Protect us one last time*." Flames may destroy the ghosts, but they haven't spread to the rest of the house yet.

A split second later, the wispy little spirit appears at Lili's side, pushing away the flames with his hands. Nicky is about to turn to look back at Lili, but she shoves him forward, doesn't let him see the Domovoy. That is her fate to bear, not his.

The glint of silver flashes suddenly, and a birdlike wrist reaches out of the smoke.

Lili has one last glimpse of the Evil Queen—plunging her glass shard into a man's neck in a spurt of blood. Auntie's eyes cut to hers for one horrific, heart-pounding moment, and she smiles through the blood. Then she dives into the flames roaring up behind Lili. Now it is only Lili's ragged breaths, her wildly thudding heart, and pure adrenaline in the race to survive.

43

Snowfall Is for Decisions

Irina inhales the sulfurous odor before she sees the blaze consuming Moscow House. The breath dies in her throat. A dazzling orange stain shifts in the black sky, the flames roaring high and hungry, burning almost as violently white as the sun. It is worse than she imagined. The house is burning down. Irina clutches Will's arm.

He insisted on coming with her after she informed him that she would be returning for Lili. This was *after* she had burst into the ARA covered in blood and ash with Seryozha and Natasha in tow. Luckily, only Will was there, and Emma hurried over to be with the children as soon as he had telephoned.

Now, Irina and Will break into a run down her street. Motorcars speed by with screeching tires and shrieking horns and flashing headlamps. Did Felix tell someone where he and his comrades were going, or was his a vigilante mission, unauthorized by the Cheka? Either way, they must be careful. Curious, half-dressed neighbors crowd the street, buzzing with talk and gossip despite the late hour.

Is Lili still in the house? Are Nicky and Madame Naroshina? Irina peers at the faces, praying to see someone familiar, but all are strangers, all wide-eyed with feverish excitement, no doubt thinking the Sherbatsky-Golitevs are finally getting what they deserve. She brushes past them roughly, Will struggling to keep up, still a few paces behind. Despite the fire's heat, the cold she felt in the ballroom seizes Irina. Her heart gives a panicked lurch.

"Wait for me here," she tells Will.

He blanches, uneasy. "You aren't thinking of going in, are you?"

"Yes, Will, I am." The words *I need to do this alone* simmer between them, unsaid.

He falls back with a worried nod, and Irina shoots toward the gate of the house. She glimpses a tall, dark-haired, dark-skirted figure, a harried-looking Madame Naroshina—thank goodness Nicky's mother is safe—but no sign of Nicky or Lili. Irina presses down her panic and hurries into the courtyard.

Pasha's ghost stands under the oak as if waiting for her. Irina thinks he whispers *Be strong*, but she cannot be sure over the crackle of the flames. She darts to the doors and pulls on the scalding handles. There may yet be time to help her sister, to save her.

"Hey!" a man shouts behind her to the wail of sirens. When did the firefighters arrive? "Hey, girl, stop!" What about the police and Cheka?

Irina pushes the doors open and leaps into the burning house.

Inside, all is coiling gray smoke, as thick as the fog at the sorcerer's cemetery. The lantern overhead bursts. Irina barely has time to throw her hands over her head as fragments of glass rain down on her. The banister of the grand staircase creaks like the rattle of a snake—maybe the Domovoy—hissing out a warning. Drapery soars, and snow whirls in through the open windows. Irina's hair flies undone, trailing small bits of glass as she shakes it out, blinking, taking in a sputtering gasp of smoke. It is ashy and rough against her throat.

She doesn't care. She dashes toward the East Wing doorway.

There, Irina peers into the rooms. She glimpses shifting figures blurred to pale transparency, and beyond them, the flames. The fire is unfurling through the house like a great orange beast. The house shakes as a gust of wind and snow blasts in. This time, ash and cinders rain down. But Irina is already sprinting toward the ballroom.

The spirits are still caught in their frenzied soirée. The wallpaper is peeling, revealing massive, moldy, watery black stains. It looks like the house is weeping. Its plaster is crumbling and crashing down along with the paintings, tapestries, statues. Irina coughs out smoke, sips at the burning, sulfurous air. Is her sister alive? Is anyone?

As if in answer, a screech resounds. Then a tittering, followed by a whistle . . . Irina's pulse speeds up. Her heart lifts in hope. A minute later, Cleo whirls up to her in a flash of jewel green and beating wings. Irina squints into the flickering distance and sees two figures materializing out of the smoke. Limping, stumbling, step after slow, painful step. Faces, grimy and soot stained. Clothes, singed. Yet it is them. Lili and Nicky.

"Lili!" Irina runs up to her sister and grasps her very hot hands. "Thank God, oh, thank God," Irina keeps saying over and over as she scans both Lili and Nikolai for injuries, signs of confusion, smoke poisoning. "Are you well? How do you feel? Any nausea or drowsiness?"

Lili merely shakes her head, body racked with rasping coughs that leave her gasping. Nicky gives Irina the barest of nods, a small sign that they are all right. Their faces are flushed and strained. Otherwise, Irina sees no other signs. She doesn't ask about Marie. She doesn't need to. What they need is to escape.

Irina hurries to reach an arm around her sister's waist, and the three of them hobble into the smoky hall, Cleo soaring overhead with wings beating hard against the stifling air. The house groans, swaying as if at any moment it will crumble all around them. But the foyer appears, then the doors, and they are leaping into the night and snow.

The fire at Irina's back is unlike the one that engulfed Moscow House. It is cozy and fragrant and safe there behind the grate. Snow whirls outside the ARA mansion in gusts. She cannot believe this is the same reception room of that party, seeming centuries ago now.

She and Will trudged through the snow with Lili and Nikolai, not wishing to take a droshky or other transport in the event they were recognized and the police or Cheka were looking for them. It was pure instinct telling Irina that with the house's death, maybe their names could die, too. On the way, Lili recounted her last minutes in Moscow House. And Irina could only thank God they were all safe.

The cold and snow recede with a warm Seryozha sleeping in her arms and Natasha dozing against her shoulder on the sofa. Irina keeps stroking their brittle hair, their soft cheeks and foreheads. Pressing them to her tight to make sure they are real.

Lili quietly smokes a cigarette on the settee across from them, Nikolai beside her. Irina wishes she wouldn't smoke, not after inhaling all those flames and so close to the children. But she says nothing. Lili takes up a glass of vodka and raises it.

"To all the dead," she says in a scratchy, low voice, "and to Moscow House."

Emma hands out vodka and pieces of bread to Nikolai, Irina, and Will, who is reclining in an armchair next to Irina. The rest of the ARA has thankfully long turned in for the night.

"We don't clink over the dead," Irina tells the Americans, raising her glass. "To the dead and the house—free now and at rest." She tips her head back and downs the vodka. The bitter spirit burns down her throat, heating her chest and belly. As she munches on the bread, a surprising contentment washes over her. Irina thinks of the house in times past, filled with light, life, and family. She thinks of Pasha and Grand-mère, noble even in death. Of Maman and Papa, forever in love. Of Xenia, as a bouncing, golden-haired little girl. Her other family, the Domovoy, all hopefully at peace. Her mind skims over Marie and Georgy, hoping they meet with the justice they deserve. Irina can no longer let her memories consume her. It is time to let go of the past, and to live.

Will clears his throat. "I know this is the worst time, but I have to say this."

Cleo screeches from her perch by the window, as if to urge him on.

"I can get you and the children out, possibly Lili, if we work fast."

Irina's heart gives a treacherous thud, recalling his offer the night of Lili's arrest.

At her questioning look, he reddens. "Remember that insurance policy? Forgive me, Irene, but I didn't listen to you"—Will glances at Lili, whose eyes widen—"and I asked my contact to prepare travel papers for you to America in case things went south. I found the children's photographs among your sister's work and had yours already. The papers are ready. And we can get papers for Lili, too. It wouldn't take long. A few days, maybe."

How is it possible? Soviet officials have likely opened an investigation into Moscow House by now, given how the men moved out and the fire. Comrade Suzhensky will be unable to help this time. Either their names will prevent travel, or they must somehow get new names. That's when it hits Irina: "You didn't use real names."

Will laughs. "Of course not. My contact is a professional."

"What will Mr. Carroll and the other chiefs think about you helping us, with Lili fresh out of prison, and our house burned down . . . under mysterious circumstances?"

Will considers. "He won't know. No one will. Besides, who says you survived?"

Her mind is racing. That was her exact thought. "How would it work?"

"A group of ARA relief workers is preparing to cross the border any day, and you can all join them. No one will expect you to have travel papers so quickly, or to be alive."

"In the meantime," Emma puts in, "you can stay at my flat with me. The Bolos wouldn't dare to search an apartment not belonging to the Soviet government and rented out by an American. At least, they haven't so far. You, Lili, and the children should be safe there."

Irina recalls her father's map. Nothing but cinders now, along with the photographs and memories. To leave, to see the world. To live that image of her going to New York City with the children. The safety, the possibilities, a future, a real one. But she shakes the image out of her mind. "No, we can find a place to live here in Moscow or in the countryside—"

"Irina, you cannot be serious," Lili interrupts. "If they find out we're alive, and they will if they see us together, they *will* come after us. Even if the remains of Felix and his men won't be identified in the wreckage, it burned down during their investigation. Neither Comrade Suzhensky nor the ARA will be able to save us from Butyrka or worse."

Her sister is right, of course. But Irina thinks of Grand-père, Pasha, Aleksei, Papa. That bygone elite who refused to leave no matter how cold Russia was to them, how difficult and bare existence became, and its cost. And yet, Marie fought to leave, seeing theirs a hopeless fight, at least for now. Though Russia is their homeland, she is an occupied, lost land. They might end up like their family, those too-proud scions of dead imperial Russia, too proud to save themselves—and worse, too proud to save their children.

Irina hears the strain in her sister's breathing; sees a haunted, maybe hunted, look in her eyes. She glances down at Seryozha's pale, shadowed face. At Natasha, thin and small as a sparrow. Irina wishes she had more time to think, to consider, to weigh her options fully, but they are out of time. No matter how much she loves Russia, a part of her screaming to stay, she cannot—will not—make the same mistake as her family. She wants more for her son, cousin, and sister. She wants more for herself.

"Very well," Irina says, giving voice to her decision. It brings on a wrenching hollowness, and a fierce ache in her heart. But somehow also a lightness. That warm contentment.

"All right," Will says with a grin. "I will let my contact know. We will prepare Lili's papers and reach out to the relief workers to see when they are setting off for Riga."

The logistics crash into Irina then. Where will they live? What will they do? How will she and her sister support two children in a country they don't know? But she looks at the children, and the panic and fear recede, just a little. It will be hard, yes, but she knows it is the right decision. The children need it. She needs it.

Lili and Nicky start to whisper to each other, Emma drifting toward them, and Irina and Will are left alone with the sleeping children.

"Why do this for me, William?" she asks quietly. "Why put your neck on the line?"

Will hesitates before reaching over and brushing a hand against her cheek. "You know why, Irene. You mean the world to me—that's the truth. And I, well, I know things are complicated, for you, us, but that makes no difference. If you cannot live here, you should live somewhere else. I . . . just want you to be happy. And maybe, when I'm done with the mission, we can pick up where we left off. That is, if . . . you would want that."

"To pick up, to start over," Irina muses, thinking, "somewhere else, without all this . . ." Who he is, who she is, an American and a Russian, unequal by virtue of the mission. But elsewhere, without office hierarchy, these jobs, Russia, maybe it could be different for them. "You don't mind that I have a son, a family?"

Will smiles, shaking his head. "Always worrying about others," he murmurs, running his fingers along Seryozha's sleeve. "I love that you have a family. Remember, it was just Aunt Mildred and me for a long time. And I've seen how your family fights for each other. I hope to be part of a family like that someday."

His gaze is so warm, filled with so much emotion, maybe even *love*, that Irina leans over Seryozha and kisses Will very softly on the lips. While she still doesn't know if she wants to be a wife, she knows Will is one of the most decent, kindest, best men she has ever met. And if she could think about a future with anyone, it would be him. Now, though, Irina is suddenly eager to leave, to escape, to make a new life for herself and the children—and to do it all herself. "I would like that very much, William. And for you to write if—" She feels her face flush. "If you wish."

"I wish it, most definitely," he says, smiling again, when Lili approaches them.

"Would you give us a minute, William?" Lili asks, throwing herself into the newly vacated armchair as Will nods easily and crosses the room to chat with Emma and Nikolai. "Well, I don't know how to say this, Irishka, but—I'm not going with you."

Stunned, all Irina can do is stare at her sister, who sighs deeply and leans back.

"The thing is," Lili says, "I think I need to stay here. Uncle Pasha has got under my skin." She gives a laugh, though flat and a little sardonic. "You know, his belief that you have to fight for something. I realized I'm not done with the ARA. And the work with former people is just beginning. Maybe if the article is published and more foreigners find out how people like us live, the more aid and support we can offer them. And"—her eyes stray to Nikolai—"well, I need to see Nicky and me through. If I leave now . . ."

"You will never know," Irina finishes for her.

"I will never know."

"But how—?"

Lili shrugs. "I can be someone new without you."

Irina laughs drily. Her instinct is to list all the reasons this is dangerous. But she cannot force her sister into coming with them. Lili is eighteen and knows her mind more than most. And Irina doesn't wish for her to live with regret. Unlike her, Lili might have something, someone, worth staying for. Perhaps no matter how cold Russia gets, no matter how difficult life here is, it can exist, even thrive. And if anyone can survive *and* thrive, it is Lili.

Irina doesn't say any of this. She simply allows Lili's arms to come around her and Seryozha.

Though they have been an older and a younger sister, divided by their ten years, by the family and their differing expectations for them, by their opposing natures and even secrets, Lili is her blood, her only sister, her best friend, and the closest person to Irina in all the world.

Everything that happened at Moscow House, almost losing each other, has brought them closer than ever. After all, sisterhood is the strongest, most powerful magic there is. Irina knows that, together or apart, in Russia or beyond, they will always have each other. That is power, that is magic. Like Moscow House, that attic, that ballroom, though reduced to cinders and ash, will live on inside them forever, they, too, will live on in each other forever. And they will see each other. When Lili's work is done, when Will completes his mission, they will all meet again.

But for now, Irina already feels very far away—from her life here in Moscow, these old mansions, Russia.

She is already in an unexplored world, starting the rest of her life.

Epilogue

Moscow Motoring

DECEMBER 1921
A Month Later

THE SUN RISES weak and watery over the buildings of Moscow. Overhead, the sky is streaked in powdery pinks and blues, and Lili is woefully late for work. She promised to meet Emma and Paulina at the old Hermitage kitchen. They will need help feeding the children today, as Will, Frank, and Harold are still on an ARA expedition into the depths of Russia, and Kirill prefers his desk to being in the field any day. But Lili cannot resist.

The street is too familiar, though it is still cloaked in gloom from the evaporating night. Snow once more blankets the city, and she thinks back to that black, snowless night, to her sister, cousin, and nephew. Lili can feel them everywhere, though they are a world and a life away in New York City by now.

She wonders what they are doing this very minute, if it is also cold in America.

And suddenly, she aches for Irina fiercely, picturing them walking together to the bazaar to barter their family's heirlooms. Now there is nothing in her hands, no one beside her. And yet, she *feels* her sister there.

Lili pushes back her newly bobbed, blonde hair. She cut and dyed it, though as far as the Soviet government and Cheka secret police are concerned, the Moscow House contingent of the Sherbatsky-Golitevs has perished in the fire. From what the Americans have been able to glean, the investigation has been closed, with it all cited as one horrific accident after another. Though there is nothing in these conclusions about nechistaya sila, as ghosts don't haunt Moscow, or exist at all. As far as anyone is concerned, Lili is Nina now, just another American in Russia, sharing Emma's flat, which is absolutely *not* owned by the Bolos.

Lili doesn't see the dome of Moscow House in the distance—that dome under which she read Uncle Pasha's words, his story, the story of their family and her. It must have caved in during the fire. Her heart clenches, regret shooting through her. *Look at this Nina*, someone might say, *one half of the Goliteva sisters, her nobility and name all but wiped away, her house and possessions gone, her coat even more impoverished and threadbare than before. And singed to boot.* Lili almost slinks past the house like a coward.

But she forces herself through the gate and into the courtyard, which still holds the memory of the flames. She inhales the acrid air, the smoke and char. Her eyes settle on the oak tree first, imagining Uncle Pasha standing on his grave. But he isn't there.

All is empty and silent and white.

Perhaps he has found peace. Perhaps someday so will she. Though she likes to think that she has moved on from this house and the past, that she is living.

"I am trying, Uncle Pasha," Lili whispers to her uncle. Both to keep her promise to live and to fight for what she believes in. She has resumed her work for the ARA and Russia's children, has submitted her and Frank's article on former people. She hopes it will be picked up by an international, maybe even an American, newspaper.

Lili turns toward Moscow House slowly. It is as if she expects it to be the same as before, savoring that remembered, familiar, grand image of it in her mind. Holding it close to her heart. She takes out her sketch pad and pencil in case she will want to commit it to memory. But what greets her is a very different house.

It is a blackened mass of pillars and caved-in walls, a twisted wreck, a deformed monster, vanquished, dead. Lili closes her eyes against the memories rushing back, of that cold ballroom, filled with gunshots and flames and Stravinsky; Auntie, that black-gowned figure in the smoke, with a shard of glass raised in her hands and blood staining her skin. Lili opens her eyes and sees the house as the wreck it is, misery made manifest.

There is nothing left here. Uncle Pasha is gone. Grand-mère, Auntie, the rest of her family, too. Even the Domovoy. Lili slips the sketch pad and pencil back into her coat.

As she starts to turn away, she thinks she catches the flicker of red eyes in the wreckage, hears the swelling strings of Stravinsky, or a ghostly whisper.

Just as quickly, it is replaced by the engine of a motorcar, slowing, then pausing there and purring. For a second, Lili's chest tightens with panic and foreboding. Perhaps they have found her, perhaps she is not as dead as she thought. But a screech pierces the air, and Cleo is sweeping toward her. The driver honks, one, two, three, four times, playful, not at all who she thought. And all is forgotten, evaporating like the night.

Lili lifts her hand up to Cleo, and the parakeet drops into her palm with a happy little chirp. Her feathers are soft and silky as they brush against Lili's fingers.

Together, they rush out of that courtyard, away from Moscow House, without a glance back—to behold the Cadillac humming at the curb, waiting for them.

Lili hops in without hesitation, with eagerness and not a little surprise. "How did you know I was here?" she asks, Cleo settling in the back seat with a contented whistle.

"A feeling," Nicky says. He leans over and slides a warm, rough hand under her chin. Then he pulls her face to his and kisses her lips intensely slow. So she can taste everything about him. That is how they kiss now. As if any kiss might be their last. Because it might. "And Cleo was worried," he adds against her lips, with a wink at the parakeet, who gives him an excited trill, liking to be acknowledged. Nikolai's knuckles graze Lili's cheek tenderly before he returns to his seat. He tightens his hands on the wheel and looks forward. "So, where to, Lil?"

Though she is late for work, she doesn't want to think about the where. She doesn't want to think at all. She laughs, shaking her head. "Just drive, Nicky." Lili is most content in this Cadillac with Nikolai and Cleo, motoring around Moscow and watching the city pass them by.

Shadows still play and flicker at the edges of the street like ghosts. But the light over the town is growing stronger, maybe a little warmer, despite a weak sun and the frosty grip of the famous Russian winter.

She flashes Nicky a wide smile, the rare one with teeth. This isn't a fairy tale, no ending in sight, happy or otherwise. Only the long ribbon of the road before them. And that, Lili thinks, is so much better.

Historical Note

Lili and Irina's story is inspired by real women, a real family, and a real house.

But first, a quick note on Russian names: A Russian person has three names, including the first name, the patronymic (derived from the father's first name), and the family (last) name. In formal settings, especially in pre-Revolutionary times and sometimes even today, the first name and the patronymic were/are used together. In informal settings, only the first name is used. Frequently, a diminutive (or nickname) is preferred. I have tried to be very clear when I use the diminutive of a name.

An even quicker note on my transliteration of Russian words: I have tried to use English words and spellings that are true to the Russian language. Whenever possible, and if it didn't interfere with authenticity, I chose the spelling most easily digestible for the non-Russian reader.

ABOUT THE FAMILY, ITS HOUSE, AND ITS LANDLORDS

I started this novel in a way that I never thought would happen to me. I was researching another story idea when I chanced upon the Sheremetev and Golitsyn families—two of Russia's greatest and oldest aristocratic clans. These kinds of families were living history, their ancestors having been around since the founding of the Romanov dynasty in 1613, and some even had the noble Rurik blood of the Vikings in their veins.

It was all the more shocking how spectacularly they fell during the 1917 Russian Revolution.

After owning countless landholdings and estates, hobnobbing with the Romanov imperial family and other royalty, and living in magnificent splendor and wealth, the Russian aristocratic families lost everything and became virtual paupers, if they kept their lives at all. Eventually, they were reduced to "former people" by the new Soviet society that had replaced the monarchy—this, after the country had been ravaged by the First World War, followed by a horrifically bloody Revolution, and then a lengthy and even bloodier Civil War.

Many of the Sheremetev and Golitsyn family members, like other former aristocrats, nobles, and intelligentsia, fled Russia. But some stayed.

This, then, is their story, the Sherbatsky-Golitev family directly inspired by families like the Sheremetevs and Golitsyns. More than that, though, this is a story about women. For it oftentimes fell on the women to take charge of what families and homes remained when their men left for war, were killed by revolutionaries or mobs, or were arrested, imprisoned, and exiled or killed by the Cheka secret police. These women held up their families. They put a roof over their heads; they found food and work; they educated and took care of their children and the older generations. And they kept their noble upbringing and past alive for the new generations.

Irina, Lili, and their aunt are inspired by such women.

Particularly Liliya Sheremetev, Anna Saburov, and Maria Gudovich, who were the widowed mistresses of the Sheremetev house. In *Former People: The Final Days of the Russian Aristocracy* by Douglas Smith (one of my inspirations and go-to resources for the book), Liliya is described as a true "lady" and "queen," while Anna and Maria shared the house's top floor and were "[a]stral specters . . . almost

Historical Note

never seen," refusing to accept their husbands' deaths. As soon as I read about these women, I knew I had to write a story not only about a family and its fall from grace but about two sisters trapped in the past, in a house that refused to let the past die.

My sisters' family and former people friends are likewise inspired by the real-life members of these aristocratic families. Some characters are named after real people, though they and their lives are fictionalized.

Moscow House is loosely based on the ancestral Sheremetev home in Moscow, the Corner House, at the real 6 Vozdvizhenka Street, where the real Liliya, Anna, and Maria lived. It was said to be stuffed with portraits, antique furniture, costly tapestries, and other tsarist treasures that evoke old, crumbling estates and decaying splendor. In short, a writer's dream. Given such a tragically romantic setting, my story had to be a gothic.

Soviet men really did move into Corner House in August 1921. In reality, it was fifty students from the Institute of Marx and Engels of the Socialist Academy, which had been in control of the house since 1918. While I was faithful to the idea of the requisition, I did fictionalize the circumstances, making it an unspecified group of Soviet officials. I also simplified the family members. In reality, three entire branches of the Sheremetev family lived in Corner House side by side with their Soviet class enemy.

The Cheka secret police, including their founding member Yakov Peters, really did burst into Corner House on November 23, 1921. They intended to arrest the family's patriarch, Sergei, the inspiration behind my sisters' grandfather, though it wasn't quite as dramatic as described in my book.

Of course, what then happens at Moscow House is fiction, and there were (to my knowledge) no violent deaths in the real house. But there may have been ghosts. That is entirely up to interpretation.

For some of the details on the Sherbatsky-Golitev past before and during the Revolution, *Caught in the Revolution* by Helen Rappaport is a fantastic and harrowing account of the 1917 Revolution and the people who lived it. For daily life in Soviet Russia, my wonderful parents and their friends were invaluable resources, as well as the Internet and *Everyday Life in Early Soviet Russia: Taking the Revolution Inside*, edited by Christina Kiaer and Eric Naiman. For cultural details, again, my family and all the books I've surrounded myself with all my life were my primary resources, but also *Natasha's Dance: A Cultural History of Russia* by Orlando Figes. For Moscow House and other mansions mentioned in this book, *Household Interior Decoration in Nineteenth-Century Russia: The Exhibition in the Pavlovsk Palace Museum* by A. Kuchumov is a wonderful Russian resource that my mom was lucky enough to snag from a little bookshop in Moscow.

THE ARA

The American Relief Administration, or the ARA, was a real humanitarian organization that arrived in Russia to help with the famine in August of 1921. Vladimir Lenin, the head of the Soviet government, had no choice but to let the Americans in, given that his country was on the brink of disaster and its population starving and dying. But he didn't like it. Raids, searches, spying, secret agent shadowing, bad press and government hostility, not to mention administrative hurdles and games, were all part of business as usual for the Americans in Russia.

I tried to keep to the facts as much as I could, but because of the complexity of the ARA and its relief operation, I simplified and fictionalized certain aspects for the sake of the story.

For example, while ARA headquarters were really at 30 Spiridonovka in Moscow, it grew from some dozen men to fifty to many more throughout the course of the mission, which lasted into 1923. It was also home to a group of Soviet officials meant to be "liaisons" between the ARA and the Soviet government. I thought this would be repetitive with the Soviet men already living in Moscow House, so I didn't include them. In a similar vein, ARA headquarters were primarily offices, the other buildings (former people mansions) more serving as both office and living quarters. For my purposes, I wanted a central location for the ARA-related parts of the story, so it made sense for my ARA men to both work and live at headquarters.

Likewise, ARA headquarters eventually encompassed many different divisions and employees. There was indeed a liaison division in reality, which Lili works for in the novel. But communications was its own division and was not established until January 1922; the historical division, too, wasn't established until July 1922. While I wish that Lili's former people project could have been real, this was purely fiction.

I also wish that I could have gone into more detail about the ARA's wonderful work. But in reality, it comprised many elements. Specifically, "districts" all over the then Russian lands, each city or town with their own ARA offices and operations. Those involved very complicated logistics, working with many kitchens, hospitals, children's homes, and other organizations to bring food, clothing, medical supplies, and other aid to the poor, starving Russian people. Not many in both the States and Russia have heard of the ARA's efforts, and that is truly a shame. Not only did it save millions of people from death (according to Douglas Smith, the ARA fed over ten million men, women, and children), but it is an example of international humanitarianism at its finest.

Unfortunately, though, the ARA was a product of its time—racism, sexism, and other issues were rampant among the highly educated white men. A few of my ARA characters are Black, namely, Emma and Frank. While there is evidence that Black people worked for the ARA (in fact, Emma is based on a real person of the same name, who worked as an ARA laundress), there is no evidence that Black people were full-fledged mission members. The same goes for American women. With few exceptions, not even wives could visit their husbands.

The women who did work for the ARA were former people and

other Russians, and in the capacities that I describe in the novel. Several inhabitants of Corner House also worked for the ARA. Socializing, friendships, romantic relationships, and even marriages were common across the entire ARA operation in Russia.

The other ARA characters are *very* loosely based on real people. Sometimes I even gave them their real names. That is mostly where the similarities end. Philip Carroll, however, was a real person and ARA chief.

The Cheka arrests of the ARA's Russian employees, some of them former people, really did happen around October to November of 1921. This was, however, largely in satellite ARA offices. For instance, in Kazan, three Russian ARA employees were arrested in a similar fashion as in this book, with a similar overarching reason—that is, the ARA hiring too many former people. The ARA in Kazan really did consider shutting down the operation, proposing to stop all ARA shipments to the Tatar Republic and insisting the ARA employees be released and permitted to return to work immediately. There were similar arrests at the ARA operations in Tsaritsyn, Samara, and even Moscow, where the ARA did try to get an employee out of prison.

While the manner and circumstances of the arrests as I describe them in the book have been fictionalized, their danger was only too real for any Russian who decided to work for the ARA.

Sadly, many of these individuals were under a permanent cloud of suspicion thereafter, and especially when the Americans left Russia. Many were arrested on trumped-up charges, including espionage and treason. This continued and even intensified during Stalin's dictatorship. Many if not most of the former people and ex-ARA employees were eventually victims in the purges during the Great Terror of the 1930s.

The best and most comprehensive resources on the ARA that I used were *The Russian Job: The Forgotten Story of How America Saved the Soviet Union from Ruin* by Douglas Smith and *The Big Show in Bololand: The American Relief Expedition to Soviet Russia in the Famine of 1921* by Bertrand M. Patenaude.

Historical Note

GOTHIC & FOLKLORE

So much of the novel is inspired by some of my favorite gothic stories, particularly by the Russian/Slavic gothic genre and the Ukrainian author who arguably founded it—Nikolai Gogol. I remember my grandfather reading Gogol's stories to me when I was just a little girl. It's true, they were a bit too scary for me at the time, but they instilled in me a very deep love for and fascination with gothic literature.

At heart, *The Haunting of Moscow House* is a ghost story. And so I am indebted to Gogol's brilliantly haunting stories for inspiring and teaching me. I reread many of them, in both Russian and English (I recommend *The Collected Tales of Nikolai Gogol*, translated into English by Richard Pevear and Larissa Volokhonsky). I would also recommend a little-known volume that was absolutely brilliant—*Red Spectres: Russian Gothic Tales from the Twentieth Century*, selected and translated into English by Muireann Maguire.

Fortune-telling makes a small appearance in this book. It has historically been (and even now is) an incredibly popular pastime in Russia. While the fortune-telling in the story is very much a work of my imagination, a few resources helped me to delve into the details of this fascinating subject: *The Bathhouse at Midnight: An Historical Survey of Magic and Divination in Russia* by W. F. Ryan and *Reading Russian Fortunes: Print Culture, Gender and Divination in Russia from 1765* by Faith Wigzell.

Lastly, while my previous novel focused on Baba Yaga and Koshey Bessmertny and the other characters of Slavic fairy tale and myth, my sophomore novel is all about the home—the spirit of the home, the spirits of departed family members, necromancy and resurrection, and other like supernatural elements. I used my imagination to come up with something of my own, inspired by Slavic pagan beliefs and lore, the gothic genre, and the many stories told to me by my grandparents and parents. The most helpful resources in English were *Russian Folk Belief* by Linda J. Ivanits, *Russian Magic: Living Folk Traditions of an Enchanted Landscape* by Cherry Gilchrist, and *Slavic Sorcery: Shamanic Journey of Initiation* by Kenneth Johnson.

FINAL NOTE

While I tried to be faithful to the historical figures, events, times, places, and pagan beliefs and lore, some have been altered or fictionalized for the purpose of storytelling. Any errors are entirely my own. Thank you for reading!

Acknowledgments

If writing and publishing a debut takes a village, then writing and publishing a sophomore novel takes a village *plus* tremendous can't-eat-can't-sleep passion, pure grit, and nerves of steel. To that end, there were many, many people who were there for me during the writing and release of *The Haunting of Moscow House*.

First, to the person who saw *that certain something* in me when I was an unpublished writer sending out her cold queries. Jennifer, my agent and mentor, thank you for being the voice of wisdom and reason, and a faithful champion of my stories. With this one, I needed your enthusiasm and belief in me more than ever, and I got it.

To Jessica Wade, I don't know how you do it, but you are an extraordinarily brilliant editor who never fails to see my vision or get me out of my head. You know exactly what to do to make my idea into a real book. Thank you for believing in me and my writing. I truly feel that my stories are made possible because of you.

To the hardworking and unbelievably talented team at Berkley and Penguin Random House, especially Gabrielle Pachon, Rosanne Romanello, Lauren Burnstein, Dache' Rogers, Jessica Plummer, Elise Tecco, and Stephanie Felty, as well as fearless leaders Claire Zion and Craig Burke, and everyone else who brought *The Haunting of Moscow*

Acknowledgments

House to life. Last but not least, to Adam Auerbach and Amanda Hudson, for the stunning (and perfect) book cover that literally took my breath away.

To my UK team, you have been rock stars from my debut to my second book. To my agent, Laura Williams, for shepherding me into the UK market; to Natasha Bardon, for giving me a chance to work with such a legendary editor and publish books in the UK (a dream come true!); to Rachel Winterbottom, for expertly taking over the reins during Natasha's leave; and to the entire absolutely brilliant Harper Voyager UK team.

To my critique partner and best friend, Gabriella Saab, for always accepting me, listening to me, and reading literally everything I write. For truly always having my back, both in publishing and in life. You might have told me that writing a second book is one of the hardest things I'll do, but you were there for me every step of the way, and that means everything. And for doing a last-minute sensitivity read on certain aspects of Emma's southern background.

To fellow author and great friend Rebecca Mildren, for the excellent transliteration help with the Russian names and words in this book, and for always being such an optimistic voice in supporting my work.

To fellow author and #HFChitChat cohost Janna Noelle, for the friendship and the generous sensitivity read of the Black characters in this book. I have learned more from you than I can say.

To my friends in the industry who never fail to hold me up, Paulette Kennedy, Rose de Guzman, Anika Scott, Rachel Harrison, Allison Epstein, C.J. Subko, Marina Scott, and many others. To the other authors who have so generously supported me and my books—namely, Kate Quinn, Chanel Cleeton, C. W. Gortner, Darcy Coates, Bryn Turnbull, Kristen Loesch, Wendy Webb, Margaret George, Hannah Whitten, Genevieve Gornichec, Molly Greeley, H. M. Long, Alexis Henderson, Sarah Porter, Elizabeth Blackwell, and Mary McMyne, I respect you and your work so much. To all the gothic/horror authors out there, you inspire and scare me in the best of ways. And to all my friends on X, Instagram, and Facebook for your wonderful enthusiasm.

To Sydney Young and the rest of the #HFChitChat community, for your passion for historical fiction and your support. It's always a bright spot in my week if we are chatting about history and books!

To Douglas Smith, for being a brilliant historian and the inspiration behind the Sherbatsky-Golitev family and this book. And to Helen Rappaport, for writing a book on the Russian Revolution that resonated with me and that finally got me out of the mentality that it would be too sad to write about such a difficult topic.

To my sister, Katerina Salnikova, whom this book is dedicated to. You have believed in me from the time that we told each other stories as little girls to the moment that I gave you *The Haunting of Moscow House*, even though you don't like scary stories. Thank you for reading anyway and for always being there to cheer me on, to support and love me no matter what. And for dealing with me during my writing and health meltdowns (thank you, Doctor!). So, to sisters! The strongest, most powerful magic there is in all the world.

To my parents, who help me day in and day out, whether it is with emotional support or childcare. Thank you for being a family that fights for each other and me. Thank you also for going to the places in this book that I couldn't visit due to COVID and being a new mom, and for answering all my questions about Soviet life and culture.

To my grandmothers and grandfathers and all the family members who are no longer with us. This is a story about ghosts, about a past that is still present and very much alive. I felt your presence as I was working on this story, as I feel you and your absence every day of my life. I remember you, honor you, and am thankful for the truly memorable moments we had together. So much of Lili and Irina's departed family is inspired by you.

To Uncle Volodya and Aunt Natasha, for keeping the memory of our departed relatives alive, and for being such an important link to both my past and childhood and my culture.

Acknowledgments

To my mother-in-law, Maureen Gilmore, for helping me with the French in this book, and for graciously coming through when I am desperate for extra childcare—you are a lifesaver!

To my father-in-law, George Gilmore, for being the number one fan. Buying (so many!) books, coming to events, and supporting me in all ways big and small. Thank you, thank you, thank you.

To my (almost!) sister-in-law, Claire Plante, kick-ass woman and cop, for the help with the investigations in this book.

To the rest of my family—to my sister-in-law and brother-in-law, Stephanie and John, for reading and supporting; to Inna, for taking such great care of my daughter and for your friendship to my family; to the Plante family in Chicago and the Hughes family in Canada, for reading (and sometimes liking!) my books when George sends them; and to one of my oldest friends Megan Bryant, for your always much needed excitement about my writing and for all the love.

To my husband, Sean Gilmore, for reading my words, for showing up to every author event, for talking ad nauseam about my stories, books, publishing, the latest drama, everything. You encouraged me not only to take a chance on my writing but to write something totally different with this second book. It is all because you believe in me (and are unflinchingly, devastatingly honest!). I believe in you just as much, and I love you!

To my daughter, Nina, for being the brightest light in my life. Even when I'm working crazy hours, just hearing your cute prattle and laughter through the door brings a smile to my face. You are the smartest, most charming (and already well-read!), most beautiful little girl, and I can't wait to share my stories with you someday.

To everyone else who ever supported me and my books, thank you so much. A special shout-out to all the wonderful booksellers (my indie, The Book Stall, especially!), libraries, book reviewers, book podcasts and bloggers and influencers, and other important voices in the reading, writing, and publishing communities.

And to you, dear reader. Thank you for picking up this book and for reading Lili and Irina's story.